I0661576

Vasara

The Vasara Chronicles, Book 3

Roland Capalbo

Copyright © 2022 Roland Capalbo

All Rights Reserved. Reproduction or utilization of this work in any form, by any means now known or hereinafter invented, including but not limited to, xerography, photocopying and recording, and in any known storage and retrieval system, is forbidden without permission from the copyright holder.

Paperback ISBN 978-1-77400-043-4
Electronic ISBN 978-1-77400-044-1

Printed on Acid Free Paper

DragonMoonPress.com

You have come with me on my journey, and one more adventure awaits. Let's go find our tree and sit under it as we let the story unfold.

Chapter 1

Zana stood on the threshold of the cottage she now occupied, although cottage was not entirely accurate. It had the simple exterior of a cottage, but if one were to go inside, it had the interior of a palace. Such was the magic here. Looking over at the stone gateway, she saw three of her ravens. The doorway to Otherwhere. That was the name of this place. She didn't name it, the ravens told her that this is what it was called. She had learned how Devon was able to communicate with these birds, and now they were hers, along with their magic. Her dark wings fluttered gently in the breeze as she pushed her black hair behind her pointed ears. *Otherwhere,* she liked that name, and she was its goddess. Soon she would be the goddess of Vasara as well. *They would pay,* she thought. *They would all pay.*

So much had changed since she spilled Layla's blood. That thought only gave her the slightest of twinges now.

"It wasn't right that Layla was chosen as Braylynn's Dragon Summoner. It should have been me," she told the ravens. "The goddess was set against anointing me." That wasn't the truth, but Zana believed it to be true.

"And now that witch, Donella has what was once my rightful place. She is barely three decades old, and even younger than that when Braylynn anointed her Dragon Summoner," she told the raven that had come to perch on her shoulder. Both Layla and she had been in their third century when Layla was anointed. But it didn't matter anymore.

"I've moved beyond being that false goddess' Summoner. I am more than a match for Donella and her dragons. I will have my own dragons at my command."

Zana smiled to herself as she opened the door to the cottage and slipped inside. Walking down the marbled halls of her domain a tall slender man came up to her. He had braided red hair with a beard to match, closely trimmed to his face. His eyes were brown, and he wore leather armor with a rapier strapped to his hip.

"Griffin, what news of our prisoners?"

"They are annoyingly positive for being stuck in here for ten years," Griffin said in his gruff voice.

"Typical," she said scowling. "Acacia was always so cloying. She turns my stomach with her sweetness. Paolo is no better."

"It won't be long before the 'heir' finds out we have them," he said with a sneer.

"You really don't like them, do you Griffin?"

"It's not obvious, is it?" he said with sarcasm. "They hold a place that is rightfully mine, and my children."

Zana knew the tale of how a queen of Vasara had been carrying twins. For a child to be considered the heir to the throne and have access to the crypt of the White Castle, they must be the eldest, but even with twins, there is always one that is born first. But in this instance, there had been a midwife with evil designs. Zana had not heard her full history from Griffin, nor did she care. But what did interest her was that just before birth, the midwife cut open the queen's stomach and pulled the twins out at the exact same moment, thereby ensuring, as far as the magic was concerned, there would be two eldest children, and two bloodlines that could ascend the throne. Stealing one of the boys she fled into the Parma Wilds and was lost to time. But that other bloodline passed down that history from father to son to this very day, biding their time to reclaim what is theirs. Zana was going to use that vengeance to further her own aims.

"Can't we at least put them in a dungeon? It might sour their attitude."

"No, I don't think even that would do it. It doesn't matter, Griffin. They are only bait. It is the Summmus Re'em that I want."

She left Griffin with a puzzled look on his face as she walked further down the corridor. Looking back, she could see him rubbing his forearm. Griffin was a tool. Someone to be used as the need saw fit. Zana had needed him to go into the crypt to steal the portal maker which allowed a person to move between one place and another by thought alone. It was shaped like a glass rod with green light sliding like sand inside it. Devon had told her of its existence, but he knew not where it lay. Zana knew about the crypt and its various treasures. She figured Trystan would have made something like that, and being Kensington is his city, the next logical step was obvious. It was only a matter of seeking Griffin out and convincing him to steal it, although it took very little convincing. That fact that Paolo and Acacia were hiding in the crypt was an added bonus. Turning a corner, she opened the oaken door to the apartments where her captives were held.

"Come to gloat some more about how all your plans are falling into place, Zana?" Acacia said as she entered the room.

Acacia was sitting in a high back chair, her long dark braid slung over one shoulder as she ran a whetstone across a deadly looking razor thin blade. Zana had allowed them their weapons on the promise they would not use them against her. For some reason unknown to her they quickly and happily agreed. They were also free to roam wherever they wanted in the daytime. They could not escape Otherwhere on their own, the magic prevented that.

"Now, Acacia," Paolo said running a hand through his sandy blond hair, "I'm sure Zana is here to see to our needs."

"You both are going to push too far one day," she said menacingly.

"Oh, I don't think we will ever get to that day," Acacia said rising and giving her sword a flourish, eyeing it closely for imperfections. "How is Griffin's arm by the way?"

Now the arm rubbing was made clear. "So that's what happened. He challenged you to a duel again. He will try and kill you. Why is it you do not kill him when you best him?"

"Because I know he cannot beat me," she said, "so for me this is just practice."

"Also," Paolo said standing up to stretch his 6 foot 3-inch frame, "his family has been told from generation to generation how they are the rightful heirs to the throne. I can understand his bitterness and anger. But maybe we can help him to see a better way."

"Good luck with that. The second he gets a chance he will gut you."

"Why don't you give up whatever scheme you have been planning all this time, Zana," Paolo said. "Nyle is out there, searching for us. He will find us, I promise you that."

"Ha! Your knight has failed you, just as he failed as one of Devon's Raptors."

The Raptors were the evil wizard Devon's elite fighting unit. After seeing Devon for what he really was, Nyle had pledged his life to Paolo.

"When he was a Raptor, he was invincible," Paolo said calmly. "After he renounced that life, he became even more."

"Ten years?" Zana said smiling. "I would say his skills are waning."

"Don't count on that, Zana. I wouldn't count on that at all. You can never win; you realize that don't you?"

"Why do you say that?" She said eyeing him dangerously.

Paolo looked at her with all honesty and sincerity in his eyes, and no small amount of pity.

"Because you are alone, Zana. Anyone in your life is just a tool, to be used and discarded at your whim. And in so treating people and magical creatures this way you can neither gain trust nor give it. It is all about connections, one to another, with all living things." Paolo looked hard at her. "There is not a single thing or person that loves you, you have never known love, and because of that, you will fail."

Zana's face contorted in anger, the blood rising to her face as her body shook. With a scream of rage, she opened her palm as a bolt of white-hot energy shot out and hit Paolo squarely in the chest, propelling him backward to slam his body against the marbled walls.

"Paolo!" Acacia screamed as she ran to him slumped on the floor, unconscious. Pulling him on her lap, she could feel a pulse as she pressed her fingers to his neck.

"You evil witch! I will kill you for that," Acacia said through gritted teeth.

Zana regained her composure and looked at the pair impassively.

"When he wakes, tell him it would be wise for him to watch what he says, or I will cut out his tongue. I just need you alive, I don't need you to be whole." She started to turn away, but paused, "Also tell him what he said was wrong."

Zana left the apartments, slamming the door behind her. Bracing herself against the wall, she closed her eyes and sighed deeply. What Paolo had said had hit a chord, and she hated him for that, because that chord had a name. Finn.

She tried to put him out of her mind. She could still see him on the canyon floor, standing on that rock after she had helped Donella defeat the shriker. His shock of bright red hair blew in the breeze as he called out to her. She hadn't heard his voice in over fifteen hundred years, and he had been dead to her in all that time. Things had ended badly between them. Now he was back, and he would try and seek her out. One more thing she would eventually have to deal with. But that could wait. The time had come to reach out to Meliakken. The one god whom it had taken five gods and a goddess to imprison. Leaving her palace, she stepped outside and spread her wings. Tying her hair in a ponytail, she took out the glass rod and held it horizontal in front of her as she pictured the place she needed to go. The ravens suddenly took flight as a bright light and a loud snap took them by surprise. They looked to where the sound had come from, but nothing was there.

Chapter 2

It had been raining all day as the man sat under the sweeping boughs of a tree. What appeared at first glance to be a very large dog sitting next to him, was in fact a wolf.

"What do you think old wolf? Will the rain stop today?"

The man looked up as water from the leaves ran into his sandy hair that now held more grays than anything else. His beard was bushy, but not very long, and his body was still muscular and quick.

"You've nothing to say to old Nyle?" he said looking down at the wolf.

Wolf just stared back at him with his mouth hanging open, panting.

"Come to think of it you really haven't had much to say in ten years. Not that I blame you," Nyle said. "I don't think I would want to talk to a failed knight either."

Wolf cried and whimpered a little at that statement, as if he understood.

Nyle reached over and scratched his head. He remembered when he first encountered this wolf. He had told his son Cathal and prince Brayton that he was going to search for the king and queen, and he would not return until he had found them. Cathal had begged to come with him. Nyle would have liked nothing better than to have him by his side. He still felt some amount of guilt for the years that he had abandoned him and his mother while he served as one of Devon's Raptors. He had done his best to make up for that and his son had said he was grateful for the life he had. Nyle knew that the king was his responsibility, just as the prince was his son's, and told him so. Cathal didn't like it, but in the end he was forced to agree.

Nyle had set out shortly after the battle that defeated the warlocks of Parma. He searched from Fenner to the Border Lands, but it wasn't until he hit the woods just above Laurel Hollow that he met his friend who was now sitting beside him. Nyle had heard some crying and yelping off the main trail. Pushing through a copse of trees he saw a wolf with its leg caught in a trap. It was large and black with gray on its muzzle and legs. Upon seeing Nyle, it growled low in its belly and bared its teeth in a snarl.

"If you don't stop that, you will be stuck there until the trapper comes and kills you for your pelt," Nyle told him.

Nyle didn't know if it was his peaceful sounding tone or the calmness in his demeanor, but the wolf stopped snarling and whimpered as it licked its trapped paw. Taking his jacket off and wrapping it around his arm he slowly walked over. Once he was in smelling distance, he held his covered arm out to the wolf. The animal growled only once, but then went silent as its yellow eyes connected with Nyle's. It was in that moment that he knew he had nothing to fear from this animal. Once free, the wolf limped for several days after Nyle put a splint on his leg, but it did not stop him from following Nyle wherever he went. He gave up trying to chase him away after many failed attempts.

Now after ten years of traveling together they found themselves back in the Parma Wilds. Of all the places they searched in that ten years, it was the Wilds they kept coming back to.

"I'm not sure why we are back here, wolf. It's not like we haven't searched the Wilds over and over again." Pan and Diminitus would help in the search from time to time, but not for several years.

"We sure could use some divine help here," he said adjusting the sword on his hip to keep it from getting rained on.

"Perhaps I may be of assistance?"

Nyle jumped up and drew his sword in one fluid motion. The wolf also got to its feet, but he wasn't growling, which struck Nyle as odd. Standing before them was a woman in a sleeveless ice-blue dress with hair the color of dancing flames. She just appeared out of nowhere.

"Who are you?" Nyle said not lowering the sword.

The woman just stared at him with a smile on her face, looking at him as if she was trying to decide if she wanted to answer.

"Sibila," she said. "You may call me, Sibila."

"Call you Sibila? Is that your name or not?"

She just kept smiling at him, looking pointedly at his drawn sword.

"Very well," he said sheathing his sword and shrugging, "Sibila it is." He didn't know why he felt no danger from this woman, but he felt she had power, and he knew she was not human.

He felt tired. As if all the years of searching had finally started catching up to him and his eyes went to the ground for the moment. Suddenly he felt a warm touch on his face as his head came up with Sibila's palm pressed to his cheek,

"Do not despair first knight, your search is coming to an end and your steadfastness will be rewarded."

"How did..." Nyle started with his eyes wide that she knew who he was and his quest, he felt his heart starting to beat faster as a warmth spread through his body.

"Shhhh," she said putting a finger to his lips. "Hold out your hand, Nyle."

He did as she bade, not sure why he was doing it. Sibila deposited into his palm a metal disc. On its surface was a raven in flight and outlined in fire. She closed his fingers over the disc.

"Take this and go find Diminitus. Tell him he must take you to Raven Rock, if he gives you a hard time, tell him one day his crankiness will go up in flames," she said smiling at him. That smile and those eyes were going right through him. *What is happening to me*, he thought. His heart was pounding like a jackhammer.

"But what…" Again, she placed a finger to his lips stopping him. Then leaning in, she pressed her lips to his. Once her soft lips connected with his, his knees went weak, and he felt himself falling as he closed his eyes only to have light explode behind them. When he opened his eyes again, the woman was gone. He stared around wide-eyed as he scanned the forest.

"By the gods, wolf! What the hell just happened."

Nyle didn't know exactly what Sibila was, but one thing he did know, she was a thief and a cruel one. Because she had just totally and completely taken his heart in that kiss, and he didn't think for a moment that it was accidental. His face and body were flush, and the feeling was not unpleasant, but he knew there would be no other woman in his life now but Sibila. He needed to find Diminitus. Something told him that Diminitus knew something about her. Nyle was still stunned, never in his life had he fallen for a woman so hard and so fast and a total stranger, yet something seemed eerily familiar.

Slinging his travel pack over his shoulder he started to make the two-day trek to Diminitus house. Arriving late in the afternoon, he knocked on the door.

"Go away! It's dinner time," came the grumpy response from inside.

Nyle and wolf exchanged a glance. "I would say he is not in the best of moods," he said to wolf.

"Really, Dim? Do you have to greet all our guests in such a manner? It's a wonder we get visitors at all," a woman's voice said just on the other side of the door.

As the door opened, a warm cozy light flooded the threshold, framing the beautiful woman perfectly. Nyle of course knew who it was, after being here so many times over the last ten years.

"Nyle! You came back!"

"It's good to see you, Ala," Nyle said as Ala hugged him.

"And you too, wolf," she said wrapping her arms around his thick neck. Wolf preceded to lick her face.

"Stop that, you," she said giggling from his wolfy kisses.

"Ala, you're letting the rain in!"

Ala stood and rolled her eyes. "You know he doesn't mean it."

"I do," he said following her inside.

After a fine meal and retiring to the library to relax and drink some wine, Nyle filled them both in since his last visit and up to his visit with Sibila. Diminitus kept chuckling to himself after hearing what she did and her message to him. Diminitus couldn't help filling Nyle in on who it was that had snared his heart.

"The Phoenix?" Nyle said, "are you sure?"

"Cathal must have told you about his visitation with her when the unicorns invoked Dodhéanta."

"That was the same person?" Nyle said startled.

"Yes, though at the time he did not know she was the Phoenix. We ran into her as well, but it wasn't until the final battle when she appeared and said that phrase you told me about that I knew for certain who she was."

Now it all came back to him. Nyle remembered sitting around a fire as Cathal and Brayton had told the story of the woman in the ice-blue dress who appeared and told them that the queen of the unicorns, Savano, must invoke Dodhéanta, which would put the grove of the unicorns in a place of her choosing, but in so doing, it would remain there for a thousand years, instead of changing locations at will, and never in the same place twice. It made the unicorns vulnerable for anyone to find them.

"Why did she do it?" Nyle asked taking a sip of his wine.

"No one knows why the Phoenix does anything she does. The best thing to do is just accept it, don't fight it. The rewards will be greater if you let it happen," Diminitus said putting an arm around Ala as she came to sit on the arm of the chair.

"Well, one thing we know is in naming herself she revealed what she is," Ala said.

"And what is that?" Nyle asked.

"An oracle," Ala replied. "Sibila means oracle."

"I don't know how I missed that," Diminitus remarked startled. "This is why I have such a smart life partner." Ala leaned down and kissed his lips.

"You will do fine," Ala said caressing his cheek.

"One of the rewards you mentioned by not fighting it?" Nyle said smiling. Diminitus just winked at him.

"So I guess now you will be heading to Raven Rock," Ala said getting up and throwing another log on the fire.

"I guess we are," Diminitus said. "But not today."

It was two days later that found Nyle and Diminitus riding through the Parma Wilds towards the southernmost tip, wolf stayed behind with Ala. Halfway through they saw a familiar figure sitting on a stump playing pipes.

"Ho Pan!" Diminitus called out.

The king of the Wilds stopped in mid-tune and looked up. Leaping off the stump he trotted over on his goat legs to where Nyle and Diminitus were dismounting.

"Dim, Nyle! It's so good to see you both!" Pan said hugging them and pounding them on the back. "Nyle, it's been years. How goes the search?"

Diminitus suggested they get off the road and find somewhere comfortable to sit and have a meal. As they were eating, Nyle told Pan everything since his last venture into the faun's realm. When he told Pan of Sibila's visit and their need to go to Raven Rock, Pan offered to show them a shortcut. Strapped to his back was a staff with a decagram, a ten pointed star on its top. Cael had given him this staff in order to defeat his brother warlocks by feeding Cael's energy into the dragons fighting them. Swirling it over his head he then lowered it and pointed it at the hillside right behind them. A tunnel, large enough to allow four horses to walk abreast opened up.

"Shall we?" Pan said.

"Show off," Diminitus grumbled. "You couldn't use that last time we traveled together?"

"Dim, please. I don't just use this willy-nilly."

"Humph," the old man grumbled under his breath. Nyle burst out laughing.

As they emerged from the other side, Diminitus could tell from the landmarks that Pan had shaved off half a day by cutting through the hillside. Another few hours of walking brought them to a glade with a huge boulder that soared up as to almost look like a cliff face. The rock was entirely black and smooth. There was no way anyone could just climb up its face.

"Okay, now what?" Diminitus said.

"I could not tell you," Pan remarked. "Believe it or not, this rock is not actually part of the Parma Wilds. The border ends just before it."

"I always thought the Wilds ended at the sea?" Nyle said.

"That is what everyone thinks, but it is not so." Pan said

rubbing his horn against his forearm. "The magic here is older than I, and even Cael's staff cannot breach it. I know, I've tried."

"Which brings us back to where we were before," Diminitus said. "What now?"

Just then the caw of a raven in a large oak off to their right caught their attention.

Nyle had a bow strapped to his back. He pulled it around and notched an arrow to it.

"What are you doing?" Diminitus asked noticing the look in Nyle's eyes.

"Shhh," he said drawing the arrow back to his cheek. He let it fly, but the raven had noticed his movement, and just before the arrow was loosed, it leapt from its perch and flew into the rock and disappeared.

"By the gods!" Diminitus exclaimed. "Did you see that?"

"I did," Pan said his eyes narrowed. "Why did you shoot at it, Nyle?"

"It was one of Devon's ravens."

"How could you tell?" Diminitus said.

"They are much larger than a regular raven for one. And also, I have seen those birds so many times when I had to report to Devon, I would recognize them anywhere." Nyle slung the bow across his back again and looked at them both. "I think I know where I have to go now."

"Yes," Pan said gravely. "I believe you do."

"Well you both have lost me," Diminitus said. "Not unless you know how to walk through rock."

"I believe with this I can," Nyle said holding up the metal disc with the fire raven image. It felt very warm in his hand now.

"If that was one of Devon's ravens, you know who is probably waiting on the other side, don't you?" Diminitus said soberly.

Nyle nodded his head. "Zana."

"Have you ever fought her before?" Pan said.

"Once, in the practice ring when I was training to be a Raptor."

"Did you win?" Diminitus asked.

"We fought to a draw," Nyle said running his fingers through his hair.

"Well that is something."

"Yes, but I was much younger then. Plus, she didn't have the power she has now. Cathal told me how she was able to stop the shriker."

"How do you plan to defeat her?" Pan asked.

Nyle paused a moment before answering. "I don't. My task is to free the king and queen. I could sure use some guidance from her oracle-ness right about now," Nyle said looking behind him to see if Sibila might appear.

Diminitus couldn't help laughing. "She is going to love to hear you call her that!"

"Yeah, well let's just keep that between us, shall we?"

"I have already forgotten it," Pan said with a wink.

Nyle squared his shoulders as he sized up the rock. He had no problem about going through, it was the unknown on the other side that had him concerned. The birds in the forest seemed to have stopped their chatter, as if they were holding their breath. He was about to take a step forward when Pan stopped him.

"Nyle, wait."

Pan took the necklace that was hanging around his neck, on it was a stone of obsidian. He trotted over and hung it from a low hanging branch, the leaves carefully concealing it.

"Is that the stone you gave Donella the first time she came to your grotto?" Diminitus asked.

"It is."

"What is it?" Nyle asked.

"It's a piece of Cael's spirit," Diminitus answered for Pan. "It will allow you to move about the Wilds unmolested by its not so friendly inhabitants."

"When you have rescued the king and queen, and you will rescue them," Pan said noticing his slightly downcast look. "Retrieve the necklace and come straight to my grotto, I can protect them there until we sort this all out."

Nyle firmly gripped Pan's hand and did likewise with Diminitus. He couldn't think of anything else to say. Grasping the raven disc in his hand he closed his eyes and started to walk forward. After several steps, he felt he should have made contact with the rock already. He was not prepared for the sight that met his eyes when he opened them.

"By the gods!"

Chapter 3

Dragonsgate was extremely busy today. It was almost mid-summer, the time of the great festival, when vendors of all stripes came to Dragonsgate for a weeklong of selling and buying. Farmers, artisans, blacksmiths, you name it, they all came. Andy was setting up a stall for Abby who planned on selling some of the library's books, at a very reduced rate, in order to make room for new books.

He stopped for a moment to just look around at the town and the people running about. This place had become home to him. Right after he and Abby had been married, they lived in the rooms at the library while their house was being built just beyond the east gate. Andy had a warm feeling of contentment as he remembered his wedding. His father, the wizard Redlin and priest of the god Trystan had performed the ceremony. It took place in the library hall which Andy felt was only fitting, given this is where it all started for him and Abby. As if thinking about her had conjured her up, he could see her driving a small pony drawn cart with books filling the back. He couldn't help smiling at the image he always saw when he looked at her, a pirate. Her dark hair hung loosely on her shoulders wearing her white shirt and leather pants with boots to match. All she needed was a sword strapped to her side and she would fit right in on one of Bowen's ships.

Abby pulled the reigns up short as she got close to Andy. Setting the brake, she jumped down and ran into his arms, kissing his lips soundly.

"And what were you thinking of just now my lord dragon?" she asked as their lips parted.

"You of course, my love," he said smiling. "And the life we have made here."

She circled an arm around his waist and laid her head on Andy's shoulder as she looked at all the activity.

"I couldn't have asked for a better life," Abby told her husband.

"Well, there are some parts I would change…"

"Shhhh," Abby said putting a finger to his lips. "Not a thing, Andros. You hear me, I wouldn't change a thing."

Abby was right, Andy thought. There was a lot of pain. Abby nearly died at Devon's hand, she did die with the guardians of death's door. But the miracle of Braylynn's gift had restored to him a loving partner that would live as long as he did. He pulled out the chain from under her shirt that held the death dagger talisman. A skull with a dagger going through the top and out of the mouth. It was always around her neck since Braylynn cautioned her to never let it out of her possession. Abby's hand closed around Andy's.

"Remembering?" she asked.

Andy just nodded soberly. He went mad when he thought he had lost her forever. It was his dragon brother, Brion, who was able to bring him back from the abyss.

"Ho, Andros!" A shout came from up the street.

"Ben!" Andy said seeing his friend walking towards him. He was as tall as Andy with dark hair and striking blue eyes.

Ben had been a godsend. Andy had met him at the Red Bull Inn about five years ago sitting in the common room drinking beers. He had just arrived in Dragonsgate and had been looking for work. Andy told him how the old town carpenter had retired to Black River, and if he was handy with wood working tools there would be jobs aplenty. Turned out he was extremely skilled, and it wasn't long before Ben had a steady stream of customers. Andy had employed him to make some additions to their house. They would work side by side for hours, talking at length. Ben came from a town just outside of Albion, his mother and father struck down by disease while he and his sister had headed north. He told Andy that his sister preferred the city life in Kensington, while he looked for a more laid back life.

"Hello, Abby!" Ben said when he reached them.

"Hello, Ben. What brings you out of your shop today?" Abby said smiling.

"I'm heading over to the blacksmith," he replied running his fingers through his thick mane of hair. "I need to have him make me more nails. I'm fixing a wagon for old man Kagen, and I don't want to run out in the middle of it. You know how he can get if things aren't finished on time."

Andy laughed out loud. Kagen was the official crank of Dragonsgate. Although the crankiness and stubborn streak of Kagen suited him well as the night guard on the eastern gate.

"Yes," Andy said. "We know all too well. We'll let you get to it then."

"If you're not busy tomorrow, after you finish your work, why don't you stop by for dinner. Andros hunted a deer in the forest and it is skinned and ready to cook."

"How did you kill it?" Ben asked with raised eyebrows.

"Not with my talons, if that is what you mean," Andy replied smiling.

"Well if that's the case, I will definitely be there," he said shaking Andy's hand before walking away.

"That's a good man there," Andy said watching him go. "What's wrong love?" Andy had noticed her scratching at her chest.

"The talisman is warm and scratching my skin again."

"I really wish Braylynn had given us an instruction manual with that thing. It seems to set itself off at really random times," he said in frustration.

"It's fine dear," she said stroking the side of his face. "Come on, let's get these books set up before lunch."

***

Tori and Cleo had been riding the countryside for weeks now. They were getting close to Dragonsgate so figured they would stop in and see Andy and Abby. They made camp for the night just off the road in a grove of pine trees. Picketing the horses nearby, they had a very small fire crackling in no time as the animal sounds of night song lulled them into a very relaxed state.

"Tell me why we are out here again?" Cleo said.

"I don't know, Boss," Tori replied. "Ever since Fallon made me his Cath Priomh, I get these premonitions I guess you can call them. Something is not right in the land."

Whenever that title came to Tori's mind, she couldn't help but think of the process that brought her to that state. She lay dying in Fenner after nearly being wiped out by a demon horde. She would have died if it hadn't been for the wizards, Redlin and Dain, stopping the source of the gods so Andros could channel Fallon's power into his sister Donella who fed it into her. When she came to, her battle skills and speed had increased a hundredfold, as well as acquiring new powers that frightened her just a little by what she could do with them.

"Can't you contact Fallon and ask him?" Cleo asked.

Tori paused before answering her friend. "I haven't been able to reach him in five years."

"What?" Cleo said stunned. "How is that possible?"

Tori was reflective as she stared at the flames. "I don't really know," she said, resting her chin on her hands. "But I believe what I am feeling now is connected to that. I can't really explain it."

"Well, we have been on our own before," Cleo said winking. "I believe we will manage."

Tori smiled at her best friend. "Have you spoken to Lyson recently?"

Cleo threw another stick on the fire. "I was down in Laurel Hollow several months ago. He and Donella are doing really well. He still likes to show off that he can fly whenever I show up."

Tori couldn't help laughing at that as Cleo joined in.

"I try to get down there at least once a year. You know," Cleo said thoughtfully, "when Donella left the first time, Lyson traveled for years, it was almost like I didn't even have a brother. Then once the demons started appearing all over Vasara, and we were chasing them, I was forced to put him out of my mind altogether. I'm so happy he is pretty much in one place again. I never want to lose that bond we have."

"You won't," Tori said in understanding. As she held her hands further over the fire, the Viper mascot Percy came slithering down her arm and over her wrist, hanging slightly to let the heat warm his belly.

"Percy, you are the strangest snake I've ever known," Cleo said.

Percy just looked at her flicking his tongue.

"We should probably turn in," Tori said. "Who's first watch?"

"I'll take it," Cleo said. "I'm not feeling very tired."

"Okay. Wake me in two hours," Tori said sliding into her sleeping roll as she hugged her swords to her side.

The next morning found them approaching the east gate. It was mid-day and the town was already hopping with visitors, vendors and shoppers all over the main square.

"Looks like we picked a good day to come to town," Cleo said.

Although Cleo and Tori were wearing their leather armor with their twin swords strapped across their backs, people didn't take much notice as they crowded around the tables and booths. It was quite the hum of voices and Tori smiled at the prosperity in the land again. She and Cleo tied their horses at the first hitching post they came to and set out on foot to examine the wares. There were goods of every kind, from food stuffs to swords. The mid-summer festival was huge and brought people and sellers from all over Vasara. The fall festival in Kensington was the only other festival that was larger. Cleo stopped at one of the booths. There was a table of jewelry, and she seemed to be looking at something in particular.

"You see something you like Boss?"

She kept staring at it. Tori looked over her shoulder. Laying on the table was a bracelet made out of a metal that is very rare, godstone. In the center was an embossed symbol, a bright red arrow on a field of black. She knew immediately what Cleo was thinking about. Bart. That archer had touched Cleo's heart more than Tori realized. A single tear slid down Cleo's cheek.

"Can I help you?" A tall man with dark hair and wearing a dark leather apron said noticing their interest.

"We will take that," Tori said.

Cleo looked at her, unable to speak but had gratitude in her eyes.

"Are you sure, it's quite expensive," the vendor said.

Tori pulled the pouch off her belt and poured out three gold coins. "Take it out of that, I'm not in the mood to haggle."

The man's eyes bulged. He took one gold coin and pushed the other two back to Tori. Walking away, Cleo put the bracelet on her wrist and connected the ends together for a snug fit.

"I'm sorry I got a little emotional back there," she said

looking down at the bracelet. "You have no idea what this means to me."

"I think maybe I do my friend," Tori said throwing an arm around her shoulder.

"Tori! Cleo!"

They both looked up as a man from one of the booths came running up.

"Andros!" Tori said as they exchanged a crushing embrace followed by Cleo.

"What are you doing here?" Andy said. "Not that I am complaining. Abby will be so happy to see you both."

"We were in this general vicinity, so we thought it a good time to visit Andros the black," Tori said giving him a wink.

Andy laughed. "Come on, grab your horses. We will go meet Abby at the library, then head up to the house for dinner. You're staying the night, it's not up for discussion."

"That sounds perfect to me," Cleo said. "I could use a break from inns and trail camps."

"You're getting soft, Boss."

They all laughed at that as they headed off to go find Abby. Later that evening found them in the sitting room of Abby and Andy's house. Cleo and Tori were sipping some fine Dragonsgate wine as Andy and Abby put the finishing touches on dinner. Suddenly there was a knock on the door.

"Tori," came Andy's voice from the kitchen. "That's Ben, he's joining us for dinner. Can you let him in?"

"Certainly," Tori responded.

Tori went to the door and opened it.

Ben stared wide-eyed for a moment.

"You alright?" Tori asked him.

"What? Oh, yes. Just startled is all. I was expecting Andros or Abby."

"I'm Tori," she said extending her hand.

"Yes, I know. Andros has spoken of you often," he said taking her hand and shaking it.

Tori felt that Ben seemed a little nervous. The god only knows what Andros has told him, Tori thought to herself.

Ben stepped inside as Tori introduced him to Cleo, whom Ben also knew based on Andros' descriptions of her.

"How long have you known Abby and Andros?" Cleo asked.

Ben rubbed his chin pondering. Tori started to feel a pressure in the center of her back.

"I would say coming up on five years."

"It's funny that our paths have never crossed. We have visited here several times in that time frame."

"It is strange, I agree," Ben said.

"Ben!" Andy said walking into the room. "You know Tori and Cleo, right?"

"He does now," Cleo said.

"I thought you had met before?"

"We were just talking about that," Tori said. "How our paths have never crossed. Just bad timing I'm sure."

"Well you know each other now. Shall we go sit down, Abby is just finishing setting the table."

They walked towards the dining room. The table looked fantastic with all the food and drink laid out. Abby and Andros never held back when they had guests over. Suddenly Tori's medallion, the symbol of her priesthood to the god Fallon burned red-hot against her chest, setting off alarms in her head. Tori knew not to give away what she was feeling. Something was very wrong in this house. Her eyes scanned the rooms quickly, looking for any threat. She could see none readily apparent. Then she caught it. The very faintest hint of sulfur. It was there for a second and then it was gone.

28

"You go ahead, I need to get something from my saddle bags," Tori said heading back to the sitting room. She grabbed her twin swords and put them in their sheaths on her back.

"What's wrong?"

Tori wheeled around as she saw Cleo standing in the doorway.

"Could you feel it? Tori said

"What?" Cleo asked looking around.

"I'm not sure, but there is danger in this house. I feel it."

"What do you want to do?"

"I'm going into the frozen moment right now."

As the Cath Priomh, and also the priest of Fallon, Tori is able to enter that space between one second and the next. Where everything is frozen and she herself is invisible since she is moving outside of time. She can't do much in it except travel while the world stands still. It is also very useful for reconnaissance, which is what she was about to do now.

"I'm coming with you."

"Okay."

Tori gripped her medallion with the twin swords embossed on it. It was her symbol of her priesthood to the god, Fallon. She didn't really need to hold it, but it helped her focus. Visualizing a tear in the fabric of reality, her and Cleo stepped through, both drawing their swords. It always took her breath away with the vibrancy of color in this altered dimension. Looking out the sitting room window she could see a robin, frozen in flight.

"Let me take lead Boss."

Cleo nodded as Tori stepped out front and into the hall. *The others must be in the dining area,* she thought. Tori scanned down the hall to the back of the house, the fire around her eyes was spinning madly.

"Can you sense anything?" Cleo asked.

"Not that way. Let's head to where the others are."

Walking slowly and peering into the empty rooms they passed they came to the dining room. Ben and Abby were seated and Andy was frozen as he carried a tray of beef to the table. The evil hit Tori like a ton of bricks as she stepped into the room. She leveled her swords and started sweeping them back and forth. Cleo also had her sword in the attack position.

"What is that?" Cleo said

Tori looked back at her sharply. "You feel it too, don't you? It's in this room."

Tori started to walk around the table slowly. When she got to the far end she was directly opposite Ben when she saw a flash of red out of her peripheral vision. Her eyes locked with Ben, and suddenly Ben's eyes flashed red.

"It's Ben!" Tori exclaimed looking incredulously at Cleo.

"Are you sure?"

"Watch his eyes. Every few seconds they flash red."

Cleo saw the truth as his eyes suddenly flashed brighter and held steady.

"What is it? A demon?"

"Yes," Tori replied, "but not like any demon we have ever encountered before."

"I have never heard of a demon coming through the Corridor and taking on the shape of a human."

The Corridor is on the eastern most section of the Border Lands. It is the only place demons can come into Vasara and take physical shape. Unless one can create portals such as the ones the warlocks of Parma used.

"It's worse than that," Tori said slowly moving, getting closer to Ben. The thing's eyes never left Tori's.

"What do you mean?"

"It has been able to befriend, work and live beside Andros for five years. Have you ever known a demon to do anything but wreak havoc five minutes after coming through the corridor? They don't get jobs nor do they make friends. And they certainly don't sit down for dinner."

"A demon lord perhaps?" Cleo said.

"At the very least," Tori said coming face to face with Ben. "There is something else."

"What?"

"This thing is aware of us."

Tori could see malevolence and hatred radiating back at her. This thing wanted to destroy her.

"I guess any element of surprise is gone," Cleo said as she walked over to the other side of Ben.

"This is bad, Boss. We had a whole conversation with him before we even sensed anything."

"Alright," Cleo said squaring here shoulders. "What's the plan."

Tori looked sadly at Andros and Abby. They were not going to understand what she was about to do to their friend.

"Tori, we aren't going to be able to prevent the shock they will experience," Cleo said seeing her friend struggle.

"I know Boss. I just wish I could pull Andros in here and explain it to him." Tori looked at Ben and felt like there was movement in his body.

"It's going to be ready for us the second we step out, isn't it?"

"Yes." Tori sighed. "Let's just get this over with. We will both move behind him and come out at the same time."

Cleo nodded. "I'll go low."

Tori nodded back. "I'll go high."

Tori focused right behind Ben's back. She held both of her swords in front of her crisscrossed. Cleo was next to her, crouched.

It was over in a second. As soon as Cleo and Tori came into real-time, Ben started to rise, but Tori was too quick. With a scissor like motion, Tori cut off Ben's head with her twin blades and sent it flying towards Andy as Cleo's swords pierced his back and came out his chest. The platter that Andy had been holding crashed to the floor and broke into many pieces as Ben's head landed at his feet. Abby let out a blood-curdling scream as she frantically patted her chest.

***

Andy was paralyzed for a moment and on instinct wrapped himself with the source, the power of the five gods pouring through his veins as he heard Abby scream and saw Ben's head go flying.

"Ben! By the gods, Tori!" Andy shouted as he ran over to Abby. "What the hell did you do?"

"Abby, what's wrong?" he said looking for a possible injury.

"It burns, it burns!" she kept saying as she tried pulling the death dagger out from under her shirt. Andy reached in and grabbed it, the talisman fitting perfectly with the branding of the death dagger that Samara had caused many years earlier when Andy had come back to Vasara for the second time. He screamed at the pain as it fell out of his hand.

Just then there was a sizzling sound. Andy turned quickly to see Ben's head turning to ash and vapor along with his body until there was only vapor left. It hovered, then sped like lightning towards Abby's chest. Upon connecting with the death dagger, the vaporous cloud exploded into a thousand sparks of light that quickly shot upward with an unearthly shriek. The force of it when it struck hurled Abby against the wall, where she now lay in a heap. Andy ran over and pulled her onto his lap, gently patting her face.

"Abby, are you alright? Abby. Abby, wake up, wake up."

He kept caressing her brow as Tori walked up and put a hand on his shoulder.

"Don't touch me!" Andy said with heat. "What is going on Tori?"

"Andros?" Abby said coming to.

"Oh thank god!" Andy said. "It's alright, I've got you. Take it easy."

"What happened?" Abby said pushing her disheveled hair out of her face.

"I don't know," Andy said helping Abby to her feet. "But Tori is about to tell us," he said looking angrily at Tori. Tori looked sadly at her friend and hung her head.

"Alright, enough of this," Cleo said stepping between them bringing some order to the chaos. "Andros, you know Tori. You know she wouldn't do something without good reason, don't you? Don't you?" she repeated.

Andy blinked at her as if he had just received a verbal slap. Whatever it was it calmed him down and allowed him to focus. He took three calming breaths as he still held Abby against his chest. Looking at Cleo, he could see the green around the edges of her eyes which only happened during great stress or anger. In his heart he knew there was more to this than what he was seeing. Shamefacedly he looked at Tori.

"I'm sorry Tori," he apologized. "I lost myself there for a moment."

"It is understandable Andros," Tori said. "To see your friend cut down in front of you would throw anyone into shock. Please believe me, there was no other way."

"I do believe you," Andy said and meant it. "Let's go outside on the porch and you can tell us what the hell just happened."

Andy and Abby sat down on the porch swing, much like

the one they used to have at the house on the banks of the Hudson River. It was actually Ben who had made this one. Andy still couldn't wrap his head around what had occurred. Tori was leaning against a porch post while Cleo pulled over one of the chairs.

"Okay, Tori," Andy said, "I'm ready to listen."

Tori told Andy and Abby everything she felt and saw from the time Ben arrived to when his head landed at Andy's feet. He could only shake his head in befuddlement as she finished her tale.

"It doesn't seem possible," Abby said. "He's had dinner here, formed friendships, friendships with us. Any book I have ever read about demon lore gives no hint to this kind of behavior."

"I have been thinking about that," Cleo said. "These demons have had some help."

"God help you mean," Andy said looking at Tori who nodded.

"Meliakken," Tori said. "There is no one else it could be."

"Something took me by total surprise though," Cleo said looking at Abby. "What was happening with you?"

"I don't know," Abby replied. "As soon as you killed Ben, the talisman flared against my skin."

"I'm wondering if it is because it's so closely associated with death and the underworld that it can somehow feel the presence of demons," Tori said.

Abby's eyes suddenly widened.

"What is it Abby," Andy asked concerned.

She looked at him head on. "You know how sometimes the talisman feels warm or itches at random times?"

"Yes of course. It happened earlier today when Ben..." Now Andy's eyes went wide.

Abby nodded in confirmation.

"What are we missing here?" Cleo asked seeing their expressions.

Abby took the death dagger out and held it in her palm. "It

hasn't always been so, but now and then, the talisman would grow warm against my skin."

"Do you know when was the first time you felt this?" Tori asked earnestly.

"I do now," Abby said. "It was the first time Andros introduced me to Ben."

Tori and Cleo exchanged a look. "What?" Andy asked seeing their exchange.

"I believe your wife will be able to sense these demons so that we may destroy them," Tori said.

"Now hold on just a minute," Andy said angrily. "Abby has been through enough. We finally have some peace, and I am getting tired of saving the world all the time."

"Andros, think about it," Tori said squatting down next to him. "This thing attached itself to you for five years. It was waiting for something."

"It's true Andros," Cleo said. "It wasn't by accident that Ben happened to settle in a town that had a dragon in it."

"Well, I'm not the only dragon now you know. Why…"

Suddenly the color drained from his face. Tori stood up quick as if her ass was on fire.

"The other dragons," Tori said. "They could be in the same danger."

"And now it is even worse," Cleo said catching on.

"What do you mean?" Abby said.

"That thing that was Ben will return to the underworld. He will report what happened."

"Can you summon your brothers?" Tori asked.

"I can try and reach them from the source."

"Take me there now."

"The source is for dragons and wizards. I don't know if I can," Andy said.

"I'm Fallon's priest. Pan was able to go there, so I'm certain you can take me."

Andy got up and sat cross-legged on the porch. Tori got down and did the same.

"Give me your hands," Andy instructed.

Tori placed her hands in his and closed her eyes. Andy sent his thought out to hers.

Tori, can you hear me, Andy said.

I hear you Andros.

Imagine your spirit separating from your body. It's going to feel weird.

I can feel what you mean. By the gods, this is strange. Then suddenly, things went dark.

Chapter 4

"Okay Tori, you can open your eyes," Andy said aloud. He could feel her spirit shaking at the experience of being pulled apart from her conscious self.

Tori did as he instructed and gasped at what she saw.

"By the gods, is this where we go when we die? It's like a paradise!"

Andy had to laugh at that. "No, this is just the wooded path that leads to the source of power of the five gods. I guess it is like a paradise to us. I come here whenever I need a respite."

"I can understand why," Tori said feeling the peace of the wood and looking at the flowers that seemed to be everywhere, dotting the forest floor like a carpet.

"Let's walk to the source," he said moving down the path as Tori followed. "I sent the call out to my brothers. They will come there if they are able."

As they got to the source with its five radiating arms, Andy held out his hands and let each energy beam brush his palms, filling him with both peace and renewed strength.

"Is this where you came when you healed me?" Tori asked.

"Yes," Andy said remembering that day of Tori's healing and how Fallon's energy knocked him unconscious for three weeks.

"I'm guessing the red one is Fallon's."

"It is," he replied. "I never felt such raw energy before or since, it was intense."

"Andros?"

Both Andy and Tori turned around to see Brion walking towards them. Last time Andy had seen him was at their yearly training with Emilia at Laurel Hollow. He walked over and embraced his brother.

"I see we've got a real lovefest going on here," came a voice from down the path, laughing.

Both men turned as Caleb, sporting a red goatee, came striding up and slapped them both on the back.

"Good to see you Bull," Brion said. "Where are you at right now?"

"In the Wilds with Brie. She's looking for some herbs, and being as I was close by, asked if I wanted to come along just in case some alfar decided to give her some trouble."

Brie is Emilia's good friend and captain of her own contingent of faeries when they go into battle. She also has the gift of being able to talk to birds.

It wasn't long before each of Andy's brothers came walking up to the source. Everyone that is but Finn.

"Anyone seen Finn?" Brion asked.

"I haven't seen him since last year's training," Jace said. The silver haired dragon was looking retrospect as he said this.

"What is it Jace?" Andy asked catching his look.

"It's nothing concrete," Jace said, "just a feeling, but I think he renewed his search for Zana."

This always troubled Andy. Since their encounter with Zana at their battle with the shriker, Finn had been obsessed with finding her. He would never talk to anyone about the depth of their relationship, but he had imagined it must have been very profound.

"Why are we here Andros?" Elek asked.

Elek was the quietest of his brothers. The most introverted until you got to know him. Andy had some deep conversations with him whenever he would come to Dragonsgate to visit. He had also been to Elek's house in Hadley several times over the years. It was a beautiful home built on a winery. Elek was very big into making wine. He loved the craft and had told Andy it relaxed him greatly to be out in the fields tending his grapes of all kinds of varieties. Abby loved his wines and had several bottles in their cellar.

"I will let Tori tell you."

"I was about to ask how she came to be here," Caleb said, "not that it's a problem or anything. Just curious."

"Because I am Fallon's priest, Andros was able to bring me along," Tori said.

Tori went on to tell the dragons about the encounter with Ben, from the moment she met him to Abby being slammed against the wall. They listened without interruption. When she had finished, it was Caleb who spoke up.

"So what does this mean exactly?"

"I know what it means," Brion said. "Which is why I assume you summoned us here, Andros."

Andy knew Brion would see the implications immediately.

"When did Ben arrive in Dragonsgate?" Brion asked Andy.

"About five years ago."

Brion turned to his brothers. "Did any of you have someone come into your lives within that time that has gotten close to you?"

It turned out they all had. Some were even women.

"But how are we to know if they are truly these super-demons you speak of?" Herve asked.

"Abby can tell," Andy said.

Tori looked at him sharply, and Andy knew why. After his declaration they had done enough, he now knew this wasn't over, they had been created for the protection of Vasara. And he knew his wife. She would not sit idly by if it was in her power to make a difference.

"If what you say is true," Caleb said, "and time is of the essence, how will she reach us all in time to find out if these people are false or not?"

"That's a good question," Brion said.

"Through the frozen moment," Tori said looking at Andy. "You could fly us to where each of your brothers are."

"How long would we be traveling?" Andy asked.

"Who is the farthest from Dragonsgate?" Tori asked.

"Probably me," Gael responded. "I'm in Akron, just beyond the Mistral Islands. I flew Emma here so she could do some more research on a place the trees have been whispering to her about, it's called Otherwhere."

"What a strange name," Brion said.

"Once the queen heard it, she asked me to fly Emma here. Also, Nia is here. She is the one that I met about five years ago." Gael looked crestfallen. Andy had a feeling some affection had built up between them. How many of these demons had worked their way into his dragon brother's hearts that they would be required to cut down. Andy put a hand on Gael's shoulder.

"She could be true, brother," Andy said to him. Gael looked at him gratefully, but something told him that might not be the case. Andy also wondered what it was about Otherwhere that would make his mother send Emma to Akron.

"Okay," Tori said, "It looks like we will probably be going to all four corners of Vasara. I'm guessing two months flying time. But for each of you, you will see us within the hour."

"That is so bizarre," Caleb said shaking his head.

"I think we better go now," Andy said. After getting everyone's location, Andy and Tori came back to their bodies.

"Well?" Cleo said when they opened their eyes.

"We've got a long road ahead of us," Tori told her friend.

Abby and Andy were in their room gathering supplies they would need. Reaching into his closet he pulled out his sword. He paused before putting it on the pile. He pulled it out of its sheath to reveal a blade that was not silver, but black. Curious patterns and designs were etched along its length.

"Remembering again?" Abby said as her arms circled his waist and she rested her chin on his shoulder and looked down at the sword.

"Yes," Andy replied thinking back to that time with his sister.

It was a couple years after the battle of the warlocks that Emilia and Andy had decided to make their way through the holy mound of the alfar to Trystan's forge, where Eriyn, their grandfather, had told them he had left something for them. After traveling through the mound together, they came to the door with the symbols of the house of Caster.

"Do you know how to open it?" Andy asked.

"Yes," Emilia said pushing her dark hair behind her pointed ears. "Mom made me practice it over and over."

Emilia traced the pattern on the door that made the design illuminate with light. Pushing the door open, sunlight greeted their eyes as they looked out onto a lush green valley. In the center was a small lake with a house made entirely of black stone situated on the water's edge. Attached to the house by a breezeway was a workshop and forge.

Andy and Emilia walked into the workshop. Tools were aligned perfectly on the wall, with barrels of scrap metal in one corner. The forge was lit and Andy felt that it burned with an eternal flame.

"Look!" Emilia said pointing.

Two pedestals stood in the middle of the room. On each

pedestal was a metal plaque. Written in beautiful flowing script were their names; Andros and Donella. On Emilia's pedestal was what looked like black metal rod in a leather strap that would fit around your bicep. On the other was a sword, wrapped in a leather sheath.

"I see you have found them," a voice from behind them said.

Both of them whirled and their eyes lit up at who they saw.

"Grandfather!" they both said at once as they rushed into his crushing embrace.

"It is so good to see you both," Eriyn said as they pulled apart. "Trystan had put a ward on these that if ever you should come I would be allowed to come back for this one moment."

Both Andy and Emilia's eyes welled up with tears at being given this gift to be with their grandfather. The last time they saw him was so fleeting.

"Can you stay long?" Emilia asked.

"I'm afraid not my dear. My time is very brief. I wanted to be able to visit with you one last time, and also to explain your gifts. Go and pick them up."

Andy and Emilia did as he instructed.

Eriyn took Emilia's gift and strapped it to her arm.

"This is a spear, Donella. One I made especially for you from a metal that Trystan himself had created. Hold it in your hand."

Emilia took the rod off its strap and held it in her palm.

"Now think of it extending."

Emilia did, and the rod snapped into the shape of a spear, not unlike a talon spear. Both ends were pointed and razor sharp, its entire length the color of midnight.

"Can you see that golden apple on the high branch over there?"

"I see it."

"Throw the spear at the apple."

Emilia aimed, and with very little effort, threw the spear

with deadly accuracy and split the apple in half. What she was not expecting was the spear doing a loop and headed directly for her.

"Hold your hand out," Eriyn said quickly.

Emilia did that and caught the spear perfectly as she grasped it in her outstretched hand.

"By the gods!" Emilia exclaimed.

"Well, one god anyway," her grandfather said with a wink. She laughed as she hugged her grandfather. "Its name is Nocte. I pray it serves you well."

"Thank you, Grandfather," Emilia said making it shrink in size and strapping it onto her arm again. "I shall never be without it I promise."

Eriyn smiled and put a hand to her cheek.

"Andros, hand me the sword."

Taking the sword from Andy, Eriyn drew it out of its sheath. The blade was black with the symbols and patterns of the house of Caster in gold along its length.

"This sword will amplify your energy, and is also made from the same metal as your sister's spear," he told Andy. "If you draw from the source and channel it through the blade, the power will increase tenfold. Also, if it is strapped to your body, when you make the change to your dragon form, it will still be there when you switch back.

"That is fantastic!" Andy said. "This is an incredible gift Grandfather, thank you."

Eriyn's eyes welled up with tears. "It is the least I could do for my only grandchildren. And hopefully it will go some ways in making up for the evil I caused in my madness."

"That has all been forgiven," Emilia said touching his arm.

"I know everyone has forgiven me my dear, I however still have a hard time forgiving myself, but I am getting there," He said smiling. "I must leave now. You will not see me again in this life."

Both Andy and Emilia looked crestfallen. Eriyn grabbed them both in his embrace. "Do not look downcast, we will all be together again one day. Remember, the house of Caster flows through your veins. I know you will lift that name to greater heights than I ever could. Be well my children, tell your mother and father I love them."

Andy could feel Eriyn starting to fade away. "Grandfather! Does the sword have a name?"

"Scáth Gealach," came the reply, "it means moon shadow." And with that, their grandfather passed from that world never to be seen again.

Andy was still staring at the sword when Abby brought him out of his musings.

"You miss him, don't you?" she said. Andy knew she meant his grandfather.

He nodded. "I've only seen him twice, but I felt like he has been a part of me for a very long time." Abby touched his cheek in understanding.

Andy had never used the sword in combat, with things being quiet for the last ten years, but he had practiced with it a couple of times. His mother, the queen of the faeries was still a little put out with him for blasting a hole through that hill in Laurel Hollow. Putting the sword back in its sheath, Andy slung it over his shoulder to rest on his back. It was too large to strap to his waist.

"Are you ready?" Tori asked popping her head in.

"Yes. We will meet you outside," Andy said. As Tori left he turned to Abby, who was just finishing strapping on her own sword that Andy's father had given her during their travels to find Samara and the death dagger. It was unlike other swords in that it could shoot lightning out of its tip.

"You sure about doing this?" he asked his wife.

Abby put a hand on either side of his face and kissed his lips soundly.

"If not us Andros, then who? We have been given these gifts for a reason and I intend to use them to the fullest to keep our home free."

Andy could only beam at the courage of this woman he loved.

"Shall we?" he said grabbing their packs and allowing her to exit first.

"Let's," she nodded striding out the door and down the hall leaving Andy smiling in her wake.

Chapter 5

Luel was staring out of the library window in Cavanah Hall, the ancient home of the queen of the faeries, her light brown wings slowly moving back and forth in a soothing, meditative way. Before marrying Redlin, she used to spend as much time away from this place as possible. She didn't realize that in trying to run away from her destiny, she wound up running right into it. Of course her goddess had played a big part in that, so she felt like she had never really stood a chance. Thinking of Braylynn brought to mind a fact that had been troubling her for quite some time. She hadn't been able to contact her for going on five years now. Tera was beside herself. She was always pestering Luel to reach out to her goddess so they could talk to her. Braylynn didn't really mind popping in for these spiritual visits, but now all contact had stopped and that worried her.

She now had another worry. Emma had come to her telling her that Arsa, the oldest tree in Vasara had kept repeating a single word over and over. Otherwhere. Her blood had drained from her face on hearing that word. Gael and Caleb had been hanging around Laurel Hollow, so she asked Gael to fly Emma to Akron to see if there was any information on Otherwhere stored in the archives on the island.

"Mom?"

Luel turned around to smile at her daughter. Her dark hair was done up in a braid and her green wings were folded behind her back, the pearl comb of the goddess tucked into her hair. She had her spear, Nocte, strapped to her bicep. Emilia had told her how her father came to her and Andy to bestow their gifts on them. Luel wished she could have seen him one last time.

"How are you dear?" Luel asked as she hugged her daughter.

"I'm good, Mom," Emilia said looking closely at her mother. "Tera said you were looking for me?"

"How is Lyson, is he with you?"

Emilia could tell something was up with her mother. "He's good. He was in his library when I left him, pouring over some scrolls he had borrowed from Stefan in Albion."

"That's a fine man you've chosen as a life partner."

"I think so too," Emilia said smiling at her comment. "Mom, is anything wrong?"

"Is it that obvious?"

"You have seemed preoccupied as of late."

Luel went back to the window to look out. From her vantage point she could see the royal garden with its winding path and many flowers arrayed on either side. Emilia came to stand beside her.

"Do you remember when you first came back from Vasara, and I told you of my encounter with my father at Trystan's forge?"

"Yes, I do," Emilia said.

"After I had come out of that place with your grandfather's crown, the first person I saw was your father."

Realization dawned on Emilia.

"That is when you saw his death."

"Yes," Luel replied looking at her daughter as a single tear slid down her cheek.

"Mom, what has happened? Is Dad alright, where is he?"

"He's fine dear. He's up in the Macedon Mountains with Loki. But there is something that's happened."

Luel told her daughter of Emma's visit and what Arsa had said.

"What does this Otherwhere have to do with Dad?"

"In my vision, your father is standing by a gateway on an island in the center of a lake. An energy bolt comes streaking out of the sky and obliterates him, all the while echoing across the world is a single word. Otherwhere."

"Have you told Dad? We should warn him."

"I haven't told him. Whenever I try to bring it up, something holds me back. Maybe he's not supposed to know. Maybe if he does know, it will come true, or maybe not. I just don't know."

"I heard a lot of maybes in there Mom."

"That is why I asked you to come. Something really tells me your father shouldn't know. But I needed to tell you. We need to protect him at all costs." She looked pleadingly at her daughter. "Emilia, I don't know what I would do if I lost your father. It is not something I ever wanted to contemplate, but when I had that vision, the worry was always present but buried for the most part. Now it is front and center and has life in it because of that one word."

Emilia hugged her mother. "What do we do, Mom?"

We just need…" Luel raised a hand to Emilia then put a finger to her lips to remain quiet. She thought she had heard something. Turning her skin the color of her surroundings Luel became nearly invisible as she flew around the room before darting behind a high back chair.

"Ow! Hey! That's not fair!"

Suddenly a silver-haired head rose above the chair with the now visible queen holding Tera under her arms.

"Alright young lady, why were you eavesdropping?" Luel said sternly.

"I don't suppose you would buy that I fell asleep, would you?" Tera asked hopefully.

The look Luel gave her clearly told her she wouldn't. Tera looked over towards Emilia for help. Emilia crossed her arms and gave Tera the same look as her mother.

"Okay, okay. I thought with Donella arriving that maybe you were going to contact Braylynn and I just wanted to be here. I didn't mean to hear about Redlin's death, honest I didn't. Is he really going to die? I'm not sure if hiding this from him is best. I can help! Let me just…"

"Tera, stop," the queen said softening. "I can't really fault you for wanting to be here, but you are not to breathe a word of this to anyone. Is that understood?"

"Of course your majesty," Tera said with all sincerity. "I know how to keep a secret.

Luel just rolled her eyes.

"What about Lyson, Mom? I don't like keeping things from him."

The queen seemed to ponder that for a moment.

"Yes, tell Lyson. It might be good to have a spy in that brotherhood."

"Your majesty! I'm shocked," Tera said wide-eyed while trying to stifle a giggle.

"Would you like to spend the next month cleaning out the Hall, missy?" Luel said with a raised eyebrow.

Tera clamped both hands over her mouth and wisely shut up.

"I know what you mean, Mom," Emilia said smiling at her sister. "He will keep an eye on Dad for us and be discreet."

"Thank you dear."

"What about Andy?" Tera said before clamping her hands back over her mouth.

"By the goddess! Absolutely not!" Luel said. "He's my son and I love him dearly, but he has never been able to keep a secret."

Emilia burst out laughing.

"It stays with the four of us," Luel said. "And you," she said pointing at Tera. "You are going to make yourself useful. Emma is in Akron looking up anything she can find on Otherwhere, but she doesn't know why. I want you to fly up to Albion and ask Stefan if he has heard or read anything about it."

"What if he asks me why?"

"You can tell him what Arsa had told Emma, that part is not a secret. Just anything about my husband stays buried inside, understood?"

"Yes ma'am," Tera said flying off at once.

"Do you think that is a good idea?" Emilia said watching Tera fly away.

"She will be fine. It will keep her busy and out of mischief. She may even find out something from Stefan. Let's go see Lyson."

***

Lyson was sitting at his large oak desk in his library that he had built adjoining the house of the Dragon Summoner. A breezeway connected the two with a kind of mini-courtyard with some benches and a garden that he found to be a perfect place for study and contemplation. He had a scroll open in front of him and was studying it intently. It was a map of the Border Lands. Lyson was no stranger to maps of his home country, he had studied them for years as a general and Border Lands warrior, but this map was different. Using his scale of distance there was an extra section in the southernmost border that wasn't on any other map that he could recall. He had gotten this map from Stefan, the baron of Albion. Stefan had told him it was buried in a cellar of the manor. It was discovered when they had started excavating to enlarge the space for storage. There was no way to tell when it dated from, but the fact that it was the Border Lands was not in doubt.

He looked up and thought for a moment. Extending his black wings, he flew to the topmost shelf on the other side of the room. He always stored his oldest scrolls here. Taking the one he was looking for, he brought it down to the desk and rolled it out. It was the oldest map of the Border Lands that he had. Looking carefully, his suspicions were confirmed, this map did not have the extra section, and this map dated back to just before the five gods departed Vasara. Lyson surmised the map he got from Stefan was probably the first ever one created of the Border Lands. Going back to that map, something caught Lyson's eye as he lifted it up and the rays of the sun hit the edges. Grabbing the parchment, he ran to the window and let the daylight illuminate what he saw. There in the corner was a symbol of two crossed swords. The only other time he had seen this image was on Tori's medallion which signified her as the priest of Fallon.

"Could this be Fallon's own map?" Lyson said aloud.

"What is that dear?"

Lyson turned quickly, startled, but visibly relaxed when he saw it was his beloved and her mother.

"Sorry if we startled you," Luel said.

"No, no. It's okay. I was just engrossed in this map, that's all."

"Did you find something?" Emilia asked.

Lyson went on to tell them of his discovery with the map.

"What do you think it means, love?"

"I'm not entirely sure. But I know if I am to figure this out I will need Tori. It is no coincidence that the symbol on the map is the same as her priest medallion."

"I believe you are right," Emilia agreed.

"I will try and contact Cleo, I'm sure she knows where Tori is."

Lyson rolled the map back up and flew both scrolls back up to the top shelf.

"Now, what brings the queen of the faeries and the Dragon Summoner to my humble library? Not that I'm complaining," he said smiling.

Luel filled him in on everything Arsa had told Emma and her vision of Redlin's death, and also about limiting its secrecy to just the four of them.

"You really think Tera can keep this to herself?" Lyson asked doubtfully.

"We gave her a task," the queen said. "As long as she has something to do and is contributing, she will see it as part of her quest."

"I've never heard of this Otherwhere," Lyson said quickly scanning his books and scrolls, trying to remember if he had read of it anywhere. "But I will keep an eye on Redlin, you can count on that."

"That actually eases my mind quite a bit. Thank you Lyson."

Lyson bowed deep to the queen.

"Oh stop that," she laughed. "I will leave you too alone now. I need to get back to send some dispatches."

After Lyson and Emilia said their farewells, they retired to the main house and sat in front of the fireplace, Emilia was on Lyson's lap as they each sipped some wine. He had created a magical fire in the fireplace. The logs burned, but gave off no heat, being that it is hot to begin with in Laurel Hollow in mid-summer; one doesn't necessarily want a real fire. But this gave the coziness without the discomfort of heat.

"Are you worried, love?" Lyson asked.

Emilia turned her green eyes to lock with his as she ran a hand along his stubble.

"I am," she said finally. "I can't lose my Dad, Lyson. I can't."

Lyson put his hands on both sides of her face as she looked at him pleadingly. There was not a thing he wouldn't do for this woman he loved.

"Donella, I promise we will find a way to make sure that doesn't happen. If I have to tie him up and lock him in a cave so he never gets near Otherwhere, I will."

Emilia laughed and then kissed his lips soundly.

Em, can you hear me?

Andy? Where are you?

"What is it?" Lyson asked as Emilia suddenly sat straight up.

"It's Andy, he's calling me."

"Where is he?"

Meet me at the glade, Andy said.

"To the glade," Emilia told Lyson.

Both of them shot out the door and flew straight for the glade where the Dragon Summoner trained with the dragons. As they reached the edge of the glade they landed and scanned the sky.

"There!" Lyson said pointing.

They could see Andy's black dragon shape framed against the blue sky as he started to come in for a landing. He seemed to be carrying three passengers. As he landed his occupants jumped off and he transformed into his human self.

"Cleo?" Lyson said as he recognized his sister running towards him. He flew to her and wrapped her up in an embrace. "Whatever are you doing here?"

"Good to see you too brother," Cleo said smiling.

Lyson smiled back. "I am glad you're here. I was actually going to contact you to see if you knew where Tori was, but I see you brought her with you."

"Good to see you again, General," Tori said.

Once Andy and Abby had caught up and gave their loved ones a proper greeting they got down to business.

"What's going on Andy?" Emilia asked. "I can't imagine this is a social visit seeing that you are all armed."

Andy told Emilia and Lyson about Ben, and the other "friends" that had come into his brothers' lives. They listened without interruption when Tori told them how they had dispatched three of these human-looking demon lords and how they were doing it.

"How can I help?" Emilia asked. "Although it looks like you have everything under control."

"We thought so too," Cleo said. "But coming out of the frozen moment and finding and killing them eats up precious time, and now they are aware."

"Em, the power these things have is more than any demon lord I have ever faced," Andy said earnestly. "We need your help, and we need to go right now."

Emilia looked to Lyson.

"Go ahead, love," Lyson said. "Help your brother and the others. I will keep watch here, as well as on that other matter the queen spoke of," he said giving her a knowing look.

Emilia nodded as Andy started running to give himself space. Once he made the change everyone climbed on his back as Tori made her slash in the fabric of reality and the black dragon plunged inside as it closed behind them, leaving the wizard of the faeries alone in the glade.

Chapter 6

The breeze was chilled up in the Macedon Mountains, even though it was mid-summer. Redlin ran his fingers through his thick mane of hair as he looked out at the falcons circling on the air currents looking for prey.

"You still thinking?" a voice said from behind.

Redlin turned his head to see Loki walk up to the wall that the wizard was leaning against, his dark hair with grey streaks blowing wildly in the wind,.

"I am," Redlin said. "It makes no sense Loki."

Redlin and Loki had both come up to the dragons' cave after a disquiet had entered their hearts in regards to the living prophecy. The cave has a chamber, the wizards chamber, which of course only wizards of the five gods can enter. It is circular and domed with the wizard's symbol carved into the center of the floor. The symbol is a sphere with five radiating beams, an exact replica of the source. Any wizard of the five, standing on this symbol and invoking the chant of seeing, will make the words of the prophecy start to appear on the walls and ceiling. There are other ways to read the prophecy without being in this room, but it is never complete or as pure as it is when read here.

"Perhaps not brother," Loki said. "But you know the prophecy, it has a mind of its own."

"I know, but this is the first time where it shows two branches, each one having a termination point. There is nothing beyond that. As if it is telling us it will cease to exist. How is that possible?"

"Still no word from Trystan?" Loki asked.

"Nothing. Not for years, which I find very troubling."

"Loki, Redlin."

Both wizards turned back towards the door of the cave to see Dain walking up, his sword from being a Border Lands warrior strapped to his hip as it always was, swinging as he walked.

"Well?" Redlin asked.

"They haven't heard anything either," Dain responded.

"What are we talking about?" Loki asked.

"I asked Dain to take the portal to Fenner to ask Rhyan and Ava if they have been able to reach Aditya."

"They haven't been able to speak to the god for about five years," Dain told them.

"For whatever reason it seems the gods have broken off contact," Loki said scratching his beard.

"But why would they do that?" Dain asked.

Just then a shriek that they haven't heard in ten years echoed off the mountain cliffs making the three wizards cover their ears. Creating a shield, they all looked up waiting for a possible attack. Then from both the east and west, two more ear-splitting screeches could be heard.

"Three shrikers!" Loki exclaimed. "How is that possible?"

"One branch of the prophecy has begun," Redlin said.

"Which branch?" Dain asked.

Redlin looked at him soberly. "Meliakken."

"The dragons are in for a rough time," Loki said watching the shrikers head off to the west.

"Are they going where I think they are going?" Dain said.

"Yes," Redlin responded. "The isle of the unicorns."

For the shrikers to reclaim their power they must fly to what is now known as the isle of the unicorns, due to the fact that they are bound there for the next thousand years.

"Don't worry," Loki told Dain. "The unicorns can protect themselves. They also have the ability to leave the island for a time if things get dicey, thanks to Pan."

"I would love to know how he managed that," Redlin said.

"You and me both brother," Loki responded, "but Pan refuses to say."

"What does that other branch of the prophecy mean?" Dain asked.

"I'm not sure," Redlin said. "Let's go back inside and look at it again."

The three wizards went back into the wizard's chamber, Redlin walked into the center while Dain and Loki remained on the outer circle. Holding his hands up, Redlin began his chant, drawing the source into himself as his hands began to move, almost as if he were writing. Thin lines started running up the walls creating a tree with many forks and branches of the past. The two newest limbs appeared as before with the ends suddenly cut-off, no new shoots to show that it would continue. Symbols and words filled the spaces between the edges of the branch. On the one were symbols of the shrikers as well as an image of the god Meliakken himself, his name written across the sky above the White Castle.

On the other branch there was only an image of a doorway of squared off stones forming the sides and the lintel with a raven perched on top. Inscribed into the stone was the letter R over a feathered quill. Above that was a single word. Otherwhere.

Redlin let his hands fall to his sides and let the images go since nothing new was forthcoming.

"Well, that helped very little," Loki said crankily.

Dain had to laugh.

"What's so funny?" Loki said with a raised eyebrow.

"You sounded just like Diminitus for a moment," Dain said after getting his mirth under control. Redlin was also smiling and stifling some giggles.

"Well, we are probably pretty close in age, maybe that's it."

Both Redlin and Dain burst out laughing anew as Loki crossed his arms and scowled as Diminitus would.

"What I don't understand is why your symbol is on the lintel, Redlin," Loki said once they had composed themselves.

"That's your symbol?" Dain asked Redlin.

"Yes. The feathered quill has always been associated with me. The image of circling dragons is Loki. We haven't discovered yours yet."

"You're still new brother," Loki said. "but it will come."

"Thanks," Dain said, "I think."

"So it looks like you are a major player in the prophecy this time," Loki said.

"It would appear so," Redlin replied. "And in true prophecy fashion, it gives no hint as to what I am supposed to do."

"All will be revealed in its proper time," Loki said slapping him on the back and smiling.

"I believe you are enjoying this," Redlin said while giving Loki a sideways glance.

"Fifteen hundred years I've been carrying your load brother, time for you to pick up the slack," he said giving him a wink.

"What are the next steps?" Dain asked.

"Try to find out as much as we can about this Otherwhere," Redlin said. "I believe I will start at the library in Kensington, it has one of the most exhaustive collections in Vasara."

"You need me to do anything?" Dain asked.

"Yes," Redlin said. "Can you go to Laurel Hollow and tell

Luel what is happening and what we are doing?"

"I will. I was heading there anyway to see Leah, she's helping the queen on some matter."

"Excellent. I will travel there as soon as I am able."

After bidding Loki and Dain farewell, Redlin traveled to Kensington via the wizard's portal. He arrived in the tower where Loki had whisked Andy away after Devon had branded his shoulder with his raven symbol. Looking around, the room was empty as he descended the stairs. Seeing a sentry, he called him over to tell him to alert Brayton to his presence. Redlin didn't want to startle or surprise anyone. As he reached the main hall he saw a familiar face.

"Cathal!"

The protector of the prince and Brayton's best friend turned as he heard his name. His face lit up as he saw the wizard and ran over to give him a rough embrace and pound him soundly on the back.

"Easy lad, you're going to rattle my bones loose."

"You're getting soft old man," Cathal said laughing. "All these years of peace have taken some of your edge."

"Well, that may be changing," the wizard said soberly.

"Redlin!"

Redlin saw Brayton come running across the hall and greeted him as Cathal had.

"Easy your Highness, you boys are going to leave me all bruised up at this rate."

Brayton was dressed in light mail with his rapier at his side making him look like a pirate with the patch over his eye that he lost in the battle on the Palatine Bridge.

"I don't suppose you bring news of my parents?"

Redlin looked at him sadly. "I'm sorry, there has been no word of them."

Brayton looked a little downcast at that, but he recovered

quickly. Redlin put a hand on his shoulder.

"Nyle is out there your Highness. If anyone has a chance of finding them, it is Cathal's father."

"That's true brother," Cathal said. "He's not stopped for ten years, he won't give up."

"I know he won't," Brayton said smiling at his friend. "I just wish I could be out there with him."

"The White Castle needs a leader," Redlin said. "And there is no better person to guard the king's throne than you."

"Well master wizard, if it is not news of my parents, what brings you to Kensington?" he smiled.

Redlin told them of the discovery they made reading the prophecy and his desire to comb through the books at the library looking for any reference to Otherwhere.

"That name sounds familiar," the prince said scratching his beard. "Come with me."

Brayton led them down to the crypt below the castle. Standing by the door he put his palm on the clear orb embedded into the lintel to gain access. Inside the crypt were sacred treasures of Vasara that only the king and his heir could procure. The crypt was actually quite large and even had a sitting and sleeping area for prolonged stays. Redlin had only been in the crypt a couple of times back when the god Trystan walked through the streets of Kensington many ages ago. He could see a lot of new artifacts had been added since that time. Brayton went down a side hall and came to a bronze door. Like the door to the crypt, this one could only be opened by the king or the heir. Upon entering, lights controlled by some magic that Trystan had put in place illuminated the space. Along the walls were shelves filled with books and scrolls. Also, there were several pedestals with ancient looking statues, orbs and devices, their use could only be guessed at. Brayton walked over to one of the far pedestals that had a thin gold tablet on it. Inscribed was a picture of a raven perched on a doorway on a small island surrounded by a lake. Across the lintel of the doorway was a single word, *Aiteile.*

"What does that word mean?" Cathal asked.

"Otherwhere," Brayton responded.

"Yes it does," Redlin said in agreement.

Redlin hovered his hand over the tablet and felt an energy there. He did not detect any wards or traps and felt it was alright to touch.

"Have you ever touched it?" the wizard asked the prince.

"Never," Brayton said. "Not that I haven't tried. For some reason, whenever I would reach a hand out, it was like another hand was gently pushing it back. As if I was not meant to touch it."

Redlin puzzled on this, wondering if he should take the risk. He reached out for it, feeling that if the worst thing that could happen was to have his hand pushed away, it was worth the risk. As his fingers wrapped around the tablet, he was not expecting what happened next.

A golden light exploded behind his eyes. Once he could see again, he was in a whole other place. He saw snowcapped mountains, taller than the Macedon Mountains, with rivers and valleys running between them. It was as if he were standing on a cliff that was high above the world and looking at a three-dimensional map. His eyesight must have been heightened because he could see birds and other wildlife far below him. His feet were shrouded in mist, and he could not see anything clearly behind him. Suddenly a rainbow started to form, one end disappearing into the mountains and the other coming to rest on a small island in the middle of a lake. On the island was the doorway that was etched into the golden tablet. Then he heard the voice.

Free me.

Redlin couldn't tell if it was coming from the island, the mountains or the rainbow itself.

Free me.

The voice didn't sound like it was in pain or anguish. It was a strong deep voice and speaking as if giving instructions.

Free me.

"Yeah, I heard you the first time," Redlin said. "I don't suppose you could tell me how to do that and why?"

Free me.

"I didn't think so."

The wizard kept stroking his beard while wondering what this could mean. He didn't think it would be helpful to ask the voice again, but he felt this had something to do with the prophecy.

Was this being some sort of god or magical creature? He thought to himself.

All of a sudden his finger started throbbing. He looked down at the ring Trystan and Eriyn had given him and his mouth fell open. Dancing along the edge was a perfect ring of fire. He wondered why it wasn't burning his hand. Something about the circle of flames struck a chord in his mind. It reminded him of how he would bring forth images in a fire by creating a ring of flames. Taking the ring off he held it up to his eyes and looked towards the rainbow. That is when he saw him. Or maybe her. Or both. The image seemed to waiver. Whatever it was it had long hair, down past its shoulders. It was wearing a plain white tunic with a gold belt. In the center of the chest was an emblem, a white sphere with five radiating arms. When the eyes of the being opened, two golden orbs connected with Redlin's eyes.

Free me wizard. Thy son must solve the dragon's maze and bring you the key.

Flames erupted around the being but did not consume it. It turned and started to walk away. Floating back on the breeze came his last words.

This time there will be a final end, for Vasara's good or ill. And it will all rest on you.

He wasn't sure, but he thought he might have heard laughter on that last statement.

"Thanks a lot," the wizard said. "Whoever you are."

For now, it's Killian. After, who knows.

The fire around the ring disappeared as the rainbow left the sky. Redlin knew there was nothing else to be learned here. He turned and walked into the mist. Suddenly he was falling as he heard a voice call out his name, and then knew no more.

Chapter 7

It felt very strange to Andy to be flying in the frozen moment. Many times he would fly past birds suspended in flight. The four people on his back seem to be resting as he gave them a bumpy-free ride. So far they have dispatched all the human-like demons but one. They were currently flying over the ocean towards Gael who was on the island of Akron. Andy had passed Bowen and his ship the Grey Morning, but unfortunately he was unable to stop and come back into the normal flow of time because of the precious seconds it would eat up.

Their last battle was with the demon who had befriended Jace in Hadley. It was well-prepared. The death dagger on Abby's chest burned when they got near him, confirming what he was. The power it had was immense. Emilia barely confined it with an energy shield that it had broken out of twice, singeing Tori and Cleo with lightning strikes. Eventually they were able to subdue it as Andy drove his black sword, moon shadow through its head while Tori pierced its chest with her twin blades. Now there was just one to go.

"Are we close?" Emilia asked.

I can see the island now, Andy said speaking to their minds.

"Do we have a strategy?" Cleo said.

"I think we do what we have been doing," Tori said. "Once Abby confirms the creature for us, we cut its bloody head off."

Andy smiled to himself at Tori's bluntness. It didn't matter that she was the supreme warrior of the god Fallon with incredible powers, she would still be Tori to the core.

"How do we know where Gael is?" Abby asked.

He said he would be near the archives with Nia and Emma on the northernmost tip of the island, Andy said.

"Hopefully Nia will not have had much time to prepare an adequate strategy," Emilia said. "But she will be the one that has had the most time."

"I think this will be our toughest one yet," Tori remarked. "Like all the others, we will just have to see what we face when we land and improvise as we go."

I really hate improvising, Andy said as he banked to the left and started his descent.

Andy could see Gael, frozen in movement and standing by a building.

There he is, Andy said, *get ready.*

"I don't see anyone else with him," Emilia said.

"We will need to move very fast," Tori said. "As soon as we come out of the frozen moment, we will get her location and dispatch her."

Andy found a clear spot and changed back to human after everyone had jumped off. Feeling behind his back he made sure his sword was there. His grandfather had told him it would be, but he liked to make sure. He still found it uncanny that it would disappear when he transformed. He couldn't help puzzling where it went.

"Andros!" Gael yelled at him as he ran over and embraced his brother.

"Quickly," Tori said, "where is she?"

"In the archives combing through scrolls with Emma. She hasn't changed her behavior at all."

"Protect our rear," Andy said as he let the source fill him. Emilia had her staff out, the pearl sphere of the goddess burning white-hot. Tori and Cleo had both drawn their swords.

"Anything?" Andy asked Abby. He wanted to see if she could feel the burning sensation that these things seemed to generate in the death dagger.

"Not yet," she answered. "We may not be close enough."

This is the part that Andy hated, for Abby had to go first if they were to be sure.

"Okay, take the lead," he told her as Abby drew her lightning sword.

The lore of the trees is stored in a domed stone building with tall oak doors. Grabbing the handle, Abby slowly opened the door and peered inside. Emma was seated next to a woman in the far corner at a table as they poured over a scroll. She had long dark hair done up in a braid and they assumed this must be Nia. The space was wide open and there was no room for stealth. As everyone filed into the room, Nia and Emma looked up, startled at all the drawn swords.

"Andros?" Emma said. "What…"

"Emma, get back!" Andy yelled.

Nia suddenly looked fearful. "Gael?"

Gael looked sick with guilt and hung his head.

Everyone surrounded Nia, ready for anything. When she stood up they could see she had a dangerous looking curved sword strapped to her hip. Andy thought it looked a lot like a scimitar, this one being long, thin and deadly.

"Abby?" Tori said.

Abby moved closer to Nia, keeping her sword leveled.

"I'm feeling nothing," Abby said placing her hand on the death dagger.

"Let me see," Tori said, the fire around her eyes spinning. "She's not a demon," she said finally.

"Demon?" Nia said flabbergasted. "You thought I was a

demon? Gael?" She looked accusingly at Gael before running out of the door, her expression like a thunder cloud, fighting back the tears.

"Go to her," Andy said to his brother. "Explain what's going on, she will understand."

Gael looked doubtful at that, but he turned and ran after Nia.

"Andros, what the hell is going on?" Emma said with a hint of anger in her voice. He had never really seen Emma angry before and figured her and Nia had become close friends.

"I'm sorry Emma, there is a reason," Andy said.

Andy told Emma everything from their encounter with Ben until this very moment. To her credit, she listened without interruption. After hearing their tale, her anger seemed to have abated.

"I can understand your reasons Andros. But I know Nia, she will be hurt by this."

"Hopefully Gael can make her realize what was going on and what is at stake," Cleo said.

"Why are you here Emma?" Abby asked.

Emma told them how she had been sitting under the oldest tree in Vasara, Arsa, and how he kept repeating the same word over and over. Otherwhere.

"The queen thought it important that I find out all I could about it, so she had Gael fly me here to research it."

"Have you found anything?" Emilia asked a little too earnestly perhaps giving what her mother had told her.

"Not yet, but I will keep looking." Emma said as she pushed her hair behind her pointed ears.

"We still have the problem of the demon attached to Gael," Cleo said sheathing her twin blades.

"Whoever it is must be in Black River," Andy said.

"Why Black River?" Cleo asked.

"That's where Gael lives," Abby said. "If there is a demon that has attached itself to him it's there. We have to talk to Gael and get more information."

"Well, one thing I can say," Tori said, "I don't believe we need to travel in the frozen moment anymore."

"Why do you say that?" Cleo said looking at her friend.

"Because Gael is in no immediate danger. Also, this demon knows we are coming, there will be no surprise. If anything, the surprise is on the demon's side, because we won't know who he or she is right away."

Tori looked seriously at Abby. "I'm afraid you are going to have to wander around Black River alone until you sense the demon. It may not know about your ability with the death dagger."

Andy let out an audible sigh. Tori looked over at him.

"Andros, if there was any other way," Tori said.

"I know," Andy said. "I don't like it, but if Abby is willing, I am behind her."

Abby tenderly touched Andy's cheek, her eyes were full of love for this man/dragon.

"I can do this," Abby said.

"We will be hidden, but not far away."

"When do we leave?" Emilia asked.

Tori thought a moment. "We have been non-stop since we started this even though the world has barely moved a day since we dispatched Ben. Let's rest here for a couple of days. Plus, it will give Gael more time to bring Nia around."

"Abby, why don't you help me search these scrolls for information on Otherwhere since you are going to be here for a few days," Emma said.

Abby's eyes lit up as a big smile spread across her face. Andy suddenly burst out laughing.

"What are you laughing at mister?" Abby said to Andy, her

eyes narrowing dangerously.

"Nothing dear," Andy said getting his laughter under control, but he had a hard time keeping the smile off his face. Asking Abby to comb through books and scrolls was like asking the mouse if he wanted to come into the pantry to sample the cheese. She just couldn't resist the urge to search the written word for things unknown.

After getting something to eat, Abby and Emma locked themselves up in the archives to see what could be found about Otherwhere. Andy went looking for his brother. He found him in the common room of the inn he had been staying at. He was sitting at a corner table drinking a beer. Grabbing a chair, Andy sat next to him noticing how tired he looked.

"How is Nia?" Andy asked.

"Hurt," Gael replied. "Although she does understand why it happened the way it did, it doesn't make it any easier. I should have known she wasn't one of them Andros."

Andy put a hand on his brother's shoulder. "Gael, I had no clue in the slightest that Ben was a demon lord, none. There is no way you could have known either way."

"So what now?" Gael said. "I can think of no one who has come into my life in the last five years other than Nia."

Andy told him of their next steps. "It's possible this being had attached itself to you or your location longer than five years ago. Whoever it is may be the first of these creatures."

"Do we even know why they are doing this or what their end game is?" Gael asked.

"Not yet, but once we have dispatched them all we will hold a council with the wizards to try and puzzle this out," Andy said running his fingers through his hair. Something was bothering him. Mainly how extensive this network of human/demons actually might be.

Chapter 8

After spending several days in Akron, Andy and Gael transported everyone aboard their broad backs. Gael took Nia and Emma, Andy had the rest. Their extra time spent on the island had paid off all around. After two days of constant talking, Nia and Gael seemed to have reached an understanding and she no longer had the desire to split him up the middle with her curved sword. He actually saw them walk into the woods holding hands, making him feel very happy for his brother. Emma and Abby had sequestered themselves in the archives where their constant searching yielded results. Apparently Arsa had written what appeared to be a book of prophecy.

"How the hell can a tree write a book?" Andy had asked.

"You got me," Emma replied. "Maybe some faerie wrote it for him and carried it here."

However it came to be, there was a passage that referenced Otherwhere.

When the morning is grey, seek the hidden passage to the cove of Otherwhere.

Abby puzzled over that for quite some time when realization suddenly dawned on her.

"Bowen!" she exclaimed.

"What about him?" Andy asked puzzled.

Emilia started to laugh. Andy scowled at her. "Alright, what?" Andy said crossing his arms.

"With all those mystery movies you used to watch, how

can you not see it?"

"He's distracted with everything going on, Donella," Abby said coming to his rescue and circling her arms around his waist. "It's Bowen's ship, the Grey Morning that the passage is referring to, love, I would bet anything."

Andy visibly relaxed and felt slightly embarrassed at not seeing the obvious.

And so it was that they found themselves circling Bowen's ship. Emma and Emilia flew everyone down as Andy and Gael transformed before dropping to the deck.

"Ho Edward!"

Andy would be very sad and disappointed on the day that Bowen didn't greet him in the manner of their first meeting, when Andy had used his middle name Edward when he first traveled abroad in Vasara,

Bowen greeted everyone warmly. The only person he didn't know was Nia, but he made her welcome like a daughter all the same. He wasted no time in asking Abby to sing for the crew, which of course she readily agreed. Abby and Andy had made it a point to sail with Bowen at least once a year, which Bowen and his crew looked forward to eagerly. Bowen had told Andy that Abby would always have a berth aboard the Grey Morning.

Abby held everyone's attention as she stood on the quarter deck with a circle of sailors seated around her. She sang an old song of sailors leaving their sweethearts to make their fortune on the open seas. Bowen was dabbing his eyes along with the rest of his crew.

"She does that to me every time laddie," the captain said to Andy who was smiling rubbing his friend's shoulder roughly.

Just then another voice joined with Abby's. Every head turned as the circle opened and Nia came to stand next to her. Abby smiled and grabbed Nia's hand as the solo became a duet, the sound they produced was achingly beautiful.

"Now they have both gone and done it," Bowen said with tears running down his stubble cheeks.

Andy turned to Gael. "Did you know she could sing like that?"

Gael just smiled expansively at his brother, beaming with pride. Clearly he did.

After their little concert everyone retired to Bowen's quarters. His cabin was unusually large for a normal captain's quarters, but Bowen had always said he wanted to have enough room to entertain his friends when on board ship.

Andy was telling Bowen about the strange passage in Arsa's book when a steward came in with a bottle of wine.

"Ah, Drem!" Bowen said loudly. "Fill everyone's cup, no skimping!"

"Of course Captain," Drem said smiling.

Andy could see it was a bottle of Fenner red as Drem filled his glass. He looked over at his wife as he swirled it around in his glass and saw a look of absolute horror on her face. Andy was about to ask her what was wrong when she shook her head quickly to silence him. Whatever she was feeling she pushed it down as Drem finished filling everyone's glass.

"Will that be all Captain?"

"Yes Drem, thank you."

As Andy watched him walk back up the stairs and close the door he then quickly turned towards Abby.

"Abby, what's wrong?" he asked

"Did something happen?" Emilia asked noting the worry in Andy's voice.

"When Drem came in the death dagger burned like a hot iron," Abby said. "It took everything I had to keep from screaming out."

"What is this?" Bowen asked, clearly agitated that Abby was in any kind of pain.

Andy explained how they had journeyed for months to hunt down and destroy these human-like demons that had infiltrated the dragons' hometowns and how Abby is able to detect them.

"It seems one of them has attached itself to you Captain," Tori said.

To say Bowen was livid was an understatement. He was already on his feet and heading up the stairs when Emilia flew in front of him to bar his way.

"Stand aside missy," Bowen scowled angrily. "No demon is going to imperil me or my crew. Stand aside!"

"No Captain," Emilia replied, her green eyes boring holes into his. "You are not thinking clearly. This thing has immense power and could destroy you and your crew in seconds." She took the comb out of her hair and the sphere lit up with power. "I love you Bowen, but I will put you in an energy bubble and leave you there if you don't turn around."

Bowen's eyes narrowed and his lips drew into a thin line. Suddenly he burst out laughing. "By the gods I believe you would do it too!" He sheathed his sword. "Okay, lass, I will follow your lead on this one."

Emilia put the pearl comb back in her hair and kissed his cheek.

"How many of these things are there?" Cleo said in frustration.

"What's the plan?" Gael said.

Suddenly the door to Bowen's quarters flew open and the bosun yelled down.

"Captain, come quick. Drem just flew up into the crow's nest!"

"It knows," Abby said.

Emilia flew up the stairs first, her staff blazing, followed by Andy, Gael and the others. Andy and Gael jumped over the side and into the ocean as Emilia created a shield around everyone on deck. A few seconds later a black and a gold dragon came spinning out of the water and flew above Drem. They quickly erected shields of their own as Drem started firing energy shots at them.

What do you think? Gael asked Andy. *We can't attack him where he is without endangering everyone below.*

We need to get him off the ship somehow. Em, are you able to come up?

Not without dropping this shield and leaving everyone vulnerable, Emilia answered.

Suddenly Andy looked below and saw Tori spinning her twin blades so rapidly that it created rings of fire. Slowly the rings started to rise up where Drem was standing. Abby was also shooting lightning strikes with her sword forcing Drem to create a shield of his own.

Emilia took her spear Nocte off her arm. Extending it she aimed for Drem's heart, if demons even had those. Drem's eyes went wide when he saw the spear. Emilia let it fly with deadly accuracy. Just before impact, Drem jumped and in his free-fall changed his form.

By the gods! Gael exclaimed. *It can't be.*

Andy was stunned, because what was now coming at them in its attack was a shriker.

Em, we need you now!

"Protect everyone as best you can," Emilia said to the others once Nocte returned and she created her Summoner link to Andy and Gael. She flew up and came to rest on Andy's back. The aerial circus began as the dragons lured the shriker away from Bowen's ship.

The shriker was spinning like a corkscrew as it came at Andy, energy bolts were impacting with his wings and chest causing him to falter. Before the shriker could cause any real damage, Emilia and Gael came up from underneath his blind spot as white-hot fire shot from Emilia's staff and hit the shriker in the side of the head, making it falter in its flight.

Why isn't it disappearing like the last one? Gael said.

Andy was wondering that as well. In the battle of the warlocks, the shriker they had fought had the ability to disappear at will in flight. It was only with the help of Emilia's dragon, Chaos, that they were able to follow his trajectory.

Maybe they all can't. Kind of how like each dragon has its own gift, it's possible it is the same with them, Andy said.

Any ideas on how to kill it? Gael said as Emilia jumped off his back to land on Andy's as he flew just below.

I have an idea, Emilia said. *You boys ever play chicken?*

You can't be serious! Andy said.

What is that? Gael asked

Andy explained to him what Emilia had in mind.

You can't be serious! Gael said. *How do we time this?*

Leave that to me, Emilia said. *I have you both tethered to me through the Summoner's link. Just let it pull you and the timing will be perfect.*

You know this scheme makes you the bait, Andy said.

I can handle it baby brother, she said smiling.

Emilia jumped off and flew straight up, enticing the demon-shriker to follow her while Andy and Gael flew off in opposite directions. Andy was a little dubious about this plan. It relied on perfect timing and also tricking the demon into a paralyzing confusion with both dragons speeding directly towards him on a collision course. Andy and Gael would have to rely on Emilia to tell them when to turn, and hopefully they turned opposite each other or it wasn't going to be pretty.

The demon had just caught up to Emilia as Andy and Gael made their turns and sped back towards one another with Emilia in the center. She had created a sphere of energy around herself as the demon latched on, beating it with its claws and fangs. The dragons put on extra speed. Andy could feel the link between all three of them, pulling them along on the inevitable collision. The demon hovered as it looked back and forth between the two dragons, realizing it was the anvil between two hammers.

You boys ready? Emilia sent.

Gael, you turn left, I'll go right, Andy said with tenseness in his voice.

You got it.

Andy could feel Emilia's tether. It was pulling tighter, letting them know the moment to turn. They were only going to turn their bodies ninety degrees, their scaly undersides facing each other as they raked their talons along the demon's body as they released the energy of the source into it.

Suddenly he felt the invisible tether tighten and force their turn. Andy flipped with one wing pointing to the sky and the other towards the earth. The demon was dumbfounded and Emilia used that opportunity to drop her shield and free fall. Andy and Gael were barely a foot apart before lightning strikes connected with the demon, surrounding it like a cage. From below came a whistling sound and as Andy flew clear of the demon, Emilia's spear Nocte buried itself in the things' chest, causing it to explode into a thousand tiny fragments before dissipating into ash. The spear started to fall and sped back to its owner as Andy and Gael flew back to the Grey Morning and transformed back into their human selves.

"Let's make a point not to do that again," Gael said to Andy. "A couple of your strikes hit me in the chest."

Andy laughed as he slapped his brother on the back. "I was never a big fan of playing chicken either."

"I can't believe Drem was one of those things," Bowen said once everyone had reconvened in his cabin. "He was one of my best sailors, never a complaint from him, a great lad." He looked at Andy sadly. "It almost feels like a great betrayal."

"I know what you mean Captain, I felt the same about Ben."

Bowen took a long draw from his ale cup. "So, let's get back to that passage you found about the Grey Morning in that book."

"Does the name, Otherwhere, mean anything to you at all Captain?" Abby asked.

"I have never heard of it lassie," Bowen said scratching his chin. "But there is something."

Bowen got up and went over to his maps case against the wall by his bed. On the top shelf all by itself was a red scroll. Taking it out he brought it over to the table and rolled it out. The skin was red, but the chart lines were done in gold. Gael whistled softly at it.

"Beautiful, isn't it?" Bowen said seeing his eyes light up.

"Very," Gael said. "How did you come by this?"

"This map has been in my family since, well I don't know how long to be honest. But it has been handed down from father to son for eons. As you can see, this coastline here does not appear on any other map I possess."

"Isn't that Parma?" Abby said pointing to the lower left corner. Although what was printed there was the word Fiain. Bowen smiled at her.

"I should have realized you would have a knowledge of maps and some of the ancient languages."

"I do know Fiain means wilds," Abby said. "But the coast-line does seem a little different."

"Exactly," Bowen said excitedly. "If you look at the depth numbers they disappear from the map right in this section. As if no one could get in there to take any measurements. A virtual hole you could say."

"What is that symbol right there?" Tori asked.

"Where?" Bowen said looking at Tori. "By the gods!"

"What?" Tori said looking around for danger.

"Your eyes, lass! They are burning like wheels of fire."

Tori relaxed. "Sorry, yes they do that sometimes."

"It's probably why you can see this symbol and the rest of us can't. The map is red, perhaps this is Fallon's map," Cleo said.

"You could be right Boss," Tori said.

"What is it you see Tori?" Abby asked.

Tori pointed to the middle of the empty space. "A rock with a raven perched on top of it."

Emilia's face suddenly went white, a stark contrast against her jet-black hair.

"Em, what is it?" Andy said seeing her eyes go wide.

"Zana," Emilia said. "She's there."

"What makes you say that?" Gael asked.

"The raven. It is Devon's ravens. The ravens that now belong to Zana."

Emilia pushed her hair behind her pointed ears. "During the battle with Devon, when I spared her life, she flew south with Devon's ravens towards the Wilds." She looked down at the map again and at that empty space. "I'm certain this is where she went."

"Then let's go there and gut her," Nia said. Gael smiled with pride at her. Andy wondered on the complex nature of this woman his brother had come to have feelings for. She could seem as vulnerable as a cornered rabbit in one instance, then fierce as a lioness in the next.

"That is easier said than done lass," Bowen responded.

"What do you mean?" Tori asked.

"Every one of my family that this map has come down to have tried to find out what is in that spot. It's in our nature to sail where others have not. We know the coordinates of this spot, but whenever we get near it, it is like the ship just sails right around it, but you could swear you sailed right through it."

"How is that possible?" Andy asked.

"I don't know lad. But as soon as I get to the edge of that spot," Bowen said putting his finger on the map, "I will look up and take another reading and find I am sailing in the totally opposite direction of where I was headed, and the ship's wheel would not have turned one degree. It is as if a hand reached down, picked the boat up and spun it around without anyone being the wiser. There is powerful magic there I have no doubt."

"I think we should take this information back to your mother," Abby said to Emilia. "I believe sailing down there now would achieve nothing."

"Yes, I think you are right," Emilia said. "We need to have a council on this and these demons."

"I agree as well," Tori said, "but first, we need to take care of the demon that is in Black River. Captain, can you take us there."

"It will be my pleasure missy," Bowen said taking out his pipe and lighting it. "As long as we can prevail upon our two young singers to ease the crews' burden as we go."

"You know you never need to ask Captain," Abby said smiling. Nia readily agreed.

After weeks of sailing from the ocean and up the Tear River, the Grey Morning entered Lake Pleasant and eventually the docks at Black River. There was a lot of commercial traffic in the harbor due to the fact it was mid-summer and the weeks long festival was still going on. It was decided that everyone would remain onboard ship while Abby and Nia searched through the city to see if the death dagger would reveal anything about whom the demon might be.

"Where should we start?" Nia asked adjusting her sword to make sure she had quick access.

Abby looked around as they stood on the corner of the main street. There were many races of beings here; faeries, humans, fauns and even a couple of centaurs. Black River was also the home of the healers whose grounds were located at the north end of the city.

"Let's go to the Shipyard Inn," Abby said. "We may be able to pick up some information."

As they walked into the common room, Abby was hit with a feeling of nostalgia. Donella had told her how she was at death's door from skull spider venom, and it was here that Dain and Leah had brought Ala to heal her. Taking a table in the corner they had ordered some wine as they watched the clientele carefully. This was a popular spot and Abby felt this was as good a place as any to begin their search.

"Getting anything?" Nia asked.

"No," Abby said shaking her head.

"Can I ask you a question?" Nia said looking down at her glass.

"Of course," Abby said.

"Am I a fool?"

Abby looked perplexed at this woman who had become her friend. "What do you mean?"

"For loving a dragon."

Understanding was written all over Abby's face. If anyone knew what emotions and doubts were plaguing Nia, it was Abby. Until Braylynn had changed her, she was right where Nia was now. Abby grabbed her hand.

"First of all, you are no fool. Never think that. And if it was like me, you had no choice in the matter. I was destined to love Andros, end of story. The fact that he would outlive me had no bearing whatsoever. Don't get me wrong, the thought always brought me anguish. But the love was much more powerful and would provide a healing balm to withstand it and focus on the wonder of it all."

A grateful tear slid down Nia's cheek and Abby could see her friend visibly relax.

Abby's hand suddenly gripped Nia's excruciatingly tight as her eyes went wide.

"Abby, what's wrong?" Nia said. Abby's back was towards the door of the inn.

"Shhh, quickly, tell me who just walked in."

Nia looked over Abby's head to see who had entered.

"It's Baron Ansgar and three of his guardsmen."

"Are they looking this way?"

"They are scanning the room with their eyes, but I don't see them settling on us." Understanding dawned on Nia. "Is it the death dagger?"

Abby nodded her head and bit her lower lip against the pain.

As if not finding what they sought, the Baron and his men turned and left the building. Abby let out a shuddering breath as she let go of Nia's hand and took a drink of her wine to help calm her nerves.

Once they got back to the ship they filled everyone in.

"Baron Ansgar?" Gael said incredulously. "It's unbelievable, he's so involved in the community. Works to make lives better. How can a demon do that! It makes no sense."

"It doesn't," Abby said sadly, "but it's the truth."

"How long has he been the baron of Black River?" Emilia asked.

"He was already here when I had gotten back from the war

with the warlocks," Gael said.

"So at least ten years," Andy said. "That is longer than any of the ones we've encountered. I think it is safe to say he was the first."

"What do we do now?" Emma said.

Tori was scratching her chin and thinking.

"I believe we need to go into the frozen moment," she said. "It's the only way we are going to get close to him."

Tori paused for a moment.

"What is it?" Cleo asked her friend.

"I'm getting a feeling in the pit of my stomach that this will be the hardest of them all. Do you remember when we were in the temple and two of the warlocks were in the frozen moment with us?" Tori said.

"Yes, I do."

"I'm getting that feeling it may happen again."

"How do we counter that?" Andy asked remembering his own limitations in fighting in the dimension. At least this time he had his sword moon shadow.

"We need to hit him from both sides at once," Tori said.

"I'm not sure I understand," Gael said.

"Some of us will confront him on the inside of the frozen moment if he is there, while the others hit him in that same moment in real time," Tori explained.

"How the hell do we do that?" Cleo asked.

"That is a good question Boss," Tori said running her fingers through her hair like a comb.

After much consideration, the agreed upon plan was to get as close to the Baron as possible, then Tori, Cleo and Andy would slip into the frozen moment. If he was there, they would distract him, then slip in and out of real time until the others had covered the distance to get within range.

Nia led them down several back alleys in order to come up on the Baron's manor unobserved.

"I'd love to know how you knew that route," Gael whispered as they came to the hedge row of the backyard of the manor.

Nia put a hand to his cheek and just smiled.

They could see two guards standing on the back patio talking as they occasionally scanned the area.

"What's your plan Tori?" Andy asked.

"Give me one second, Andros the Black," Tori said smiling right before a red slash opened up in front of her as she disappeared.

Andy looked towards the patio and saw Tori standing there waving her hand to come up, the guards unconscious at her feet.

"It's very unnerving to be on this side of that frozen moment," Emma said as she flew up to the patio with Emilia. Andy and the others did a quick jog after pushing through the hedge.

"Gael, do you know the way to the main room where Ansgar does his business?" Tori asked.

"Yes, I've been here many times. Follow me."

Gael led them up a short flight of stairs before traversing a long narrow hallway. On one side were doors, on the other there was an inner courtyard and a small open-air garden. Andy could see people strolling about, but fortunately no one was looking up. Suddenly Gael stopped. The hallway made a sharp turn and they could see an arched opening in the center of the next hall.

"The Baron's meeting hall is through there. If he is there, he will see us as soon as we step inside."

"Okay," Tori said. "This will be the tricky part. Andy, Cleo and I will go into the frozen moment just as you start to gather your power, do not get close to him. Range weapons only."

"That means just me and Gael then," Emilia said as she

took Nocte off her arm and extended it as well taking out her comb to transform into her staff.

Tori nodded.

"Let's do this," Andy said.

Tori took several deep breaths. "Now!" she said. And then all hell broke loose.

***

Tori ripped open the fabric of time as she, Andy and Cleo jumped through, just as Gael and Emilia were winding up their magic. Before entering the frozen moment, Tori's eyes connected with the Baron's and knew he was not taken unawares.

As Tori closed the portal she could see Ansgar looking at her the way Ben did, his eyes following as the three of them separated and formed a semi-circle around him. Suddenly Ansgar smiled and he started to laugh.

"I have a feeling this is not good," Cleo said with both of her twin blades crossed and held out in front of her.

Tori likewise had her blades out and Andy drew his black sword as the baron started to divide in two. Now there were two Ansgars in front of them. One frozen and the other very much mobile. Ansgar walked around the desk. He was well over six and a half feet tall with long flowing blond hair, looking almost angelic. Then Tori noticed something else. Two guardsmen stood on either side of the baron's desk, and both of them could see her.

"Oh hell! He's not the only one," she exclaimed.

"Very observant, Cath Priomh," Ansgar said smiling wickedly. "We have been following your progress with the others you have vanquished. I'm afraid you are at a serious disadvantage here."

"We've handled tougher than you, dirt bag," Andy said.

"You've handled no one like me, first dragon."

"Can we stop with the monologues and just get to it," Cleo said getting frustrated.

"Patience, Viper Captain. Are you so eager to die?"

"You seem to know us all," Tori said with her eyes narrowing.

"I've watched you all for a very long time. You have only just scratched the surface of what we are, and more importantly, what we are capable of."

Ansgar started to move his hands in a circular motion creating an energy sphere.

"Quick, get behind me!" Andy said. He raised his shield. He couldn't enclose Tori and Cleo but he could act as a wall for whatever Ansgar threw at them.

"How is he able to use his magic?" Cleo said falling in behind Andy.

"As I said," the demon snarled, "you have never encountered anyone like me before." Ansgar released his energy and directed it straight at Andy's chest. The impact threw all of them against the far wall.

"By the gods," Tori said groaning as they worked to get quickly on their feet.

The power is in your hand, a voice said.

"Who said that?" Cleo asked.

Ansgar also was looking around for the source of the voice.

The power is in your hand, the voice repeated.

"I'm not sure, but it sounded like my grandfather," Andy said.

Andy looked down to the only thing in his hand, his black sword, moon shadow, and understanding lit up in his eyes.

Call its name.

"What does that mean?" Cleo said, "moon shadow?"

"No," Andy said. Grabbing the sword by the hilt and aiming at Ansgar's chest he called out the sword's ancient name. "Scáth Gealach!"

The energy of the source that was inside Andy flooded into the blade, turning it white as mini lightning bolts danced along its length. With the strength of a dragon he let the sword fly. Ansgar, being too stunned to move at what was speeding towards him, gaped with an open mouth as the sword buried to the hilt in the center of his chest, the energy encasing his body like an electric storm. His eyes were bulging, turning black and smoking. They could all see he was about to explode.

"Tori!" Andy yelled.

"Already on it!" Tori said as she opened the portal and time started to flow again.

"Em!" Andy shouted once they jumped through.

"I know," Emilia said as she aimed her spear. "Nocte!"

Like Andy's sword, Emilia's spear flew straight and true as the spear turned white, alive with energy as it pierced Ansgar's chest on this side of the frozen moment. But Emilia had learned something in her years of practice with the spear her grandfather had made. Making twisting motions with her hands, the spear flew through the baron, turned, pierced him again, before turning one last time and burying itself in Ansgar's skull. He put both hands on the side of his head, as if he thought he might be able to hold it together. But the combined energy of the sword and the spear was too much as the demon exploded, body parts spraying everywhere before turning to ash. The two guardsmen were easily dispatched as Gael obliterated one with liquid fire while Tori slipped quickly into the frozen moment only to appear by the other demon as her twin blades made a scissor motion and cut off its head. Both demons evaporated as silence filled the room with the exception of everyone's heavy breathing.

Tori picked up something that she had dropped by her feet. It was Andy's sword that she had retrieved while inside the frozen moment.

"Figured you would want this back Andros," Tori said throwing it to him.

"Thanks Tori," Andy said smiling as he caught it. "How did you know to call out the name of the spear Em?

"I heard grandfather's voice," she responded. "I assume you must have heard it too."

Andy nodded in the affirmative.

"What happens now?" Abby asked.

Suddenly a shriek and a cackle blasted everyone's ears as they stared open-mouthed at what had just flown into the room.

Ansgar circled their heads twice before coming to hover near the top of the fourteen-foot ceiling.

"Did you really think it would be that easy?" he hissed. "I told you, you've not encountered someone like me. A new god is rising, and yours have all fled. This world will be ours."

"Over my dead body!" Andy yelled.

"That is the idea, first dragon."

Ansgar's eyes then turned towards Abby.

"As for you, death's mistress, someone will be coming for you real soon," Ansgar said as he cackled some more.

"Bite me! You bastard of hell," Abby said in her New York slang as she leveled her sword and sent several white-hot lightning strikes streaking towards his face.

Ansgar folded his hands over his chest and spun, deflecting the bolts before disappearing through the wall as the acrid smell of electricity hung on the air.

"Bite me?" Andy said looking at his wife.

Abby just shrugged as she sheathed her blade. "Seemed appropriate in the moment."

Tori burst out laughing. "Your bride has bite Andros."

"What did he mean, death's mistress?" Nia asked.

"I'm not sure, but it probably has to do with the death

dagger," Abby said.

"It also means he knows how we are finding them," Cleo said. "You are marked now, you know that."

"Don't much care," Abby said pushing the hair out of her eyes. "I'm tired of all these creatures trying to threaten and take my life. It's time I found out exactly what this thing can do," she said taking the death dagger out from under her shirt to look at it.

"Braylynn did say you may come to learn its powers in time," Andy said as he put his hand on the charm, it fitted perfectly with the brand on his palm that the witch Samara had put there.

"Where to now?" Emma said.

"Laurel Hollow, we need to see the queen and gather everyone together to discuss what all this means," Emilia answered.

"Well brother," Andy said to Gael. "You ready to be a taxi service again?"

Gael nodded in agreement, "Let's do this."

"I'm coming with you," Nia said.

Gael looked like he was about to protest. Instead he smiled as she took his arm and squeezed it before following everyone out to find an open space.

Chapter 9

A golden dragon was circling the temple of the warlocks, the warm updraft allowing him to soar to a great height. Craning his neck back towards the shoreline he could see the herd of unicorns gathered together in what was now their new home. With his dragon sight he could see a lone black unicorn standing on a huge boulder looking up at him. The queen of the unicorns had always made him nervous. Spying a place to land he circled once more before descending. Once on the ground he changed, and where a gold-colored dragon once stood, there was now a young man wearing clothes that looked like black dragon scales set against a mane of red hair.

"What the hell are you doing here Finn," he said aloud to himself looking around to see if any being or creature was about.

Finn knew exactly why he was here. Zana. Every dragon has a gift that is their own that doesn't require the source. For Finn, that ability was to sense those whom he had a strong connection with and follow that connection to wherever they were. He had another gift that Cael had given him, but could be used only once, and the god gave explicit instructions that no one was to know about it.

After Donella had freed himself and his brothers from that cave, Finn could not sense Zana anywhere, which he found very strange. It wasn't until the battle of the warlocks when she came to help with the shriker that the connection blazed in him on the ground of the battlefield. When he called out to her, he could feel her hesitation and indecision, but she flew off and the connection dropped.

Finn didn't know if she had found some way to block him, for she did know about his gift. Or maybe she was in a place where his ability could not reach. For ten years he had searched. Every once in a while, he would get small quick bursts of a connection but then it would disappear. Most of them came from near the Parma Wilds, and he had combed that area for years, finding nothing.

Suddenly however, the connection was strong while he was at the Mistral Islands, coming from the West. He flew immediately and the connection brought him here. He could still feel it, Zana was in that building.

Going inside was not a good plan he felt. He would wait here and see if she came out. Sitting on a rock he ran his fingers through his hair as he thought back on his past. He smiled as he remembered the first time they met.

Finn had found a quiet secluded pool deep in the southern woods of Laurel Hollow. He would like to come here at times to sit cross-legged on the grass and meditate, which is what he had been doing that day. All of a sudden, he heard a crashing sound in the brush behind him. He turned around just in time to see a lynx come flying through the air and over his head as it splashed in the water and started swimming to the other shore. Following close on his heels with a spear extended was a faerie with wings the color of midnight. Seeing she wouldn't be able to check her speed in time she dropped her spear and collided with Finn, spilling them both into the pond as her arms wrapped around him.

After they both broke the surface of the water their faces were inches apart and their arms were still around each other. There was a momentary awkward silence and then the faerie threw her head back and started laughing. After a few moments, Finn joined in.

"I'm sorry to have disrupted your hunt," he said once they had climbed back onto the shore. "My name is Finn."

"Zana," she replied wringing the water out of her jet-black hair.

Finn's heart was in his throat. The way the droplets of water seemed to cascade down her body and the musical sounding lilt of her voice made his face flush.

Using the source, he gathered some of the dead branches nearby to put in the ring of rocks he always used to build fires. Extending his hand, a single flame shot out of his palm to ignite the pile of wood. Very quickly there was a merry little fire going.

"This should help you to dry out faster," he told her.

Zana looked astonished at what she had seen.

"You are a dragon, aren't you?" she said with wonder.

"I am," Finn said hoping that it might impress her a little.

Finn didn't know what was happening to him. Out of all his brothers, he was the family skeptic. He didn't believe in love at first sight or any of that romantic nonsense. But this woman had affected him in a way no other ever had, faerie or human. He shook his head in bewilderment.

"Everything okay?" she asked with a fetching smile and a slight tilt of her head.

He paused for a moment before answering. "Yes, I believe it is," he responded.

They spent several days by that pond just talking. Finn would fish and cook their catch while Zana would talk, he was grateful for this since he was not a big talker himself. They found they could talk about anything. Her greatest aspiration was to be chosen as Braylynn's Dragon Summoner one day. Zana also had a great interest in magic and asked Finn to tell her everything he knew about the source and the wizards. They spent many months together. Their friendship grew deeper and richer until they both finally admitted what they knew all along, that they loved each other. Finn however wanted to keep their love a secret from his brothers.

"Why?" Zana had asked him.

"I'm not really sure," Finn had said. "Maybe because my brothers and I are so tightly bound together, I just want something that is apart from them for now."

Zana had understood and abided by his wishes. She didn't even tell her best friend Layla. It was a time of peace in Vasara and not much was going on that really required the assistance of dragons. Finn and Zana spent many years alone together, their love growing stronger. She would ride his back as they flew to every corner of Vasara.

And then suddenly, all that changed.

"What is wrong?" he asked her when she seemed particularly moody and snappish.

"Nothing," she replied turning away from him.

Finn walked up behind her and wrapped her up in his arms. She visibly relaxed against him.

"Tell me," he said.

"You must know by now that Layla was chosen as Dragon Summoner."

"Yes, I felt her link some time ago."

Zana stiffened and pulled out of his embrace.

"And that is part of the problem!" she yelled.

"What do you mean?" Finn asked sounding perplexed.

"She will have a connection to you I can never have. I should've been named Summoner, it was supposed to come to me. Braylynn set herself against me. Layla knows nothing about magic or power."

She was raving now and it scared Finn a little with the wild look in her eyes. The woman he loved was changing right in front of him.

"Zana, you are upset and not thinking clearly. Let's go somewhere and think this through."

A wild hope lit up in Zana's eyes as she grabbed both of his arms.

"Finn, let's leave here."

"Leave? What do you mean?"

"There are other places, other worlds. We could keep searching until we found a place where we could be equal to a god and goddess. Please Finn, come with me right now."

"Zana, stop. You know we can't do that. We both have duties, you to your queen and goddess and me to my brothers and the gods. We can't just leave."

Zana let her arms drop as she hung her head. She looked up at him as if she suddenly despised him.

"You are a weakness to me Finn, and I hate weakness!"

She turned and ran before leaping into the wind and flying away.

"Zana! Zana come back," Finn yelled to no avail.

All it took was that one moment for Finn's heart to break. He would see Zana now and again but the passion that used to be in her eyes was gone. More often than not he would see her in the company of the wizard, Devon. This gave him a small measure of hope, for Devon was wise and if anyone could make her see reason in regards to not becoming the Dragon Summoner it would be him. Little did he know at the time that this would seal her fate forever.

Although Finn did not necessarily believe that. When he had called out to her at the battle, he had felt that tug of hesitation. A part of the woman he loved was still there, buried deep inside her, he was sure of it.

Finn was brought out of his musings by an explosion of rocks right next to him. Grabbing the source, he quickly created a shield as he looked back towards the temple. Zana was standing on the stairs holding a staff made of ash with a black sphere on top, looking exactly as she did on that day on the cliff face. The wind was blowing her hair as the sun shone behind her as she lifted off the ground and flew close to where he was.

"This is your only warning, Finn, if you wish to keep on living for a while longer, leave me alone," Zana said with hatred in her eyes.

"You don't have to do this," he said sympathetically.

"Keep your pity, I don't need it."

Finn kept his eyes locked on hers. Where once he saw the reflection of forest pools there was now only darkness and his heart wept to see it.

"Zana, you once asked me to go away with you. Let's do it right now, just us. I know how to get to other worlds, we can make our own way."

She just stared at him. Finn couldn't tell if her mind was warring with itself or not.

"That ship sailed an age ago, Finn. I'm claiming this world now, and there will be a new god, and I will be his goddess."

"What are you talking about?" he said startled. "What have you done Zana?"

"Go home, Finn," Zana said dispassionately. "Go back to that witch you call a Dragon Summoner. Let her make you dance with her invisible strings," she sneered, as the blood rose to her face in anger. Finn could see some inner battle was going on inside her when her eyes took on a panicked look.

He watched as she held out a glass rod and closed her eyes. There was a bright light followed by a loud snap that made Finn wince. When he could see clearly again, Zana had vanished. Finn hung his head in utter despair. He felt what Zana had become was all his fault.

***

When Zana suddenly appeared back in Otherwhere her breath was heaving, her chest rising and falling as she tried to get her breathing under control.

What had just happened? she said to herself.

She hugged herself as her body shook.

"Damn you to hell, Finn!" she screamed aloud.

"Zana, Zana! They're gone!"

Zana turned towards the cottage to see Griffin running towards her, his arm in a sling and a sword cut across his brow.

"What are you talking about? Who?"

"Paolo and Acacia," he told her with fear in his eyes.

"That is impossible!" she said, her eyes blazing. "There are wards everywhere, they can't just walk out of here!"

She leveled her staff at an enormous oak tree and blew it apart with a bolt of white energy in frustration. She then pointed her staff at Griffin.

"Tell me everything, including your failure to do the one task I entrusted you to do!"

Sweat was pouring off Griffin's brow and into his cut making him wince in pain as he told his tale.

Chapter 10

Nyle was not prepared for the image that greeted him when he walked through Raven Rock. A carpet of lush green grass ran before him and ended at the edge of a crystal clear lake. Ringing the lake were flowers of every color. Just off the shore was a tiny island with what looked like an open doorway of stone upon it. Two ravens sat on either side of the doorway. He knew they were Devon's ravens by their size and by the way they were looking at him. He felt he had just lost any element of surprise.

The ravens leapt into the air, circled once and disappeared as they flew through the opening. Nyle could not tell where they had gone, because when you looked through the doorway all you could see was the other side of the lake. He started walking towards the water and as he got closer, he could see the bow of a small rowboat hidden in the reeds.

"Well, that is mighty convenient," he said aloud.

Jumping into the boat he rowed to the island. Once on land he walked up the steps and stood by the doorway and stared through apprehensively. Nyle was a soldier, he didn't like magic all that much, he preferred settling all his issues with his sword if he could. He took several deep breaths.

"You will eventually need to walk through," a voice said behind him.

Nyle drew his sword and spun around.

"Sibila, will you please stop doing that!" Nyle said ramming his sword back home in its sheath.

Sibila couldn't help laughing. Nyle loved her laugh and he shook his head because it affected him in ways he still hadn't come to grips with yet.

"I don't suppose you could tell me what's waiting for me in there?"

"I'm sorry first knight. I can only reveal knowledge in its proper time. This is your part of the ultimate quest and some things need to be puzzled out on your own."

She suddenly got real close to him and placed both hands on his muscular chest, the heat she was generating made him slightly dizzy. "But that doesn't mean you need to face this alone," she told him as she leaned in and kissed his lips.

As with her first kiss, his body was suddenly infused with power and vigor, he actually felt himself getting younger, his muscles tighter. As he felt her lips pull away he opened his eyes, but she had vanished.

"I really wish you would stop doing that," he yelled to the sky.

He turned around and squared his shoulders. He no longer hesitated as he drew his sword and stepped through the doorway, ready to meet whatever challenge came at him, but now he no longer felt alone.

As he walked beneath the lintel it felt as if he were parting an invisible curtain. The scene changed from a view of the lake to a well-worn dirt path leading past a cottage and then disappearing into the woods. He expected to be met with some form of resistance since the ravens had seen him. When he got closer to the cottage he came upon a large open-air aviary. There were many perches and each one had a raven on it. These were definitely Devon's ravens. But something was wrong. Or maybe something was right, because every raven had their heads tucked as if they were sleeping. There was no crying out in alarm as he quietly stepped past them. Dead silence. Nyle wondered if this was Sibila's doing. He could feel that this place radiated magic. Being in Devon's service for so long had made him attuned to it, like it almost had a smell. He was certain there would be traps, so he scanned the immediate vicinity looking for the one person he knew had to be here, Zana.

Nyle opened the door and quickly stepped inside.

"By the gods!" he exclaimed quietly, staring in wonder at the palatial inside.

His Raptor training took over. Feeling youthful, thanks to Sibila, he moved quickly from column to column in what he assumed was the great hall. Suddenly he heard footsteps and quickly ducked into a darkened alcove.

Peering out, he could see a tall man with long red hair done in a braid, walking down a hall, followed by two servants wearing black aprons carrying laden trays with food and drink. Nyle assumed they must work in the kitchen. After letting them get a good distance away he proceeded to follow them. They took a left turn and walked down a narrow corridor. He ran to catch up with them, stopping just short of the room they had just entered.

"Ah, Griffin, is it that time again?" Nyle could hear the king's voice say.

"It is the same time every day, Paolo," a gruff voice said. Nyle assumed this must be Griffin.

"Care for some more practice?" came Acacia's voice with the sound of a sword swishing back and forth.

Good, Nyle thought to himself. *They are both in there, and at least Acacia has her rapier.*

"Nothing would give me more pleasure," Griffin said. "But Zana is returning soon. I believe your time is starting to run out."

Nyle was surprised to hear that. He ran his fingers through his hair as he thought of his best line of attack. He couldn't have picked a better time with Zana away. Nyle reasoned the red-haired man was Griffin and the one currently in charge. The other two were just servants and most likely didn't have any training at arms. He started thinking through a plan. If he could somehow alert Paolo that he was here, Nyle was sure the king and queen would know what to do to give him a distraction.

Suddenly it came to him. The room that Paolo and Acacia were in must butt up against an open-air garden because he could hear birds chirping. When the war with Devon was over, Paolo had rebuilt the White Castle and the existing gardens, he also brought back with him a specific bird that he always admired from the village where he grew up. It was cornflower blue in color with red eyes and a body similar to a robin. It was called a star thistle, and it made a very distinct sound. The king would know it, and he was pretty sure Griffin wouldn't know one bird sound from another.

Nyle rubbed his sweaty palms on his pants before drawing his sword. Taking several quiet deep breaths to give him focus, he pursed his lips and made the sound of a star thistle. He would have no way of knowing if the king heard it or not. He paused a few moments before he strode through the door.

"What the…?" Griffin said drawing his own sword. "How did you get in here?"

Nyle could tell Paolo had gotten his signal because he was already moving as Acacia threw him his sword. One thing Nyle didn't count on was the other servants who had drawn swords as they threw off their aprons. Griffin held a black disc in his hand and he was pressing it.

The air was suddenly charged. Nyle could feel the electricity of magic, something was about to happen.

"Glad you could make it," Paolo said smiling as he engaged one of the servants.

"Sorry I'm late your Majesty," Nyle said as he crossed swords with the other servant.

"It's of no moment," Paolo said casually. "I knew you would be along presently. I never doubted it my knight."

Nyle's heart was in his throat. There was nothing he could say to that. The faith of this man in him was humbling beyond measure.

With Paolo and Nyle facing off against the servants, that left Griffin for Acacia.

"Well Griffin, looks like we get our match after all," she said slowly swinging her rapier back and forth as her long braid down her back kept her centered as she carefully balanced herself on the balls of her feet.

"This time it is to the death!" Griffin said as he attacked.

Acacia easily parried his blade as she ducked down and spun, coming up behind him as she cut his forearm.

"Ahh!" Griffin screamed applying pressure to his cut.

The swordsman Nyle was facing was an excellent duelist, easily underestimated when first viewed as a servant. But Nyle was a former Raptor, put through the rigors of training that was akin to torture. In the training ring there was always one that came out either severely wounded or dead. Those times would always haunt him, but the training was second nature to him and the sword became an extension of his arm as he blocked each thrust. As his foe raised his sword for a crushing overhead blow, Nyle took that opportunity to slide on his knees as he thrust upwards into the man's lower rib cage and came out his back. The man's sword fell from his lifeless hand as it clanged onto the marble floor. Nyle quickly withdrew his blade before the man had a chance to topple on top of him.

Paolo had disarmed his man and had him against the wall with his sword at his throat.

"Leave now," the king had told him sparing his life. The frightened servant bolted and could be heard running down the hall and out the door.

"Do you need any help love?" Paolo called to his wife who moved like a cat playing with a mouse as she battled Griffin.

"I've got this one, dear," she said fiercely.

Nyle watched as Acacia was basically performing almost dance like moves as she circled round and round Griffin. She would occasionally whip her braid as a distraction. This caused Griffin to receive a deep gash across his brow.

Griffin, seeing that he was now alone, threw his sword at Acacia and bolted for the door.

"Don't think this is over!" he shouted as he exited and fled.

After the fight they exchanged hugs and Nyle told them quickly of his search including and up to when he had arrived in the room.

"I know there is much more to the story," the king said, "but you can tell us when we have more leisure. For now, I think it is best we get out of here."

They started running back towards the main hall and were just about to the door when a curtain of fire shot up in front of them.

"Everyone back!" Paolo shouted.

But flames had erupted behind them from floor to ceiling.

"We're cut off," Acacia said. "Any ideas?"

"I think the first order of business is dealing with them," Nyle said with unusual calmness pointing with his sword to the left.

Paolo and Acacia looked to where he pointed to see nine hulking demons standing arrayed against them with swords and clubs.

"So what do you think?" Acacia said flourishing her rapier. "Three each?"

Both Paolo and Nyle looked at her. Nyle with astonishment and Paolo with pride.

"That sounds fair. What do you think, Nyle?"

"I will follow your lead sire," Nyle said while taking some quick practice strokes with his sword.

"Let's go," Paolo said.

The three of them slowly spread out, causing the demons to follow suit. The hall was enormous which gave them plenty of room to maneuver. Acacia wasted no time engaging her demons, preferring to stay on the offensive. She darted in and out like a faerie, her movements were a blur as she would strike and counter-strike. She took some grazing cuts but for the most part was not seriously injured. One demon fell at her feet as she drove her rapier through its head, its body turning to vapor as its scream echoed through the hall.

Paolo had two down, but the third was more agile and quick, parrying all the king's strikes. Sweat was streaming down his face from the exertion and the flames.

Nyle was engaging two at once while the third hung back, why he couldn't tell. He had fought more than one opponent together and easily fell into a rhythm. The trick was to lure them into a position so that once you delivered the killing strike to one you could immediately follow it up on the other. The moment came quicker than he thought as he dispatched the first demon and then the second. The vaporous cloud that formed had obscured the third demon, so Nyle never saw the spear that was thrown until it was sticking out of his chest. He oddly felt no pain as he sank against the wall.

"No!" Paolo shrieked as he rushed to his friend's aid after killing the demon he faced.

As Acacia killed her last demon, she ran over and slid on her knees to where Nyle sat bleeding out. His eyes started to pool with blood as his face turned ashen.

"I'm sorry my king," he wheezed as blood dribbled down his chin. "I really had hoped I could've rescued you."

"Don't talk Nyle," Paolo said. "You did free us. We are getting out of here and you are coming with us."

Both Paolo and Acacia had tears running down their cheeks. "Hold on Nyle," Acacia said. "We are not finished yet."

"I'm afraid we are my queen," the knight said looking past her.

The king and queen turned to look behind them. Circling them so there was no possible chance of escape were nine more demons. Paolo started to shake in rage at the hopelessness of their situation.

"Damn you Zana!" he yelled to the ceiling as the demons started their slow torturous advance.

Suddenly a bright light descended through the ceiling to land between them and the demons, momentarily blinding everyone. Once they could see, a woman with hair the color of flames wearing a sleeveless dress to match stood facing the demons with arms outstretched. Nyle smiled weakly.

"Sibila," he said as he forced himself to stay alert.

Sibila turned her head quickly and smiled. Then with all the natural force and magic of the phoenix, she drew the flames that barricaded them into herself, for a moment she was encased in fire before releasing it at the demons. All nine turned to instant vapor as their screams flew upward. Clapping her hands together, the fire instantly went out. Turning she knelt by Nyle as Paolo and Acacia stared open-mouthed at what they had just seen.

"I guess this is the end, Sibila," Nyle said as he coughed up blood. "I would have been curious to see what might have been."

"This is not the end my knight," she said gently caressing his cheek.

"Can you help him?" Paolo asked anxiously.

"Do not worry, his task is not done, but I will need the help of you and your queen," Sibila said.

"What do you need us to do?" Acacia asked.

"You hold onto the spear while your husband holds him from behind. When I say now, I want you to pull the spear out of him quickly."

"Why do I feel like this is not such a good plan," Nyle said trying to manage a smile.

"Brace yourself my knight," Sibila said. "Are you ready queen of Vasara?"

Acacia grabbed the shaft of the spear close to Nyle's chest. "I'm ready."

Sibila's eyes were the color of autumn with auburn rings around them that were spinning like a ring of flames. Nyle was drawn into them and when he focused all his attention on her eyes he could actually feel their warmth starting to spread through his body.

"Now!" Sibila said.

Nyle felt the king's arms tighten around him as Acacia pulled with all her might. The scream that tore from his throat blasted his ear drums. Suddenly Sibila's hands were on his chest and he could feel fire flying through his veins and encasing his heart. Something was happening to him. He was changing, and the screams never stopped. He felt like a baby being pushed out of the womb into a new existence, kicking and screaming the whole way through just before he passed out onto the cold marble floor.

***

Nyle felt something wet against his left cheek, then against his right, and eventually all over his face. Opening his eyes, he could see and feel wolf giving him a face bath.

"Stop old wolf, I'm awake, I'm awake," he laughed.

Nyle looked around and saw that he was in an alcove made out of stone surrounded by a garden with a small running stream making peaceful gurgling sounds as it ran over the stone bed. He knew where he was, Pan's grotto. How he had gotten here he had no idea.

"How long have I been out wolf?" he said scratching behind wolf's ears.

"About a week," came a familiar voice from behind him.

Nyle turned and stood up as he ran to embrace his king.

"I'm glad to see you whole my champion," Paolo said.

Nyle looked a little downcast at that.

"What's wrong?"

"I don't know that I am necessarily whole, Sire," Nyle said as he looked down at his hands. "She changed me."

The king put a hand on his shoulder. "I know, Sibila told us, although she wouldn't say anything specific. She said she had to speak to you first."

"I feel it Paolo. You can't see it, but the flames are running through my body right now, I'm not even sure I have a heart anymore, or if I am even human."

"Well of course you have a heart my love."

Nyle looked behind him and saw Sibila had come into the alcove followed by Acacia.

"As for being human, I guess you could say you are, but at the same time you are not."

She put both hands on the side of his face and Nyle could feel the heat radiating between them both as she kissed him. The flames in his body suddenly flared up, but Sibila's breath in his mouth provided a cooling balm that kept his body in check, or he was sure he would burn to a cinder.

"If you really want to know what this duality is like you should speak to Andros the Black, for this state of being is similar to what dragons experience," Sibila told him.

Nyle again looked down at his hands. He started to see something, lines trailing up and down his fingers. They were lines of fire. He focused harder on them and they began to grow. All of a sudden, his hands burst into flames, but it did not hurt or burn him.

"By the gods!" Acacia exclaimed.

"Actually, goddess would be more accurate," Sibila said smiling, as she closed her hands over his and the flames went out.

"Sibila, what am I?" Nyle asked.

"What you were always meant to be my knight. This was always the purpose of your birth, and part of my existence as well. So that we could come together at a time when our power would help to tip the balance."

"You know I have no clue what you're talking about, right?"

Sibila gave out a rich and beautiful laugh to Nyle's ears. "You will my love, you will."

"By the goddess is right," Paolo said, "because this has Braylynn written all over it."

Sibila looked at each person in turn. "A great battle is coming," she told them, "and as of right now the scales are so evenly balanced that it will not take much to tip it either way."

"So, what is our next step?" Nyle asked.

"We will go to Laurel Hollow. We will take council there with others who travel there even now. Also my love, they have a place there to practice your new found powers."

"I can't wait," Nyle said a little nervously as he scratched wolfs' head.

"What about Brayton, shouldn't someone tell him we have been rescued?" Acacia asked.

"I will take care of that, queen of Vasara. He too shall be there along with the queen of the unicorns."

"What's this?" Paolo said.

"Oh, I think in all the hustle of trying to escape I forgot to mention that part. Brayton is the Summus Re'em, the unicorn master," Nyle said.

Paolo and Acacia went from open astonishment to beaming with pride.

"Are you people hungry or what?" came a cranky shout.

"We better go," Paolo said. "Dim gets downright cantankerous when he's hungry."

Everyone laughed at that and it made Nyle feel somewhat normal to know that some things will never change.

Chapter 11

Brion was heading up the road to Baron Stefan's manor with a book under his arm that he had retrieved from his library. Shortly after Andros and the others had dispatched the demon lord that had wormed its way into his life, Tera had appeared. She claimed to be on some special mission for her faerie queen about seeking information of a place called Otherwhere. The silver haired faerie was throwing out questions a mile a minute, driving everyone to distraction. It was at this point that Brion remembered a book he had in his possession that he had gotten an eon ago from Baron Galvyn, the baron of Albion at the time. Brion had been surprised to have found his home still intact when he arrived back in Albion after the battle of the warlocks. He had come to learn that when he and his brothers had been imprisoned, Loki had done the only thing he could do for them, and that was to put enchantments around all their homes, so they would never know rot or decay. He also put wards on them so that no one could enter. There were centuries of dust on everything, and it had taken him almost a month to get everything back the way he wanted, but he was grateful for what Loki had done.

His books were his prized possession and he had quite a collection of rare and unique editions. One of them was the book he now carried. It was actually because of Tera that he remembered it at all, for on its cover was a silhouette of a faerie that very much resembled Tera. There was a passage with a reference to ait eile, which roughly translated meant otherwhere.

Walking into Baron Stefan's study, Brion was immediately assaulted by Tera.

"Did you get it?" Tera asked. "Where was it? You were gone a long time. Did you have trouble finding it? Do you think it will help us?"

"Tera, please," Brion said holding his hands up in surrender.

Tera grabbed the book and flew over to the pedestal in the corner of the library where Stefan was combing through a large tome. Tera placed the book in front of him.

"Here, you read," Tera instructed.

Brion could tell Tera was taking her mission from the queen very seriously. Donella had asked him to keep her sister out of trouble and assist her however he could. Stefan and himself went out of their way to be accommodating.

"Any particular place I should start?" asked Stefan directing his question to Brion.

"Page twenty-five," Brion replied.

Stefan flipped the pages to the place Brion had instructed and read aloud.

"When the silver hair stands on the steps of ait eile with prophecy's wizard, know that the end is nigh."

"What does that mean?" Tera asked. "It's gibberish!"

"Calm down Tera," Stefan said. "It reads like a prophecy, and if that is what this is, a prophecy is meant to obscure as well as reveal things in order to protect its message."

"But that doesn't stop us from coming up with theories," Brion said, "does it?"

"No, it does not," Stefan said as he closed the book and traced the image on the cover then looked at Tera closely.

"What are you thinking Baron?" Brion said.

"If I remember my history, Baron Galvyn was obsessed with prophecy. In his diary he wrote how he would often sit with the wizard Redlin at the library in Kensington pouring over books like these. I'm not sure why he would give this one to you though."

"Maybe some other power ordained it," Tera said in all seriousness.

Both Brion and Stefan looked at her sharply. All trace of her whimsical personality had disappeared as she said this.

"What makes you say that Tera?" Stefan said.

She looked back and forth between them. "Because I believe the silver hair is me."

Stefan nodded. "Yes, that is what came to my mind as I read it. I believe it is you too."

Tera suddenly flew into his arms and hugged him fiercely.

"Do not be frightened Tera. If you are ordained to be this person, you will have the strength to do whatever is necessary."

"But what if I do it wrong?" she said looking at him, her bottom lip trembling slightly.

"I don't think you can," Stefan told her. "Whatever strength or talent is required will be given at the appropriate time if you don't already possess it."

"Who do you think the 'wizard of the prophecy' is?" Brion said. "Has to be one of four if you now include Lyson."

"No, it will only be one of three," Stefan said. "The prophecy was created by the five, it will be one of their wizards, but which one I couldn't tell you."

Tera was thinking hard. "I bet it's Redlin," she said.

"Why Redlin?" Brion asked.

Tera put her hands over her mouth knowing she had revealed too much.

"Is anyone hungry? I'm really hungry. Is that coffee brewing

I smell?" Tera said as she started to fly towards the door.

"Hold it young lady!" Stefan said sternly. "Come back here right now."

Tera hung her head as she did a reluctant half circle and flew back.

"Okay, spill it," Stefan said.

"I'm not sure what you mean?" Tera said as she nervously kept pushing her hair behind her pointed ears.

Both Stefan and Brion just looked at her with arms crossed.

"Alright," she said finally. "But you can't tell Luel it was me that told you," she said shaking a finger at them.

"Never," they both swore with a straight face.

Tera went on to tell them how the queen had seen Redlin's death on the threshold of a place called Otherwhere and that this was the reason she had been sent to Albion to gather information.

Stefan was scratching his chin in thought.

"I don't believe it was a coincidence that you were sent here, Tera."

"Really?" Brion said.

"Really," Stefan affirmed. "The prophecy is guiding things and I think it was letting us know that Tera would be present at this moment of Luel's vision. Again, what you are supposed to do I do not know, but I am certain when the time comes all will be revealed."

"What do I do now?" Tera asked.

"I think now I should fly you back to Laurel Hollow. Events are starting to move and I am getting a feeling things are going to be revealed there. Are you ready?" Brion asked her.

Looking at him soberly, Tera replied, "Yes, let's go."

***

Cavanah Hall was crowded with faeries, humans, dragons and various other magical creatures. Luel sat on her throne as she listened to the various conversations going on. To anyone else it was a hum of activity, but one of the powers she had learned of the jewel of her father's house was that she could isolate multiple conversations at the same time.

"I've gotten used to it," she heard Brayton tell his parents about the patch over his eye.

"I wish I had been there, son," Paolo said putting a hand on his shoulder. Acacia had her arm linked through his and seemed not about to let go.

"It is still such a shock that you are truly the Summus Re'em," Paolo said. "Even though I knew the possibility existed, to see it come to fruition is another thing altogether."

I was skeptical at first as well, king of Vasara, Savano said. The queen of the unicorns was standing on the other side of Brayton, the prince flanked by two queens. Her black horn gleamed in the light of the hall, giving it an otherworldly glow.

"I will be glad to give you back your throne, Dad. The people need their king."

"We will speak more about that later," Paolo said. "First we must deal with the battle that is coming."

Luel's attention shifted to Lyson. He was off in a corner at a table with Tori and Cleo. Lyson was showing them the map with the extended section and its image of two crossed swords that was the symbol of Fallon.

"What do you think?" Lyson asked Tori.

Tori smoothed out the parchment as the ring around her eyes turned to circles of fire.

"Can you see anything?" Cleo asked her as she shifted the swords on her back that were poking her as she leaned down to try and see what Tori might see.

"Yes, something is coming through, the lines are starting to fill in," Tori said.

She started to squint as she tilted her head to look from another angle. "By the gods!"

"What is it?" Lyson said startled by her exclamation.

"I know you can't see this," Tori said, "but there is a three-dimensional image here."

"What do you mean?" Cleo asked.

"I can see the land and all its characteristics. Every hill, tree and river, only miniature. It looks nothing like the rest of the Border Lands."

"So how do we find it?" Lyson wondered aloud.

Tori got lower to the map. "This border here," she said pointing, "there are two columns not unlike the pillars of Fallon that guard the Corridor."

Luel remembered that the Corridor is where the demons came into Vasara to obtain physical form. It was marked by four pillars with a power orb on top of each one. Devon had stolen one which rendered the Corridor nearly useless until Andy and Emilia had helped Tori and Cleo to retrieve it and put it back.

"I believe with my sight, I can find these pillars," Tori said.

"Then what?" Cleo asked her friend.

"I guess we go and find out," Lyson said with a wink.

"We will need a ride," Tori said smiling at the adventure at hand. "I know just the dragon."

The queen turned her attention to the small gathering sitting in chairs by the hearth. Nyle, Sibila and Cathal were in a semi-circle facing each other. This was the first time in Vasara's history where the identity of the Phoenix was known before transforming into the magical creature of legend.

"So what does this mean, Dad? Are you human? I mean what are you exactly?"

Luel could tell Cathal was having a hard time trying to understand the transformation his father had gone through.

"For the most part I still feel human," Nyle told his son. "Except for the fact that I feel like I could burst into flames at any moment."

Cathal had to laugh at that which helped to dispel the uneasiness. He reached down to scratch wolf on the head. Wolf seemed to know that Nyle and Cathal shared the same blood and proceeded to lick his hand. "This is all very strange, but I always knew you were destined for great things. Does this mean I will no longer see you?"

"Absolutely not," Sibila interjected. "He is as much your father now as he has always been, he is just taking up the task he was created for."

"And will he burst into flames and be reborn as another creature as you do?" Cathal asked her."

"No, prince protector," she said. "He is not a true phoenix as I am."

"You never did explain to me what I have become," Nyle said.

Sibila looked back and forth between them.

"You my love, are Sol. The power of the sun is yours to command, and in time you will learn how to command it. But that time is very short for we are now hurtling towards the final battle."

"Damn, you've got to love these tight time schedules the prophecy keeps throwing at us," Cathal said.

Nyle smiled with pride as he mussed his son's hair.

Luel looked to the very center of the hall. Rhyan and Ava had traveled all the way from Fenner to be here. The priests of the god Aditya were in a circle with Andy, Abby, Emilia, Gael and Nia. They were dressed for battle with their bows slung over their backs. Among the arrows in their quiver, Luel could see the red godstone arrow of Bart the archer sticking out among them.

"I find it very peculiar that he called you death's mistress," Rhyan was saying in reference to the title the demon/baron Ansgar had given Abby. "That name has a familiarity to it."

"You have heard it before?" Abby asked.

Rhyan was silent for a moment as if weighing what she would say.

"I really wish Redlin were here," Rhyan began, "but I believe I will not violate my oath in telling you this."

"Are you talking about what you swore to Samara?" Andy asked.

"Yes, what I tell you does not directly involve her. When I linked with the sonipes, what I saw with regards to the death's mistress and the death dagger was the ability to communicate with the dead."

"You mean like Diminitus?" Emilia asked.

"No, not like a necromancer, that is not the impression I got. I believe you will need to figure this out for yourself," Rhyan said to Abby.

Luel saw the door to the hall open, though no one else had with all the conversations going on nor did they see it was Brion and Tera entering.

We need to speak to you, Majesty, Brion spoke to her mind.

Luel nodded. *Come to the library*, she told him.

Luel excused herself as she made her way down the hall to the library. Brion and Tera were already there. Tera flew into the queen's arms and started crying as Brion filled her in with what they had found in the book and about Tera's role in the upcoming battle. Luel knew the pressure that Tera was putting on herself. The queen sat down and made Tera stand in front of her. Pushing Tera's hair behind her pointed ears she tenderly touched her cheek.

"Tera, I am trusting you with one of the things I hold most dear to my heart, the life of my husband."

"I know," she said fighting back the tears. "That is what has me the most fearful, that when the time comes I will fail to do what I need to do out of fear. And Redlin will die because of my failure."

"Tera, do you know why I trust you?"

Tera looked down and merely shook her head. Luel lifted her chin up and made her look at her.

"You are so young in the manner of faeries," Luel said, "but since my children first came back to this world you had fought beside them every step of the way, never flinching once. Without knowing it, you were already helping to protect my family. Your heart is honest and pure, and I know when the time comes you will be there for my husband as well."

Luel then took Tera's hand and let it rest on top of her own as she touched the jewel in her father's crown. Tera's eyes went wide as a blue nimbus seemed to surround them both as care and worry left her body.

"How did you do that? That was amazing? That thing is incredible, what else can it do?" Tera started rambling.

"It's good to see you back to your old self," Luel said smiling as she winked to Brion who smiled and winked back.

Suddenly there was a knock on the door.

"Come," the queen said.

An attendant poked his head in. "Your husband and the other wizards are here your majesty."

And so now it begins, she thought as she stood up with Brion and Tera following her out of the library.

Chapter 12

Abby sat and listened as Redlin stood on the raised dais in order to be seen and heard, standing next to her husband was the queen. When Redlin arrived, he went straight to the queen's chambers with Loki and Dain. After coming out, the wizard talked to everyone in turn, learning all that had transpired. He was now telling everyone what had happened to him.

Abby couldn't believe what was going on. It was like they had a span of peace and then suddenly their very existence was being challenged from forces on all sides arrayed against them. At one point Abby had been only half listening when Redlin had mentioned the dragon maze and the key that Andros must find. Her eyes went wide and she gripped her beloved's arm.

"Abby, what is it?" Andy asked concerned.

"The dragon maze," she whispered. "We need to talk to your father."

After Redlin had finished giving account of all that had happened to him, the crowd started to disperse. There was going to be a meeting later of key people to discuss the next steps to confront the storm of war that was coming.

Abby and Andy ran up to Redlin as he was walking off the dais.

"Dad!" Andy said.

Redlin embraced his son and Abby.

"It is so good to see you both," the wizard said. I'm sorry we couldn't speak earlier, but your mother and I had a lot to talk about."

"That's ok, Dad. Abby needs to speak to you."

"What is it Abby?"

"This being you saw, Killian, you didn't really describe him, but did he have golden eyes?"

Redlin appeared stunned. "Abby, how did you know that?"

"I didn't really. But my father had once told me of a legend he once heard, about the key of golden eyes and his magical maze."

"What did your father say about it?" Redlin said his curiosity keenly piqued.

"That's the problem, I can't remember. I was very young when he told me. The only thing I do remember is the part about golden eyes and his key."

Redlin looked slightly disappointed. "Well, if anything it is confirmation that all this exists."

"I was thinking though," Abby said with a brightness lighting up in her eyes. "I discovered something just recently that could help us."

"What do you mean?" Andy asked. Abby looked at the man she called husband and saw concern in his eyes.

He probably already knows what I am going to propose, she thought. Which is understandable because it will involve some level of emotional pain.

"I want to talk to my father," she said. Abby went on to explain to her father-in-law what she had found out from Rhyan about being death's mistress and what that entailed.

"Are you sure you want to do this?" Andy asked her.

"I know it won't be easy, but I feel like I need to try, for all our sakes."

Redlin put a hand on her shoulder. "Abby, you are as much my daughter as Emilia is, and I will help you anyway I can."

Abby was grateful for this man she had come to regard as a second father.

"Will you come to Dragonsgate?"

Redlin smiled at her. "Of course I will. I would not pass up the opportunity to meet my son's father-in-law."

Abby wrapped her arms around him in a fierce hug.

"Come on," Redlin said. "Let's go meet with the others. There are plans to be made."

Abby took two steps then fell to her knees as she clutched her chest.

"Abby! What's wrong?" Andy cried out in alarm.

"The dagger," she said between clenched teeth, "it burns. There is a demon lord in the Hall."

Redlin and Andy quickly scanned the area.

"There are too many!" Andy said.

"Can you walk Abby?" Redlin asked her, helping her up as she grabbed onto Andy.

"Yes," she answered.

They started walking among the crowd, weaving in and out of clusters of faeries and humans. There were some puzzled glances in their direction but nothing that pinpointed to who it might be. Hanging onto Andy's arm with her hand on her chest, Abby was trying real hard not to let the pain show on her face, for alerting the potential enemy was the last thing they wanted. The force against her chest had her moving towards the far open window. The faeries were starting to leave to continue with their day, so many were flying out of the doors and windows at the same time, making it hard to pinpoint anything. Suddenly Abby stopped and her hand dropped.

"They've gone," she said looking back and forth around the room. "I am certain it is a faerie though."

"What makes you say that?" Andy asked still holding onto her arm.

"Because the dagger was leading me to this window, and

only a faerie can escape this way. It would be too obvious for a human."

"I believe you are right, Abby," Redlin said as he gazed out the window. "There is nothing we can do about it now, and we have no time to look for this person. Events are moving too quickly, and we have to keep ahead of it."

"I really thought Ansgar was the last one. We should tell Mom," Andy said running his fingers through his hair.

"My thoughts exactly," his father said. "Her people can take whatever precautions she thinks necessary. Let's go."

***

The library was crowded with people, but big enough that all could sit comfortably. Redlin chose to stand by the hearth in full view of everyone. Nyle and Sibila had left saying something about going to practice Nyle's newfound abilities.

"I think it's time to split up," Redlin began.

"I really hate when we have to do that," Andy whispered to Abby. Redlin smiled at him since he was close enough to hear.

Luel sat on the other side of him. His conversation with his wife when he had gotten back seemed a little strange, as though she were holding something back. Redlin had pressed her on it, but she had reassured him that everything was fine. Redlin knew his wife, and if there was something she wasn't telling him she had a good reason and she would reveal it when it was time. He trusted his Luel implicitly. Redlin felt Andy didn't know, or he would have spilled the beans long ago. That boy could not keep a secret if his life depended on it.

"So what are your thoughts brother?" Loki asked him.

Redlin paused, gathering his thoughts as he settled all the different pieces in his mind.

"I will be going with Andy and Abby to Dragonsgate for

starters to see what information can be gleaned there."

"Can you take Tera with you?" Luel asked.

Redlin looked at his wife with puzzlement. "Are you sure that's necessary dear?"

Luel returned his gaze with resolve. "Yes, I do. If anything, it will keep her out of mischief," she said smiling at the silver haired faerie.

"I am at your disposal, master wizard," Tera said saluting smartly. Redlin rolled his eyes and groaned inwardly.

"Sure you won't change your mind," he said to his wife under his breath.

Luel winked and shook her head no.

"Very well," Redlin said. "Lyson, Emilia, Tori and Cleo will be traveling to the Border Lands to investigate what they have found in Fallon's map."

"Brion will accompany us and has agreed to fly us there," Lyson said.

"I have also been in contact with Caleb, who should be flying here now. With Gael already here we should be able to provide transportation to wherever anyone needs to go."

"Excellent," Redlin said. "I was going to suggest that very thing."

Just then Leah burst into the room, her face was like a thunder cloud with a ragged cut above her eye, which thankfully was not deep.

"Leah," Luel said, "What's wrong?"

"I was flying past the Hall when your personal assistant flew out of a window like a demon out of hell."

"Keary?" the queen asked.

"Yes," Leah answered.

"Hold still sister," Emilia said as she placed her hand on Leah's forehead over her cut, allowing her healing energy to flow through. When she pulled her hand away the cut was completely gone.

"Thank you, sister," Leah said smiling.

"Leah, what happened?" Luel asked.

"Keary and I collided. When we became untangled, she looked back towards the window like she expected someone to be following her. She hissed at me and drew her talon dagger. She got one cut in before I had my spear out and leveled it at her throat. Then with speed I had never seen in a faerie, she shot straight up and disappeared from sight. What the hell is going on Majesty?"

"She's the one," Abby said. "The one I sensed in the Hall."

"What are you talking about?" Leah asked.

Redlin told them of the demon Abby had sensed with the death dagger and how it had escaped through the window.

"Do you want me to go after her Luel?" Leah asked with anger in her eyes as she tested the edge of her dagger. "I believe I owe her one."

"Absolutely not," the queen said. "These things are too powerful."

"And what do we do if she comes back," Leah said putting her blond hair in a ponytail as if she were going into battle. "Once everyone leaves on their various quests, we will be a little short of firepower."

"Em?" Andy said to his sister.

"I'm already on it," Emilia said as she closed her eyes as the eye in her dragon crown started to glow.

"What is she doing?" Rhyan asked.

"She is summoning the rest of our brothers," Brion answered.

Luel was shaking her head. "I can't believe Keary is one of those things. She was a trusted advisor, a friend."

"They duped all of us Mom," Andy said. "We still don't know what their ultimate endgame is."

"Perhaps I can help with that," said a deep resonant voice

from a darkened part of the room.

Everyone gasped as Meliakken stepped into the light, his penetrating ice blue eyes connecting with all who gathered there. Emilia had her staff out and Luel jumped up to stand next to her daughter.

"Come to try your luck again?" Emilia asked smirking.

The jewel in Luel's crown was blazing as Andy and Redlin took up positions on either side of them. Pretty soon every being with power formed a semi-circle facing off against the evil god.

"I will never underestimate you again Summoner, or your faerie queen mother. You should all just relax, I am not here to harm anyone," the god said as he looked around at the circle of power facing him.

"Easy thing to say since you are outnumbered," Lyson said, the power of the goddess clearly visible in the little bolts of lightning dancing on his upraised hands.

Meliakken laughed at that. "You are the newest to come into his power, general. I would tread lightly if I were you."

Lyson suddenly got belligerent as he slowly walked forward, his black wings extended. "You forget, it was the power that is flowing through me now that tipped the balance and imprisoned you forever."

A flash of anger briefly crossed the god's face. "Yes, Braylynn was the one thorn in my side that I was not expecting, but she is not here right now, or any of the gods for that matter. Been having trouble contacting them lately?" Meliakken said knowingly.

"What do you know about that?" Redlin said as he kept a tight hand on the source.

Meliakken said nothing, just stared at the wizard with undisguised hatred.

"Enough of this back and forth," Loki said. "You said you

could explain these demons and their end game. Why tell us?"

"You were always the more sensible one when it came to my secret plots Loki."

"Whatever that means," Loki said. "Say what you have come to say and be gone, because I doubt you are truly here and there is not much we can do against an illusion."

"You are right that there is nothing you can do to me here, but I assure you I am no illusion."

Just then a black energy stream shot out of Meliakken's hand and attached itself to Tera's chest as he lifted the little faerie off the ground.

"Ahhh!" Tera cried out in pain. "It burns! It burns!"

"Meliakken stop!" Luel roared.

Suddenly Andy jumped up, swinging moon shadow. As soon as the black sword connected with the energy beam, it severed the link to Tera, but the force knocked Andy back against the wall. Brion, who had been underneath Tera, caught her as she fell unconscious into his arms, but she was still breathing.

"You insolent pup!" Meliakken screamed.

Luel and Emilia started walking forward. Emilia was holding Nocte as well as her staff. Luel was making movements with her hand as if starting to cast a spell.

"We may not be able to harm you," Luel said, "but we can prevent you from harming others here."

Meliakken's eyes narrowed and he smiled wickedly as they continued their forward pace, as if he were waiting for something. Once they stepped in the direct line of one of the windows he spoke.

"Now you will see one of the reasons for my pets being among you."

Just then there was a crash as a redhaired faerie with

translucent purple wings flew into the room and straight at Emilia. There was no time to react.

"Keary!" Luel shouted.

Keary collided with Emilia and pulled out her medallion with the power of a goddess in it. Yanking the chain with the strength of a demon lord it broke from around Emilia's neck, leaving a deep gash in her skin as blood formed around her neck like a necklace. Emilia fell to the floor gasping in pain as Keary fled through the back door before anyone could stop her.

"Donella!" Lyson screamed as he ran over to his beloved. Putting a hand to the back of her neck, he poured the healing energy of the goddess into her body, closing the wound.

"You bastard!" Redlin screamed. His ring was a wheel of fire as he aimed it directly at the god and unleashed his power. As if some signal had been given, everyone else in the room unleashed whatever power was in their own personal arsenal.

Meliakken however had already erected a shield around himself when Keary had broken into the room, and just stood there with a self-satisfied smirk on his face.

"Stop!" Loki yelled. "This is pointless."

Everyone turned off their power like water from a faucet as Loki's words penetrated.

"As I said Loki, you were always the sensible one. Now I have one, one more to get. Say goodbye to your little witch."

There was a bright flash as everyone shielded their eyes. Once they could all see again, Meliakken had vanished.

"What did he mean by 'say goodbye to your little witch'?" Dain asked.

"Samara!" Redlin said his eyes lit up with fear. "Rhyan!"

"I'm on it!" Rhyan said. "Brion, I need you."

"I'm coming too," Ava said. "No arguments, you aren't facing this alone."

Brion carefully handed Tera to Andy as the three of them fled from the Hall.

"Will someone tell me what the hell is going on?" Lyson said helping Emilia to her feet. "You alright love?"

"I'm fine, thank you dear," Emilia said touching his cheek. "I can't believe I let her take it," she said shaking her head.

"Don't beat yourself up sweetheart," Redlin told his daughter. "Meliakken played us from the beginning, none of this is your fault."

"Was he really here?" Lyson asked.

"No," Loki answered. "If he were totally free from his prison, no one would be alive right now. But to be able to project himself here and use some of his power, he must be very close to breaking out."

"Who is the witch he spoke of?" Nia asked.

"Samara," Redlin answered. "She has the other medallion with the power of a god inside, Emilia's held the goddess. There is no doubt he plans to absorb their power somehow."

"Why send Rhyan?" Gael asked.

"Because she has a link to that medallion and can locate the blood forest where Samara lives," Redlin explained as he walked over to the window and looked out. "I only pray she gets there in time."

He said this with such sorrow that Luel came over and put her arm around his waist as he lay his head on top of hers.

"What is it Dad?" Andy asked.

The wizard looked sadly at his son. "Samara has had a hard life that most don't know or would understand. I don't want to see that life snuffed out in an instant by Meliakken. She has suffered enough."

"What happens now?" Dain asked.

Redlin suddenly became all business as he outlined his plan, giving everyone their roles for the next step in their quest to save Vasara. After the meeting broke up Redlin kissed his wife goodbye. Abby, Tera and himself, climbed aboard Andy's back as he lifted off and started winging his way to Dragonsgate for their appointment with Abby's father.

Chapter 13

Samara was walking the paths of her blood forest, deep in thought. She was wearing her sleeveless red dress with her belt of gold half-moons. The breeze on her skin was warm but not hot. She was fingering the god medallion around her neck that she had traded for the death dagger with Andros. He had felt such loathing to give it up and for good reason, immense power resided inside, the power of a god. There were many times over the years that she thought about releasing its power. The how was never an issue, she knew just where to go to do it. It was the why that always held her back. Plus, that pesky little priestess Rhyan had put a charm on it. As soon as she did it, Aditya's priest would be on her quicker than thought. But still, even that wasn't what prevented her from releasing them. It was Andros himself. When he thought his love was dead and his mind had shattered, the outpouring of love and support for him from others was immense and intense. There was a raw power in it and even she was caught up in helping him.

She always had thought she didn't need anyone, being abandoned and unacknowledged by her father at birth had hardened her heart to believe this. Her mother had died in childbirth which piled guilt into blaming herself. She was raised by a decent enough family, but by the time she was a teenager her powers had started to appear and out of fear they turned her out. The one gift her father did give her was the Blood Forest. At least here she was somewhat protected since it constantly moved its location. Also, the various spells and wards she put on the place kept unwanted visitors out. But there was a hole in her soul now that longed to be filled, and Andros had awakened the ache of it.

"Damn you, Andros!" she cursed to the sky.

She kept walking up the path when she noticed someone coming towards her. He had shoulder-length dark hair with a closely trimmed black beard that set off his amazing blue eyes. It was Ferris, her youngest conscript who had indentured himself to her for a certain spell. It was actually quite easy and harmed no one. All he wanted was a belief in himself. She tried to tell him he could achieve this without her help but he was adamant. Out of sympathy she granted his request. The terms of the deal was servitude for six months, that was ten years ago. He found he liked living in the Blood Forest and asked to stay on. She initially thought to refuse him, but again she felt sympathy for him. He became her aide that she would send out into the world to gather information. He was exceptionally gifted in this and kept her updated on the goings-on in the wide world.

Suddenly the hair on the back of her neck started to rise and she stopped walking. Something was off. Her eyes went wide as she suddenly found she could not move her arms. Ferris kept getting closer and his eyes suddenly turned red.

"Ferris, what is happening?"

"I'm sorry, Samara, but I need this," Ferris said ripping the god medallion from around her neck.

"Why are you doing this? You can't do anything with that."

"But I can," a voice from behind her said.

Samara was released from whatever was holding her and she spun around.

"Meliakken," she said with fire in her eyes as her hands began to move with power.

"I wouldn't advise that if I were you," Meliakken said. "I still haven't decided if I want to kill you or not. Do that though and I definitely will."

Samara stopped what she was doing as her eyes narrowed at the god. Ferris walked over and deposited the medallion in Meliakken's open hand. The god held it up and looked at it, then taking out the medallion he stole from Emilia he pressed the two together until they melded into one.

"You have the other?" Samara said stunned.

"I do," he said in a matter of fact tone. "Although the Dragon Summoner suffered more hurt than you in relinquishing it if that makes you feel any better."

"It doesn't," she said angrily as she turned her eyes on Ferris. "What exactly are you, Ferris?"

"He's a very special demon lord," the god answered instead. "One of a select group of demons bred for my cause."

"And you were able to wait ten years for your plan to bear fruit? You are patient," Samara said.

"Oh my little witch, I have waited much longer than that. Now everything is aligned and perfect for me to execute my final plan."

He held up the now one thick medallion. "When I release the power of these two into me, not even the five and that irksome goddess will be able to defeat me."

Samara started to laugh.

"What's so funny?" Ferris asked sneering, all pretense of friendship gone as his true demon nature came out.

"What is so funny my dear demon is that there is only one place where that power can be released, and not only do you lack access, you also lack knowledge of where it is."

Meliakken shook his head sadly. "You know Samara, there was a time when I thought we could align together. We both have been wronged by the same person."

"What are you talking about?" Samara said. "You know nothing of my pains."

"Oh but I do," the god said. "I have watched this world since its creation, and some I have watched most carefully, weighing when I would need certain alliances."

"You are like a circus magician," she said with heat. "You make generalities and guesses. Are you going to guess my age and weight next?"

Meliakken chuckled at that. "I know your father cast you out by his failure to acknowledge you. Just as he tried to cast me out when this world was formed."

Samara started to shake as tears slid down both cheeks, but she kept silent.

"I see I've hit the mark. Trystan put me in a prison and thought to leave me to rot. Just as the god put you in a prison to rot by not claiming his only daughter."

Samara let out an ear shattering scream as energy bolts shot out of her hands and raced towards Meliakken. The god easily deflected them and wound-up hitting Ferris instead, incinerating the demon on the spot as his body turned to ash and a black oily smoke went shrieking through the woods.

Samara lowered her head and her hands, realizing the futility of trying to harm the god. The tears kept falling, but she lifted her head with a look of defiance.

"Trystan did not put me in a prison, although I did hate him for what he did. I shall never call him father, but I didn't waste my life in bitterness or tried to seek useless revenge. I went my own way and made my own choices."

"Bravely spoken," Meliakken said. "Keep saying that and one day you may even convince yourself. But it doesn't matter, now I must away to your father's forge, so I may release these deities and claim their power."

Samara was shocked that he knew where to go. "You will never be allowed in there," she said.

The god just gave her an evil smile. "We will see my little witch. And now I think I have come to a decision."

"What decision is that?" she said drained and weary, both physically and emotionally.

"About letting you live," he said as if he were talking about how blue the sky was today. "I think you really need to die. Even though you are insignificant, you could still be a thorn in my side. This is not personal."

Samara just stood there defiantly, resigning herself to her fate. Her one regret was that she couldn't warn Andros, to be able to help them all in some small way.

Meliakken started to raise his hands to deliver the killing strike when he suddenly sensed something. Looking behind him and up, he saw a red godstone arrow speeding towards his back. His posture quickly turned from offensive to defensive. Then came the shout.

"Samara! Jump!"

Samara looked up to see a red dragon with wings outstretched descending. On his back were two women, one being Aditya's priest, Rhyan whose hand was outstretched. The other holding a bow in her hand was identical to Rhyan in every way. Samara knew this must be her sister, Ava. It must have been Ava who had shot the godstone arrow. It only took a matter of seconds to take all of this in. Running forward while Meliakken was distracted she leapt up and grabbed Rhyan's hand as she was pulled onto the dragon's back.

"Brion, now!" Rhyan shouted.

Hold on, Brion spoke to Samara's mind.

Brion went vertical with amazing speed as he did a half

loop to head back in the direction they had come as he dodged curses and lightning strikes from the angry god. They broke through the barrier of the Blood Forest and flew south as if all the demons of hell were after them.

"I think you can slow down," Rhyan told Brion.

The red dragon slowed to a steady beat of wings as a cool breeze made Samara's hair trail behind her. Gathering it up she tied it into a ponytail much like in the manner of her rescuers.

"I never thought I would say this, but I am happy to see you, priestess. I assume this is your sister."

"Ava," she said introducing herself.

"That was a good shot," Samara said. "It saved my life."

"It was the godstone arrow of Bart the archer, it is for occasions such as this that he would have wanted it to be used, even though I am sure Meliakken has turned it to dust by now, but it gave us the distraction we needed."

Samara looked sadly at Rhyan. "He has both medallions now."

"I know," Rhyan said. "We will stop him."

"He also knows who I am, or rather where I came from."

Rhyan put a hand on Samara's shoulder. "It is nothing to be ashamed of you know."

The emotion running through Samara was raw and for a moment she cursed it as weakness, but then all of a sudden something inside her broke as she collapsed into Rhyan's arms sobbing. After her tears had run its course she wiped her face.

"I was never ashamed," Samara said. "Divinely hurt is more to the truth. And I can't honestly say I didn't enjoy playing the victim to excuse some of the actions I had taken over my long life."

Care to share what you mean? Brion said.

"It's a private wound, Brion," Rhyan said.

"No, I am done with the hurt and the wallowing. I want a

better path. I have been wanting it for a long time now. The god Trystan is my father."

Brion faltered for a moment in mid-flight at what he just heard.

"Whoa!" Ava said astonished. "I did not see that coming. You sure know how to keep a secret, sister."

"I made a vow, as you know," Rhyan said to her sister.

"I release you from that vow," Samara said.

"So what happens now?" Ava said.

"Meliakken is heading for my father's forge so he can release the power of the god and goddess in the medallions."

"Can he actually get there?" Rhyan asked.

"If I remember correctly, only Luel and Donella have the knowledge to open the door that leads to that valley that lies through the holy mound of the Alfar," Ava said.

"He's a god," Samara said. "He may not be able to go physically himself right now, but I am certain he has agents he can send."

Who would he trust with such a task, Brion said as he started to bring his flight lower to the ground so as to not make himself a target for any potential enemies the god might send.

"There is only one person that comes to mind," Rhyan said looking at her sister.

"Zana," Ava finished for her.

Chapter 14

Zana was not looking forward to this encounter with the angry god as she transported herself once more to the warlocks' temple. The summons had been hard and painful as he assaulted her brain with his need for her presence. She sometimes had doubts about allying herself with Meliakken, but she would never turn back now. She had tasted his power, bathed in it and let it lift her up almost to the point of ecstasy. Power was all now. She knew exactly when she had set herself on this path, though at the time she didn't realize it was Meliakken pulling the strings even then.

Her mind went back to that day. That day when she committed the ultimate sin against her friend as well as being forsaken by her goddess. Finn was out of the picture by then. Layla was the Dragon Summoner, and she thought she had come to accept that as they worked together to keep Vasara safe. Zana had no idea of the darkness that had encased her heart like a box.

They were in the Baron's house in Hadley after summarily defeating a host of demons that had broken through the Border Lands and was invading the mid-towns of Vasara. They rode the dragons together, killing any demon foolish enough to come in range. Layla had been on Finn, when together they had destroyed the demon lord of the host, using their combined powers to do it.

"Did you see, Zana," Layla remarked as they sat in high back chairs sipping wine as she recounted the battle. "When

Finn and I had joined our power, it was like a flood of energy."

Zana's eyes narrowed slightly. Layla didn't say this as any kind of boast or as if she was bragging, she just wanted to relay to her friend what she had felt.

Something was happening. Zana was feeling hot and her breathing was becoming slightly labored, but Layla noticed none of that. Then Zana started to hear Devon's whispers in her ears. Layla got up to go over to the mirror. Taking her auburn hair out of its ponytail she picked up the brush on the vanity table and began to brush it out. Zana looked at Layla's glass of wine sitting on the end table. Taking a small vial out of the pouch belted to her side, she poured the contents into the glass.

"This has been a good day," Layla remarked sitting down and taking a long sip of her wine.

"Yes, it has, sister," Zana said with a slight smile.

Her mind had totally gone over now. All she had to do was wait. After a few minutes, Layla said she felt tired and was going to lay down. The potion Zana had given her was going to make her sleep deep. When she felt enough time had gone by, Zana walked into the bedroom with her dagger drawn. She leaned against the door frame and just watched Layla's steady breathing. It was hard and deep, and Zana knew she would not wake up. She was amazed at the amount of bitterness that was in her heart at this moment.

"You have taken everything from me Layla," Zana said not expecting any response. "All that you are, everything you have become should have been mine. You are not worthy of the power you hold. And Finn..."

A burning rage came over Zana as she quickly walked over to the bedside, grabbing Layla by her hair, she tilted her head back and sliced her throat. Blood splattered across her chest, but she was numb to it. Layla had opened her eyes but could not make a sound. They locked with Zana's as they just stared at one another as her life drained away.

Zana felt hollow, without remorse or guilt. There was however a part of her mind that had cut itself off from everything, and in that part of herself was an image of a woman scratching her eyes out and screaming, but she could not feel it. It was screaming still.

Coming back to the present, Zana shook her head, telling herself that dwelling on the past would serve no purpose. Her soul was sold, her life committed. She had more power coursing through her body than any other time in her life.

Walking up the temple steps she opened the big red doors that gave her entrance. She looked back behind her one more time to make sure she wasn't being watched, more specifically that Finn wasn't there. All was silent. Walking down the hall she came to the door with the letter M embossed on it in a circle of shrikers. She was about to turn the knob when the door opened on its own.

"Come in Zana," Meliakken said.

Stepping into the room the god was seated at a high back chair staring out the window.

"You summoned me, my Lord?"

Meliakken turned in his chair and smiled at her. "It pleases me that you know your place Zana, and your ambition is tempered to grow only to the level you know is safe. I knew your heart with Devon and how it chastened you to basically be his lackey."

"He lied and betrayed me," Zana said not flinching from the god's stare. "In the end he tried to kill me."

"And yet he is dead and you survived, that says something. But you survived because of the intervention of the Dragon Summoner."

Meliakken walked over to her and stood but a finger's width apart. He was much taller than she and his short-cropped hair gave him the appearance of a ruthless creature who would snuff out your life as soon as look at you.

"I have to wonder Zana, do you feel any obligation towards her because of this."

Zana flinched only slightly, but not out of fear, but because the raw power being directed at her mind was overwhelming.

"The score between Donella and myself is even. I helped save her life as she once helped me, not that I needed it. I owe her nothing, but she owes me everything, and I plan on collecting."

Meliakken took a step back as he probed her eyes for a few moments before speaking again.

"Good. I can see you mean what you say. I have a task for you, and this will truly prove your loyalty to me."

"What is it?" Zana asked.

"I need you to get me into Trystan's forge."

"I'm assuming something prevents you from going there," Zana said.

Meliakken seemed annoyed at her response.

"Yes, this prison prevents me. Though enough of my bonds are gone, I still can't move freely at will or with my full power. And I certainly can't get into the one place where I am sure there are many wards to prevent me from entering."

Zana pondered on that for a moment. The god needed her. His plans could not move forward without her. That thought alone gave her such a feeling of power.

"How are we to achieve this?" she asked.

"You will use the glass rod that brought you here. It is Trystan's rod and it knows where it came from."

Meliakken waved his hand in the air and the image of a

door with intricate scroll work appeared. "You must learn the pattern that opens this door."

Zana watched in amazement as a line of light traced an intricate path along the scroll work.

"Did you make this door?"

"No, but I controlled the man who did for a time," the god answered. "Have you committed it to memory?"

"I have," Zana said.

"You will need this," Meliakken said as he handed her a round black stone.

"What do I do with this?" she asked as she rolled the stone in her hand.

"When you reach the forge, put it on the anvil and smash it. You will also need to take Griffin with you."

She looked up sharply. "Why? He would only slow me down."

"Let's just say it's necessary and leave it at that."

Zana was getting a bad feeling down her spine.

"How are things with your captives?" Meliakken asked her.

Zana told him everything about what had transpired in Otherwhere, including the intervention of the Phoenix and the transformation of Nyle. Everything suddenly went black, and before she knew what had happened, she was picking herself up from the other side of the room, pain was shooting from her feet to her head.

"Incompetence!" the god shouted. "Do you realize what you've allowed to happen?"

"What!" Zana said angrily. She knew the god could turn her to dust, but she hadn't got to be where she was by showing fear. If she had shown that the god certainly would have destroyed her.

Meliakken just stared at her, his eyes narrowed to slits. Suddenly he let out a loud laugh.

"Very good my pet, you have mastered your fear. The pain you are experiencing now is punishment enough. What you have allowed to happen is that Sol is now loose in the world."

"Why is that a problem?"

"Because he brings the power of the sun, but it will take him awhile to come into his full power."

"Can you not handle him?"

Meliakken looked irritated by her question. "I know that you are brave, but don't push it. Of course I can, it's just an added thorn to have to deal with. Our timetable has moved up. Go fetch Griffin and get to Trystan's forge. I will see you there."

And with that, the god disappeared leaving Zana alone in the room. She was getting tired of being some magician or god's plaything. A pawn to do their bidding, but Zana had aspirations beyond what Meliakken was willing to give her. She just needed to bide her time and play his game. Eventually her time would come.

Chapter 15

Nyle was getting discouraged. He and Sibila had come to the glade of the Dragon Summoner in order for him to harness and control his new powers, but he wasn't having very much luck.

"Why can't I grasp this?" he asked Sibila.

"You are trying to force it my knight," she said smiling at him. "It is like love, you need to relax and just let it flow through you."

"Yeah, well I haven't really had that much practice at love either if you want to know the truth."

Sibila looked at him with something akin to sadness in her eyes. Nyle saw it and instantly berated himself for it.

"I'm sorry if I have caused offense, Sibila. I didn't mean that."

"It is not for any imagined offense that makes me sad my Sol. It is that your life has been missing out on a more complete happiness, and it is only because of some supposed guilt that you would not allow yourself to feel it."

"What do you mean?" Nyle said, his body starting to shake a little.

Sibila put both hands on his shoulders. Her wind-blown autumn colored hair was proving to be a little distracting for him, but in a good way. Sibila smiled at him, knowing what he was thinking.

"Look into my eyes, sir knight."

Nyle's eyes locked with hers. Once again, as in Otherwhere,

rings of fire circled around the edges of her eyes as images started to appear. Images of his youth, when his father would beat him with the blunt end of a sword for losing a match at the soldiers' academy. Then during his time in the ring with his best friend for Raptor training, where only one person could come out alive.

Nyle could not look away, tears were streaming down his face. "Sibila please."

Fire was streaming from Sibila's hair, the rings around her eyes spinning faster as each pain in his life was brought to the surface.

"You have carried the guilt and shame long enough," she said. "It is time to forgive yourself."

It was then that Nyle let himself go as his back arched and he let out a blood-curdling scream. If that scream had physical form it would resemble a black cloud leaving his body. Breath heaving and crying, he collapsed into Sibila's arms and knew no more.

He didn't know if he was out for moments or hours, but he felt newly made. As if a giant stone were lifted off his chest and he could breathe again.

"Now you are Sol," Sibila said smiling. "I can feel the flow within you. Much easier now?"

Nyle took several deep breaths. He did feel the fire and blood within him moving freely together without impediment.

"Now look around you and tell me what you see," she told him.

Nyle started to really see things for the very first time, and he was in awe at what he saw. He could see the vapor of fire in the air, moving and undulating like a ribbon as it ran across the sky. Looking at a tree he could see a faint line of fire as it outlined its shape. All the trees had this. A rabbit darted through the glade and it too was illuminated by fire.

"Sibila, how is this possible?"

"Every living thing has some element of fire my love. You, me and the gods are the only ones who can see it." Sibila thought for a moment. "It's possible the Cath Priomh could see it."

"Tori?"

"Yes, but I have never asked her, so I don't really know."

Nyle smiled at her. "I thought you knew everything my love."

Sibila gently patted his cheek. "I'm an oracle my knight, not a goddess. Now, to work."

Nyle closed his eyes. He envisioned the elements of heat and fire all around him. Stretching his arms out, he started pulling all of that energy into himself.

"Not too much love," he heard Sibila say, "and only a little from each thing. You are only borrowing, not stealing."

He modified his pulling in. Taking some from the trees, the air and the grass. The fire was flying up and down his body in a repeated loop, going faster and faster. Every nerve felt like it was aflame. He opened his eyes and looked down at himself, shocked at what he saw.

Nyle's entire body was outlined in flames. He could feel its heat, but his flesh was not consumed. Even his hair seemed to be dancing flames. Also, within that heat he felt its raw power. Moving his hands in a circular motion he created a ring of fire directly in front of him as if it were the most natural thing to do.

"Very good my love," Sibila said with approval. "Your instincts are very quick. I want to show you something. Make it go faster."

Nyle concentrated as the ring started to pick up speed. He was feeling something coming off of it, as if the fabric of air and space was changing from his immediate surroundings. Suddenly there was a bright flash and the image he was seeing through the ring had changed. Instead of the grassy glade, what he saw were snowcapped mountains under a blue sky.

"By the gods! Is that place real?"

"Yes, it is," Sibila said smiling. "And we can even step through. You have learned the first of your many powers my love, you've created a portal."

Nyle was feeling pleased with himself that he finally had created something.

"Shall we?" he asked meaning to step through.

"Not there. What you produced was random. Now I want you to think of a specific place. I want you to think of the White Castle and take us there."

Nyle tried that. After letting the ring drop, he created another. As its rotations went faster, he thought of the White Castle, but once the flash of light happened he was staring at an ocean of grass.

"Fenner," he said. "I don't understand, I was thinking of the castle."

"You can't just think of it," Sibila said patiently. "You must feel it. Feel its connection, otherwise the portal will just open to random places."

Nyle tried again. This time, instead of just trying to see the visual picture of the place in his mind, he reached out to the strongest connection he had to that place, his son Cathal. The flash of light was very bright this time and now he could see the soaring turrets of the White Castle.

Sibila kissed his lips. The fire surrounding his body didn't seem to have any effect on her, in fact his flames encircled her as he held her and kissed her back.

After breaking their kiss, she grabbed his hand and led him through the portal.

A deer stood on the edge of the forest, its head turned quizzically as it watched a ring of fire shrink to nothingness before winking out of existence with a fiery snap. Startled it bounded through the woods, not likely to choose that path again.

***

The wind was warm blowing through Abby's hair as she rode on Andy's back with Redlin and Tera. It was nighttime and the stars were incredibly bright tonight as they got closer to Dragonsgate.

Should we go to the house? Andy asked her.

"No, let's go to the library," Abby answered with a little nervousness in her voice.

Abby felt a hand on her shoulder. She turned her head to see her father-in-law looking at her with compassion.

"Abby, you don't have to do this if it is too much for you."

Abby was grateful that Redlin had come with them. She had no idea what to expect in what she was about to try.

"I can do this," Abby said, "as long as the people I love the most are with me."

"We would never let you face this alone," Redlin told her.

"I should say not," Tera said pulling out her spear and extending it. "I've got your back sister."

Instead of laughing at Tera's statement, a tear of love slid down her cheek and she hugged the young faerie fiercely. Tera for a second seemed startled since she was usually the one giving the hugs. Redlin looked at her knowingly.

"You have grown quite a bit, Tera. Quite a bit indeed."

"I'm the same size I've always been master wizard," she said.

Redlin and Abby both laughed at that.

Andy started to circle around Dragonsgate until he came to the field he usually landed in when coming home, which happened to be just behind the library. After everyone got off his back he made his change.

"You lead the way Abby," Redlin said.

Abby led them to the hedgerow where the secret gate was that led to the garden area of the library. Once they entered the garden, she took them down a short path with dwarf trees on either side to form a kind of tunnel. Upon reaching the end of the path there was a small grove with a bench and a single white headstone. Abby had built this little garden herself because she knew this is where her father would want to be buried, on the grounds of the place he loved the most. On the stone was the image of an open scroll with her father's name and inscription underneath.

"Neil, father and curator. Words are alive and keep us out of bondage," Tera read aloud what was written. "Did you write that?"

Abby shook her head. "It was one of my father's favorite things to say. It summed up his entire belief system, so I thought it fitting to have it here so anyone would know what he believed." Abby brushed a tear that had escaped the corner of her eye as she took a deep breath.

"Are you ready Abby?" Andy asked his wife.

Abby grabbed his hand and nodded.

"This part is all you Abby," Redlin said. "I can't even begin to tell you how to do this."

"I understand, I'm ready."

Abby let go of Andy's hand and took several deep breaths. She had an idea of how to proceed here. She needed a guide, and she was going to contact the only one associated with the death dagger.

"Here we go," she said as she clasped the pendant in her hand until the point of the dagger pricked her palm, causing blood to flow. Suddenly a door opened in her mind. Abby knew there was a presence in the pendent when Andy had touched it in the Blood Forest and the sing-song message in the ancient language was revealed to him. Stepping through the door she was face to face with a tall figure in a cowled robe. Its features were concealed in the shadow of the hood.

"Welcome Mistress," it said in a very deep male voice. "I figured sooner or later you would come."

"How do you know me?" Abby asked.

"When the goddess gave you the pendant to bring you back from the dead, she had to go through me and seek my permission."

"Thank you, I guess?" Abby said with uncertainty.

"Thanks are not necessary, Mistress. Something for something, that is how all things work."

"And what do you get out of all of this?"

"That is not needful for you to know," he said.

Abby ran her fingers through her hair at the strangeness of all of this.

"Do you have a name at least?" she asked.

"You may call me Bas," he said.

"Very well, Bas. I need to speak to my father who has died and is buried in this very spot. I was told with the pendant I may be able to raise the dead."

Abby could hear Bas chuckling.

"You go right for the hard stuff, don't you," Bas said.

"Is it true then, can I raise the dead?"

"This is not necromancy," Bas told her. "You are not calling forth a person's spirit to commune with them. Death is but a door to another existence, what you are doing goes against the natural order of things."

Abby noted for the first time that the robe Bas wore was fluttering around his feet, even though there was no wind. Abby felt wherever he was talking from was a different place altogether.

"What exactly does that mean?"

"You are asking me to guide a person from where they exist now, to pass through the door and back into this world. Which is possible, but if they linger too long, they would be stuck in a world that nature intended them to leave and will not be able to get back to the place they belong. Eventually madness would set in, and they would not live long. A second death would take them to where the demons reside, eventually becoming demons themselves. Something for Something."

Bas looked into Abby's eyes intently. "Are you sure you want to risk this with someone you love, Mistress?"

Abby was troubled and uncertain.

"How long after being summoned do they have to get back?"

"That is never set, Mistress. Sometimes minutes, sometimes days. It is a risk you take."

Abby was conflicted. Could she risk her father's eternity in this manner? But she knew they needed the information that only he could give. Something in her heart told her she had to do this.

It will be alright Abby.

"What did you say?" Abby asked.

"I said nothing," Bas responded his arms crossed on his chest.

It's okay, the voice said again.

She couldn't tell who it was. Was it her father, or one of the gods she wondered? In any event her decision was made.

"Bas, bring my father to me."

"Very well Mistress. I should tell you that whenever you do this, your physical form will be altered slightly."

"How do you mean?"

Bas had already left and the door to her mind closed.

"Well?" Andy said when she opened her eyes.

Abby told them of her encounter with Bas and all that he said.

"So I guess we just wait," Redlin said looking down at the gravestone.

"Abby?" a voice said from behind.

Everyone turned. Standing at the end of the path was a tall man with silver hair and a dark scruffy beard. Abby couldn't move although her body started to shake. Tears were streaming freely down her cheeks, could this truly be happening she thought.

"Abby?" the man said again with a catch in his voice as he moved towards them, his arms starting to open.

Abby just started walking towards him, forcing her legs to move as her shoulders heaved and the sobs came.

"Daddy! Oh god, Daddy!"

Then she was running, and Abby's father caught her up in a tight embrace as he lifted her off the ground and hugged her to him. She put her head on his shoulder and just let him hold her. He even smelled the same, pipe tobacco with a hint of wild cherry. Abby felt like she was home after a long absence. God, how she missed him. But Abby knew time was short and broke from their embrace.

"Andros," Abby called.

Andy walked up almost shyly.

"Daddy, this is my husband, Andros."

"It is a pleasure to meet you sir," Andy said shaking his hand. But Neil would have none of that and hugged Andy as fiercely as he hugged Abby.

"I can see you have made my daughter very happy, and by your dragon clothes I am assuming you are also a dragon," Neil said.

"How did…" Andy started but never finished.

"I am a curator, lad. Once a curator, always a curator," he said winking. "I made a great study of dragons when I lived in this world." Neil looked past Andy to the others. "And I see

149

you are accompanied by a faerie and the mighty Redlin."

Seeing Andy's look of astonishment, he responded, "A curator also would know the wizard Redlin by sight anywhere."

"He is also the father of Andros, Daddy," Abby told him.

Redlin and Neil embraced each other. Tera, in typical Tera fashion, smothered him in hugs and kisses.

"I can't tell you how happy this makes me," Neil said. "Wait until I tell your mother. She sends you her love."

Now it was Abby's turn to look astonished. Abby never knew her mother, she had died giving birth to her. All she knew about her mother were stories her father had told her. To know that she lived and that they were together started her tears flowing anew.

"Tell her I love her too, Daddy," Abby said with a catch in her voice.

Neil wiped the tears from his daughter's face. "Bas told me you had summoned me. I don't know how all this works, but I am sure my time is short."

"It is, very short," Abby told him, "and I will not risk your time here anymore than is needful, though I wish we could have a lifetime."

"Don't worry, dear, we will all be together again one day. Tell me what you need."

"I will let Redlin explain," Abby said.

Redlin told Neil as quickly as he could all he had seen in his vision and what Killian had said.

"Ah, the dragon maze," Neil said scratching his chin. "I remember telling Abby the story when she was young. The story of golden eyes and his magical key."

"Do you remember it?" Redlin asked. "Can it help us?"

"I originally heard the story as a boy from an old woman who lived in the woods not far from our village. We always thought of her as a witch, although whether she was or not, I really have no way of knowing."

Neil paused for a moment in thought. "She used to tell it in a way that golden eyes was something to be feared, and that he would trick unsuspecting travelers into solving his maze to find the golden key, and untold riches would be theirs, but all who tried had failed. The witch also told us that because of all the dangers of the maze, only a dragon could survive it. Of course, when I walked this earth, there were no dragons in Vasara at the time, so a boy's imagination would run wild on how he could solve this riddle."

"Did you actually try and find the maze?" Andy asked.

Neil smiled at him. "Young boys from a remote village will try any adventure. But as I grew older, I realized it was just a tale told by a crazy old woman trying to keep us boys from trampling through her garden. But I always felt there was something to it."

"You used to say in every myth and legend there is an origin of truth to it," Abby said.

"Very good my little scholar," Neil said smiling proudly at his daughter. "Yes, and that is what kept the fire inside burning to find out more. And I believe it was that tale that set me on the path of becoming a curator."

"What do you mean?" Tera asked.

"Our village was in the south, below Hadley and in the center just north of Laurel Hollow and the Parma Wilds. Anyone traveling south to either of those destinations would pass through our village because we had the only inn for many miles. Traveling merchants would be coming and going all the time. A considerable amount of them were book merchants. After that I had found my addiction so to speak. One never went through our town until I had gone through every book in their wagon. I developed quite a collection, but it was a while before I happened upon the one that I believed touched on the legend of golden eyes and his magic key."

Neil paused with a confused look on his face.

"What's the matter Daddy?" Abby asked her father.

"It just occurred to me. The man who had the book I mentioned was dressed like a traveling bard. He didn't have a wagon, just a satchel with about a dozen or so books. And I wasn't even looking out for merchants that day. It was like he came upon me."

"Can you describe him?" Redlin asked intently.

"He was as tall as you, with ocean blue eyes and a beard of white. I remember thinking as he walked about with a staff made of white ash that he almost looked like a wizard."

"Reika," Redlin said.

"Who is that, Dad?" Andy asked.

"He's a wanderer," Redlin said. "He's kind of like Diminitus, he's always been here. My brothers and I would come across him from time to time over the centuries. He always had something prophetic to say."

"Is he a prophet then?" Andy asked.

"Who knows," Redlin told his son. "There are many things in this world that we don't know or understand."

"It's funny that you should say prophet," Neil said, "because that book he gave me read like something a prophet would recite."

"Do you know where this book is now?" Redlin asked.

Neil turned to his daughter. "Abby, has my office changed very much since I was last here."

"It hasn't changed at all," Abby told him. "After you had died, I couldn't bear to go in there, so I boarded up the door. No one has been in there since."

Neil could see the pain on his daughter's face and he

hugged her to him. "I'm sorry I left you here alone Abby," he whispered in her ear.

Abby wiped the tears on his shirt and pulled herself together. "I'm okay Daddy."

Neil turned to Redlin. "In my office is a picture of you. Behind it there is a stone panel that is opened with the curators' pin. The book is there. Oh my," Neil said as his eyes widened.

"Daddy, what is it?" Abby said alarmed.

"I'm feeling very strange." He looked sadly at his daughter. "I think my time here is finished."

Abby wasn't ready. She wanted more, she had so many questions. So many things she wanted to know. She felt as if her heart was ripping out of her chest all over again, just like on that day he died.

"Oh Daddy, I'm not ready."

Neil put both hands on the sides of his daughter's face. "You were always ready my darling, to face whatever life had to throw at you. But now you are never alone in this world," he said looking at Andy and the others.

He kissed his daughter on the forehead. "Bas said you had to send me back, or not."

Abby, with fresh tears streaming down her cheeks closed her eyes and hugged him as tight as she could. Holding the death dagger in her hand she forced the words out. "Go back Daddy, go back before it's too late. I love you"

Abby didn't open her eyes, but she felt his body becoming insubstantial. She thought she heard him whisper, I love you, and in the next instant she was hugging only air. She let out a despairing wail as she collapsed into Andy's arms.

When Abby finally pulled her head off Andy's chest, she could see tears standing in everyone's eyes.

"Are you alright?" Andy asked his beloved.

"I am now dear," she said stroking his cheek.

"Abby, your hair!" Tera exclaimed.

"What about it?" she asked puzzled.

"Oh my," Redlin exclaimed. "There is a streak of white like silver moonlight on your right side."

Abby put a hand to her head. She could tell where the streak was without even seeing it. It felt different from the rest of her hair, much silkier.

"Bas did say my physical form would be altered anytime I did this. I guess this is what he meant. How does it look?" she asked Andy nervously.

Andy smiled at his wife. "It looks fine Abby," he assured her. "If anything, it makes you look kind of magical."

Abby kissed his lips. "I think I'll keep you," she said patting his cheek.

"What now?" Tera asked.

"We go to my father's office and get that book," Abby said.

They entered the library, passed through the rotunda and went to the left down a side hall. It was dark so Abby lit one of the sconces.

"I take it that it has been a while since you've been down this way," Redlin said. Abby nodded in reply.

Once they came to the end of the hall there was a boarded-up door.

"Could you?" Abby asked the wizard.

"Of course."

Redlin concentrated and held out his hands. The boards suddenly turned to ash and fell in a miniature heap on the floor. The door was a burgundy color with a brass handle and lock. Abby produced a key and unlocked the door. Stepping inside, Redlin created a sphere of light, illuminating the entire room. They located the portrait and walked over to it.

"Not the greatest likeness," Tera said with a raised eyebrow.

"I'm sure this was done by someone who was painting from memory, since I have never sat for a portrait."

Tera seemed unable to stop giggling, which brought a scowl from Redlin. Andy took the portrait down as Abby inserted the curator's pin into the outline on the stone panel and pushed. The stone below popped out to reveal a drawer. Inside was a thin book with a gold cover that had a twisting red dragon on it. Abby opened it and started to skim through it. Nothing seemed to be jumping out at her, so she turned to the bookmarked section that undoubtedly her father had made.

"What does it say Abby?" Redlin asked.

"You must go to where the inside is bigger than the outside. Going high before you go low will get you moving in the right direction. The key is not what you think, and to find it you must follow your heart and not your eyes. Run when you want to fly and fly when you want to crawl. To succeed you must be the first and not the second or even the third, the fourth can give you a clue but no others can. As in all mazes, the key is in the center, but the way out will not be the way you came in. Reach the wizard before another gets the key, because what is released is neither good nor evil, until the person that releases it makes it so."

Everyone was silent for a few moments.

"What the hell is all that supposed to mean!" Andy exclaimed. "I really hate puzzles, I really, really do."

Redlin put his hands behind his back and started pacing as he puzzled out the meaning in the book.

"We need to break it down one section at a time," the wizard said. "Going to where the inside is bigger than the outside, I believe that is Otherwhere, exactly where I do not know."

Now he stopped and scratched his chin as he looked at Andy.

"The second part about the key and following your heart, we will probably not know what that is until you are in the maze, same thing about the flying and crawling. The next bit about the first second and third has me totally stumped."

"Me as well," Andy said. "It seems like gibberish to me."

"Really?" Tera said. "That part seems the easiest to understand."

"I would love to hear your analysis, Tera," Redlin said with a totally serious face.

Tera pushed her silver hair behind her pointed ears. "Well, I think it refers to the dragons. Andy is the first. Brion and Caleb and the others can't perform this task and it seems like the fourth dragon, Daragh, holds a clue that could help you."

Redlin looked astonished. "I think you may have hit the nail on the head, Tera."

"But what clue could Daragh have, Dad?" Andy asked.

"I don't know, and I doubt he even knows himself. On our way south we will stop and see him."

"That last part seems pretty straightforward," Andy said. "I'm not going to be the only one after this key, whatever it is."

"That part actually worries me," Redlin said.

"Why is that?" Abby asked.

"Because when I asked that being his name, he said to call him Killian for now, after that we will see. Whoever gives him his new name by way of the key will determine if his nature will be for good or evil."

"What's next, Dad?" Andy asked.

"Let's go find Daragh," Redlin said.

"Where does he live?" Tera asked.

"In a cabin just outside of Hadley," Andy said. "He's always preferred living in the forest as opposed to cities or towns."

"Let's go," Redlin said.

After leaving Dragonsgate, Andy flew straight towards

Hadley. Once reaching the town he veered left, that took him to an open meadow. Daragh had created this meadow to give himself a place to land whenever he would change to fly. Andy landed, and after everyone jumped off his back, he made the change. Daragh must have seen them flying in because he was running across the meadow to greet them.

"Back so soon?" Daragh said embracing his brother and the others. "I was just getting ready to fly to Laurel Hollow after receiving Donella's summons."

"We need to ask you something," Andy said.

Andy went on to explain everything that had happened in Laurel Hollow up to the point of the words written in the book about the dragon maze.

"We are not entirely sure what having a clue means and why you might have it, but we were hoping something might occur to you," Redlin said.

Daragh ran his fingers through his thick mane of brown hair while thinking.

"Redlin, I was never good at these prophecies and riddles. That's more Brion than me."

"Nothing is coming to you at all?" Abby asked.

"Well," he replied thinking, "the only thing that truly sets me apart from the other's is my gift. The one where I don't need the source to be able to tap into it."

"You mean your empathic abilities?" Andy asked.

Daragh nodded in reply. Everyone looked at Redlin. The wizard seemed deep in thought.

"That must be it," Redlin said finally. "Probably, whatever the key is, empathic abilities are going to be needed to acquire it."

"But how does that help me?" Andy asked. "I have no idea how to use that ability."

"Daragh, can you show Andros how you do it with your

gift? And then maybe he can use the source to do it."

"We can try," Daragh said. "Andros, join my mind and see if you can follow what I do."

Andy did that, but this felt different from any kind of linking he had done before. When Daragh let him in it was as if he latched onto his consciousness and it melded with his. He saw and felt things much differently than in the waking world.

I can feel you are with me, Andros, Daragh said. *Are you ready?*

Yes, Andy said, but he was not prepared for the flood of emotion that suddenly washed over him.

Gods! Andy said with tears streaming down his face.

You're letting too much through, Daragh said.

I'm not doing anything. I'm just connected to you.

Yes, but you are not filtering what's coming from me.

How do I do that?

Imagine a wall, Daragh said. *Then picture holes in it that will allow the emotions to come through in a manner that does not overwhelm you.*

Andy grabbed the source and made a wall in his mind and the feelings and emotions instantly stopped. Now he pictured little sliding doors throughout the wall and opened them one by one. Doing this he could sample what was coming through. He could feel sadness and anger, as well as happiness and various other emotions. It was all jumbled together with no direction to it.

Very good, Daragh said. *Right now you are just accepting in all the emotion that is in the general area. Now we will try and focus it. Use the source and see if you can see the aura around each person here.*

Andy felt the source coursing through him as he enhanced his vision to see what Daragh saw. Looking at his father first he could see a multi-colored aura around him.

I can see it, Andy said.

Now touch each color in the aura.

Andy did this, and he could start sensing his father's feelings. Each color band was different in size of its thickness. With the thicker ones he could feel the emotion strongly, the thinner ones only trace amounts.

What does the thickness of the color bands signify? Andy asked.

All feelings are usually present in a person, but the thicker ones will be what they are currently feeling, Daragh answered.

Andy could feel determination and resolve coming off his father and very minute traces of apprehension. He turned his attention to Tera and was suddenly taken aback at what he saw there. Their eyes locked and Tera's eyes went wide because she guessed what Andy must have seen by the expression on his face.

Andy saw fear and panic in Tera's aura as well as secretiveness. He had never seen this side of Tera and it disturbed him greatly. He could tell she was struggling with something.

"Andros, stop," Daragh said. He had seen it too, Andy thought.

"I'm sorry," Daragh had said. "This was probably not the best way to achieve this, but I knew time was pressing and I saw no other alternative."

"What's wrong?" Abby said.

Daragh looked shamefully at Abby, no doubt blaming himself. "I never use this on people I know, especially not friends. Feelings and emotions are a very private thing, and it is almost a violation of a person to feel them this way."

"Daragh is right," Andy said, "I should have seen this myself."

It was Tera who spoke up next which surprised Andy.

"It's okay," Tera said. "I know Andy needs to learn this if we are to win."

Andy had noticed a significant change in Tera. It was like his father had said, she had grown noticeably. She had always been so flighty and whimsical, and now there was a seriousness about her. Andy had picked that up in his reading of her as well. There was a task she had to perform he could tell, and the enormity of it, whatever it was, had her on the brink of being overwhelmed. He wondered if he should ask her about it, but he knew it was sometimes difficult for Tera to keep a secret. In the end he decided he would talk to Abby about it later.

"I think you are ready, Andros," Daragh said. "You have picked this up rather quickly. But I must warn you, the interpretation of feelings is the most crucial and also the hardest part to accomplish."

"What do you mean?" Andy asked.

"Just because you feel anger or some other emotion coming off someone, it will not tell you why. This is where you must use intuition and context."

"Context?" Abby asked.

"Yes," Daragh said turning towards her. "The best way to do this is to engage that person or being in conversation. The feelings that come off them in regard to your words will be a good guide to what those feelings represent."

"I think I understand what you mean," Andy said.

"I knew you would, brother," Daragh said putting a hand on his shoulder.

"We better go," Redlin said. "We are going to Laurel Hollow, Daragh. You may as well come with us."

"Gladly," Daragh said.

Andy and Daragh made their change so now there was a black and red dragon leaping into the air. After gaining altitude, they veered off to the southwest in the direction of the faerie kingdom.

Chapter 16

The wind was blowing Tori's hair around wildly as she rode on Caleb's back as they headed towards the Border Lands. She tied it into a ponytail wondering why she hadn't done that in the first place. Cleo, Lyson and Donella also rode with her. Brion was originally going to fly them, but he had been called to help in the rescue of Samara. Tori wondered if they had been successful. Caleb arrived shortly after Brion left with Rhyan and Ava and had graciously offered to take them where they needed to go.

Anyone care to give me a little direction? Caleb said. *We are coming up on the edge of the Border Lands.*

Lyson had written the geographical coordinates on a piece of parchment while the map itself was in a tube slung over his back. Using a modified sextant, he was able to tell Caleb where to go.

"Start veering a little southeast," Lyson said.

You got it, Caleb responded tipping his wing to make the turn.

After another hour's flight, Lyson instructed Caleb to land. After everyone climbed off his back, he changed back to human. They landed right on the outer edge of a forest as they stood there looking around for any kind of landmark to show them which way they should go.

"I think you need to take the lead now, Tori," Lyson said.

Tori started the fire in her eyes spinning as her gaze scanned left and right. After several moments she brought her eyesight back to normal.

"I'm not picking up anything," Tori said.

"That's very strange," Lyson said. "The boundary of it should be right here."

"So what do we do now?" Cleo said adjusting her swords.

"I have an idea," Emilia said.

"This isn't going to be anything exotic, is it love?" Lyson asked with a raised eyebrow.

Emilia patted him on the cheek. "Trust me."

"I hate when people say that," Caleb remarked as he latched onto the source just in case.

Emilia just winked at Caleb.

"Lyson, where is the point that the boundary of Laurel Hollow meets the Border Lands?"

Lyson took Fallon's map out of the tube and unrolled it. Taking some string from his pocket he took some measurements and wrote them down. Standing up again he made some adjustments on the sextant as he looked through it.

"That should be it right there," Lyson said pointing at a lone talon tree.

"In a way that seems fitting that Laurel Hollow should end there," Caleb said.

Emilia took the sphere off of the end of her staff and held it aloft, causing the field to be awash with a white light of the goddess.

"Tori, stand directly in front of me and try again."

Tori walked over and stood in the light, illuminating her body in an otherworldly way. She started the circle of fires around her eyes to spin again. Then she saw it, two pillars just like the ones in the Corridor of the Border Lands. One was actually superimposed with the talon tree, as if it existed inside of it. The other stood approximately ten feet north of it. Now she understood why Donella did what she did. One pillar existed in Braylynn's lands and the other in Fallon's. It required the magic of both the god and goddess to be able to see it.

"It is there," Tori said as Emilia put the sphere back on her staff. "How did you know to do that?"

"Plain faerie intuition," Emilia said. "I had a feeling that the borders must touch, and Braylynn will always want to be a part of something that touches her lands," she said smiling.

Walking over towards the talon tree, Tori took the lead. She looked at one pillar and then the other. She knew the others couldn't see them. Why Fallon and Braylynn chose to make them invisible was a mystery. On one pillar was a red jewel of Fallon, and on the other, the pearl sphere of the goddess.

"Can you see it?" Tori asked Emilia.

"I can now."

"I think we are supposed to do this together," Tori said.

Emilia nodded.

"So what happens now?" Cleo asked as she drew her swords.

"Now we go forward," Lyson responded.

Emilia had her staff out with its power glowing. Tori grabbed her hand as they passed between the pillars, Lyson put a hand on Emilia's shoulder, as Caleb and Cleo put a hand on Tori's. The scene before them suddenly changed. What had been forests and sparse grassland turned into a lush green valley with snowcapped mountain tops beyond. They could see six different rivers coming together to form one massive river. The entire area was teeming with life.

"By the gods!" Lyson and Caleb said at the same time, although Lyson had said goddess."

Caleb looked sharply at him. "You feel it too?"

"Yes," Lyson replied.

"What is it?" Tori asked drawing her twin swords.

"The source," Caleb said. "I was holding onto it when we entered, but once we crossed over it feels like it's been magnified a hundred times, and also…"

"Also what?" Cleo asked when he paused.

Caleb was scratching his chin. "I don't know how else to describe it except to say it feels perfectly pure. It's as if the gods are standing right here with me, pouring their energy directly into my body."

"That's exactly how I feel," Lyson said.

"What do you think it means, love?" Emilia asked.

"I haven't a clue dear," he told his beloved.

They started walking towards the point where all the rivers converged into one. It looked almost like an oasis with a beach by the water's edge and palm trees in a semi-circle around it. Deer, rabbits, otters and various other animals were drinking the water together without any fear of each other or the group that was approaching. Off to the left and standing by a palm stood a man wearing dark buckskin leather pants with an open collar white shirt. As they got closer, Tori could see he had a closely trimmed black beard with hair to match. His eyes were grey like a wolf.

"Greetings travelers," the man said. "I've been expecting you."

"You have?" Lyson said. "We didn't even know we were coming ourselves until a little while ago."

"I am an instrument of the prophecy," he said. "It is part of my job to see that all the proper pieces are in play for their given tasks."

"Do you have a name?" Emilia asked.

"My name is Tutore," he said.

"And just what are our tasks?" Caleb asked.

"That is not for me to tell you, third dragon. I am only here to make sure all those that arrive are the ones that have been destined to be here and guide them on their way."

"And I don't suppose you can tell us where we are going?" Tori asked him.

"Nay, Cath Priomh. That is for you to discover."

"I really hate riddles," Caleb said, "I really really do."

Emilia laughed. "So does Andy. It must be a dragonish trait."

"Okay," Cleo said sheathing her swords. "Obviously Tutore can't help us anymore, so maybe we should just push on."

"That is not necessarily true, Viper Captain," Tutore said.

Tori saw Cleo wince at the title Tutore had called her. No doubt the pain of losing her entire squad still pained her greatly.

"What do you mean?" Lyson asked.

"The last thing I can tell you is that you must travel by the river. If you leave it at the wrong place and time your tasks will fail, and with it Vasara."

"What are we supposed to do," Cleo asked hotly, "swim?"

"No, you will travel in this," Tutore said with a sweep of his hand.

Everyone's mouth hung open at what they saw.

Gliding up to the beach was a ship, but it was unlike any ship they had ever seen. The entire ship was made out of white crystal, even the masts. The strangest thing about it was there were no sailors manning the ship.

"Does this thing steer by itself?" Cleo asked.

"No," Tutore replied. "It is driven by thought."

"Who's thought, anyone's?" Tori asked.

"It must be a dragon or wizard," Tutore answered.

"I'll let you do the steering," Caleb said to Lyson. "Any of my brothers will tell you my thoughts tend to wander."

Lyson laughed at that. "Very well, let's get on board."

Tutore waved his hand once again and a gang plank was lowered to the beach as everyone boarded.

"Any last words of advice?" Caleb yelled down to Tutore.

"Yes, don't get yourselves killed, or we are all lost." With that, he promptly disappeared.

"Okay General," Tori said looking at Lyson, smiling. "I guess you have been recommissioned to Captain. Lead on Captain."

Lyson closed his eyes as his hands rose.

"Can you feel it, love?" Emilia asked.

"Yes," he said. "There is a flow to it. I can see the source of the goddess."

Lyson opened his eyes and the ship started to move back out into the current of the river. Lowering his arms back to his side he let the ship be pulled down river, steering around any rocks or small islands. Tori kept a keen eye out on either side of the riverbanks. She thought that whatever properties were in the water was extremely beneficial in the promotion of life evident by the lush vegetation.

"So, does anyone know what we are doing or where we are going?" Caleb asked in his logical dragon fashion.

Everyone kind of looked around at each other. No one really had any idea of what their task might be or where they might go. There were benches over by the main mast and Lyson walked over and sat down as the others followed his lead.

"What are you thinking, Lyson?" Emilia asked as she retracted her wings to get more comfortable.

"There is a reason this map came into my hands," Lyson said holding up the tube with the map inside.

Tori suddenly had an idea. She looked up towards the quarter deck and saw a pedestal near where the ship's wheel would be on any other vessel.

"Lyson, take out the map and follow me," Tori said getting up and walking up the stairs to the upper deck. Once everyone was around, Tori told Lyson to put the map on the pedestal. Her eyes started the wheels of fire spinning as she looked at the map. Once again, she saw the land features with such clarity. She zoomed in on the river on which they were traveling, bringing it more and more into focus.

"There," she said pointing at something on the map that no one else would be able to see.

"What is it?" Cleo asked squinting at the map.

"It's hard to tell clearly but it looks like a statue in the middle of the river."

"Can you make out what the statue represents?" Lyson asked.

"No," Tori responded. "It is as if the map is purposely blurring its features."

"I don't think you'll need the map to see its features," Caleb said.

Everyone looked at Caleb and saw he was staring down river. Turning to look they all gasped.

"By the gods!" Cleo exclaimed.

It was still some ways off but that only gave evidence to the size of the statue.

"You are close to the mark, Boss," Tori said in wonder. "It is one of the gods. It's Fallon's likeness."

"Are you sure?" Emilia asked.

"A hundred percent sure," Tori said with certainty. She knew without a doubt it was his likeness since she had spoken to her god face to face when he had given her the medallion she now wore designating her as his priest.

It took another twenty minutes to reach the base of the statue where Lyson brought the boat to a stop. Everyone craned their necks to see to the top which seemed to touch the sky. On the statue's base was an inscription which Tori read aloud.

"You travel the river of the gods and goddess, but just because you are here doesn't mean you are meant to be. Choices you must make, and in that choice, your true nature will be revealed, as well as whether or not you will be allowed to continue."

"What is the choice?" Caleb asked no one in particular.

"Look!" Cleo said pointing to the left of the inscription. "There is an indentation that looks like the size and shape of your medallion."

Tori considered this. "You think I should push my medallion into it?"

"Can't lose anything in trying," Lyson said.

"Unless it's the wrong choice," Caleb said matter-of-factly."

Tori took the medallion from around her neck and pushed it into the spot on the base. Suddenly two huge walls shot up out of the river at forty-five-degree angles to the statue causing the river to fork.

"I think you just created our choices," Emilia said astonished.

"Now there is something you don't see every day," Caleb remarked.

"Caleb, fly down one fork and tell us what you see," Lyson said.

"You got it," Caleb said as he started running for the port side of the boat. Just before he reached the edge he came to a sudden halt.

"What's wrong?" Emilia asked.

Caleb turned and looked at her. "I can't change, Summoner."

"What? How is that possible?" Emilia asked.

"I don't know," Caleb said walking back. "I can feel the source and manipulate it," he said as he created a fireball in his hand, "but something is blocking me from changing shape."

"It's not going to let us avoid the choice this way," Tori said. "We have to choose according to our nature as the inscription says."

"What does that even mean?" Cleo asked clearly frustrated.

"I don't know, Boss."

Suddenly from down one fork they started to hear sounds, battle sounds. There was the clash of sword upon sword as well as the screams of soldiers dying. They could hear the screeching sounds of demons on the attack.

"There is a battle down there," Cleo said. "We are warriors, clearly that is the path of our nature. Lyson?"

Lyson was scratching his chin, deep in thought. Then came the sounds from the other fork. But instead of sounds of battle, they heard laughter, children's laughter as if in play in a field on a sunny day.

"That way is obviously a trap," Caleb said.

"What makes you say that, Caleb?" Tori asked intently.

"That way has to be false. It signals something too good to be true in my book. It seems like the obvious choice, but to me it feels like a trap.

"By the gods!" Cleo said. "Trying to puzzle this out could be maddening."

Lyson walked up to the prow of the ship and closed his eyes, listening.

"Tori, which way pulls you the most?" Lyson asked suddenly.

"The left, where the battle is," Tori answered.

"Why?" he asked.

"Because we are warriors, General. We go where there is fighting."

"But why, Tori? Why do we do that?" Lyson said looking at her intently, his eyes lighting up.

All of a sudden it dawned on Tori and her eyes went wide. "Because we want peace. Because we want our families, our children, to live in happiness," she said eyeing the fork where they heard the children laughing.

"And that is our true nature," Lyson said, "to find peace and laughter in our lives."

Lyson started the boat moving towards the right fork. Once the stern was past the statue the other fork disappeared followed by a wail of agonizing loss.

"I wonder if that sound meant we made the right choice?" Caleb asked.

"I guess we will find out when we reach our journey's end," Lyson said.

It was a day later when they reached the next statue and brought the ship to a stop. The statue in front of them was of a man with close-cut hair, almost a buzz cut, wearing what looked like an animal vest and pants to match. He had a wineskin slung over one shoulder and carried a staff. He looked like someone who would be at home in the wilds.

"It is Cael," Caleb said.

"Are you sure?" Cleo asked.

"I am," he said. "The image of all the gods are imprinted on the dragons."

"I wonder what his choices will be," Tori said.

"I guess it is time to find out," Lyson said.

Tori once again took out her medallion and touched it to the place on the base. The walls came up causing the river to fork. This time there were no battle sounds or laughter. Instead, on the right fork, the river became placid, like glass, while the other fork became a raging cataract.

"Okay, I don't know about the rest of you, but I don't fancy a ride in a crystal boat over a waterfall when I have no ability to fly off of it."

"What do you think is the test here?" Lyson asked no one in particular.

"Well, the last one we didn't take the one that represented battle and struggle. Maybe the raging river represents the same, and we should take the calm and peaceful waters," Cleo said.

"I might just agree with you sister," Lyson said.

"I'm not sure," Emilia said.

"Why do you say that, love?" Lyson asked.

"It is something Caleb said. That he didn't want to be in a crystal boat going over a waterfall."

"That makes sense to me," Tori said.

"It would if we knew that taking this ship that way would result in its destruction."

"What are you saying?" Caleb asked.

Emilia looked at her brother's brother. "I believe this is a choice of faith. Cael is the god of the Wilds, a country that is sometimes full of chaos and mayhem due to its wild nature of the magical creatures that inhabit it. I believe the turbulent waters represent that, and I further believe we need to put our faith in him that we will emerge unscathed at the bottom."

"So, I guess the choice has to do with our nature of whether we have faith in the gods or not," Lyson said. Emilia nodded.

"What do you say, Captain?" Tori asked. "Calm waters or plunging death?"

Lyson smiled at her and closed his eyes as the ship moved forward. He took the fork and as soon as the prow hit the fast movement current it shot like an arrow in a headlong flight toward a multi-level waterfall. For a moment, the ship was suspended in mid-air before it started to point downwards. Everyone was open-mouthed and wide-eyed at what happened next. As the ship started its deep descent with the onset of sharp rocks waiting at the bottom of the first waterfall, an amazing thing happened. What could only be described as wings, two masts shot out on either side of the ship, slowing their speed and raising the prow of the ship. Slowly the ship left the water and began a gentle glide over the waterfalls. Lyson kept his focus on guiding the ship through the air for the bottom level of the falls was coming up. To keep the ship from belly-flopping on the hard surface, Lyson provided a little wind to the sails to help propel it forward enough that it would skim across the water.

After a gentle landing the side masts retracted, and the fast-moving current came to a gentle crawl.

"Well, if it's all the same to the rest of you, I'd rather not have to take anymore leaps of faith," Caleb said wiping the water spray off his face.

"I'll second that," Cleo said.

It took another day's travel before they reached the next statue.

"Rafael," Caleb said looking up.

"I really wish Ala were here for this one," Emilia said.

"I wish we had every priest of the gods here," Tori said. "I don't like having to solve these riddles without a little guidance."

"I don't know," Lyson said, "we've done pretty good so far."

"Bite your tongue, brother," Cleo said. "I would knock on wood, but we don't have any on this ship. Perhaps I should use your head?"

On hearing that everyone burst out laughing.

Once again Tori put her medallion on the recessed spot of the statue and the walls came up. This time, floating above the water was a large bottle that everyone could see. Written on it was the word poison with skull and crossbones underneath. Over the other was a bottle of wine, and not just any bottle. It was an Albion red with the year just before Devon overran Vasara with his evil scheme. There was a corkscrew in the bottle as if it was about to be opened.

"By the gods!" Caleb said frustrated. "What the hell does one have to do with the other?"

"Let's think this through," Lyson said scratching his chin. "The bottle, I would say, represents victory, being opened now after Devon's demise. Also, it represents toasting good health."

"And poison?" Cleo asked.

"Poison is poison, nothing more that I can think of," Lyson said.

"Well, since Rafael is the god of healing, don't you think

it would make sense to go with the fork that symbolizes the wine and good health," Tori said.

"What are you thinking Summoner?" Caleb asked noticing Emilia intently looking at the bottle of poison.

"Only this," Emilia said, "that when I was dying from the skull spider venom, it was poison that Ala used to heal me. She also did the same with Ava when she was struck by the Alfar arrow."

"What are you saying exactly?" Cleo asked her.

"That sometimes, poison can be the most powerful healing agent of all."

"Well Captain," Tori said to Lyson, "which way?"

"You love doing that, don't you Tori," Lyson said with a raised eyebrow. "We go with the poison. The fact that my beloved has a life experience associated with this choice lends great weight with me." Emilia smiled at him.

"You sure you are not biased?" Caleb asked him.

"Of course I am, that doesn't mean I'm wrong," he said with a wink.

"I hate when he does that," Cleo said running her fingers through her hair.

Lyson started moving towards the fork with the poison. As he did there was a shattering of many bottles as the other fork died away.

"We're committed now," Caleb said as he looked down river for the next statue, if there is one on this fork, he thought to himself.

Like clockwork, another day brought them to the statue. This one was a man with his hair pulled back in a ponytail and a bow slung across his back.

"Aditya," Caleb said identifying the god. "God of the horse lords."

"I'm curious to see what this test is," Tori said as she pushed the medallion into the base.

The walls came up and the river forked. On one fork stood a man with red hair and dressed in buckskin. On his belt was a huge hunting knife with a longbow strapped to his back. In his hand he held a red arrow.

"Bart," Cleo said with a catch in her voice.

Tori came up to her friend and grabbed her wrist. "It's ok Boss."

Cleo looked at her friend gratefully.

They all turned and looked towards the other fork. Nothing appeared.

"Well that is quite odd," Lyson said. "Where is our other choice?"

"I say go with what we know," Caleb said. "I never met Bart, and only know him from Andros' stories, but I am comfortable with taking the fork he represents."

"I see no reason why not," Lyson said. "It's a fifty-fifty chance."

"Yes," Emilia said, "but the wrong choice will end it all."

Everyone was silent for a moment, trying to weigh out the risks.

"I see no clear path here," Lyson said. "Maybe it is another leap of faith."

"Let's just do it," Caleb said. "If we are wrong, we will figure out a way back. No choice is just as bad as the wrong choice in my opinion."

"I fear you are right," Tori agreed. "Let's take it now before we over think it."

Lyson closed his eyes and began his turn.

"Wait!" Cleo said suddenly.

Lyson stopped the boat and turned towards Cleo. "What is it Cleo?"

Cleo was staring intently at the image of Bart who now had his arms crossed on his chest with his red arrow between them.

"That is the wrong way," Cleo said.

"Why do you say that Boss," Tori asked her friend.

Cleo smiled at Tori. "Because Bart's nature was protection. He sacrificed his life for those he loved, and he would always put himself in the middle of danger to block the way so others wouldn't get hurt. He would not want us to go that way."

Lyson gave a low whistle. "You're right. That is exactly what Bart would do." He walked over and hugged his sister, Lyson knew of Cleo's feelings for the archer. "We almost made a grave error, thank you Cleo."

Cleo hugged him back and gave him a punch in the chest. "Our parents told me I always had to look out for you. I'm just keeping that promise," she said winking.

It was a pattern now. A day later brought them to the statue of Trystan. Tori did her thing with the medallion and the walls shot up.

As they stood looking from one fork to the other a bright light flashed in the sky and streaking down came Andy's black sword, moon shadow. There was another bright flash and out of the sky to come and rest over the other fork was Emilia's spear, Nocte.

"I guess we choose between your spear and Andros' sword," Tori said to Emilia. "Although I can't see how one choice is any better than the other."

"Is there any differences between the two weapons that could help us decide?" Lyson asked his love.

"Other than that, one is a spear and the other a sword," she replied. "They are both made of the same metal that Trystan created and my grandfather forged into these weapons."

"They both have their own unique powers," Cleo said, "I've seen that. Maybe that's it."

"But which one would you decide over the other," Caleb asked, "and why."

Nobody had an answer.

"Perhaps because the choices are pretty much equal, there is no choice," Emilia said.

Caleb was furiously scratching his head. "Have I mentioned that I hate riddles? Who is going to solve this one?"

Tori noticed that Emilia seemed to be deep in thought as she scanned the statue up and down.

"You're thinking something, Summoner. What is it?" Tori asked.

Emilia continued looking up as she spoke. "I'm thinking back to when our grandfather gave us these weapons and all he said. I feel that episode in our lives has significance here."

"Was there anything he said that stood out?" Lyson asked.

"There is," she replied. "Right before he left he said, 'Remember, the house of Caster flows through your veins. I know you will lift that name to greater heights than I ever could'."

She kept scanning the statue as if looking for something.

"There," Emilia said pointing.

Everyone looked. "I can't see anything," Cleo said.

"I can Boss," Tori said. "It's a pattern inscribed on the god's chest."

"Not just any pattern," Emilia said smiling. "It is the pattern of the house of Caster. The kind that opens hidden pathways."

With that she leapt off the deck and started to fly upward.

"I guess she's allowed to fly off the ship," Caleb remarked as he shielded his eyes from the sun to see better as he followed her flight.

"I have a feeling certain things are allowed in conjunction with the given challenge at hand," Lyson said. "For myself, I can't fly off of this ship either. Probably because Donella is the only one able to trace the pattern that will open the door to show us the way, flying is essential for her."

Everyone watched as Emilia traced the pattern known only

to the descendants of the house of Caster. Once complete the statue started to move upward. Emilia immediately flew down to the deck. The statue of Trystan kept rising. Soon everyone could see an opening in the base as it rose out of the water, stopping only once it was higher than the mast. The river looked like it sloped down as it rushed under the statue and was lost in shadow.

"I guess our direction is down," Lyson remarked.

"Shall we?" Tori said waving a hand in the direction of the water tunnel.

Lyson started the ship moving. Once the current took it, it was like the ship was on ice, sliding down. It was dark, so Caleb created spheres of light and placed them in the center as well as the bow and stern of the ship. The light reflected off the walls which were solid crystal.

"I can see light up ahead," Cleo said. "I think we are about to emerge."

Sure enough, they shot out of the crystal tunnel and found themselves in the middle of a lake whose waters were like mirrored glass. Ringing the lake was lush grass and many flowering trees. The flowers were all the colors of the rainbow and actually gave off their own light. In the very center of the lake was the last statue, although this one was not as monstrously tall as the others had been.

"Braylynn," Lyson said.

"It is," Emilia agreed. "This statue seems almost life-like."

No sooner had she said this, than rays of color started exploding out of the statue, momentarily blinding everyone. Once they were able to see again, everyone just stared with open mouths as the goddess herself stepped out of the light. Emilia flew towards her like an arrow.

"Mother," she cried as she embraced her goddess.

Lyson slowed the ship once it reached the pedestal on which she was standing.

"It is good to see you my daughter," Braylynn said as she held Emilia tight.

Braylynn took hold of Emilia's hand as they jumped the short distance to the ship. The goddess greeted everyone warmly then she looked long at Lyson.

"You have done well my wizard. You puzzled out the riddle of the map and made your way here as is your destiny."

"Well, I did have some help," Lyson said smiling.

"Damn right he did," said Caleb speaking up. Everyone laughed at that.

"I thought you could never come back to Vasara?" Emilia asked.

"You are no longer in Vasara," Braylynn responded.

"Where are we then?" Tori asked.

"This is the place where my brothers' and I take counsel with one another. It is similar to when the dragons' journey to their source. Only difference is, we are really here."

"Braylynn, can you tell us what our reason is for being here?" Lyson asked.

"I cannot tell you everything, General," Braylynn said. "But I will tell you that your being here has everything perfectly balanced."

"What does that mean?" Cleo asked.

"It means the battle for Vasara can go either way. There is one act that will decide the outcome, of course I cannot tell you what that is. None of us even knows if it will happen, not even the prophecy."

"Do you know what our next step is?" Tori asked the goddess.

"A day's journey from here there is a temple. However, there is a guardian there." She looked at each of them in turn.

"You need to get past him."

"And I'm assuming you can't tell us anything about him," Tori said.

The goddess shook her head.

"I can tell you what he guards is essential to your quest. You must take it to Otherwhere, that is where the final battle will be."

Braylynn smiled at Tori. "Before you ask, I cannot tell you where the road to Otherwhere lies."

"I sure have missed you and your cryptic ways your worshipness," Caleb said.

Braylynn raised an eyebrow as her wings folded behind her back. "You know how I feel about that Caleb," she said with the slightest hint of a smile. Caleb just winked at her.

"You must go now. And take with you a goddess' blessing."

She wrapped each one of them in a hug, coming lastly to Emilia.

"I am well pleased with you my daughter, know that I have never left you."

"Will you be at the last battle, Mother?" Emilia asked.

"No. I will never set foot in Vasara again, for the moment that I do, Abby's life will end. I could not do that to her, or your brother."

Tori remembered how Braylynn had to give up her existence in Vasara in order for Abby to be raised from the dead.

"Do not let it worry you," Braylynn said. "Another is coming into his power that will help make up some of the difference. Go now, time is running short."

They left the goddess behind, and the temple came into view a day later. The temple was white with gold lines along the edges, as well as four turrets on each of its corners. There was a dock with a marble walkway leading to the temple's entrance where they could see a black door with a gold knocker in the shape of a miniature dragon.

Lyson brought the ship to a gentle halt where the port side of the ship connected with the dock and everyone got off and walked up to the door.

"You want to do the honors, Caleb?" being that the knocker is a dragon.

"Why not," Caleb said grabbing the knocker and hitting the strike plate three times, the sound reverberating all around them.

"Did you have to knock so hard?" Cleo asked rubbing her ears.

"Sorry," Caleb said. "I didn't realize it would do that."

Once the sound died down there was an audible click and the door started to open inward. No one was quick to rush in, instead they just peered inside.

"Tori, why don't you go into your frozen moment and look around," Lyson said.

Tori focused for a moment. "It appears I am not allowed to use that power here."

"Let's just go inside and deal with whatever is in there," Cleo said drawing her twin swords. "We are supposed to be here, so we should be able to handle whatever comes along."

"Well said Boss," Tori said pulling her own blades.

Lyson, Emilia and Caleb had their hands on their own source of power as everyone entered the temple. Inside was like a great hall with marble columns stretching from the floor to the ceiling some fifty-feet high. In the center was a dais with an altar of alabaster white stone. It was hard to tell from this distance, but some objects seemed to be laying on it.

"Any idea where this guardian might be?" Caleb asked looking around.

"No place that I can see," Lyson said extending his wings. He also drew his Border lands sword. Being a wizard he didn't really need it, but after wearing one for so long he felt naked without it.

That hadn't walked more than ten paces, when all of a sudden, a beam of intense white light shot out of the ceiling to land on the floor in front of them. Once the light died away, they were astonished at what they saw.

Staring at them was the face of a man with yellow eyes and mane of flowing flaxen hair. The face was beautiful, almost feminine. Once past the neck, all sense of humanity was gone. He had the tawny body of a lion, with eagles' talons for feet. On its back were a pair of white wings as one would imagine an angel having.

"By the goddess," Emilia exclaimed. "It's a sphinx!"

"What's a sphinx?" Cleo asked.

"In the world where I grew up, there were people known as the Greeks. They had many gods and goddesses and several mystical creatures, the sphinx was one of them," Emilia explained. "Although in that world the sphinx was a woman who would ask riddles of travelers. If you guessed correctly you were allowed to pass, if not you were eaten."

"I tell you, I just love these life or death choices," Caleb said sarcastically. "Keeps things interesting."

"I know of your love for riddles, third dragon," the sphinx said in a deep resonant voice, "perhaps it should be you who answers."

"You trying to be funny?" Caleb said. "And it is nice to know you're able to speak our language."

The sphinx smiled at him and winked.

"Since you know Caleb is a dragon," Lyson said, "I'm assuming you know the rest of us."

"It is my job to know all who journey here, wizard of Braylynn."

"You mean there have been others?" Emilia asked.

"Many others, Summoner. And none have made it past me."

"Who were they?" Tori asked.

"That is not needful for you to know, Cath Priomh."

"Alright, time is a wasting," Caleb said running his fingers through his hair, "what is the riddle?"

"I was teasing before, third dragon. It is not for you to answer."

"Who then?" Cleo asked.

The sphinx's eyes bore down on Cleo. "You, Viper Captain."

"Why my sister?" Lyson asked perplexed and with no small amount of concern.

"That is not needful for you to know, wizard."

"Seems like a lot of things that are not needful to know," Caleb said.

Cleo was staring hard at the sphinx. Just as she was about to say something the sphinx stopped her.

"Before you speak Captain, know that you still have a chance to turn back. If you accept this challenge and are wrong, all of you will perish. Such is the magic of this place," the sphinx said swishing its lions' tail.

Cleo paused before answering, looking at each of her friends in turn, lastly coming to Tori, who knew what she was thinking.

"Boss, we are in this together, you don't need to base your decision on us."

"If I don't do this, Vasara falls. If I get it wrong, Vasara falls."

"Two chances to fail, one to succeed," Caleb said. "I can handle those odds."

Cleo smiled at this brash young dragon. Although he was not really young, he just acted like it. Cleo turned back towards the sphinx.

"I'm ready," she said.

Somewhere within the temple a gong sounded. Tori didn't necessarily like that and stood ready for anything.

The sphinx took two steps forward and hovered just above Cleo's head.

"Words give shape to reality, and in some ways are even more real than the reality itself. Think hard on your answer. Get it right and a reward awaits you, get it wrong and your souls are forfeit. I ask you one last time, do you agree to this challenge of your own free will?"

"I do," Cleo answered with resolve.

Again, the gong sounded.

"Here is your riddle," the sphinx said. "I am straight when relaxed but bend when I'm stressed. My companion leads the way and saves me from danger. Who are we?"

Tori watched as Cleo struggled in thought.

"Are we allowed to help?" Caleb asked.

The sphinx shook his head no.

"Probably for the best anyway," Caleb said, "because I haven't a clue."

Cleo looked at the ground and started to pace as if seeking the answer there. The others watched helplessly.

"Is there a time limit?" Lyson asked.

"No wizard," the sphinx replied. "But you cannot take forever. Meliakken will soon be free, and if she doesn't solve this riddle by then, it will no longer matter."

Cleo kept pacing, mouthing the words of the riddle over and over as she rubbed her head.

"There must be a way to help her," Emilia whispered to Tori.

"I don't believe there is," Tori said. "I don't have any idea what the answer could be, do you?"

"Not really," Emilia said. "At least nothing that really fits the words in the riddle and makes me scream out, that's it. That is the one thing about these riddles, once you hear the answer, you think yourself stupid because it seems so blatantly obvious."

Cleo stopped pacing and sat crossed legged on the floor

with her eyes closed in a lotus position, her mouth moving rapidly now.

"Lyson, what is she doing?" Caleb asked him.

"She's done this before, many times as a matter of fact, in Lyonsdale."

"But why?" Caleb asked.

"Before a battle, she would study the battlefield on the map and commit it to memory. Then she would do what she is doing now. In her mind she is centering herself as she draws up every possible battle line, strike and counterstrike until she has everything accounted for."

Everyone watched intently as Cleo performed her ritual. Tori then saw her friend reach for the bracelet around her wrist that they had purchased in Dragonsgate and closed her hand around it. Her eyes snapped open as she looked at it. Then in one swift motion she leapt to her feet and stood in front of the sphinx.

"The bow and arrow," Cleo said with confidence. "That is your answer."

The sphinx smiled, and just as before, the bright light shot down from the ceiling momentarily blinding them, but once they were able to see again, the sphinx was gone, and Cleo started trembling at who was standing in front of her. Tears started to run down her cheeks as she stifled a sob and threw herself into the arms of the man she loved.

"By the gods!" Tori exclaimed. "Bart!"

It was the archer, He was wearing a buckskin vest and pants with his bow slung across his back. Exactly how Tori remembered him. He was holding Cleo tenderly as he stroked her hair. Cleo looked up at him as he wiped the tears from her eyes.

"Bart," Cleo started. "I never got to say..."

"Shhhh," he said putting a finger to her lips. "I've always known without you saying it. I love you too." Cleo buried her face in his chest one more time. After several moments Lyson coughed rather obviously. Bart laughed.

"It's good to see you again, General," Bart said.

Tori and Emilia broke and ran to hug the archer along with Cleo in one big group hug.

"Well, well," Bart said chuckling. "I never thought I would be missed this much. Although there is a dragon here I haven't met yet."

"Caleb," the dragon said shaking Bart's hand. "Andros has told me a lot about you."

A momentary pain crossed Bart's face. "How is he, and Abby?" he asked Emilia.

"They are doing so well, and I know they will be crushed that they were not here to see you."

"I really wish it had been different," Bart said.

Emilia put a hand on Bart's shoulder. "They understand, and they know you are in a better place."

"But you are here now, aren't you?" Cleo asked. "Here to stay I mean."

Bart caressed her cheek. "I am afraid not my love. I am here to explain certain truths, and as the solver of the riddle, you have a choice."

"What choice is that?" Cleo asked.

"We will get to that in a minute, but first I must show you these."

Bart walked behind the altar as the others came forward to see what lay there. There were six necklaces, each with a gold disc attached. Stamped on them were the symbols of each of the five gods, although two of them had the image of a rearing horse.

"These are the talismans' of the gods," Bart said. "You will note that there are two with the same symbol."

"I was just about to remark on them," Tori said.

"They are the talismans for Aditya," Bart explained. "Each talisman must be given to their respective priest. You need to make sure Ava and Rhyan get these. It is imperative that all the priests are wearing them at the final battle."

"I don't suppose you could tell us why?" Caleb asked.

Bart just smiled and shook his head no.

"I thought I would give it a shot," Caleb said.

Lyson was about to reach out and touch one of them when Bart stopped him.

"I wouldn't do that General," Bart said as Lyson's hand stopped in midair. "Only a priest of the gods may handle them. Which means you are going to have to carry them all and make sure they get to their proper owners on time," he said to Tori.

"Looks like I'm going back into the frozen moment," Tori said.

Tori picked up the talisman that was Fallon's and put it around her neck.

"By the gods!" Tori exclaimed. "There is a power here that is immense, but it sleeps."

"Yes," Bart said nodding. "It will awake at the proper time. You must never lose these, and the enemy must never find out that you have them."

There was a leather satchel on the table with the symbol of a sphere with five radiating beams of power. Bart picked this up and handed it to Tori.

"Put the talismans in here. The satchel is basically invisible to the ordinary person, so they should be safe there. It is not invisible to Meliakken however, and possibly one other."

"Zana," Emilia said.

Bart nodded at her soberly. "Protect them at all costs."

Tori collected the other talismans from the altar and placed them in the satchel.

"Now for the choice," Bart said looking at Cleo.

"You my love can come with me, right now. You can leave the pains and hurts of this world behind and never experience death. This has been granted you by the gods since you bested the sphinx. What do you say Cleo?"

Cleo just stared at Bart for a few moments, her back rigid as if she were about to take a step forward. Then she turned to look at her friends, but they were not just her friends, they were her family. Tori walked over and put both hands on her shoulders.

"Boss, no one would blame you at all if you decided to take this jump. Although I will miss having you sleep next to me on the trail under some tree root for the thousandth time," Tori chuckled as her eyes welled up with tears. Cleo's likewise was full.

"This is a choice you will not get again Cleo," Caleb said.

Emilia also put a hand on Cleo's shoulder. "I know what it means to be separated from the one you love," Emilia said looking over at Lyson.

Cleo looked over at Lyson who was strangely silent and looking slightly downcast. She went over to him and put her hands on both sides of his face forcing him to look at her.

"What should I do brother?"

Lyson appeared to be warring with himself, but finally his body relaxed.

"You are the only sister I have. Since our parents died it was just us, and even though you said you promised them to look out for me, I have always looked out for you as well. I always felt I would die first, and not have to bear the anguish of watching you die before me. But since Braylynn changed me, there is little chance you will outlive me."

Lyson now put his hands on Cleo's face and pressed his forehead to hers. Choking back the emotion he whispered, "Go Cleo, you have done more than your share. Put your burdens down and be happy."

Cleo then hugged him fiercely. Letting go she kissed his forehead and walked over to Bart and hugged him just as fiercely.

"I'm staying," she told him.

Bart smiled and caressed her cheek.

"I knew that would be your answer. You stayed true to your nature," Bart told her, "which is what this has all been about. You chose not to leave your path at this time, and for what it is worth, I believe you are making the right choice."

"Cleo, are you sure?" Lyson asked her. "Think of what you are giving up."

"That is exactly what I am thinking of brother. Bart will always be waiting for me, but I feel Vasara still needs me. My family still needs me, and I need them."

"You are correct my love, I will be waiting for you, which for me will be the blink of an eye. There is just one more thing I must do before I leave you," Bart said. "Since you have chosen the path of your true nature, I am allowed to give you something. Remove your swords Cleo."

Cleo did as Bart instructed and laid her twin swords by the altar along with their sheath.

"Take this bow," Bart said as he took it off his back. "You will never again be the Viper Captain. You are now the Archer, Vasara's Archer."

Cleo's hand grasped the bow as Bart still held onto it. Blue energy ran through Bart's body into Cleo's causing her to throw her head back as it flooded her being.

"What are you doing?" Tori asked alarmed by what she was seeing.

"Fulfilling a destiny," Bart told her after the energy had completely transferred. "Cleo, sling the bow over your shoulder."

Cleo did this. Once it was in position a quiver of arrows appeared on her back as well.

"What the hell?" Cleo exclaimed.

"You will never want for arrows," Bart told her. "No matter how many you shoot, this quiver will always remain full. You will also be able to hit whatever your eye can see, no matter how far away it is."

Caleb gave a low whistle as he remarked, "That is a deadly weapon to have."

"She will need it in the battle that is coming. You will all need to be ready," Bart said with great urgency. "Now I must go, and you must continue your journey."

Cleo quickly latched onto Bart and hugged him as if she would hold on forever. She could feel his body starting to feel less real.

"I love you," she whispered into his chest.

"I love you too, my darling," Bart said as he started to disappear.

"Bart!" Lyson shouted. "Where are we going from here?"

"Otherwhere," came the ghostly reply as Bart the archer vanished from sight.

There was a profound silence as everyone looked to the spot Bart had just vacated. It was Cleo who turned around and got everyone moving.

"I guess we get back on the ship and sail on to Otherwhere."

"And where would that be my dear sister?" Lyson said arching an eyebrow.

"I'm sure it's that way, somewhere," she said waving her hand in no meaningful direction.

Caleb burst out laughing as he followed Cleo out to board the ship to who knows where.

Chapter 17

Meliakken was walking in his garden deep in thought. The god was imprisoned on the island with its castle and palatial grounds. Most people thought the underworld was in total darkness with nothing but sorrow and suffering. There were places like that in the underworld, but this wasn't one of them. The Five and that pesky goddess did make it so he couldn't leave physically, but he was able to have influence with events throughout the history of this world. He was a god who subjected worlds to his will. Ones that he had created and ones that were created by others. He wasn't going to stop until he was the god of all worlds. This was the first time in his existence that he had ever been bested, but it didn't matter, time was always on his side. He was the oldest of the gods, the first created by the father of the gods. These younglings had no idea of the power that resided in him. They could imprison him, but they could not destroy him.

"Master," a voice called from the top of the garden steps.

"What is it Ansgar?"

"Everything is moving according to plan," Ansgar said coming to stand next to him.

"Everything that is except for your expulsion as the Baron of Black River," Meliakken said sneering.

Ansgar held his tongue, he knew better.

"You have started to grow back into my good graces Ansgar, by not trying to come up with some pathetic excuses."

Meliakken rubbed his hand over his short cropped hair as two separate shrieks came from a darkened alcove in a far corner of the garden.

"It seems your pets are growing restless," the demon said.

"Only two left to be freed," the god said.

Just then two dragon-like heads peeked out from under the archway, shrikers.

"One is for my apprentice, whom she will ride into the final battle once she has fully come into her power."

"Do you think she suspects?" Ansgar asked.

Meliakken's eyes narrowed. "Don't think to presume to know my plans or thoughts, demon."

Ansgar shrank back from that stare.

Meliakken swept his hand across the vast expanse in front of him.

"This world is a chess board Ansgar. Have you ever heard of that game?"

"I have not lord," Ansgar replied.

"No, I wouldn't think you had. In chess, as in life, everything is move and countermove. Being able to read your opponent and anticipate the moves he must make in reaction to your own. Nothing is ever set-in stone, there is always the variable of the unknown that always makes the game interesting."

He looked hard at the demon lord.

"And I, Ansgar, am a master chess player. Of course sometimes I invent my own rules as I go along," the god said with a very evil grin.

Ansgar fell in step with Meliakken as he continued his stroll through his garden. The god leaned down to examine a particular flower. It had blue petals with a white center. Meliakken sniffed at it and made a sound that was not all too pleasant. Apparently, the flower was not to his liking. Closing his hand into a fist he crushed it and turned it black. Likewise, all of its mates started to wither and blacken as well.

"Did I ever tell you of the world I conquered before I came here?"

"No lord, you did not."

Meliakken paused in thought. "It was very much like this one, but there was a single god and goddess, but they were no match for me. I trapped them in here," he said holding up the medallion that he had fused together from the two he had taken from Samara and the Summoner.

"Actually, that is not entirely accurate. They were originally trapped in rock and came hurtling toward this world when I blew up theirs."

"Why did you destroy their world?" Ansgar asked.

"I found them offensive," the god said offhandedly. "And the creatures they created were amazingly primitive and I had neither the time nor inclination to sit around and watch them evolve. But you interrupted my original point Ansgar, don't do that again," he said dangerously.

Ansgar bowed deep in apology.

"Once the rocks impacted with Vasara, Trystan found them and fashioned them into medallions. He did this in a vain attempt to keep me from releasing their power. But I know where his forge is as well as the means to unlock them."

"What happens now?" Ansgar asked.

"Now, my pet demon, you will travel to the Border Lands and aid the demon lords there in breaking the last seal that holds my two remaining friends there," Meliakken said pointing towards the shrikers. "Go now Ansgar, I find I no longer desire your company."

The demon promptly disappeared as Meliakken continued to walk and ponder all the chess moves coming up and what his response to them will be. There is one unknown in this game of chess he can never have a counter move ready for, and that unknown is Killian. Not even Zana knows he is in Otherwhere. Meliakken himself is not entirely sure what Killian is, but he knows he has immense power, which is why he imprisoned him. In the eons since Vasara's creation, that being had seemed content to remain neutral in all events, but he now felt a stirring come from him making him slightly uneasy. He did have an ace in the hole. His prison was warded with special magic, he just needed to get someone there first.

But there was another thorn in his side, Andros the Black. That insolent pup of a dragon had thwarted all his plans with Devon. It was true that Devon had brought about his own demise, but the god had spent centuries grooming him and swaying him to his side of thinking. But Devon craved power not just in this world but others, which is probably why it was so easy to turn him. In many ways Devon was like himself. Then Andros was drawn here by the prophecy and destroyed everything. Although the prophecy started drawing Andros to Vasara long before he physically arrived there.

Meliakken saw everything, he saw when the dragons were created. He felt their spirits and he knew there were ten, even though everyone thought there to be only nine. The god had watched that tenth dragon for eons in the realm where the prophecy had hidden him. It never moved, never spoke, it just watched. And that dragon spirit watched him. Its eyes were always on him. What knowledge it gained, Meliakken was not sure, but Andros arrived and it moved for the first time. Like a lightning streak it penetrated Andros' body, and the rest as they say is history. Whatever insight that spirit gleaned from watching him, he was pretty sure Andros knew nothing about it, he sensed his lack of knowledge during their brief encounter.

"That damn sword though, how the hell had he come by it," Meliakken said aloud. "And the spear the Summoner held."

Meliakken knew they were made from the same rock that had held the god and goddess that now resided in his medallion. He could feel its power as that boy sliced his energy beam that had held the squealing little silver haired faerie. His anger started to rise at that thought.

"You will die very painfully, Andros," he said as he looked up. "And I am going to enjoy that very much."

There was one other chess piece Meliakken was considering, the Summus Re'em. The unicorn master who also happened to be the heir to the throne. Zana had failed to bait the prince into rescuing his parents when she held them in Otherwhere. The creatures of this world were one of the reasons the god would not destroy it once he had conquered it. There was so much mystical power in the land and its magical creatures that Meliakken would absorb it all. The power the unicorns have is immense and varied, to capture all that energy would be a crowning achievement. But on the other side, he didn't want to have that same energy in battle arrayed against him.

The plan had been to capture Prince Brayton and subjugate him to the god's will. Turning him by force if necessary until he had none of his own will left.

Zana had failed in her mission, but like all good chess players, Meliakken had several pawns to use in any given attack, so that when one failed, he would fall back to another. This pawn had been in place for a very long time, just waiting for the right moment to make his counter move. Meliakken had always had a pretty good idea who the Summus Re'em was, and one of the god's pets had grown up with him. Meliakken started to laugh hard.

"This betrayal will be so sweet," he said to himself. "The

prince will be shaken to his very core, and that is when I will take him. Time to wake up my pet"

His garden continued to ring with the echoes of his laughter that grew louder and louder causing demons to pop out of the woodwork, wondering at the maniacal sound the god was making.

Chapter 18

It was a warm day as Brayton ascended the marble steps to the main doors of the White Castle. He scratched an itch around the corner of the patch that covered his missing eye. Life felt whole again with his mother and father back where they belong. Paolo had assumed his duties as king, but once again had hinted about stepping down. Brayton wasn't prepared to think about that, so he pushed the thought aside.

Upon entering the castle, he spied Cathal on a bench along one of the walls. He appeared deep in thought.

"Cathal," the prince called out.

Cathal didn't answer. He seemed to be staring at a spot on the opposite wall.

"Cathal?" Brayton asked as he got closer. The prince's presence still didn't seem to register with his friend. It wasn't until he put a hand on his shoulder that Cathal finally looked up.

"Oh, I'm sorry your highness, I didn't see you there," Cathal said.

Brayton sat down next to his friend and protector.

"Is everything alright Cath?"

"What? Alright? Yes, yes everything is fine," he responded. "I'm just feeling really out of it for some reason today, like I am having a hard time focusing."

Brayton was concerned for his friend. It almost seemed like his mind was only half there.

"Come with me," Brayton said getting up.

"Where are we going?" Cathal asked.

"To get some fresh sea air to help clear your head."

They both started walking out the back gates and down to the docks. Upon reaching the harbor they walked to the farthest pier where his ship, Boreas, was tied up. The crew was not on board, but Brayton could see the captain, Colton was wandering the quarter deck as he inspected various parts of his ship. Nothing ever got past his sharp eyes.

Colton had taught Brayton navigation at a very early age, and once Boreas had been built, Colton had Brayton try his hand at every single position on the ship. From the lowliest crewman to first mate, he made Brayton master them all.

"You need to know every man's job if you are ever to be captain of a ship, laddie," Colton told him.

They wouldn't be able to put out to sea without the crew, but they could lounge on the decks and cast some fishing lines. Brayton found that nothing could calm a man more than the sea and an afternoon of fishing with good companions.

"Well, your Highness, to what do we owe this visit?" Colton called from the gangway.

"Just trying to get some air. May we come aboard Captain?" Brayton asked.

"Of course, of course. Come up, both of you."

Cathal grabbed Brayton's arm to stop him. When he looked at Cathal's face he could see the pupils of his eyes were very wide.

"Bray, something's wrong," Cathal said.

Brayton knew something was wrong with his friend. He almost never used his boyhood nickname unless he was under some great duress.

"Cathal, what is it? What's wrong?"

Cathal was looking from side to side, scanning the crowd on the docks.

"I don't know, but there is some evil about, I can feel it. In here," he said pointing to his chest.

"Come on, let's go up. Some fishing and a drink of Colton's ale will make you feel better."

The two men who had been like brothers since Cathal arrived at the castle so many years ago walked side by side up the gangplank to the awaiting captain. Once they neared the top, Brayton could smell a foul odor in the air, like sulfur.

"I've been expecting you, your Highness," Colton said.

"You have?" Brayton asked puzzled. "I didn't even know…"

"Brayton!" Cathal yelled.

That was the last thing Brayton heard before he was enveloped in a black cloud and fell to his knees choking, unable to even see his hand before his face. He thought he heard the thump of a body next to him before his mind clouded over and he knew no more.

***

"Brayton?"

Brayton could feel his consciousness returning long before he could move any muscle in his body. His eyes felt as if they were open, but he couldn't see anything. There was a sharp pain, like a knife, buried deep into the top of his head.

"Brayton? Can you hear me?"

"Is that you Cathal?" Brayton managed to croak out of his raspy throat. He felt like whatever that black cloud was had burned the inside of his throat and lungs. "I can't see you."

"Your vision will return soon."

"Colton, is that you?" Brayton knew it was the captain's voice.

"Yes. Don't bother to struggle, you are securely bound."

Brayton now could feel the ropes that bound his arms and legs to what he assumed was a chair.

"Colton, what is going on? What did you do?"

A low evil chuckle came from Colton's mouth.

"I have finally liberated myself, that is what I have done."

Brayton felt the bitter taste of ash in his mouth at this betrayal. Colton had been one of his earliest confidants. A mentor and almost a second father. Many was the time when he would get into a scrap at the dockyards, and Colton was always there to bail him out of whatever trouble he was in. He had even introduced Brayton to his wife so many years ago. A single tear slid down his cheek as the enormity of what Colton was came crashing down on him. He is what Andros and the others had been chasing all over Vasara. A demon in human form.

"I see realization has come to you," Colton said dispassionately.

Brayton lifted his head to where he knew the demon must be. "Yes, I realize that my friend has died, and I mourn him."

"Don't bother," Colton said.

"Where are we?" Brayton asked.

"The place you call the warlocks' temple."

Brayton's eyesight was coming back. He looked over and saw Cathal was similarly tied up.

"Cathal, you alright?"

He could see that one of Cathal's eyes was closed shut from swelling.

"Don't worry about me, I'm okay."

"Did you do that?" Brayton asked the demon.

"Your friend is something of an empath, at least when it comes to threats involving you," Colton said. "He knew something was wrong and fought to try and protect you."

"So what do you want Colton?" Brayton asked.

"It's more what I want," a voice from behind him said.

Brayton turned his head around and saw Meliakken standing behind him.

"I really should have put it together that you were behind all this," Brayton said.

"Don't beat yourself up princeling. You are way out of your depth with me."

"Then why am I tied up? What are you afraid of?" Brayton asked with contempt.

The god's face took on an angry hue as his face hovered inches from Brayton's face.

"Moderate your tone prince, or maybe I will take your other eye just for the fun of it."

"Do your worst. Whatever it is you want you will not get it from me."

Meliakken burst out laughing.

"So bravely spoken," the god said. "But since you brought it up, let's talk about what I want. I want you to summon the queen of the unicorns."

Brayton's eyes narrowed as he struggled against his bonds. "I have no way of contacting her."

Suddenly a force like none he had ever experienced picked Brayton up and flung him against the far side of the room, smashing the chair and leaving him in a crumpled heap on the floor. Brayton was dazed, but he still had a moment of clarity. He used that moment to see the one being he thought could help him right now. Closing his eye, he focused everything inward. When he opened it again, he was in a whole other place.

"Well, well my prince, it has been awhile," said a voice from the other side of a crystal-clear stream.

"Caomhnoir," Brayton said. "I need your help."

The white unicorn with the rainbow-colored horn slowly walked over to the stream and bent to take a drink. The guardian of the gate to the paradise of the unicorns looked intently at the heir to the throne of the White Castle.

"No, hello Caomhnoir, how you been?" the unicorn said.

"I'm sorry, but it's urgent," Brayton said.

"I'm only jesting Summus Re'em," Caomhnoir said. "How can I help?"

"Meliakken captured Cathal and myself. We are in the warlocks' temple on the island of the unicorns."

"What does Meliakken want with you?"

"He wants me to summon Savano."

"Do you know why?" Caomhnoir asked with some urgency.

"No. Meliakken slammed me against a wall before he had a chance to tell me. I doubt he will clue me in, but I can't imagine it is anything good."

Caomhnoir was silent for a few moments. The birds in the woods seemed unusually loud as well as the stream that cascaded over the rocks.

"Wait here," he said suddenly as he trotted over to the gate that let travelers' journey to their afterlife.

Putting his horn to the lock, the gate swung inward. There was a bright flash as Caomhnoir disappeared through the gate. Brayton waited for his return. He didn't know if it were moments, weeks, months or years, time had no meaning here, but eventually he could see Caomhnoir returning as the gate swung shut behind him.

"You must leave Summus Re'em."

"What? Why?"

"I did not realize it was that time already. I am afraid you are on your own. Follow your instinct and your nature, prince. You must go. Now."

Before Brayton could answer he was back in the temple and picking himself up off the floor since the ropes had loosened after the chair had broken. He shook his head trying to understand what Caomhnoir meant. *Follow my nature?* he asked himself. *What does that mean?*

"Now, prince," Meliakken said, "you will summon Savano, or you will watch your friend be slowly torn apart before your eyes."

Brayton understood now why Cathal was here. To be used as leverage against him.

"To hell with that Brayton," Cathal said fiercely. "Just spit in his eye and let his godly plots fall all around him. Ahhhhh!!!!!"

Cathal was suddenly screaming in intense pain as his body shook uncontrollably in his chair. Blood and spittle was forming at the corners of his mouth as his head started bouncing back and forth.

"Stop!" Brayton yelled. "Enough! I will do it."

Cathal's pain suddenly stopped as his head slumped onto his chest as he passed out.

Meliakken crossed his arms with a self-satisfied smile on his face as Colton stood behind Cathal, ready to do his master's bidding. Brayton didn't know what to do. He said what he did to buy some time in order to save Cathal's life. Reaching into his shirt he drew forth the talisman that was the symbol of who he was, the master of unicorns.

"I know what you are trying to do," Meliakken said. "Unless you want the torture to begin anew, you better start cracking."

Brayton knew he could stall no longer. Follow his nature Caomhnoir had told him, and his nature was to protect Cathal. The only way to do that was to summon Savano.

Holding the horn tightly in his fist he closed his eye and projected his thoughts outward.

Savano, he said. *Can you hear me?*

I hear you Summus Re'em. You sound very close.

Cathal and I are in the warlocks' temple, Meliakken captured us. He tortured Cathal to make me summon you to come here. It's a trap Savano.

Of course it is, the queen replied. *I am on my way.*

Brayton let the connection drop. It wasn't long before they heard hoofbeats coming down the hall and the queen of the unicorns stood in the doorway, her black coat gleaming in the light of the torches.

"Welcome Savano," Meliakken said. "My heart rejoices to see you here."

I don't believe you possess a heart, Meliakken, Savano said as she looked over at Brayton and Cathal, assessing their condition.

Her horn was glowing, and Brayton could feel she was putting a shield around them.

"There is no need for that," Meliakken said sensing what she was doing.

What do you want? Savano asked.

"Just your magic, Savano."

"No!" Brayton said.

Savano looked steadily at Brayton. *If you forbid this, you bind me to your choice as the Summus Re'em.*

"He will kill you," Brayton said his eye welling up. He couldn't let this stand "Savano, as Summus Re'em…"

Brayton, Savano said speaking to his mind alone. *You have the power to make this choice, I want you to search your nature, and trust me.*

Brayton was warring within himself. He knew for Savano to give the god her magic she would most certainly die. He already had bound them to an island for a thousand years because of his choice of invoking dodhéanta. He looked at Savano, she returned his gaze with love and understanding. She didn't blame him for dodhéanta, and she didn't blame him for this. He silently nodded as he put his trust in the queen. She bowed her head in return.

Very well Meliakken, Savano said, *but the prince and his protector are to be released.*

"They are free to go," the god said. "I can always kill them another day."

Go now, the queen said to Brayton. *Take Cathal, Tilmin is waiting outside.*

Brayton untied Cathal and helped him to his feet.

"Can you walk?" Brayton asked his friend.

"Yes," Cathal answered. "I'm sore from my hair to my toes, but I can walk."

Brayton put one of Cathal's arms around his shoulder as his arm circled his waist and he walked them out into the hall.

"Can you make it to the entrance?" Brayton asked.

"What are you going to do?" Cathal asked with concern written on his face.

"I don't know, but I have to do something. I'll meet you outside."

Cathal was too weary to argue, and with the resolve he saw in his friend's eye, he knew trying to talk him out of it was pointless. He nodded and started to limp as fast as he could towards the entrance as Brayton silently crept back towards the doorway.

"I have been waiting for this day for centuries," Brayton heard Meliakken say.

Get on with this, Savano said defiantly.

Brayton peered around the door frame. Meliakken was so totally absorbed in what he was doing that he never even sensed that Brayton was there. Colton stood off to one side with his arms crossed over his chest as his eyes followed his master.

Meliakken wrapped his hand around Savano's black horn.

"There is a proper way to do this," Meliakken said into her ear as he flicked his wrist and gritted his teeth as he ripped the horn off her head.

Brayton's eye went wide as his body went into total shock at what he had just witnessed. His mind silently screamed at all the blood that was pouring out of the spot where her horn had been. Meliakken held up the bloody end and examined it closely as he opened his mouth. Colors of the rainbow, not unlike the colors in Caomhnoir's horn, poured out and flowed into the god's body.

Savano's legs buckled as she knelt on all fours, unable to hold herself up from the loss of blood. Her head slumped, but before she lost consciousness she glanced towards the door and her eye met Brayton's.

Run Brayton. Run now! She said. *Remember me.*

Brayton's heart was in his throat as he watched the queen of the unicorns roll over on her side and die. Heeding her last command, he ran down the hall and out the door where he saw Cathal astride Tilmin, standing next to him was a blond color unicorn that Brayton didn't know.

My name is Fynbar, Summus Re'em. I will bear you to the grove of the unicorns.

"What does that mean?" Brayton asked while getting on Fynbar's back. "This whole island is the grove of the unicorns."

Not any longer, Tilmin said as he turned and they started to gallop towards the East.

"How is that possible?" Brayton asked.

Dodhéanta ends with the death of the queen, Tilmin said. *The grove is moving, and we must get with the herd as quickly as possible.*

"Wait, you knew this was going to happen?" Brayton asked in disbelief.

Her majesty had a strong feeling about it, Fynbar said, *which is why she had us come along with explicit instructions of what to do in case her worst fears were realized.*

Brayton's mind was on overload. He needed a minute to center himself. He focused everything inward to take his spirit to see Caomhnoir.

"Damn!" Brayton exclaimed.

"What's wrong?" Cathal said with his arms wrapped around Tilmin's neck since he lacked the strength to sit up.

"I can't get to the garden where the gate to the unicorn paradise is, I think Caomhnoir is blocking me."

"Why would he do that?" Cathal asked.

"I don't know. Let's just get to the other unicorns, and we can sort it out then. Tilmin, do you know where the grove is going next?"

I'm afraid I don't, Tilmin replied. *As you know dodhéanta has never been invoked before, and none of us have a way of knowing what happens after it is removed. Blind chance is now guiding us I fear.*

Brayton grabbed on tight to Fynbar's mane as the unicorns raced across the flat expanse to where the unicorns waited. If the grove should suddenly appear in a place far from the White Castle, he wasn't sure what he would be able to do to get back.

Tilmin and Fynbar had to slow their gallop somewhat as they started to get near the coast and the ground became rocky. Brayton could feel and taste the sea breeze as they came over a rise and the beach and shoreline opened up before them. He could see the unicorns, but they were doing something odd. They were all running together in a counter-clockwise circle on the beach.

"Tilmin, why are they doing that?" Brayton asked him.

Once we start to feel the pull of the grove, we all run together so we don't accidentally leave anyone behind, he answered. *A unicorn can live outside the grove for a period of time, but eventually must find their way back or they will die.*

It's starting, Fynbar said.

Brayton looked and could see a rainbow-colored cloud starting to envelope the unicorns.

Quick, there is not a moment to lose, Tilmin said.

If Brayton had thought they were at their top speed in getting here, he was proven wrong as Tilmin and Fynbar took it to a whole new level. Everything around them became blurred as the two unicorns sped through the sand and at the last possible moment they jumped and went sailing over the unicorns to land in the middle of the circle. No sooner had their hooves skidded to a halt that the cloud enveloped them like a dome and everything went dark. There was a loud crack and a snap.

When Brayton could see again, all the unicorns were standing still as the dome started to recede. Once it was gone, the prince found they were in a glade in a valley that was encircled by tall mountain peaks.

"Tilmin, where the hell are we?" Brayton asked.

This is a day for firsts, your highness, Tilmin said. *I haven't the faintest idea. I do know this, we are not in Vasara.*

Chapter 19

Andy was standing on the quarter deck of the Grey Morning. After dropping Daragh off in Laurel Hollow to help protect the faerie kingdom, Andy had flown Abby, Tera and his father to Bowen's ship, Gael and Nia came as well. Redlin thought it a good idea to have backup by bringing Gael, and there was no way in hell Nia was going to be left behind.

The plan was to use the captain's ancestral map to try and enter Otherwhere. They had been sailing for two days now, and of course Abby and Nia had sung for the crew both nights. Andy heard footsteps coming up behind him, and from the heavy booted step knew it was Bowen.

"It's a pleasant day for sailing laddie," Bowen said.

Andy smiled. Even though he was a grown man, his friend still thought of him as a youngster.

"That it is Captain," Andy said. "Any idea how long until we are there?"

"We should be there by midday tomorrow if my calculations are correct. What happens after that is anyone's guess."

Just then there was thumping against the hull of the ship.

"I don't believe it," Andy said rushing to the port side and looking down. Abby came running up from below to join them.

"Is it?" Abby asked excited.

"Yes," Andy said smiling. "Tagen."

Andy's mind connected with the dragon-like sea horses.

The images he got back were unlike any he had gotten from them before. They stopped thumping the sides of the boat and four tagen stood up on their tails with most of their bodies out of the water and their eyes locking with Andy's.

"By the gods!" Bowen exclaimed. "I have never seen them do that before."

"What are they doing?" Tera asked as everyone came over to see what was happening.

"They are trying to tell me something," Andy said.

"Any idea what they are saying?" Redlin asked his son.

"They are sending me images of the ship following them through a channel, past an enormous whirlpool, or maybe through it, and emerging under a marble gateway."

"I'm getting them as well," Gael said.

Andy looked over at his brother. Of course, it stands to reason that the tagen can talk to Gael as well as himself since they were both dragons.

"So what do you think?" Nia asked as she put her hair in a ponytail to keep the wind from blowing it in her face. "Do we follow them?"

"I believe so," Andy said scratching the stubble on his chin. He hadn't shaved in several days and had started to get a short scruffy beard. "Something tells me they are a part of this and that they know the way."

Andy closed his eyes and concentrated, communicating with the tagen that they were ready to follow. In unison, the four tagen did a backflip and briefly swam under the water only to emerge a few yards down from the bow as they slowly started to swim forward.

"Helmsman!" Bowen shouted to his pilot. "Unfurl all sails! Follow those creatures!"

"Aye, Captain!" the helmsman responded.

As the sails came down the ship picked up speed to maintain a consistent distance behind the tagen.

"Captain, how sturdy would you say the Grey Morning is?" Andy asked.

"She's the sturdiest ship afloat lad, I can promise you that. Why do you ask?"

"Just curious is all," Andy answered.

He didn't want to voice his real reason and risk frightening everyone, but the whirlpool he had seen was massive and strong. He caught Gael looking at him in understanding. His brother was thinking the same thing.

After a day and half of following the tagen, they saw it. Everyone's mouth dropped open at the size of the whirlpool that seemed to have opened up in the middle of the ocean and stretched as far as the eye could see. They were still some distance away but the pull of the current was substantial.

"Furl all sails!" Bowen shouted. "Lower the sea anchor!"

"Why the anchor?" Nia asked.

"It's to provide some drag, lassie. To slow us down a bit as we figure out a plan to navigate around that thing."

Andy watched as the tagen swam right into it. They were circling the outer rim and picking up speed. They seemed to reach a certain point when all of a sudden, like a stone out of a slingshot, they were out of the whirlpool and onto the other side.

"Please don't tell me we have to do that Captain," the helmsman said.

Bowen looked at Andy. "Is this why you asked about the structure of my ship?"

Andy mutely nodded as Bowen blew out a heavy breath.

"I don't think the Grey Morning will break apart in that. My concern is pulling out of the current before it pulls us into the center of the vortex. No ship would survive that."

"I have an idea," Gael said.

"Let's hear it lad," Bowen said. "If it saves our lives and the ship, I'm all for it."

"What did you have in mind, Gael?" Redlin said. The wizard had his palms facing forward, pushing against an invisible wall before the current became too strong and propelled the ship forward before they were ready.

"Andros and I can fly ahead of the ship as it makes its run. We will hold onto ropes in our talons that will be tied to the railings, and when the time comes, with the aid of the speed from the ship, we should be able to pull it free of the current. What do you think brother?"

Andy pondered if such a plan could work without pouring them into the abyss.

"Let's do it," Andy said.

Kissing his wife, Andy jumped over the side following Gael as they disappeared under the water. Once they emerged, two dragons, one black the other gold were winging their way into the sea breeze before circling back towards the ship.

Bowen, can you hear me? Andy said to his mind.

I hear you Andros, Bowen replied.

We are going to swing around once we go past the ship on either side. Do you have the ropes ready?

All set lad, the Captain said.

Andy and Gael went a half mile from the stern of the ship before crisscrossing and heading back. Two huge, muscled sailors stood on the bow swinging one end of the ropes as the other ends were tied securely to the ship. As the dragons got close, the sailors heaved them into the air. With perfect precision, Andy and Gael caught the ropes in their talons and started to fly until the lines became taught.

Ok, Dad, Andy said. *You can release the ship.*

Letting it go now, Redlin said. "Bowen, you can pull the anchor up."

"Raise anchor!" Bowen shouted to his crew as four large men turned a huge wheel, bringing the anchor back up to the surface.

They picked up speed as the current grabbed the ship and propelled it forward. Andy and Gael had to fly faster to keep the ropes taught. As soon as it hit the top most rim of the whirlpool, the prow of the ship started to angle down into the vortex. Andy spoke to Gael, who was on the outer side of the whirlpool.

Gael, you need to pull your side up or it's going to go down!

I'm trying, Gael shouted. *This current is so strong!*

Andy could hear the timbers of the ship starting to creak and groan from the stress being put upon it.

Andros, you need to get us out after one circuit, or we are not going to make it, Bowen said to his mind.

Dad, when we get to the spot where the tagen exited, can you send a blast of wind behind the ship to help push it out? Andy asked.

You got it, Son, Redlin responded.

Andy and Gael were beating their powerful wings, trying to keep the ship as straight as possible as it made its way around the circle. Suddenly there was a loud crack and a couple of curses from the sailors as pieces of the deck buckled and broke apart, sending splinters and wood shards everywhere. The speed of the ship was increasing, and the dragons were struggling to stay ahead of it. They were almost at the point where the tagen exited.

Gael, you ready? Andy asked. He was struggling as his wings started to ache from the strain.

As ready as I can be, he responded.

Andy needed to time this perfectly. He felt if he didn't pull them out at just the right spot they would not get to where they needed to be. He could see a slight break in the water and knew that was the spot he was aiming for.

Andros? Gael asked.

Not yet.

It was so hard to hold back until he felt the right moment. Suddenly he saw a flash.

Now! Andy yelled. *Dad, now!*

Both Andy and Gael flew ninety degrees from the ship slowly getting the prow to point out of the whirlpool. Redlin lifted both hands and a great force was pushing from behind. Andy could feel the ship straining to want to keep circling, then all of a sudden, the ropes went slack as the ship shot out like a stone skimming across the top of the water. The dragons had quickly dropped the ropes and flew straight up to avoid being hit by the tall masts of the ship. Andy watched as the ship looked like it was being pushed by a gale. They needed to slow it down before it crashed into something. Andy had an idea.

Dad, can you make an energy parachute?

Great idea, Son!

What's a parachute? Gael asked.

Watch, Andy replied.

Redlin was rapidly moving his hands in an intricate pattern, as if he were knitting something together. Andy could see lines of energy connecting, forming a half dome and extending behind the stern of the ship, catching the air and providing enough drag that the ship started to slow. They were about a mile distant before the ship came to a complete halt. Andy and Gael hovered over the ship as they made their change and dropped to the hard deck.

"Everyone all right?" Andy asked.

"As alright as we can be," Abby said picking herself up from the deck and running over to hug him. Nia was only two steps behind her as she jumped into Gael's arms looking wide-eyed.

"Well, that was an adventure," Nia said a little shakily, then kissed Gael soundly.

"Oh my," Abby said looking over Andy's shoulder.

Everyone turned to see what she saw. The ocean was as calm as a pond and rising out of the water were two black obelisks. The tagen were bobbing in the water right next to the gateway, the sun reflecting off their golden scales. Andy now understood the flash he saw that told him when to exit the whirlpool.

"Any doubts that is the way to go?" Tera asked rhetorically.

Bowen steered his ship in between the two obelisks. As they passed the tagen, Andy gave them a silent nod and an image of thanks. The tagen bowed in return, and in unison, backflipped into the air and quickly disappeared beneath the water.

"Well, that was something," Andy said running his fingers through his hair.

"You were a little reckless back there, husband," Abby said squinting at him.

"Were you worried, love?" Andy asked as his arms circled her waist and he quickly kissed her lips. Abby's demeanor softened at the kiss.

"Maybe not as much now," she said smiling at him.

"Will you two stop that," Tera said buzzing back and forth between them, her wings beating as fast as a bee's.

"By the gods!" Bowen exclaimed.

Andy and Abby quickly whipped their heads around. Once the boat was all the way through the gate, the scenery vastly changed. They were perhaps a hundred yards offshore from a crystalline white sandy beach, with a tropical jungle beyond.

Looking with his dragon sight, Andy could tell that the forest was so tightly woven together that passing through it was going to be near impossible. Suddenly Tera started to speak.

"You must go to where the inside is bigger than the outside. Going high before you go low will get you moving in the right direction," she said.

"You are right Tera," Redlin said putting a hand on her shoulder. "This place is definitely bigger than the outside."

"And if we are going to get past that jungle, we will need to go high for sure," Andy remarked.

"Are you thinking what I am thinking?" Gael asked his brother.

"Yes. It looks like the dragon taxi service is in business again," Andy said.

"Captain, can you hold here until we find what it is we are looking for?" Redlin asked.

"If it is all the same to you master wizard, I would like to come along."

Redlin seemed about to go against that request when Bowen continued.

"It's like this Redlin," Bowen began taking a puff on his pipe. "Since your son arrived here, all of my interaction has been on the sea, which I am not complaining about mind you. But just this one time, I'd like to be front and center to witness what happens here." Bowen looked around retrospectively. "Besides, this place is closely linked with my family line, and I would love to be able to fill in that empty hole on my map."

Realization dawned on Redlin's face as he smiled and clasped the captain's hand.

"Of course you may come, Captain," Redlin said. "Andy, Gael?"

With no more prompting than that, both men jumped over the side and made their change.

Once everyone climbed aboard the dragons, Andy and Gael started winging their way inland. The jungle was extensive. Andy was glad they had decided to fly over it, for it would have taken weeks to work their way through it. He would have also worried they might have missed the maze if it weren't for the line in Abby's father's book.

The land below had started to change. Forest started to give way to foothills which eventually ran up into mountainous peaks.

Does anyone know what is next? Nia asked from Gael's back.

Well, Redlin said, *the second half of what Tera had recited said to go high before going low. I think we need to start looking where to go low.*

What do you think go low means? Andy asked.

I have a feeling the maze goes under those mountains, Redlin said.

Gael let out a deep sigh.

What's the matter Gael? Andy asked his brother.

Sorry, Gael said. *I forgot we were mind speaking. No one was supposed to hear that.*

What's troubling you? Redlin asked.

I'm just being ridiculous, master wizard, Gael said. *It's just that I have spent fifteen hundred years under the earth, and since I've been freed, I have been in no big hurry to go underground again.*

I'm the one that needs to solve the maze, Gael, Andy said. *I wouldn't think of making you go inside if it bothers you that much.*

It's alright, Andros, Gael replied, *I know you would go in if the situation were reversed.*

And this time there is a difference, Nia said.

What is that, love? Gael asked.

I will be right beside you.

Using the empathy skills Daragh had taught him, Andy

could feel happiness and gratitude radiating off his brother.

After flying another thirty minutes, Andy looked down and saw they were flying over a bowl shaped glen at the base of a huge mountain. In the glen was a lake with what looked like a large cabin. Leading away from the cabin was a ribbon trail leading into the face of the mountain. It was then that Andy saw it.

Dad! he exclaimed. *I think I found the entrance.*

Where? Redlin asked.

Can you see that cabin? Follow the trail that leads from it to the base of the mountain. It looks like there are two dragon statues on either side of the path.

I will have to take your word for it son, it is still too far for me to see.

I can see it, Gael said.

Just then there was a loud shriek followed by a dark shape that shot past them and down towards the dragon statues.

A shriker! Andy exclaimed. *What is it doing here, and where is it going?*

Suddenly Tera started to recite from the dragon maze book.

Reach the wizard before another gets the key, because what is released is neither good nor evil, until the person that releases it makes it so, she said.

I was really hoping we got a step up on that part of the riddle, Andy said.

As they got closer to the ground, they could see the shriker begin to change, and standing before the gate looking up at them was a man who ran between the statues and disappeared.

That thing was just like Drem! Bowen exclaimed thinking about his former steward who was actually a demon that turned into a shriker.

"Andy, land us down by the cabin," Redlin said, "we need a plan."

Andy and Gael banked left to land them in an open field where everyone got off and they made their change. The cabin was made out of red-wood logs with spacious windows and a white door. The roof seemed to have some sort of white stone on it which shone in stark contrast to the dark red wood when the sun's rays hit upon it. Opening the door everyone stepped inside. Andy looked around and noticed a fire blazing in a hearth on the far wall. The cabin was a single room with a long table in the center and a candle lit chandelier hung over it. High back chairs and divans lined the walls for comfortable sitting.

"Do you think someone lives here?" Nia asked as she slid her curved sword into its sheath feeling there was no immediate threat.

"I don't believe so," Redlin said. "I have a feeling that fire burns continually, giving the evidence that there is no ready source of wood lying around, nor are the logs in the fire burning down at all. Same with the candles," he said looking up.

"So who built it and why is it here?" Andy asked his father.

"My guess, and this is just a guess, is that this building exists because of the maze. Whoever created the maze made this as well. What for, I couldn't tell you. Maybe as just a place to rest and prepare before venturing into the maze."

"What is that?" Tera asked pointing at a picture over the hearth.

Everyone walked over for a better look. The picture had many curious patterns and designs on it and Andy thought it almost looked maze like. In the center however was a being with blond hair and sharp angular blue eyes. The shape of the eyes looked almost like a cat's, with small ears but pointed on the ends with a definite feminine look. It was strange, but Andy felt like she was looking directly at him.

"She's definitely not human," Gael said. "If it is a she, that is."

"I think she may be the key," Abby said.

"What makes you say that lassie?" Bowen asked as he made a few notes in his journal that he had brought along to record landmarks and general observations.

"The fact that she is centered in what appears to be a maze makes me think that she is."

"The key is not what you think, and to find it you must follow your heart and not your eyes," Tera said reciting another piece of the riddle

"I believe you are right," Redlin agreed.

"So what do we do now?" Andy asked.

Redlin looked long at his son with no small amount of concern.

"I believe this is where you go on alone," his father replied.

"Do you want me to come with you?" Gael asked him.

Andy looked gratefully at his brother. "Thanks, but I don't think you can. Killian told my father I must get the key, as well as the passage in my father-in-law's book."

Andy put a hand on Gael's shoulder. "I would also feel better if you were here protecting everyone in case another shriker shows up, or even Meliakken himself."

Gael nodded, letting him know that he would protect everyone with his life.

"I guess I shouldn't delay this any longer," Andy said.

Abby pulled him into a fierce embrace as she whispered in his ear, "Please come back to me."

"I will," he whispered back, "I promise."

Everyone took turns hugging him and wishing him luck. Once outside the cabin he saw a corral that he hadn't noticed before. Penned up inside was a horse the color of midnight looking passively at him.

"I guess whoever built this place really aimed to provide

everything," he said to himself.

Opening the gate the horse calmly walked out and stood next to Andy. Grabbing a fistful of mane, he pulled himself up as the horse leapt to the trail and onto the dragon gate. It was a short ride, but Andy was grateful to not have to change back and forth.

"Thank you, horse," Andy said stroking his long neck.

The horse whinnied as he turned and galloped away. Andy took a closer look at the statues before walking between them. They were patterned after the dragons of Vasara of that he was sure. One was black, the other silver. He wondered if it was just symbolic or did it mean that only those dragon colors could enter, which would mean only himself, Herve, Irwyn and Jace would be allowed entry. The shriker was black so it made sense that he was allowed in if his theory held true.

Taking a deep calming breath, he walked between the silent sentinels to the cave mouth beyond. But once he was through, everything changed. Instead of a mountain in front of him he was in a forest. Whether this was real or not he had no way of knowing, plus it didn't really matter much, he had to solve the riddle of the maze no matter what he faced, truth or illusion.

Before taking another step, he made sure he could still touch the source. Focusing everything inward he reached out and felt the energy of the gods flow through him. He breathed a sigh of relief; it was still there. He twisted his shoulders and adjusted his sword moon shadow on his back. Andy still had that to fall back on if there were any funny business with his power suddenly leaving him. Now came his first decision. There were five paths before him that went different ways into the forest. The trees were tightly bound together to make almost a hedge row, which made it impossible to see where each path led or what was beyond.

"Ok, a little help here maybe?" Andy asked to the sky, not really expecting an answer. "God, I hate riddles and puzzles."

He surveyed each path one by one, looking for some clue that would tell him which way to go. There was absolutely nothing.

"Damn!" he shouted to the sky. Then Tera's voice came back to him as she recited from Abby's father's book.

"The key is not what you think, and to find it you must follow your heart and not your eyes," she had said.

"That's it!" Andy exclaimed as the realization hit him.

He needed to use what Daragh had taught him. He latched onto the source and imagined a wall with holes in it. Then he began reaching out for emotions, directing his thoughts down each path. One by one he would discard them as he felt nothing, then on about the fifth path he tried he felt something, hatred. Its color was black. He wondered if that was the shriker. He kept probing until he felt something coming down another path, fear and loss, the colors were pink and red. Andy figured the obvious choice was the fear and loss. But what if the shriker was fearing Meliakken for losing his way in the maze. Daragh was right, the interpretation of this was difficult. He decided to go with the obvious and assumed the hatred radiating from the one path was from the shriker given their true nature.

Andy walked the forest path as it twisted and turned. If he hadn't been following the raw emotions, he was sure he would have taken the many false turns that sprung up in his path. He found it strange that there were no animal sounds whatsoever. Suddenly there was a scream from a side path followed by a shadow that was racing towards him. Andy drew moon shadow and planted his feet. The creature stopped inches from the point. It was the shriker in its human/demon form. He had blond hair with a scruffy beard. He looked so human, although the red eyes gave it away that he was not.

"You may as well turn back," it hissed. "If anyone will get the key, it is me. Leave, and I will spare your life."

Something was wrong here. Andy focused all his empath abilities on the demon. It was there, the fear and the loss was strong. Realization hit him like a rock. He was lost, and so was the demon. Andy needed to think fast, or this thing would follow him wherever he went. He thought of changing and flying over the treetops when he heard Tera's voice again, "Run when you want to fly and fly when you want to crawl."

"Run when you want to fly," Andy thought to himself. "But run where?" he wondered.

He thought maybe he should just try and slay it, but that fight could take forever. Andy was sure this thing would just play dodge since it was on a quest of his own and wouldn't risk being annihilated. He needed to figure out how to make himself invisible, but first he needed to know where to run too. Keeping moon shadow leveled at the demon, he sent out his empathic thoughts again, sweeping in a circle around him. Just off to his left, he felt it, black hatred, but when he looked at where it was coming from, it was a solid wall of green vegetation.

"How can I run through that?" he said to himself. "Unless it is an illusion."

He figured he had nothing to lose by running that way, but how to mask it so the demon can't see where he was going. Suddenly Andy smiled.

"What's so funny," the demon asked sneering at him.

What had Andy smiling was something he remembered from his training with Emilia, when they were facing off against Braylynn as she was preparing them in their fight against Devon. Plunging himself into the source he pulled in all the moisture that was in the surrounding air. He let it build before starting to slowly release it as a mist.

"What are you doing?" the demon asked looking at the fog billowing at his feet.

Andy didn't move his sword, keeping the demon in place as the fog billowed around them, covering their legs, their chests and eventually their entire bodies.

"Where are you?" the demon shrieked. "Where are you?"

Andy didn't waste a second. He closed his eyes, he couldn't see anything anyway. He latched onto the black beam of hatred that he saw with his empathic mind's eye, and he ran. He ran and he didn't stop running. He felt he had passed where he should have encountered the wall, but he didn't slow down. He took several twists and turns, not knowing if they were correct or not, he followed his instinct. After about ten minutes of running, he let the fog go as he fell to his knees panting. As the fog lifted Andy looked around dumbfounded at what he saw. He had managed to stop at just the right moment, because what was in front of him was a canopy of vines with six-inch thorns all along their lengths. It would have been all too easy to accidentally impale himself if he hadn't stopped. He walked over to one of the vines and ran his hands along one of the thorns. His body started to shake as he realized the thorns were metal. And not just any metal. These thorns were dragon piercing thorns. He had felt this metal just once before, as an arrow that had pierced his wing in the battle of the White Castle where they had destroyed the evil wizard Devon. There was no way he could fly through that, he would need to crawl through.

"Fly when you want to crawl," he could hear Tera say.

"Tera, you want to come do this?" he said to the air in frustration. 'By the gods, I hate riddles."

He stood looking at the canopy of thorns that encircled him. How was he supposed to fly through that without tearing his dragon body to shreds. Andy needed help, but he didn't know where to turn, there was no one around to help him in any case. "Or was there?" he asked himself. Suddenly he had an idea. There was only one other person other than a dragon who knew all there was to know about dragons, Loki.

Andy sat cross-legged on the ground and turned his thoughts inward. He was going to the source to try and reach Loki. He knew what he was doing was risky and left him vulnerable without anyone to watch over him, but he didn't think he had any choice. Once he crossed over he immediately sent out his thoughts to Loki. As he walked the forest path he came to stand beside the source of the Five gods. The five rotating arms around a sphere of energy always soothed Andy's spirit.

"Andros?"

Andy turned around and saw the man who was a second father to him. The fact that he himself was a grown man now didn't matter. He ran up to the old wizard and hugged him in a crushing embrace.

"Well well, it's good to see you too lad," Loki said once he got his breath back.

"Sorry," Andy said smiling. "Hopefully I didn't break anything."

"I don't think you can in this place," the wizard said.

"Where are you now?" Andy asked.

"I am at the White Castle with Dain and Leah. Sibila and Nyle are here as well. The prince and Cathal have gone missing, lad."

"Oh no! How, when?"

"Shortly after you left."

Loki went on to tell Andy how the last time anyone had seen Brayton and Cathal was on the prince's ship with the captain.

"At some point the ship must have sailed," Loki said. "But the strange part is the entire crew was on shore leave. And we questioned all the ships that arrived in port over the last week and none reported seeing anything matching the ship's description."

"What will you do now?"

"Sibila believes that Nyle can locate his son through his connection to him and create a portal. But that is our job, lad. How can I help you?"

Andy outlined his dilemma with the canopy of thorns and his effort to move forward. Loki scratched at his beard deep in thought as he paced. Andy remembered whenever Loki was very deep in thought he would pace in a circle.

"There is something," Loki said coming to a stop. "I remember Cael and I were discussing the powers and limitations of dragons and one thing that came up was something called phasing, but he said only one dragon would have that gift."

"What is phasing?" Andy asked.

"It is basically changing your molecular body structure that allows it to pass through solid objects." Loki paused for a second. "Andros, what is your gift? What is the one power you have that you don't require the source to perform it?"

"I don't have a gift as far as I know," Andy replied. "I always thought it was because I wasn't physically born in Vasara."

Loki seemed to ponder that. "No, every dragon has a gift, and I know that none of the other nine have this ability."

"How am I supposed to know?" Andy asked.

"I'm afraid I can't help you there, lad. The others just knew from the moment they were born, or so they told me."

"I guess I'm the odd man out Loki, because I feel no gift inside me."

Loki sized Andy up as he was deep in thought trying to

find an answer to this puzzle. Andy was glad that Loki was here because he is the master of riddles.

"From the very beginning you have been a child of the prophecy. It has guided your steps and brought you to this moment. For whatever reason I believe it has blocked your gift from being revealed until the proper time. Maybe that time is now."

"So how do I unblock it," Andy said getting really frustrated. Suddenly he felt like he was back in the dragon cave the first time Loki had pulled him out of the White Castle to escape Devon. And all he knew was he had become a dragon with lots of questions and no answers. Loki saw the pain on Andy's face and put both hands on his shoulders.

"Andros, do you trust me?" Loki asked smiling.

Andy nodded mutely.

"I know you have never liked being in this position, it is just who you are, but I am here to help you. Help will always come to you when you need it most. And it always has, hasn't it?"

"You are right, I'm being childish. I'm sorry."

"No apologies necessary lad," the wizard said. "We've all been there. Now, I want you to stand with your back to the source."

"How come?" Andy asked as he turned around.

"There is something you have never gone through, that all your brothers did at the moment of their creation."

"What is that?"

"It is a baptism of energy. Each new dragon stands before the source as the power of the gods fill every cell in their body with magic. I wasn't thinking of this before when you first came here because I didn't fully understand how each dragon's gift worked. But listening to you, I think I have finally figured it out. The reason a dragon can use his gift without touching the source is because the source of energy that is linked to each gift is embedded in their very being. Hold still."

"Will this hurt?" Andy asked.

"I'm pretty sure it will. Your brothers certainly screamed a lot."

"Couldn't you just lie to me?" Andy asked groaning.

"Brace yourself lad," Loki said.

Andy locked every muscle in his body. Loki stood in front of him with his arms raised. He seemed to be chanting something, but Andy couldn't really make it out. It was as if he were calling something by the tone of his voice.

Suddenly Andy felt something. It was like vines circling his feet that started to climb up his body, but instead of vines it was the five energy beams of the gods. He turned around and looked back towards the source and his mouth dropped. The arms were no longer rotating around the sphere. Instead they slithered on the ground like snakes and attached themselves to Andy's body.

Then the pain hit. He could feel each cell one by one being infused by the energy of the gods. It was as if they were being blown apart and re-made, billions of cells and he felt them all as well as the deafening scream that was being ripped from his throat. For a millisecond he felt like he only existed as pure energy, but then he started to feel a cooling balm starting at his feet working its way back up to his head, like he was being made anew. As it got to the top of his head he felt something very different, excruciating pain in his shoulder where Devon had branded him with the symbol of his raven many years ago. It felt like a knife was digging into his back. Realization came to him in a flash. With no time to bid farewell to Loki, he quickly went back into his body. Andy lay on his back and when he opened his eyes a silver blade was descending towards his heart.

His hands shot up to grip the arm that held the knife. It was not the same demon he had met earlier, this one was muscular with red hair and a cheeky grin on his face. He reminded Andy of an Irishman he once knew back in his old world. The demon was hissing and spitting in his effort to overcome Andy's strength and plunge the dagger into his heart. He could feel the blood pooling under his back from his first wound. He needed to stop the bleeding before he bled out.

Andy saw moon shadow laying on the ground behind the demon. There was no way he was going to reach that. First, he had to stop his bleeding. Andy was never very good at healing others and even worse at healing himself. He did the only thing he could do. Feeling the wound with his mind he reached out to the source for fire and slammed it into the slice to cauterize it. He screamed as the pain ripped through him, but it gave him the strength to keep his arms locked on his assailant's. Once it was closed, Andy hit it with a cooling balm. It didn't take away the pain of the stab, but it did lessen the burn. Now he could focus on what was in front of him and suddenly a great rage came over him as his eyes turned red.

Then he felt it. He felt his gift. Every cell in his body was alive and burning. He could see the form of his being and how it was made, and he could see how to shape it to be slightly different from everything around him. Andy felt like his hair must be standing on end, he could see between the minute spaces of all things and how he could adjust his phase to them. He did this. The demon whose arm he was holding was suddenly free and with the downward force no longer held back, the demon's blade buried itself in the dirt. Andy stood up and passed right through him.

The demon looked up startled, turning his head from side to side. Apparently, the demon couldn't see him in this altered state of reality. He walked over to moon shadow and phased back to normal as he picked up his blade and turned. The demon upon seeing Andy reappear, ran towards him and leapt into the air, ready to split him down the middle.

Andy phased out again, and thankfully, such is the magic of the sword that moon shadow phased with him. Stepping behind the demon after he landed, Andy came back and split the demon from head to toe. As the halves split apart and dissolved, a black angry smog went screaming into the air to disappear.

"By the gods!" Andy exclaimed aloud. He realized what a powerful gift he had. Now it was time to put it to use. Grabbing its sheath, he rammed moon shadow home and slung it over his back. He phased one more time.

Now came the tricky part. Could he transform into a dragon in this state he wondered. He was about to find out. Turning his thoughts inward he saw his dragon self, just slightly different from what he was used to. Pouring his being into it he made the change. He moved his wings which were already at the level of the roof of the canopy, passing through the thorns without hurt. He still felt the pain in his shoulder blade from where the knife went in. He buried the pain and started to beat out a rhythm as he lifted off the ground.

Andy was headed higher when he looked down and saw the extent of the tunnel of thorns. It was immense, and he could only imagine that it would've taken weeks to crawl through all that. Once he felt he was high enough he phased back into normal reality. Using his empathic skills, Andy picked up the trail of hatred that led him onward. He found himself flying through a network of canyons, banking left and right to navigate the many twists and turns. Twice he had to double back because the turns were so sharp he went in the wrong direction before realizing the trail of hate had dropped off.

Suddenly the twist and turns stopped and he was flying down a straight corridor that opened up into a huge amphitheater. Andy pulled up short and settled to the ground. Now he understood the hatred. In the center of the amphitheater on a raised circular stone platform was the key. She looked just like she did in the painting in the cabin, apart from a score of demons surrounding her. Her feline like eyes looked over at Andy and connected, and in that instant, Andy felt another emotion coming through, relief.

The demons sensing something all turned to where the key was looking. Seeing Andy they started whipping themselves into a frenzy, but they didn't break ranks. Andy assumed they must have strict orders to keep the key prisoner at all costs, but then why not hand her over to the demons that were trying to find the key as well. He was sure everything would become clear eventually, but first things first, he had to deal with this mob, and he wasn't exactly sure what the best approach should be. Once again, he heard Tera's voice.

"To succeed you must be the first and not the second or even the third…"

"Only the first can succeed," Andy mused to himself, "the first dragon." It has to be because of my gift."

Andy pondered on that thought. Feeling he had nothing to lose and no better plan of attack, Andy phased out and walked through the ring of demons. As he passed through them he knew they felt him because of the hideous noises they were making, but still they made no move. One thing he did know is that the key could see him. She followed his every move until he was standing right next to her.

"Welcome, first dragon," she said in a vibrant voice that had a feline sound to it.

"You know me?" Andy asked.

"I have known you since the five departed Vasara and the prophecy had been created. A long time my young dragon."

"Why haven't you just left?" Andy asked her, he felt like she must have immense power.

The key swept her hand in front of her, encompassing the demons.

"My guardians," she replied. "The moment I move, they will be allowed to attack, and because of the magic of this place, I have no power against them and I will be killed."

Andy was shocked as he looked around at the slobbering demons who had been standing here for eons just waiting for a chance to rip her apart.

"Do you have a name?" Andy asked.

"I am the key," she replied. "No other name is required for now. Later, well that will depend entirely upon you. It is your task to free me from here without being torn to shreds. How will you solve this riddle, first dragon?"

Andy thought she was almost smiling at him, as if she knew his detest for riddles, which she probably did. Andy heard Tera's voice again.

"To succeed you must be the first and not the second or even the third. As in all mazes, the key is in the center, but the way out will not be the way you came in."

Understanding lit up in Andy's eyes and the key saw it and smiled.

"Wasn't that hard, was it?"

"Well no it wasn't, thanks to a little silver haired faerie whose voice seemed to be rattling around in my head spouting prophecy." Andy wondered if somehow it had been ordained that Tera was with them and not just a whim of his mother. He remembered when he was practicing his empathic skills that a great responsibility hung around Tera's spirit, perhaps this was part of that.

"Are you ready then?" the key asked.

"Why yes, I believe I am," Andy replied feeling a little better about his riddle solving skills.

Andy phased back into reality, the demons started to salivate, getting ready to pounce.

"So how exactly do we get out of here chief dragon?" the key asked him.

"Well, certainly not the way I came in," Andy replied.

Andy looked up. Thousands of feet above was the roof of the amphitheater and also the underside of the mountain. His plan was simple. Only problem was, he was not entirely sure it would work. He was going to transform back to a dragon, grab the key, then try to phase them both out together.

Andy made his transformation, the place where they stood was large enough to fit his big body.

"You do know that the second you touch me, the demons will be free to attack."

I know, Andy said speaking to her mind. *But I know of no other way.*

"I am ready when you are, Andros," the key said.

How did you know my name? Actually, never mind I already know, prophecy.

The key smiled at him knowingly.

Okay, it's now or never.

Andy focused everything inward. He could see the cells of his body, their molecular structure. He then looked at the key to see if he could see hers. He could, but it was very intricate and complicated. Andy needed to touch her and then force her cell structure to phase with his. The concentration this was taking had sweat forming across his dragon's brow. The demons were moving within their circle now, making a clockwise rotation. Apparently within that narrow band they were allowed to move but not out of it. Andy stretched forth his dragon claw so his talons would close around the key's torso. The demons were in a hyper frenzy now, clawing and climbing over each other in their frustration to break loose. He could see that some of them were flying demons and would no doubt give chase, but by then it wouldn't matter. At least he hoped that was the case.

"It's time", the key said.

Trying to hold everything together in his mind, Andy's claw grasped the key. Then all hell broke loose, literally.

The demons were running and flying towards them at an incredible speed. Andy could still feel a demon's hot breath on his neck just before he phased out with the key and the demons blew right through them. They circled and clawed the air of where Andy and the key stood but, they could not touch them. Gathering his legs under him and stretching out his wings, Andy leapt into the air as he propelled himself upward, the key held firmly in his grasp. Looking below the demons gave chase, the ones that could fly anyway. Swords were out and the demons were slashing at anything and everything, but were unable to connect. Andy saw the roof coming closer.

I really hope this works, Andy said.

It already has my young dragon, the key replied as they shot through solid rock and continued up and up, to the top of the mountain. Andy flew for all he was worth. Even though he was phased to pass through matter, it still caused a drag on his flying and he had to exert more energy than if he was flying through plain old air. Suddenly they broke through and out into the night sky. Andy phased back, and as he hovered, placed the key on his back. The exertion had left him breathless and he was taking great dragon gasps of air to bring his breathing under control. Andy looked around and realized how high they were. Looking up he felt like the stars were so close he could touch them.

Where are we? he asked.

"We are above the highest mountain in Otherwhere," the key answered him.

Andy turned his long neck to better see the key. His empathic ability could feel her joy at being free.

What happens now? Andy asked.

"Now you must take me to thy father, so that he may complete his task."

Using his dragon sight, Andy could just make out the cabin at the base of the mountain. Wheeling to the left he started his descent. Even being so high, the wind was warm as it rushed past them. Distance was deceiving as it felt like it took a lot longer to reach the ground then he would have thought, but eventually he reached the base of the mountain and landed in a field on the far side of the cabin. Seeing their flight, everyone had come outside to greet them.

After introductions were made, Andy gave them a full accounting of what had happened. There were a lot of open mouths when Andy told them about his gift.

"By the gods!" Gael said. "That is a mighty gift, brother."

"It actually makes me feel complete now," Andy said. "For the longest time I always felt I was meant to not have a gift, so I never really missed it, until it came."

Redlin put his hands on his son's shoulders. "It also makes me very happy," the wizard said. "In a small way I had blamed myself for your lack of a gift by having you born in another world."

Andy hugged his father. "It's alright now, Dad."

"Yes it is," he said smiling. "Now, I suppose you can tell me what happens next?" Redlin asked the key.

The key just shook her head. "That is your quest master wizard, but I will tell you this, it won't unfold the way you think it will."

"Great, you sound just like Killian," Redlin said as the key stood there smiling at him.

"So what now Dad?" Andy asked his father.

Redlin was scratching at his beard, thinking, suddenly he had an idea.

"Everyone on the dragons," he said. "We are going up."

Andy and Gael were walking further out into the field to give themselves room to change.

"Do you know what he has in mind?" Gael asked his brother.

"I have no idea," Andy said as he changed into his dragon self.

***

Redlin scanned the night sky from his son's back. Abby and the key were with him. Bowen, Tera and Nia rode on Gael.

Dad, what are we looking for? Andy asked as his wings beat a steady rhythm through the night air. Every once in a while, he would catch a warm updraft and let it take him higher.

"I will know it when I see it son," Redlin replied. "For right now, I want to get between the mountain you came out of and the island in the middle of the lake, once we find it that is."

I think the sun is coming up, Redlin, Gael said. *It's getting lighter over there. It's hard to tell but that could be a body of water.*

"You could be right," Redlin replied. "Keep heading east."

Redlin had thought about what he would do once this moment came. When he first had his vision of Killian, he had been standing on the middle of the rainbow that had connected the island and the mountain, and that is where he was going to look for him.

The sun broke the horizon and momentarily blinded everyone in the process.

That's definitely water, Andy said. *And I think I see an island.*

"Yes, that is it I'm sure."

Now where? Gael asked as he caught an updraft and started to soar to give his wings a rest.

"Just a little bit more, and then I want you both to hover."

Not for too long I hope, Andy said. *We are pretty high up and I would hate to start free falling from exhaustion.*

"Trust me," the wizard said. "Abby, could you do me a favor?"

"Of course," Abby replied.

"I want you to keep aware of anything the death dagger may tell you when we meet Killian."

"Do you think he may be a demon impersonation?"

"I have no idea what he is, but let's not take chances."

They flew for another thirty minutes. Redlin looked over at Bowen and smiled. The captain was writing furiously from his vantage point aboard Gael's back, Nia looking intently over his shoulder. Tera seemed to be in a meditative state. Since Andy arrived back with the key, Tera had withdrawn into herself. Something was up with her, and Redlin had promised himself once they dealt with the situation with Killian, he would sit down and have a talk with her. Judging they were equidistant between the island and the mountain, Redlin had the dragons hover. Removing his ring that Trystan and Eriyn had made for him, he put it up to his eye as the flames started to dance around the band. The rainbow appeared in his vision as he suspected it would. At the crest of the rainbow, he saw a golden door, which he was pretty sure the key would be able to open.

"Andy, start flying straight ahead."

Ok Dad, Andy replied.

As Andy started flying, Redlin would tell him to veer left or right. Suddenly they passed through some invisible barrier and the door became visible to all.

By the gods! Gael exclaimed.

Before the door was a big expanse of rock with enough room for the dragons to land and transform. Redlin took the lead as they came up to the door.

"Do we knock?" Nia asked.

"I don't think that is the kind of door you put your hand to, lassie," Bowen remarked as he took a few more notes.

"The captain is right," the key said. "It is death for anyone to touch this door but me."

"Well madame," Redlin said. "If you please."

The key smiled at Redlin as she walked up to the door and placed both hands on it. There was a white nimbus that surrounded her hands and slowly spread up her arms and eventually her entire body. There was a humming sound, and to Redlin it looked as if the door was vibrating. Then there was a loud crash, like the detonation of crystal that sent shards flying straight up, leaving a wide opening.

Just then, Killian came flying out and grabbed Redlin by the throat and started to squeeze. Both Andy and Gael had grabbed onto the source and were ready to unleash a hellish fury against this person.

"Killian! No!" the key shouted.

Hearing her voice, Killian dropped the wizard and turned to face the woman who spoke. Redlin was gasping for breath as Tera flew over to him to help him up, with concern and anguish written all over her face.

"I'm alright Tera," Redlin said coughing.

"Tallika," Killian said as he embraced the person everyone called the key. "Finally, I am free."

"Tallika?" Abby asked.

"That is her name, death's mistress," Killian said.

"You know me?" Abby asked feeling stunned.

"I know all of you, but I did not know who waited outside my door until it was finally opened."

"Abby?" Redlin asked.

Abby just shook her head, indicating that she felt nothing with her death dagger. Killian chuckled.

"I see," Killian said. "You thought I might be one of Meliakken's impostors."

"For someone who has been locked away for eons, you seem to be well versed in what has been happening," Redlin said with wariness.

"My prison was not like you think, master wizard, but my origins will not be told here, that is for another story. Come inside."

Everyone followed Killian through the opening that had only recently been occupied by the golden door. Once passing through, everyone gasped at what they saw. It was like stepping into a world bursting with so much color that it dazzled the eyes. It was a land of rolling hills that was teeming with wildlife. Multi-colored birds were circling overhead as they walked up a set of marble stairs to a porch that surrounded what appeared to be a mini-mansion in Redlin's mind. Killian had everyone sit down on the chairs and benches that were available and produced drinks and bowls of fruits and everyone had their fill.

"So what happens now that you are free?" Redlin asked taking a sip of his wine. "This is most excellent by the way."

"I'm happy it is to your liking, it is made here from the

grapes in the valley just below the house. As to your question, what happens now is we get ready for the battle that is coming. Meliakken and I have opposed each other since the dawn of creation itself. His power however has long surpassed mine. It was he who imprisoned me and set the magic as such that whoever freed me I would be bound to join them in battle."

"So if one of his demons had gotten the key before me, you would be fighting against us, is that right?" Andy asked.

"That is correct first dragon, thankfully it hasn't gone that way."

"First thing we do is wait," Killian said.

"Wait for what?" Redlin asked.

"A visitor, master wizard. One who must give you something prior to the battle. She is on her way here now."

"She?" Redlin asked.

"All will be revealed in time. For now, I have something for some of you, gifts you could say."

"What sort of gifts?" Redlin asked warily.

"Do not worry master wizard," Killian said laughing. "They do not come with any attachments. Most of you have been rewarded in the past with gifts or powers from the gods and goddess. But there are three here that I am instructed to pass on special instruments of power. Captain, will you come here please?"

Bowen walked over to where Killian stood next to a pedestal. Picking up a long burgundy colored wooden case, he handed it to the captain. Bowen opened it and peered inside.

"By the gods!" Bowen exclaimed. "It's a solid gold spyglass," he said lifting it out.

"It is more than that Captain," Killian said. "Think of a place and put it to your eye."

Bowen did as he was instructed, and his mouth fell open as he started shaking.

"Bowen, what is it?" Andy asked concerned for his friend.

"The Grey Morning, I can see it. No matter where I point this, I can see exactly where it is and what is happening. By the gods! They've opened up the ale barrel and the crew is lounging around drunk. Oh, there will be hell to pay when I get back," Bowen said huffing.

Everyone had to laugh at that.

Bowen tenderly put the spyglass back in its case. "Thank you, sir, this is an amazing gift."

"It is well earned, Captain. For all the service you have provided Vasara without question. Nia."

Nia got up and walked over.

"You are the newest to this company, but your contributions have been more than you know. This gift is actually for you and the one you love, but it is you who must safeguard it."

Killian picked up a necklace with a small charm made of silver attached to it. Stamped on the face of it was the image of an hourglass with running sand. Killian put it around her head and let it fall upon her chest.

"As long as you wear this about your neck, it will stop the aging process. Take it off or lose it and your body will continue to age as it normally does."

It took a second for it to register in Nia's mind what this meant, and her eyes went wide. Killian smiled to see her wonder.

"Yes," he said, "as long as you wear this you will live as long as your dragon."

Abby jumped up and hugged her friend fiercely as the tears were streaming down her cheeks. Geal's eyes were also full as he looked on in happiness at what they had been given.

"Now this is no shield," Killian explained. "It cannot stop you from getting killed or anything like that."

"It's okay," Nia breathed clutching the charm in her fist. "It is more than enough, and you have no idea how happy you have made me," she said looking over at Gael.

"Tera," Killian called.

Tera stood up and folded her wings as she walked over to Killian. Redlin noted that she walked as if carrying a great weight.

"Come inside with me," Killian said. "Your gift I must give in secret."

The wizard watched as they disappeared inside the house.

"Why do you suppose they did that Dad?" Andy asked his father.

"I don't know," Redlin answered. "But I think we would do Tera a great service if we didn't ask her about it. If we are meant to know, she will tell us."

Andy nodded in agreement.

It wasn't long before Killian and Tera came walking out of the house. Redlin could see a necklace around Tera's neck that also had a charm like Nia's but he could not make out what it was. It's as if the image was obscured by magic. Tera herself still seemed to be carrying a great weight, but he saw resolve in her eyes. He felt like she was going to be alright.

"So how long do we have to wait here?" Andy asked now that everyone had their gifts. "We are running out of time."

"Oh, I don't think time means very much to this individual," Killian said pointing down the path.

Everyone turned to where he was pointing and sat stunned at who was approaching.

Chapter 20

"Loki, what's wrong?" Dain asked startled as the wizard sat bolt upright after being at the source with Andros. Leah was with Dain and ran over to help Loki to his feet. They were in the sitting room of the castle library.

"Andros, something has happened," Loki said with concern written all over his face.

Loki went on to tell Dain of his encounter with Andros at the source and how they were trying to figure out if he had the gift of phasing.

"What do you think happened to him?" Dain asked as he automatically readjusted his sword whenever there was talk of a threat. Being a wizard he no longer needed it, but he always felt naked without the sword with the serpent wrapped hilt that was the mark of all Border Lands generals.

"He was alone in the dragon maze when he contacted me, with no one to watch him as he traveled to the source. My guess is he was attacked by whatever was in the maze with him."

"By the goddess!" Leah said pushing her blonde hair over her pointed ears. "Do you think he is alright?"

"I have absolutely no way of knowing. I don't even know if he got his gift," Loki said clearly frustrated and worried. "Come, we will see if Sibila can see anything with her sight."

As they left the library, they traversed the outer hall of the castle that eventually brought them to the rear garden. Paolo and Acacia were standing next to the fountain with the rearing unicorn that was the symbol of the house of Taiyo, with them were Nyle and Sibila. Several groomsmen stood behind them holding the reins of seven horses.

"Ah, Loki!" Paolo said hailing the wizard. "We were just about to send for you, we have been discussing our next steps." Paolo took one look at the wizard to know something was amiss. "What is wrong?"

"I'm not sure your Majesty," Loki replied. "Sibila, would you be able to see something for me."

"If it is within my power, master wizard," she replied.

"Loki, what has happened," Acacia asked.

Loki went on to tell them of his encounter with Andros and all that had transpired.

"You want to know if he is safe," Sibila said, "and if he has found his gift."

"Yes," Loki responded. Loki had never felt more worried for the dragon/man that he regarded almost as a son.

Sibila closed her eyes as a fiery nimbus encircled her body. She stood like this for several minutes, probing and searching the stars and universe for direction and guidance. Finally the glow around her body dissipated as she opened her eyes.

"Of Andros the black and the others I can see nothing. It is as if they are being shrouded from me on purpose."

"Why would that be?" Nyle asked.

Sibila smiled at the man she loved and placed a hand on his cheek.

"Because my knight, if certain things are obscured to me, it also means they are obscured for Meliakken as well."

"So there is no way of knowing then," Leah said.

"Not so," Sibila told her. "There is knowing, and there is knowing."

"By the goddess, Sibila. You're talking in riddles like the

first time we met," Leah said blowing a lock of hair out of her eye in frustration.

Sibila winked at her.

"What exactly do you mean?" Loki asked her.

"Just this, that if Andros had failed or been killed, the pain and grief would be screaming through the universe at what had been lost. At the very least I think we can say his part of the quest has not failed as of yet. We all have our parts to play in this to keep everything in balance until the final meeting. I suggest we concentrate on ours, lest we be the ones that bring about Vasara's demise."

"Well that is succinctly put," Dain said. "So what is our next move?"

"Now it is time for Nyle to take us to the prince," Sibila said.

"If I can," Nyle said with a small amount of apprehension.

Sibila placed both hands on the side of his face. "You can do this my Sol. The sun touches everything on this world, and somewhere it is hitting your son and the prince. This is why we are by the unicorn statue. There is a link here between the unicorn and the Summus Re'em. You must find it and follow it. This is in your hands now my love."

Nyle looked over at Paolo. "There was a lot less pressure when my only job was to protect your life, Sire."

Paolo laughed and slapped his friend on the shoulder.

"I have always trusted you with my life Nyle, since that first day when I didn't even have a crown. I still do. And I don't hesitate to trust the life of my son in your hands as well."

"Nor I," Acacia said hugging her friend as she pushed her rapier to the side to keep the hilt from jabbing Nyle.

"Thank you, that means a lot to me. I guess I better get started with this."

Nyle closed his eyes and held one hand towards the sun and the other towards the statue.

"Sibila, what is he doing exactly?" Loki whispered.

"He is feeling for the life force of the sun that is currently touching the prince and the unicorn. He is also trying to draw a connection between himself and his son, Cathal."

"What if the sun isn't visible where they are?" Dain asked.

"Shhhh," Acacia said. "He doesn't need any doubts just now."

"Oh, right. Sorry," Dain said.

Nyle had beads of sweat running down his forehead. Loki could see the sun's rays clearly defined as Nyle slowly manipulated them, as if he were searching for just the right one. It was dizzying how fast he was cycling through them. Then he stopped.

"I think I have them," Nyle said excitedly. "It is very faint, but I believe it could be them."

"Well done my love," Sibila said. "Now take us there."

Nyle's hands started to make a circular motion as he drew his fire from the sun and everything around him. A ring of fire twelve feet high appeared in front of them. Now his hands were moving faster now, making the ring spin at an incredible speed. Suddenly there was a loud snap and everyone gasped at what they saw.

"By the gods!" Loki exclaimed. "Where is that?"

What they saw through the portal were tall mountain peaks that formed a ring around a valley.

"It is Otherwhere," Sibila said. "At least a part of it."

"Are you sure they are there?" Dain asked. "I don't see any movement."

"It is where I feel them," Nyle said with some effort as he strained to keep the portal open. "I think we better go in quickly, I'm finding it hard to maintain the connection."

"Everyone mount up," the king said.

They all went to their horses that were standing by. Paolo took the reins of Nyle's horse and led it through so Nyle could hold the portal open. Once everyone was on the other side, Nyle stepped through and let the portal close behind them.

"I must say, that is a lot smoother traveling than the portals we use Loki," Dain said smiling.

"Hmmm," Loki said with his eyebrows drawing down. "We can't all travel the same way, Dain. How boring would that be."

Leah burst out laughing.

"I'm going to scout ahead," Leah said extending her talon spear and lifting off into the air, her lavender wings beating a rhythm to take her higher.

"Be careful, love," Dain called after her.

"You know me," she called back before disappearing from view.

"Yes, I do," Dain said to everyone around, "that is why I said it."

"Paolo, you've been here for ten years," Loki said. "What can we expect?"

"I'm sorry Loki, Acacia and I have never been in this part of Otherwhere. In fact I thought the area where Zana held us captive was all there was to this place."

"Otherwhere is bigger on the inside than on the outside," Sibila remarked.

"More riddles?" Loki asked.

"No master wizard," Sibila said. "That is just the magic of this place. The further in you go the bigger it gets. You have to experience it to understand."

"I think I know what she means Loki," Nyle said.

"I'm all ears," Loki responded.

Nyle was running his fingers through his hair as he framed his thoughts.

"When I first came here to rescue the King and Queen, I came upon Zana's cottage. It was small and unassuming, but once I stepped inside it was like I had stepped into the grand hall of the White Castle. It was huge. I have a feeling this whole world is like that."

"That would mean this place is practically limitless," Dain said in awe. "I would think this would be the place where only gods can live."

"You are not too far off the mark, General," Sibila said.

Suddenly Leah came flying back in a hurry.

"Prepare yourselves!" she shouted as she flew low over their heads before turning around to head back the way she came.

"Dain, shield everyone with me as we ride!" Loki said.

"You got it!" Dain replied.

Everyone spurred their horses forward to meet whatever threat was headed their way while the two wizards plunged themselves into the source of the gods to create a dome of protection over all of them. As they crested the hill they stopped and could see down into the valley. Coming out of a cave mouth at the base of one of the mountains was a swarm of demons. Some running and some flying. Loki could see Leah impaling demon after demon, her spear was a blur as it rapidly found its targets.

"Leah, come back!" Dain shouted.

Leah broke off and flew back to the protection of the shield as she settled behind Dain on his horse.

"What is the plan?" Paolo asked. "I don't believe we have long before they are upon us."

No sooner had Paolo spoken than the entire horde of demons stopped. All the ones that were in the air settled to the ground.

"Now that's a first," Dain said. "I've never seen an army of demons stop their forward movement once they had already committed to battle."

"Something is coming," Loki said. "Look, their ranks are parting."

As everyone watched a wide swath appeared as the demons in the center pushed to either side. Something large was coming out of the mountain. As it got closer, they could see it dwarfed the demons easily, but as it got even closer, the demons started to look like children in comparison. It was now close enough to give them all a clear view. It was a being with a man's torso and face that was bearded except the beard appeared to be moving. It also had very large black wings. Under a heavy brow, two red eyes peered back at them. His hair, like his beard was black and moving. It was made up of scores of snake heads, each hissing and blowing fire.

"By the goddess!" Leah exclaimed. "What is that thing."

"He is the god of monsters of the underworld," Sibila said, "which means he can touch all worlds. If Andros were here he could probably tell you its name from the world he was born in, for it is the same here."

"And what is that?" Acacia asked.

"Typhon," Sibila said.

For some unknown reason that name filled Loki with dread.

"Well oracle," Loki said. "Any guidance on how we should attack him?"

Sibila smiled at him. "This is part of Sol's task, master wizard."

"Me?" Nyle asked. "You have a lot of faith in me Sibila."

"More than you could imagine my Sol," she said smiling.

"And I suppose while Nyle is dealing with Typhon, the rest of us have to take on that host of demons by ourselves," Leah said.

"As long as Typhon is on the field of battle, the demons will not move without his leave. He knows that Sol is here, no doubt he was sent by Meliakken," Sibila said. "He will want to fight him in single combat."

Sibila took both of Nyle's hands in her own. Fire erupted around her entire being as she nodded to Nyle. Understanding, Nyle nodded back and his body also burst into flames.

"This is your task Sol. Fail and Vasara fails with you. In all things, even in your doubts, follow your nature and use that disciplined military mind of yours. As oracle and your mate, this is all the advice I am allowed to give," Sibila said. "Are you ready?"

Nyle nodded and took what he truly believed to be the hardest steps of his life.

***

Nyle walked forward, and as he did, Typhon started to advance as well. The rest of the demons stood still. Apparently, this was going to be single combat. He could tell from Typhon's steady advance that he viewed this as a competition of equals. Why the god of monsters would view him in that light he wasn't really sure since he didn't feel himself anywhere near his equal in strength and power. But Nyle used this time to his advantage. He knew Typhon would not attack until they had sufficiently stared each other down. He was savoring this to make his victory all that much sweeter.

It was time to focus. Time to bring his military mind to bear. Typhon had certain advantages that were visible, his wings for one, which meant he could fly. His size was another, but that could be turned to a disadvantage in his maneuverability. Third was the hundred or so snake heads that made up his hair and were spewing fire.

Nyle decided to tackle the problems one at a time. First was flight. He started feeling the fire flowing through his veins. As it raced up and down, he brought all his focus to one spot, right between his shoulder blades. He was a manipulator of fire, so he imagined the shape of fiery wings in his mind. Slowly he pushed the fire outward to fill that image. His eyes were closed, but he could hear everyone behind him gasp, so he assumed it must be working. The image was taking hold and Nyle felt it become a part of him. He opened his eyes and folded his wings forward to look at them. They were translucent with veins of fire running through them like veins on a leaf, the edges were dancing flames. He slowly moved them back and forth, feeling their lift.

He raised his face to the sun and began to draw its power. Typhon followed his gaze to see what he was looking at. Suddenly the monster chuckled and that did not make Nyle feel good at all. What did this god know that he didn't. Typhon spread his hands and started moving them in a circular motion. At first Nyle didn't know what the beast could be up to. After a few minutes it became clear. A large cloud bank was moving in, covering the area on which they were standing effectively blotting out the sun. Nyle could still feel its power but it was greatly reduced.

"Well played," Nyle said, but he was not beat yet.

Nyle started drawing energy from everything around him, including the demons, which gave him a vast source of fire. He let it build up, felt it filling his entire being. Typhon started to lift off the ground as his wings created a mighty wind. Nyle had to brace himself from being pushed backwards. He started his own wings moving and feeling their rhythm through his shoulder blades, they became a natural extension of himself. The wind that Typhon was creating lifted Nyle up on a blanket of warm air. Never having flown before, Nyle was having a crash course on how to keep his balance while in flight. It seemed awkward and jerky as he tried banking left and then right.

Typhon let out a roar as every snake head shot liquid fire at him. Nyle created a shield of fire which effectively absorbed most of the shots, although some did get through. Being made of fire, he figured he would not be hurt by it, but this fire was different, it burned hotter than any flame he had ever experienced, more so than his own.

Sol, can you hear me? Sibila's voice came to his mind.

I hear you, Nyle responded dodging more fire blasts as he decided to use his maneuverability and streaked low over the demon horde, Typhon's fire blast taking some of them out.

Beware of hell's fire my love, it can kill you.

I was actually coming to the same conclusion darling, Nyle said as he picked up speed and started to fly straight up, leaving a trail of fire in his wake.

Suddenly Typhon stopped and hovered. In a big booming voice, he called to Nyle.

"I know thee, Sol. Our spirits have contested over the ages and on many worlds. The outcome is always the same, you die. Fortunately, you are spared the memories of this disgrace."

Nyle slowed his speed and hovered just above Sibila and the others.

"I wish to make you an offer," the god of monsters said.

Nyle was puzzled. Why was he doing this he wondered. The demons as one were looking skyward, salivating, waiting for the word that would release them. Nyle decided to hear him out. If nothing else, it gave him time to think on a strategy.

"What is your offer?" Nyle asked as he yelled across the space.

"You may not realize your full power yet, but you have the ability to move between worlds. I can show you this power and you can take your friends and leave Vasara alive, never to return."

"And surrender the rest of Vasara's inhabitants to Meliakken's oppression," Nyle said.

"He is going to take it anyway. This way you and your friends here can live out your life in peace."

Nyle didn't respond. He just hovered, thinking, his raptor training kicking in. Nyle knew Typhon would not make this offer unless he thought the battle was in doubt. But the god had told him that Sol had lost in all their encounters. "Thank god I don't remember any of those losses," Nyle thought to himself.

"What is thy answer, Sol?" Typhon asked, the snakes on his head whipping back and forth in a frenzy, itching for someone to bite and burn.

Sibila, what do I do? Nyle asked speaking to her mind.

You must decide according to your nature my love.

Nyle already knew what his nature would say, fight. The biggest weapon in the training ring was surprise, and suddenly he had an idea as he smiled to himself.

Sibila, when I tell you, can you blast an opening through the clouds?

Nyle could actually feel her smiling as she guessed what he was planning.

Just let me know when my knight.

He was about to deliver his answer, before Typhon had a chance to speak again or raise any defenses. Nyle started streaking towards him, a trail of fire racing behind him. Typhon was momentarily taken aback to see Nyle racing at him without any warning at all. The god of monsters was so puffed up with his own self-importance that he couldn't comprehend an enemy not engaging in dialogue with him, even if to shout their defiance. Nyle was going to show Typhon this was not the same Sol he's faced many times over the eons.

He could now see Typhon was regaining his composure from his surprise and was preparing to strike.

Now Sibila!

The oracle was on fire as she clapped her hands together and a beam of fire shot up between Nyle and Typhon. Sibila must have spoken to Loki and Dain, because the wizards had also added their power to hers to rip a hole in the cloud cover. As soon as Nyle reached the hole, the sun's rays hit his body. The power now surging through him was almost euphoric as it filled his being. Taking his aim, he held his hands out in front of him as the power of the sun was shot directly at Typhon's chest. It hit squarely and the god went tumbling end over end as his back finally slammed into the mountain. Scores of his snakes had disintegrated in the blast, making it seem like half of his hair was burned off.

Typhon roared in pain and fury. Nyle assumed it was probably the first real pain he had ever felt. Sibila and the wizards couldn't keep the rip open forever and let the clouds come together because they hastily needed to raise a shield as Typhon released an assault on them.

"How dare you!" Typhon screamed. "You have abused the trust of adversaries. I had hoped the battle would be restricted to just you and I, but now you will bring death upon your friends."

Typhon yelled something in a guttural and savage language as he released the demon horde. It was now thousands against seven. Six really since he would need to concentrate all his efforts on Typhon. He needed to think quickly because the god was gathering himself together to strike. His one asset now was maneuverability, and he began to employ it.

Nyle started flying in a zig zag fashion, banking left and right at random, Typhon firing hellfire at him in an effort to land a strike. Most missed and some took out a few score demons. Nyle suddenly had another idea.

He created a shield of fire and extended it in front of him as he flew low to the ground, when he was about three feet off the ground he flew directly into the demons. Any that were before him were instantly vaporized. What he was counting on however, was that in his rage, Typhon would rain hell fire on his own demons. Large gaps started appearing in their ranks, but that is when Nyle had suddenly realized there was something he didn't account for, demon lords.

The demon lords had magic and ten very large flying ones had zeroed in on him. Energy bolts encircled his body, disrupting his concentration and flow of energy. Suddenly he hit the ground and was tumbling end over end like a rag doll as his body impacted with a boulder. As his eyes refocused, he looked up and saw a star descending from the heavens. As it got closer he realized it wasn't a star but Sibila in all her fiery glory, her hair lit up like dancing flames as she landed with the force of an explosion where the wind repercussion wiped every demon within the immediate vicinity on its back.

Nyle shook his head and hit it with his hand to clear his mind as Sibila quickly erected a shield of fire around them.

"Thanks for that, love," Nyle said kissing her cheek as he gathered his power.

Sibila could see the fierceness and resolve in his eyes.

"You know what to do now my Sol," she said smiling.

"Yes I do," he responded. "It's time to end this. Get yourself clear as soon as I leave."

Sibila nodded in response.

Nyle spread his wings of fire. Typhon was headed right for

them and he needed to lure him away from Sibila. Shooting off like a rocket, he sped directly for Typhon. The god was shooting hellfire but Nyle, with precision and accuracy was able to swerve slightly left and right to avoid being hit.

Just before he came within a hundred yards of Typhon, Nyle shot straight up for the clouds.

"Come back you coward!" Typhon screamed. "You cannot hide from me in the clouds."

Hiding was not Nyle's plan. He took a quick look behind him.

"Come on you bastard, follow me," Nyle said aloud to himself.

Nyle smiled as he saw the enraged god take the bait. Now he needed speed. Using every ounce of firepower he had in him, he shot like an arrow towards a target. He was taking a risk by using all his energy, but he couldn't think of anything else to do. Now he was in the thickness of the cloud bank, totally cut off from gathering any fire from below. Nyle could hear the snarls of Typhon coming below him and gaining speed. He knew the god could no longer see him, so he flew horizontally through the cloud cover so Typhon wouldn't know where he came out. Nyle kept flying, waiting for a certain sound. His reserves were almost gone when it came. Typhon screamed his fury as he exited the cloud bank and came out on top.

"Sol! Where are you? Fight damn you!"

Nyle smirked as he shot straight up.

"I'm here you pathetic excuse of a god," Nyle said as he threw his curse and the full power of the sun ignited his body.

Nyle made two slashing motions. He wasn't using hellfire, but fire from the heavens that sliced across either side of the god's head, cutting through all the snake heads as they fell to the earth far below.

Typhon roared with anger. A whip of fire suddenly appeared

in the god's fist as he whipped it towards Nyle with deadly accuracy. It wrapped around his body and pinned his wings and arms to his sides. Typhon started to descend as he swung Nyle around his head in a circle like a lasso. Nyle struggled to break free, but the whip was made of hell fire and it was starting to cut through the shield he had erected around himself. He was losing his concentration and focus which made it very hard to use his power effectively.

Fight according to your nature my Sol, came Sibila's voice in his mind.

Even though he was spinning through the air about to be dashed against a mountainside, Nyle fell back on what made him the most fearsome raptor captain ever. It was something his father had taught him, through fear and pain of course as was all his father's lessons. His father would take Nyle up to the high peaks in the Macedon Mountains. He would set him on a narrow cliff face where the wind was whipping in all directions with incredible gusts that threatened to blow you off. His father would leave him there for a day. If he came back and Nyle was in anything other than a calm and steady state, he would leave him there for another day. He endured a week of clinging to the rocks and screaming every time his father returned. It wasn't until that last day that he saw something, a hawk. Another raptor who seemed to be hovering on the air currents right in front of him. As if it were studying Nyle in curiosity. What struck Nyle was the free-flowing movement the bird exhibited, as if he were his own master and he either bent the elements to his will or he rode along with them, and suddenly everything clicked into place. The next day Nyle's father found him sitting cross-legged on the very edge of the cliff with his eyes closed and a look of peace on his face as the winds shrieked around him.

Nyle closed his eyes and felt the circular motion the god was putting him through. He could feel the lines of force, his mind's eye slowly touching it, almost caressing it until it became a part of him, and once he stepped into it, no matter how fast he was spinning, in his body and soul he was still and stationary. He felt the power of the sun once more, but in his heightened state he could see what he was missing. He had only been drawing from the outer edge of the sun's corona layer. Now he could see all the way to the core.

He was hesitant to reach out for it. His senses could feel the enormity of it and on some level he feared it.

Reach for your birthright my love, Sibila's voice came to him once again.

Nyle looked past his fear and stretched out with his mind. When he connected with the core, a bright light exploded behind his eyes and he found himself in a totally different place. He was standing on a precipice overlooking the core of the sun. Looking down it was the most incredible sight he had ever seen. It was like a ball of molten fire. It pulsated from dark red to intense white. Nyle assumed he was here in spirit since he doubted his body could ever withstand the heat generated by the core. Suddenly he saw a figure walking towards him. He was robed in black and had a snowy white beard and red hair. His eyes were a piercing corn-flower blue.

"Welcome Sol," he said.

"You know me?" Nyle asked.

"I have never met this incarnation of you, but only Sol may come here."

"What is your name?" Nyle asked.

"Ilios," he said. "I am the guardian of this place."

"Well, Ilios," Nyle said. "Are you able to tell me what I am supposed to do?"

"No mystery there my friend," Ilios said smiling. "Jump."

Nyle stared at him for a few moments before it sunk in what Ilios was asking. "What will happen when I do?"

"You need to take the step to find that out," Ilios said.

Nyle took a deep breath and looked down. "Well, I guess I have done this before in some past life."

"Actually, this will be the first time Sol has jumped in the core," Ilios said.

"What do you mean?" Nyle asked surprised by that statement. "I thought you said only Sol could stand here."

"That's true, only Sol can, I never said that one ever has. For whatever reason, you are the first."

Nyle pondered that for a moment. "Could it be that no other Sol before him had ever tapped into the core of the sun's power?" he said to himself. He wondered if maybe this was why Typhon had always won all their contests.

"I guess this is a leap of faith," Nyle said aloud.

"Most things are," Ilios said.

"You wouldn't care to jump with me?" Nyle asked.

Ilios actually laughed at that. "I can always give you a push if you need it."

Nyle smiled. He found himself liking this guardian. He knew he needed to do this, otherwise why was he here. Taking three deep calming breaths, he put a hand over his heart as he stepped off the precipice. Nothing could have prepared him for what happened next.

As he fell, Nyle crossed his arms over his chest and closed his eyes. This was not his body that was falling, but his very soul and the essence of all he was. His entire life was laid bare before him, all his failures and triumphs, his sadness and fears as well as his joys. He was being made anew. Anything that was buried was purged, like metal in a crucible when all the dross is burned away. Nyle was slipping into the core now, becoming one with it, formless and pure energy. He knew his body was feeling it, the power was almost uncontainable, and he was certain that anyone looking at him right now would be instantly blinded. The sun was accepting him as Sol, baptizing and purifying him. How long he stayed in the core he had no idea. It could have been moments or eons, whatever it was he felt that time had not moved where his body was.

Nyle found himself starting to ascend. As he exited the core he looked at himself. He was pure fire in the shape of a man. He truly was Sol now. Stepping back onto the precipice he came to stand next to Ilios.

"Well that wasn't so bad, was it?" Ilios asked.

Nyle couldn't help it, he had to laugh.

"And that response right there, my friend is what this was all about," Ilios said.

"What do you mean?" Nyle asked.

"When you arrived here, all the shame and guilt of your life, the many lives you took, even the failures with your own son, hung around your neck like a black chain attached to a boulder. You could never have become all that you were truly capable of until you had let that go."

Ilios put both hands on Nyle's shoulder. "I know the pain and hurt your own father has caused you. Know this, I am not only the guardian here, but the sun's very spirit, and this day forward, you are my son."

Nyle broke in that moment. A grown man crying for the father he should have had and also for the one who claimed him now. Ilios held him until he was spent, his purification now complete.

"Now my son, you have the power to defeat Typhon. Go and show the god of monsters what it means to burn."

Ilios touched Nyle on the forehead and he momentarily blacked out. When he opened his eyes, he was back in his body, one hand on Typhon's whip, but he was no longer spinning. His eyes locked with the god's and he saw fear there. The hell fire that once burned him felt like it had no effect. Nyle sized the god up.

"Size," he thought to himself. He felt it was time to put things on an even footing. Focusing, he felt his body expand, getting larger until he was as big as Typhon.

"Let's finish this you and I," Nyle said in a booming voice that everyone could hear clearly.

Seeing his whip no longer had an effect, Typhon let it disappear.

"I am a god," Typhon said snarling. "Do you really think you can destroy me?"

"I'm not a god," Nyle said, "and I guess we are about to find out."

The cloud cover was back, but it didn't matter. Nyle carried the sun's core within his spirit. He didn't need to draw fire from the things around him. Thrusting both hands in front of him, Nyle released his attack as two razor sharp energy bolts went streaking towards Typhon. The god quickly erected a hasty shield only to have it shatter, and even though the impact was less it created a burning hole in Typhon's chest. As he crashed against the mountainside, he caused an avalanche that took out several thousand demons, but there were still many thousands more. Being occupied with Typhon kept Nyle from helping the other's. Suddenly he had an idea. He knew they were close.

Cathal, can you hear me? He sent out to his son.

Dad, where are you? came Cathal's reply.

No time son, is the prince with you?

Yes, and the unicorns.

Excellent, I had hoped that was the case. Listen carefully, you need to follow my thought and lead the unicorns to where we are. I sense you are not far. Can you do that?

I can Dad, answered Cathal. *I don't know how, but I can feel where you are. We are coming now.*

Thank you, son. And Cathal.

Yeah Dad?

I love you.

Nyle could feel the emotion coming through as Cathal responded.

I love you too, Dad.

Nyle knew this is what it was all about, love. Love for family and friends and even people you didn't even know. This is what separated them from their enemies. All they knew was power, and that in itself was such a hollow thing.

Typhon was getting up now. He wasn't so hasty that he would charge Nyle. Instead, he stood there as if trying to decide how to handle this threat that he never had encountered before. Nyle too waited, but for a different reason. He turned his head slightly and listened. Then he heard it. The sound of a thousand hoof beats. Cresting the hills into the valley was a sea of unicorns, their horns blazing as they out flanked the demons. Sibila and the wizards were holding their own against the horde that was attacking from the front. Great clouds of black oily vapor from the dead demons were being carried away by the wind. Still, there was a sizable army still left to fight. Nyle just hoped they could hold them off until he dealt with Typhon.

It was time to finish this, and for some reason Nyle needed a weapon that was up close and personal. Drawing on the power of the core he created a sword of power. Typhon looked at him and smiled. He too created a sword out of hell fire. This is what Nyle was hoping, that in his arrogance, Typhon would accept a challenge of personal close quarters combat.

Nyle started his flight directly towards the god. Typhon likewise had pushed off the mountainside and propelled himself forward. There was no bellow of challenge from either of them, they were both laser focused on ripping the insides out of each other.

As they got closer their sword arms reared back, the energy running along the blades was almost too bright to look at. As they came together, they made a resounding crash as the impact created such a wind that anyone directly below them was immediately knocked to the ground.

Now it was hack and slash as these two titanic forces did battle with each other. Nyle thought that Typhon would be a poor swordsman given that he probably never had to fight anyone in this fashion. He was wrong. The god was able to parry all of Nyle's strikes and even managed to get in a few of his own as he sliced open Nyle's brow. It was an aerial acrobatic dance as they circled and clashed, neither one gaining the upper hand. Nyle then did a quick twisting motion with his hand and deflected the god's blade while at the same time cutting Typhon's hand off at the wrist. The god howled in rage as he made the sword appear in his other hand to continue to battle on. It was hard to tell how long this fight lasted, but Nyle could start to feel fatigue in his arms. He needed to end this now or the god would finish him. He pulled out one last trick. One that had sealed forever his place among the raptors and at the same time had killed his best friend. He had never used that maneuver since that day. It was not without its element of risk.

He waited for the right moment to draw the god in. After a series of strikes and counter strikes, Nyle allowed Typhon to knock his blade wide exposing the whole front of his body. He kept his eye on the blade as Typhon started to make his thrust for Nyle's heart. At the very last second, he twisted his body taking the blade in the side where it caught in his rib cage. Nyle knew he only had seconds. This wasn't a blade of steel like the one his friend had pierced him with. This was a blade of hell fire that was already starting to burn him from the inside. As quick as a thought he slashed the god across the throat with his blade of core fire.

Typhon looked at him dumbly. His eyes wide as realization of what just happened hit his brain. Nyle thought the god was about to say something, but he was unable to make his mouth work. Then, as if in slow motion, his head toppled and fell crashing to the earth below as a black oily cloud poured from his body and was taken on the wind followed by a despairing wail.

Typhon's sword disappeared from his body, but he still had his wound and blood was pouring out of it. Nyle didn't have the strength to close it as the flames of his body disappeared along with his wings and he began to freefall towards the ground below. He thought he heard a scream just before he blacked out and knew no more.

Chapter 21

"Why do I have to go along?" Griffin asked.

"Because Meliakken said you have to," Zana responded furiously. "Do you want me to take you to him so you can ask him?"

Griffon shrank back from her anger and said no more about not going.

"How are we going to get to Trystan's forge?"

Zana looked at him dangerously, wondering if he really was worth all this trouble.

"What? Can you not even tell me that?" Griffin asked.

If it were up to her, she would have gotten rid of Griffin long ago. Although he had proven his usefulness in getting into the crypt of the White Castle as well as providing an adequate jailer for the king and queen for the past ten years. She really didn't blame him for their escape. There was no way he was any kind of match for the phoenix.

"With this," she said holding up the glass rod that Griffin had stolen for her out of the crypt. "This will create a portal to the place where it was created by Trystan himself."

"When do we leave?" he asked.

"Right now," she said as her wings folded behind her back.

Zana held the rod out in front of her, the green light within pulsating as the sand in the rod moved from side to side. To locate a place, she first needed a point of reference. It was easy if it was a place she had already been, but she had no idea where Trystan's forge was, but the sand had memories of where it had come from and she fixed her mind on that. It was hazy at first, but then an image started to come into view, a door with an intricate pattern on it. This was the pattern that Meliakken made her memorize.

"Let's go," Zana said.

Griffin was sweating profusely as he followed her through the portal. Standing before the door, Zana traced the outline as the god had instructed and the door opened onto a valley with lush green grass surrounding a lake. On a hill overlooking the water was a building made of black obsidian.

As they walked towards the lake, Zana noticed a small black stone with a curved top.

"Looks like a grave marker," Griffin commented. "I wonder whose it is? Should we go look?"

"No," Zana said as she continued to walk towards the building that contained the forge. "It doesn't concern us."

Once reaching the doorway, Zana peered inside. There was enough sunlight streaming through the door and windows to see that it was the workshop of a god. Though the forge had probably not been used in a very long time, the room was spotless. The black anvil, mounted on a bench in the center of the room looked newly made, as well as all the forging instruments that lined the walls. On the far wall was a fire pit still burning. Zana felt sure that fire had been burning since the first day that Trystan lit it.

"What happens now?" Griffin asked.

Zana walked into the forge and stood before the anvil. Taking out the black stone that Meliakken had given her, she placed it on the anvil. She suddenly heard a slight humming sound from the stone as it touched the metal. Now she needed to break it open.

"Fetch me that hammer," Zana said.

Griffin walked over to the wall and pulled down a hammer made of silver with a foot long handle and a squared off face on one end and sharp point on the other. Zana could tell he did not like the look of this instrument at all. He gingerly handed it to her.

Zana took her aim, and with a strength that surprised even Griffin, she brought it down to smash the rock. As the hammer made contact, the rock exploded, sending shards everywhere as Zana raised a shield to protect both herself and Griffin. A black oily cloud drifted up from the center of where the rock had been. Zana looked out of the doorway they came through and could see that the sun's rays no longer penetrated inside. In fact, it looked like a very dark cloud had come to hover over the entire valley.

The oily cloud that came out of the rock started to coalesce into a shape, eventually becoming the evil god. Once he was solid, Meliakken laughed.

"Well done my dear!" Meliakken praised her. "You have destroyed the last bond that held me prisoner in the only way possible. I so love the irony, that the very tools used to form my prison are the very ones to set me free. Trystan never did have any foresight," Meliakken said rather proud of himself.

Zana stood passively to one side as the god continued his monologue as Griffin was shaking beside her.

"What now my Lord?" Zana asked.

"Now we release the power that will make it so those five younglings and that pesky goddess can never dominate me ever again. Even if they try and come back here, they will never be a match for me. It will be check and mate, and this world will be mine. I will take great pleasure in making slaves of all those who dared to cross my path."

"How, how do we release it?" asked Griffin while still shaking.

"It's funny you should ask that, Griffin," the god said putting an arm around his shoulder as he walked Griffin to the anvil, taking the hammer from Zana. "Your help to us has been invaluable and we could not have gotten to this place without you."

Griffin started to relax a little, but then his eyes suddenly went wide as he looked down to see the pointed end of the hammer sticking out of his chest. He couldn't speak as blood poured out of his chest and mouth, covering the anvil. His eyes stared out into nothingness as his spirit left his body and he slumped to the ground as Meliakken, holding onto the handle pulled it out of him as he fell. The god gave his body a swipe with his foot that sent it flying to the far wall. Meliakken looked over at Zana who kept a neutral expression on her face.

"I would love to know what is going on behind those eyes of yours my dear," Meliakken said. "Did that bother you?"

Zana knew her answer would be important to the god regarding her loyalty.

"I assumed it had to be done," Zana said shrugging her shoulders as if Griffin's death meant nothing to her.

The god appeared to be mollified by that as he nodded once.

"The anvil needed to be tainted with the blood of a sacrifice to allow what comes next."

Meliakken pulled the medallion that held the power of the god and goddess and laid it on the anvil. After a few moments, he flipped it so that both sides were covered in blood. Closing his eyes, he waved it over the hammer as he spoke an ancient chant. The hammer turned from a bright silver to black, though you could still see Griffin's blood dripping from the point. Zana watched in amazement as everything around them was drained of color. The wood, the forge, even looking outside the grass had turned to a monochrome grey.

"What is happening?" Zana asked in stunned disbelief.

"This will never be used again by any god or creature. I am sucking out the very magic of this place," Meliakken told her.

Meliakken then took the hammer and raised it above his head, and in a tongue Zana did not understand he uttered the words, "Rialaim thu go deo," as he brought the pick end of the hammer down on the medallion. The impact blew Zana against the far wall as she hastily created a shield around herself to keep from having her body snapped in half.

Two lights of energy, one black the other gold, appeared and intertwined as they circled the room of the forge. Meliakken had his hands spread wide and his face was lit up in ecstasy from the power that was infusing his body. The power of the god and goddess was circling faster, their ring becoming tighter as they totally encased Meliakken's body. Once the energy beams had been absorbed into himself, the god brought his hands together in a thunderous clap which exploded the roof off the forge as well as blowing out the walls. The only thing left was the foundation and the anvil. Even the fire that had burned since the forge was built was gone, never to be lit again.

Zana was shaking as she realized that Meliakken had grown in size, he was twice his original height. Although she knew the god could be any height he chose, she found this significant that with the absorbing of the god and goddess' power, his physical attributes seemed more defined, more powerful and in a way, more cruel. For the first time since joining with him, Zana felt fear, and in that fear had sunk to a knee.

"What now lord?" Zana asked.

"It pleases me to see you are willing to bend a knee Zana, I have had my doubts."

"I will never fail you or prove myself false to you," she said shaking as she felt the force of his will override hers. All her thoughts were laid bare, even her desire to one day usurp his power which was thoroughly crushed by the power of his mind. That part of her that was locked away when she killed Layla was screaming once again.

"I know you won't, my little faerie. For my will is now yours."

Meliakken walked down towards the lake and looked upon Eriyn's gravestone. With just a thought, the stone crumbled upon itself and turned to dust that was carried away on the breeze. What was once vibrant and colorful was now desolate and reeked of death. Zana shuddered to think that the stronghold of one god was laid to waste by another. She knew without a doubt that Trystan would never be allowed back here. Meliakken had created an abomination that would forever repel Trystan or any of the five for that matter. Zana was wondering why she even cared.

"I am free of this prison," the god said. "Able to walk the world once more, with no gods or goddess to stop me. Time is always on my side and in the end, everything comes back to me."

He turned to look at Zana and cupped her chin. "There is a magic that permeates this world unlike any other I have conquered, and that magic has a name. Vasara."

***

"Your Majesty, what's wrong," Brie said with concern written all over her face.

Luel had stood up and held her hand over her heart as the jewel embedded in her father's crown blazed and her breath came in gasps.

"An abomination," the queen said wide-eyed as she looked at Brie. "A great evil is loose and war is coming."

"Coming where?" Brie asked unconsciously while pulling her spear off her arm and extended it.

"Otherwhere," she responded. "Assemble the host of faeries."

"All of them?"

"All of them," Luel answered her. "Every last faerie."

"But who will protect the kingdom?" Brie asked as she tied her hair in a ponytail as she prepared for battle.

Luel placed both hands on Brie's shoulders. "If we do not win this battle that is coming, nothing will be able to protect Laurel Hollow."

Brie sobered up and her focus was back in her eyes.

"So, it is to be one of those battles," Brie said knowingly.

Luel nodded, knowing what she meant. It was going to be all or nothing, winner takes all, and there was no point in holding anything in reserve.

"Which dragons are in Laurel Hollow?" Luel asked.

"All of them," Brie answered, "except for Andros, Brion, Caleb and Gael. Oh, and Finn as well."

Luel was troubled by Finn. Emilia had told her of Finn's feelings for Zana and his absence was concerning.

"Are there any dragons currently in the hall?" Luel asked Brie.

"Jace is there."

"Could you ask him to come in?"

"Of course, my queen," Brie responded as she flew out the door.

Luel smiled as Brie departed and she walked over to the window to observe the activity outside. Ever since making Brie her general of the host, Brie insisted on formality, and she found it hard to get her to drop it when they were alone. Luel also found it interesting that Jace was the one lingering about the hall. When the dragons were first rescued, Jace and Brie had struck up a fast friendship. The queen would often see them together over the years and wondered if more than just a friendship bond was forming between them.

"You sent for me, Majesty?" a voice from behind her said.

Luel turned to see the silver haired dragon who just entered with Brie by his side.

"Ah, Jace. Yes, I need a favor."

"Anything," he responded readily.

"I need you to fly me to the far western border of the Parma Wilds."

"Not a problem. May I ask why?"

"I want you to take me to Otherwhere," Luel responded with deadly seriousness.

"Otherwhere?" Brie asked astounded. "You know another way to get there?"

"I do now," Luel answered.

"How?" Jace asked her.

"Tera is there," the queen said. "As queen and priestess of the goddess I can sense the general whereabouts of any faerie by focusing on them, and Tera is to the west."

Jace ran his fingers through his long silver hair. "When do you want to leave?"

"Right now," Luel replied.

"What about the host?" Brie asked.

"That general is your job," Luel said smiling. "Assemble them and follow as quickly as you can."

Luel handed Brie a silver disc with the image of a moon above two upraised palms.

"My father gave me that when I was a little girl," Luel said. "Pour your thoughts into it and you should be able to follow us. It will make sense the first time you do it."

"Yes, your majesty," Brie said turning the disc over and over in her hand.

"Let's go," Luel said to Jace.

"Be careful," Brie said. Luel was sure that was meant more

271

for Jace and smiled to herself.

They exited the hall and walked the path to the dragon's glade. Jace made his change and Luel climbed aboard his silver back. Jace gave a mighty thrust of his powerful wings and was climbing high into the morning sky. From this height Luel could see where the border of Laurel Hollow ended and the Parma Wilds began.

Which way, Majesty? Jace asked.

Luel closed her eyes and reached out with her mind and found Tera.

"South-west if you please, Jace."

You got it.

Jace's silver wings beat out a steady rhythm as they crossed the Wilds. Looking down, Luel could discern no movement of any kind. The thick vegetation obscured most things anyway. Her natural reaction when flying over the wilds was to always be on the lookout for alfar. She knew none of their poisoned arrows would reach her up here, still, old habits die hard.

After a day of flying, Luel had Jace land them in a valley near a cliff face. After the queen flew off his back, Jace turned back into his human form.

"Is this it?" he asked.

Luel started to run her hands along the rock. She could swear she could feel some very slight indentations.

"Tera's path lies on the other side of this."

Jace looked at the rock with skepticism. "Unless there is a door there, I don't see how we are getting through."

Luel turned back towards the dragon and smiled. "Jace, you are a genius."

"I am? What did I say?"

"Can you create a fog just above our heads, enough to block out the sun?"

"Sure, but why?" Jace asked as he plunged himself into the source to do as the queen asked.

"You'll see."

As Jace created the fog and obscured the sun, the jewel on Luel's crown blazed, illuminating the fine crack lines in the rock. Her heart leapt as she saw the pattern emerge.

"By the gods!" Jace exclaimed. "Who chiseled that?"

"My father," Luel said, "or one of his ancestors. That pattern is of the house of Caster."

"Can you open it?"

"Yes, I just need to trace the pattern."

Not yet.

"What?" Luel said.

"I didn't say anything," Jace said perplexed.

Luel looked at the pattern once again. She was about to raise her hand but stopped. She knew she heard a voice tell her not yet. If it wasn't Jace, then who was it she wondered, it was not a voice she recognized.

"What are your thoughts?" Jace asked her.

Luel kept staring at the pattern. It wouldn't take but a moment to open the door, gateway or whatever entrance manifested itself.

"Let the fog go, Jace," she said.

"Are you sure?"

She turned around to face him. "Yes, we will at least wait for Brie and the host." She turned back towards the door.

"Something tells me that once we open that door, the final battle will have begun, and there will be no turning back."

***

Neala sat astride her chestnut stallion as she looked over the vast expanse of the Corridor, the place where demons enter to take physical form. Her dark red hair was done up in a ponytail, the end coming to rest between the shoulder blades of her leather armor. It is ever the duty of the Border Lands warriors to fight back the scourge that would invade Vasara. Neala was the general of a very special elite force that had but one duty, to guard the seals to the underworld. Behind her was a building in the shape of a pyramid. Inside on the floor were two stone tablets that were warded by magic. Every so often, demon lords would try and assault the pyramid in hopes of breaking the seals and releasing what lies beneath.

"General," a voice called from behind.

Neala turned to see her captain, Kendal riding up to her position.

"What news, Kendal?" she asked as he stopped his horse next to her.

"The patrols are just coming back," Kendal said, "there has been no movement within a five-mile radius."

"None at all?" she asked adjusting her serpent hilt sword that is the symbol of all Border Lands generals. "The demons seem very quiet today, and that worries me."

"Should I send the patrols out for another circuit?" Kendal asked.

Neala rubbed her chin in thought.

"No," she said finally. "Have them fall back to the pyramid. My gut tells me something is coming. I'm going to go inside and join the detail guarding the seals."

Kendal saluted and rode off to inform the outer patrols. Tying her horse up to the rail, Neala entered the pyramid. She walked down a long torch lit hall with doors on either side leading to offices and sleeping quarters. Upon entering the center of the pyramid, it opened up into an enormous, vaulted hall. The floor was marble and in the very center were two large, rounded stone tablets that were so heavy, a team of horses would not be able to budge them. On their surface was embossed the letter M. Only the warriors slated to guard the pyramid are ever allowed inside and are bound by their oaths to not reveal what it contains. For eons it has been this way to maintain the secrecy of what they guarded against. Etched into the floor around the tablets was a circle that had a star symbol every ten feet. There were twenty such stars, with a warrior standing on each one. This was the most arduous and tedious task in the Border Lands, but also one of the most important.

Neala walked around the circle, inspecting each warrior as they looked straight ahead, hands resting on their sword hilts. Once the patrols returned, she would change out these twenty for fresh troops. As mind-numbing as this task could be, every warrior knew the risk if they were to let their guard down for even a second.

Suddenly Neala felt the hairs on the back of her neck rise. She turned to look back down the hall she had just come through. A group of warriors were headed her way. She had a puzzled expression on her face because she felt Kendal could not have reached the patrols and returned so quickly.

As she looked more closely, she could see the lead warrior was carrying something, almost like a rounded stone. He gave it a mighty heave as he swung his arm and the object sailed through the air and came to land at her feet. She stared in horror as Kendal's sightless eyes stared up at her.

"Swords!" Neala shouted.

The twenty warriors drew their blades as one, leveling them at the twenty warriors that had come into the pyramid.

"Who are you?" Neala asked.

The one who had thrown the head had spoken up first.

"Ansgar, at your service," he said with a flourish of his hand as he bowed.

"The baron of Black River?"

"Well, ex-baron we should say. The job didn't quite work out, but that is another story. You have a choice to make, General."

"And what is that?" Neala asked.

"Your time in this world will be ending soon anyway. You and your warriors may leave after you drop your weapons," Ansgar said.

Neala didn't answer. She was stalling for time.

"If you are waiting for your patrols to arrive you wait in vain," Ansgar said guessing her intent. "No one is coming."

Neala was sure he was not making an idle boast, and there was no way she could surrender her position.

"Always fight to the last warrior," her mentor had told her many years ago, "because you never know what that sacrifice will bring about."

That mentor had been general Lyson, before he had become Braylynn's wizard, even before Andros the black had set foot in the Border Lands. This was one of those last stands the bards would sing about for many generations to come. Neala would make sure it was a song worth singing. She turned to face her team.

"Warriors!" she shouted. "Today we will do our duty, as every warrior has since the dawn of time. For them to achieve their goal they will have to do it over our dead bodies. In the end they will still be bound to their hell as we move on to Fallon's paradise. Stand ready!"

Every warrior went from a defensive posture to one of attack with the point of their blades facing forward.

"Such a waste," Ansgar said shaking his head.

He made a gesture with his hand and the twenty warriors parted and lined the inner wall of the pyramid. Suddenly they changed and to Neala's dread she saw them for what they were, demon lords, but they weren't engaging them. Then she understood why. The sound of many feet came running down the hall.

"Demons," she said aloud.

"I tried to give you a chance," Ansgar said as he too stepped aside, and the inner chamber became flooded with demons.

The battle lasted longer than even Ansgar expected. Many more demons had to be summoned to replace the ones struck down by the warriors, but eventually the law of attrition took over as each warrior fell and their blood covered the stone tablets. One lone warrior remained.

"Stop!" Ansgar commanded. The demons howled in fury at being denied the fun of ripping this warrior's body apart.

Neala lay panting against the wall, her legs no longer able to support her as one arm hung lifeless at her side. There were many cuts on her neck and face and the blood was flowing freely as she struggled to remain conscious. Ansgar raised his hand as heat radiated from his palm and he cauterized her wounds.

"Run me through and be done with it, demon," Neala said through clenched teeth as she fought back the pain.

Ansgar squatted and brought himself down to her level.

"No General, you will bear witness to what will happen here. You will also carry the shame of losing your entire command, and that will cause more hurt than dying."

Neala watched as Ansgar walked over and took up position where he had a foot on each tablet. The other demon lords took up positions on the star emblems where her warriors had stood. All the other demons had left and she could clearly see the bodies of the fallen. Brave souls that were now safe with Fallon. But Ansgar was right. The shame and guilt of losing them all was overwhelming. If Fallon had not forbidden any warrior from taking their own lives she would have impaled herself right then and there.

"Swords!" Ansgar commanded.

The demon lords held their swords in front of them. The blades were black with a ruby stone embedded in the hilt. Ansgar held up his own sword above his head as the rubies shot forth an energy beam that connected with the tip of Ansgar's sword, infusing him with its energy. His blade burned an angry red as he let the power build. Neala could feel the heat of the energy being generated from where she sat. Then with a loud cry, Ansgar swung his blade down in a sweeping arc across both tablets causing them to break open.

An ear-piercing shriek came from below, followed by an identical shriek. Neala never knew what the seals held back but, she was about to find out. Ansgar jumped as the ground suddenly erupted and two dragon like creatures came streaking out of the hole and flew through the roof of the pyramid. Brick and mortar came raining down with one large piece landing on Neala's leg crushing it. But none of it mattered anymore. Two shriekers had been let loose upon the world and she allowed it to happen. She could hear Ansgar laughing in triumph and she tried to push herself up to go and rip his heart out if he had one. But the pain had finally hit her brain and everything went black before her eyes and she knew no more.

Chapter 22

Samara looked down as they flew over Cavanah Hall in Laurel Hollow.

"Is it just me, or is there no one around today?" Samara asked. "Can you see anything with those dragon eyes, Brion?"

No, Brion answered. *Not a soul.*

"Take us to the dragon's glade," Rhyan said, "we'll see if Donella or Lyson are about."

"Good idea," Ava told her sister.

Ever since fleeing Meliakken's assault in the Blood Forest, Samara had been thinking long and hard of what she would do next. She would always remain neutral in the events of the world, taking no one's side but her own, but here she was drawing a line and choosing a definite side. She didn't know if her powers would be of any use, but whatever she could do would be done in the service of Andros the black.

As Brion touched down in the glade, everyone climbed off and Brion made the change back to human. Walking the path, they came to the Summoner's cottage. Ava pounded none too lightly on the door.

"Donella? Lyson?" she called out.

They waited several moments. There was no answer.

"This is very odd," Rhyan said. "Can you sense the Summoner?"

"No," Brion said. "But I do sense some of my brothers off to the West somewhere."

There was an ear shattering shriek coming from the glade.

Both Rhyan and Ava took the bows from around their backs.

"I know that sound," Samara said. "A shriker."

"Quickly," Brion said, "let's move."

They raced back to the glade and stopped just before the opening. There in the center stood a shriker. Black as midnight with its two sets of wings outstretched and a double row of razor-sharp teeth showing as its mouth opened wide to let out another banshee like cry.

"Can we defeat that thing?" Ava asked notching an arrow to her bow.

"Not by ourselves," Rhyan said following her sister's movement.

"Brion! Shield!" Samara yelled just in time as the shriker stretched forth all its claws and energy bolts came flying towards them.

Both Samara and Brion erected shields around themselves and the twins as the energy bolts impacted and cascaded upward like a wave.

"We need help," Samara said.

Just then the attack from the shriker stopped as it looked towards the far side of the glade. Arrow after arrow came streaking out of the woods. The shriker barely got its own shield up in time before a rain of arrows struck. Screeching in frustration, the beast lifted off the ground and was away in seconds. Once it was out of sight, Brion and Samara allowed their shields to drop.

"Is there an army of archers out there?" Brion asked peering into the woods.

"If it is, they came just in time," Ava said. "They must be excellent marksmen. Never have I seen a cluster of arrows hit the same mark."

Suddenly a person stepped out from under the trees.

"Brion, can you tell who that is?" Samara asked him as

she danced lightning between her palms just in case it was an enemy.

"By the gods!" Brion exclaimed. "It's Cleo!"

Just then another figure stepped out and stood next to Cleo.

"And Tori," Brion said as everyone started running towards them.

As everyone gathered around, each gave a high-level summary of what had been happening to each other.

"You actually saw Bart?" Ava asked still stunned that the archer had visited them.

"I did," Cleo said, "and he whispered something to me that the others did not hear. He said to tell the twins their father is fine, and they will all be reunited one day."

A few tears slid down both Ava and Rhyan's face.

"Thank you for that," Rhyan said gratefully.

"Come," Tori said. "We need to leave, and you are coming with us."

"Why, where are we going?" Brion asked.

"Otherwhere," Tori answered as she turned back to the rip in the fabric of reality she had created. "I have something for both Ava and Rhyan. You will understand once we are inside."

Samara had been watching all this with great interest. Never before had she seen such power displayed by the gods. Events were moving fast and only the gods knew where it would all wind up in the end. Upon stepping through the rip, Samara expected to be still standing in the glade with everything frozen in time, except it wasn't.

"What is this?" asked a stunned Samara.

They were standing on the edge of a river with a white crystalline boat anchored to a dock by the shore. And unlike everything else that was frozen in time, the boat and the river were moving.

"Ahoy there!" a shout came from the deck.

Samara looked up and saw a man in dragon clothes with red hair waving at them madly.

"What are you doing here Bull?" Brion shouted.

"Well, since you were off doing god knows what, someone had to give these people and faeries a ride. Actually maybe just one faerie. Lyson, are you considered a faerie now?" Caleb asked talking to someone on the other side of the ship.

Suddenly everyone saw Lyson and Emilia fly up to where Caleb stood at the rail.

"Let's just say, wizard, and leave it at that, shall we?"

Everyone onshore laughed.

"Let's get on board," Tori said as she adjusted the twin swords on her back, "I have something to give you both," she said to Rhyan and Ava.

As they walked up the gangplank, they heard a shout from down below.

"What the hell is all that racket up there! A man can't get any decent rest on this thing. I'm starting to doubt why I came along on this trip anyway."

"Dim," a female voice said, "there is no need to be so disagreeable."

"Diminitus, Ala!" Ava cried out as she saw them emerge from below decks and ran to hug them.

Samara had heard the story of how Diminitus and Ala had saved Ava's life from a poisoned alfar arrow. She couldn't help wondering why they were here. Then one more figure emerged from below, his horns emerging before the rest of his head. It was the king of the Parma Wilds and priest of Cael, Pan.

Tori filled everyone in on why Pan and Ala were there. Samara was fascinated by the golden discs hung around their necks, that Bart had told Tori to deliver to each priest of the gods. Rhyan and Ava now wore theirs. The moment she saw them, something started to stir in her breast.

"May I see Trystan's?" Samara asked Tori.

They all knew now about Trystan's relationship to Samara. Tori pulled it out of the bag and held it up for the witch to see, a gold disc with the symbol of an open scroll embossed on it, Trystan's symbol.

"May I hold it?" Samara asked.

"I don't think that is a good idea," Tori answered. "Bart said only priests of the gods could handle them."

"Please, Cath Priomh," Samara said with pleading eyes.

"Tori, it's ok," Rhyan said. "I have a feeling about this."

Tori looked skeptical, but she deposited the disc into Samara's outstretched hand. As soon as the metal made contact with her skin she suddenly found herself in a totally different place. There was a bright white sun hanging in a cloudless blue sky. She was standing on a well-worn red dirt path that wound through a forest of evergreen trees. Flying among the branches were birds of every color and size, it was a virtual paradise.

"Samara," a rich deep voice said from behind her.

Tears started to fall down her cheeks. She knew exactly who it was. She heard that voice in her mind every time she rose in the morning and every time she closed her eyes at night. That voice represented loss and abandonment, grief and pain.

She turned to see the god Trystan standing before her. He had always seemed tall to her, although she supposed a god could be any size he wanted. His flowy blond hair set off his azure-colored eyes.

"I hate you," she said.

Samara could see the pain in his eyes.

"I know," he said.

"You knew I would touch the disc you gave Tori, didn't you?"

A bird with white wings and a red body landed on the god's shoulder. He gently stroked its head as he answered her.

"Yes, the suggestion was there in case you ever got close to it," Trystan said.

"Why?" she asked, her shoulders slumped with heavy emotion. Samara didn't know if she was going to be able to handle this.

The god waved the bird away while at the same time creating two chairs right in the middle of the woods.

"Samara, please sit."

Reluctantly she sat down as her father did the same. Father, that name held nothing but pain for her.

"Why did you do it, why did you abandon me? Why did you never acknowledge me? Meliakken nearly killed me because of you."

She could tell her accusations hit the mark. She didn't know if a god could be emotionally wounded, but Trystan certainly appeared like he was.

"There is something you should know, gods are not perfect like everyone assumes. We make mistakes."

"Loving my mother was a mistake? Having me be born was a mistake?" Samara was shouting now, the rage building in her body.

Trystan looked at her with patience and kindness, and also understanding at the hurt he had caused her.

"No," he replied gently. "That part was perfect. You, are perfect."

Samara was shaking now. She didn't want his kindness, she didn't want to feel kindly towards him. She did not want to be robbed of her anger; it was all she had.

"Why couldn't you love me?" She finally said it. That which she had screamed to the heavens since she was old enough to walk, she had finally said it to the person who needed to hear it the most. The dam broke and the choking sobs came. Trystan got up and walked over towards her and folded her up in his arms. At first she resisted and twisted her body to get away. She knew it was useless, and the part of her that didn't want to get away took dominance and allowed herself to be held. She buried her face in his chest and let the tears run, cleansing her and making her pure. When the tears had run their course, Trystan cupped her face and had her look into his eyes.

"Samara, out of all that I have created in Vasara, you are the most important. I loved you when you were first conceived in your mother's womb, and that love has grown with the passing of every second and is now bigger than a universe. It is not containable."

He stood her up and grabbed her hand as they walked for a bit. For some reason she felt almost childlike to have this god holding her hand like he was. She was many hundreds of years old, but that amount of time was insignificant compared to the life of a god.

"Leaving you was never my intent," he said. "Right when you were born, my brothers and I realized we needed to leave Vasara."

"Why?" Samara asked, the edge in her voice no longer there. She desperately needed to know.

"Meliakken," he said. "Our physical presence gave him leave to work some of his powers that we could not counter, weakening the seals of his prison. By leaving, we limited ourselves in that world which in turn would limit any god or goddess."

"But why did you cut yourself off from me?"

Trystan stopped and turned to face her with pain in his eyes.

"It was the hardest thing I have ever done in the history of my existence, but I had to, because it creates a physical link between the two of us. A link that Meliakken can use to reach back to me."

"Is he really that much stronger than you?"

Samara was surprised by his direct answer.

"He is."

"Then we can't win," Samara said matter-of-factly.

"What makes you think that?" the god asked. "Do you really think we would be doing all of this if there was no chance at all? There is always a chance my daughter, when we are all united. The five of us and Braylynn were able to imprison him. Now we have a chance to destroy him forever."

Samara looked at him with worry in her eyes.

"What's wrong?"

"Meliakken has the medallions of the god and goddess that you had forged. He's going to release them, he may already have," she said reluctantly.

"He has released them, but don't despair. A lot of power is being brought to bear."

"The only way there will be enough power is if all of you are there," Samara said.

Trystan smiled at her knowingly.

"What? Are you saying you will be there?"

"There are some things I cannot reveal, even to you my daughter. But there is one thing I can tell you."

He put both hands on her shoulders and looked at her with deadly seriousness.

"Stay centered. Protect the vessels."

"What does that mean?" she asked.

"You will know when the time comes," he answered her.

"Riddles of the gods," she said while blowing a stray lock of hair out of her face.

Trystan smiled and winked at her.

Suddenly a thought had just occurred to her.

"What if I hadn't come? What if my bitterness towards you had thrown me to ally with Meliakken?"

"The prophecy works to make sure all the players are in place to bring forth its best outcome for Vasara," he said. "So it sent to you the one thing that would help thaw your heart."

"Andros," she said with certainty.

The god nodded. "That boy wasn't born just to free Vasara, he was also born to help free you."

She pondered that for a while as they continued their walk. Eventually they came to a small lake where a woman was kneeling as she ran her hands through the water. She wore a sleeveless burgundy dress with her jet-black hair braided and coming to rest in the middle of her back.

"I was wondering when you two would turn up," she said without turning around.

Every muscle in Samara's body locked as she heard the voice that spoke to her only once at the moment of her birth. That voice lived in Samara's soul and to hear it again now rocked her to her very core.

The woman stood up and turned. Her eyes were green. Samara still remembered those eyes. They were imprinted in her memory even as a baby as she had looked upon her daughter for the first and last time in that world. The tears were again running freely down Samara's cheeks. She woodenly started moving forward as her body was still in shock and trying to catch up to her brain. Once it did, Samara ran into her mother's open arms. She was stroking Samara's head as she made little shushing noises.

"I'm so sorry mother," Samara said when she found her voice. "I'm so sorry you had to die because of me."

"There is no need to be sorry my dear," she said. "You being born was the greatest gift I could ever have. Lay aside your

guilt and pain my darling, everything is right and whole now."
Samara's mother looked over at Trystan. "She is all we ever
hoped for, isn't she my love?"

"Yes she is, Maeve," Trystan said, "and so much more."

Maeve gently lifted her daughter's face and peered into her
eyes. "I do believe you are right. There is a power there, a very
great power."

"What do you mean?" Samara asked.

"I believe your father would say something like, you will
know when the time comes."

Samara laughed between sobs of joy as she wiped the tears
from her eyes. She then did something she had always wanted to
do. She grabbed her mother around her waist and walked over
to her father and wrapped her other arm around his waist. Both
Trystan and Maeve encircled her with their arms and crushed
her to them. She closed her eyes in happiness and basked in their
presence as the warmth flooded her body. When she opened her
eyes again, Tori was looking at her with great concern.

"Samara, are you alright?" Rhyan asked her.

She looked down at the ground and for a moment she was
crestfallen. And then she felt it. In the very depths of her being
she felt the link her father had kept from her for all these eons.
That link that only existed between a father and his daughter,
and even more so when your father is a god. She was not
alone, and she would never be alone ever again. Her body
started to glow with a blue radiance.

"By the gods, Samara!" Brion exclaimed. "You're glowing!
Glowing with the color of Trystan."

Samara felt the power that was there, more than she had
ever experienced in her whole life. She was sure it was there to
do the task her father had given her, to protect the vessels. She
just hoped she knew what that meant when the time came.

Chapter 23

Redlin was stunned to see who was approaching Killian's house. It was Tori and following behind her was quite the gathering of people. His daughter flew past all of them and into her father's arms.

"Emilia, what is going on?" Redlin asked. "How did you get here?"

"A lot Dad, but I'll let Tori fill you in."

Once Tori reached the house, she gave a full account of everything that had transpired from when they boarded the boat on the river of the gods until that moment. Redlin and the others listened without interruption.

"And where is that boat now?" Redlin asked her.

"Gone. Once we docked here it disappeared just before we came out of the frozen moment. I guess we are traveling by dragon now."

Redlin could see they certainly had enough dragons to transport everyone with Andy, Gael, Brion and Caleb.

"I was instructed to give you this, master wizard," Tori said as she handed Redlin the golden disc of Trystan.

When Redlin touched it, he sensed something and looked over at Samara. Samara nodded once knowingly. Redlin smiled to himself because he knew what that meant, she had been reconciled to Trystan. He put the necklace with the disc on it around his neck and could feel the power of the god resting against his chest. He was not sure what all this represented or why all the priests of the gods were together once again. The last time was to pass the barrier that allowed them onto the island where the temple of the warlocks was, but he felt now they were together for an entirely different reason.

"What do we do now Dad?" Andy asked his father.

"Now it is time for the last battle," Killian answered instead with his arm around Tallika.

"Are you coming with us?" Redlin asked.

"Not now, but I will be there for the final face off with Meliakken."

"Do we have a chance?" Nia asked as she absently rubbed the charm that would allow her to live as long as her dragon.

Killian smiled at her. "A chance?" he looked up as he pondered that statement. "There is always a chance my dear. One set of circumstances where everything comes together at just the right moment that guarantees success." He looked back at her. "So yes, there is a chance for success, but there are many more chances for failure."

"Somehow that doesn't really make me feel better," she said with one eyebrow raised.

Killian just winked at her.

"Where do we go now?" Brion asked.

Killian walked to the edge of the porch and pointed.

"Fly between those two peaks. As you do you will see a cottage. Go through the door and the battle will be there."

"Inside the cottage?" Caleb asked with skepticism. "You wouldn't care to elaborate, would you?"

Again, Killian just smiled.

"It gets bigger the further in you go," Tera said absently.

Redlin looked over at Tera and saw the worry had returned, but she wasn't pushing it down and she wasn't running away from it. Whatever her task was, Redlin was never prouder of this little faerie that his wife had made him bring along.

"I guess it's time," Lyson said.

"And about time," Diminitus said crankily.

Killian burst out laughing. "I have missed you Diminitus," he said when he got his laughter under control.

"Do I know you sir?" Diminitus asked squinting at Killian with one eye.

"You did once," Killian said, "though you were just a young lad at the time."

"Now Diminitus as a boy is just something I cannot imagine," Caleb said.

"Why you insolent pup," Diminitus started to sputter.

Ala put a hand on his arm, smiling she said, "Just let it go darling."

"Alright brothers," Gael said. "Shall we change and give these good friends a ride to the battle of the ages?"

"You are just a little too enthusiastic brother," Brion remarked good naturedly.

"Before you leave, I must speak with the Summoner and her brother," Killian said. "Please come inside."

Andy and Emilia followed Killian inside the house as Redlin pondered what he was telling them. He looked over at Abby who seemed to have concern written on her face. He walked over and sat beside her.

"What's wrong Abby?" Redlin asked.

"What? Oh, sorry, I was just wondering what they might be discussing," she said as she fidgeted with the death dagger on its chain.

"Was that all?" Redlin asked sensing that there was something more.

At first Abby looked at him as if she were deciding how to answer. Then she lowered her head.

"I'm afraid," she said quietly. "I'm afraid with this battle coming I'm going to lose many that I love."

"So am I," Redlin responded as he looked out over the yard watching everyone in quiet conversation with each other.

"You are?" Abby asked shocked. "No offense, but I didn't think you were afraid of anything."

"When you died, Abby, and Andy lost his mind, for a moment I was too afraid to move," he said as his eyes connected with hers. "But I knew there was a job that had to be done, one that only I could do, and I took comfort that all of us would be reunited again one day. At the time it did not lessen the pain very much, but it did allow me to move forward."

Abby smiled at him gratefully as she hugged him and he hugged her back.

"Don't despair, Abby, we aren't dead yet and we just may come out of this alive after all," he said winking.

Just then the door to the house opened and Andy and Emilia walked out. Redlin noticed they had puzzled expressions on their faces.

"You guys alright?" Redlin asked his kids.

"We are okay, Dad," Emilia answered. "Killian just wanted to give us some advice and warnings about the coming battle, but he made us promise not to discuss it."

"Yeah, not sure why though," Andy added.

"It's alright kids," the wizard said, "with Killian, everything is for a reason, and it will all make sense when the time comes."

"I suppose you're right," Andy said. "Are we ready to go then?"

"I believe we are," Redlin replied.

"Let's do this, brothers," Andy said as he, Brion, Caleb and Gael walked a little way from the house to make their change.

Four dragons stood in the field as everyone climbed aboard.

"The gods be with you!" Killian shouted from the porch with his arm around Tallika once again.

You want to lead the way? Brion asked Andy.

You got it, Andy responded as he spread his black wings and lifted off into the warm air current.

This was the beginning, Redlin thought. So much power was assembled here, winging its way towards a confrontation that was meant to destroy a god. He looked over at Samara and wondered what part she had to play in all of this, something told him it would be significant. In fact every little piece would need to be just right to tip the balance in their favor.

Redlin cast his eye to Tera who was sitting next to him looking pensive.

"Are you ready?" Redlin asked knowing she had some great task to perform that would have no less impact than anyone else's. Such a large responsibility on those small shoulders he thought, but she answered him with absolutely no hesitation in her voice.

Meeting his gaze, she replied, "I am."

***

Andy soared a little bit higher as he caught another warm updraft. The distance to the peaks were a little further than it first appeared as they flew for half a day. Passing between them Andy started his descent as he saw the valley with the cottage.

Let's land to the left of the cottage, Andy told his brothers, *there is more room there.*

One by one the dragons landed, as everyone jumped off, they made their change. Andy looked around and noted how many of his loved ones were here. All fighting for one cause, the existence of Vasara. He knew the battle was starting today, and once it began it would not stop until they were either victorious or dead. Just then Abby walked up to him.

"What are you thinking my love?" she asked snaking a hand around his waist.

He looked long at this woman he loved. Several times in their history he thought he had lost her. He had vowed that would never happen again. If this was to be the end, they would go out together, he knew that for a fact.

"Just wondering if we are going to win," he said kissing her forehead.

"Can you tell me what Killian had said?"

"He did say I could tell you," Andy said. "He said something would happen that would rock the very foundation of my world, and to not despair. He also told me to beware of Meliakken's voice and believe nothing he says."

Andy thought for a moment. Killian specifically told him he could tell Abby without Andy even asking if he could. It was as if for some reason Killian wanted Abby to know, but no one else.

"Are you alright, Andros?" she asked squeezing him tighter.

He kissed her forehead and held her tight in return. "I am love, as long as we are together, I am."

Everyone had reached the door of the cottage. It was just a plain brown wooden door that you might see on any house. Two windows sat on either side of the door, but nothing was visible as Andy peered inside.

"Well Dad?" Andy asked.

"I guess we go inside," the wizard responded. He waved his hands over the door, the ring of Trystan glowing as he did so.

"What are you doing, Dad?" Emilia asked.

"He's looking for spell wards," Samara replied. "Your father is very good at breaking those as I recall."

Andy saw his father wink at her as Samara gave him a frosty smile.

"It seems safe," Redlin finally said after his examination of the door. "Everyone be ready, I have no idea what is on the other side.

Andy had plunged himself into the source and he could feel his brothers had done the same. Emilia then linked with all of them and felt her power surging back and forth. He looked over at her and saw nothing but readiness and resolve. Killian had told her the same thing he told him, minus the part about Abby, that Killian had spoken directly to his mind. He wondered if Killian had said she could tell Lyson.

Redlin opened the door, and everyone stepped through, dumbfounded at what met their eyes. Instead of the inside of a house, what they saw was a great expanse of hills and flatlands. What was amazing was how eerily quiet it was. No animals could be seen. No birds flying through the air. Far in the distance was a lake that shimmered in the sunlight.

"Well one thing for sure, this is definitely a place to have a battle," Caleb remarked.

"I'm going up for a look around and see what can be seen," Brion said.

"I'm coming with you," Emilia added.

Brion nodded as he ran further out and made his change as Emilia flew onto his back and they both climbed into the sky.

"Should we move forward, Dad?" Andy asked his father who was a little pensive. "What's wrong?"

"I don't know," Redlin said, "and that bothers me."

Redlin looked back at his brother wizard.

"Lyson, can you sense anything?"

Andy watched as Lyson closed his eyes and probed with his mind.

"It is very faint, but I am sensing faeries, a host of faeries, there," he said pointing off to the east where a cliff face reared out of the ground.

Andy looked and all he could see was solid rock with his dragon eyes. Thinking of faeries made him look at Tera who seemed to be fidgeting with the talisman Killian had given her, like she was waiting for something. Her breathing looked a little shallower, as if she was going to great lengths to calm herself down. Andy could feel his own breathing getting rapid as the hairs on the back of his neck stood up.

"Dad, something is happening!"

Suddenly everything went into slow motion in Andy's mind as several things happened at once. First there was a bright flash that momentarily blinded everyone, followed by the cliff face opening up as a host of faeries with five dragons poured through. He could see his mother out front with the jewel of her crown blazing. The last thing that happened and the most devastating was descending from the sky. Two figures, Zana and Meliakken, floating like a god and goddess, were moving into position on the field of battle. Zana had created a shield around them both. Meliakken's gaze was directed at one person and one person only, Trystan's priest, one of the three wizards of the gods, the father of Andros and Donella and husband of the faerie queen.

Andy's head turned slowly towards his father and their eyes met. Redlin gave his son a look of both sorrow and acceptance, as if what was about to happen was fated from the beginning of time. Redlin's eyes closed as a single tear ran down his cheek and he crossed his arms over his chest as the power of two gods and a goddess left Meliakken's hand and blew his father apart along with Tera who had drawn her talon dagger and stood in front of him. The earth exploded from the strike and knocked everyone to the ground. When Andy got up with tears streaming down his cheeks, there were two things he would always remember for the rest of his life, the scorched burn mark of where his father had stood and the shriek and cries of his mother as she flew straight at the god.

Chapter 24

He was numb, and disbelief ran through his mind and body. Andy couldn't believe his father was gone and Tera as well. He didn't know what to do. Suddenly his body wanted to change and transform into a dragon.

"What the hell?" he asked aloud. "What is going on?"

His brothers seemed to be in a similar state.

"Your sister is overriding our will," Gael said as he started running. Caleb likewise was being forced to run and make his change.

Em! Em! What are you doing? You need to stop! Andy sent to her mind.

She's not listening, Andros, Brion said. *She has sunk herself deep in our minds, her grief is overwhelming everything.*

Andy watched as Emilia, standing on Brion's shoulder, started flying low as she sent energy bolts flying at Zana and Meliakken. Brion was also shooting lightning out of his talons, charging the air with so much electricity that Andy could feel its energy racing along his body.

"Abby! Find cover," Andy shouted over his shoulder. "Emilia has lost her mind."

All the dragons were on the field now and streaking towards Brion and Emilia. All except Finn. Andy had no idea where he could be nor how he could be resisting Emilia's summons. The link between the Dragon Summoner and her dragons was unlike anything Andy had ever felt before. This was something different.

As Andy came up alongside Brion, Emilia looked over and her eyes connected with his. He recoiled at what he saw, her eyes were no longer green, they were black as midnight.

Em, what is happening? Andy asked.

She just kept looking at him, expressionless. One thing he did notice, there was a steady stream of tears leaking out of the corner of her eyes and a look on her face that radiated undisguised hatred. The death of their father had caused Emilia to slip into an altered state of being.

Brion, what do we do? Andy asked his brother. *I can't break away.*

There is nothing we can do, Brion answered as the dragons formed up into a v-formation behind Andy and Brion. *She has tapped into a power that I have never felt in any previous Summoner.*

Emilia! You need to let us go! Dad would not want this!

Emilia's face twitched slightly, but she still did not release the dragons' will. She started using the dragons as weapons, forcing them to pour every ounce of power they could muster into assaulting Meliakken's shield. Jace and Gael were in a complicated zig zag pattern that was dizzying to watch as they sent a barrage of energy bolts at the shield. Andy knew if he couldn't figure out something, Emilia would exhaust them, and they would be unable to fight.

Suddenly the cliff face exploded as Finn entered Otherwhere. His flight was erratic as if he were fighting something. Andy assumed Emilia was really trying to force her will on him, and he was resisting with everything that was in him.

Finn, are you alright? Andy asked sending his thoughts to his brother.

No, your sister wants me to kill Zana.

Finn was doing targeted strikes at Meliakken's shield, some

even impacting on Zana's own shield. How they were getting through, Andy had no idea. But he was pretty sure Emilia did since she was using Finn as her sword to strike out at her most formidable enemy and the one person who has been trying to take everything away from her since the day they met.

Andy was circling now and he felt like Emilia was going to have them do something that would get them all killed. He hadn't had time to think of his own grief, but he could tell it was consuming his sister. There was only one thing he could think of to do.

Lyson, we need you! Andy called out to the man his sister loved. *Em has overridden our will and we can't stop her.*

I'm on my way, Andros.

Andy could see the wizard as his black wings beat a quick rhythm up to where Brion was flying and settled onto his back. Because of the link and maybe because Lyson was sharing his thoughts with the dragons, Andy could hear everything Lyson said in his efforts to reach her.

"Donella, can you hear me? You must stop this!"

Emilia gave a flick of her hand and sent Lyson flying.

Em, what are you doing? That's Lyson! Andy said.

Andy could feel a shift in his sister's psyche. Lyson wasn't put off by Emilia's violent outburst as he flew right back up to her and put his hands on her shoulders.

"Donella, you will see me," Lyson said as his eyes bore into hers.

An orange nimbus like flames started to surround Lyson. Andy knew he was bringing all his wizard powers to bear.

"You are the Summoner of the goddess, but I am her wizard." Lyson paused and then pulled Emilia to his chest. "I am also your love as you are mine, and no power of god or goddess is ever greater than that."

Andy heard a sob break through Emilia's granite exterior, and then she broke. The link between them broke and the dragons were free of her will and veered away from Meliakken's shield. He watched as Lyson lifted her up and cradled her head as he flew her to the ground.

Andy now turned his attention to the next problem, his mother, and reached out to the one person he thought could help.

***

Luel had traced the pattern on the door after the faerie host had assembled behind her. Jace and his brothers were in a semi-circle behind them, ready to change as soon as they got through. With the pattern complete, the door dissolved and started to expand. The queen flew through first and several things met her eyes at once. There was a wide expanse that let her know this had to be the place of the last battle. The other was off to her right, there was a large group of people, faeries and dragons. Even from this distance she could see Redlin and Tera. The color drained from her face as she realized where she was, Otherwhere.

"Your majesty, watch out!" Jace yelled pointing skyward. "Brothers!"

The dragons were running as they made their change. Luel was looking at what Jace had pointed at, Meliakken and Zana descending from the sky, and she saw where Meliakken had started to direct his power, directly at her husband. Her worst nightmare was coming true right before her eyes. Her mind snapped as she saw Meliakken obliterate Redlin and Tera. Someone was screaming a cry of enormous grief. It took several moments before it registered in her brain that it was her. One thought occupied her mind. One thought obsessed her entire being. One thought was all that mattered in her existence right now, to kill the being who just ripped half her soul from her. There was a loud buzzing in her ears. Someone may have been calling her name, but she couldn't be sure. None of it mattered. Nothing mattered anymore. The man that she loved and had spent hundreds of years of life with was dead. Dead. That word was a knife slowly twisting in her heart and she felt the anguish as it ripped through her being. She was flying straight for Meliakken's shield. All thought for her own safety was gone as the tears coming from her eyes were captured by the wind as she flew faster and faster. The jewel of her father's house was blazing, as if it sensed the grief, anger and anguish of Luel's soul and was answering in kind. She felt a power within her that she had never felt before. It was the god killing kind of power, and she was aiming it straight at this abomination that destroyed her heart.

***

Loki had just finished closing Nyle's wound with the source and he was starting to come around. Leah had flown up and caught him after his fight with the god of monsters in which he took Typhon's blade into his own side to be able to cut off the god's head.

"Dad, are you alright?" Cathal asked his father as his eyes started to flutter.

After reaching out to his son, Cathal and Brayton had ridden the unicorns to battle against the demon horde. There were none left on the field. Loki felt exhausted after his battle with the demons while trying at the same time to shield everyone as best he could. He knew Dain felt the same.

"Can you rise my love?" Sibila asked Nyle.

As Nyle was falling, Loki had noticed Sibila had fear written all over her face, as if she had not known what the outcome of their battle would be. Loki knew a thing or two about oracles over his long years of life, and he knew they could only reveal what the universe chooses to tell them. The fact that she is also the phoenix makes no difference. Nyle sat up and grabbed Loki's hand as he helped him stand.

"I'm alright," Nyle said to his son and his beloved. "Let's just hope I don't have to fight anymore gods."

"Just one more, my knight," Sibila said smiling.

Nyle started laughing. "You know, after all of that I had totally forgotten about Meliakken."

"Trust me, he hasn't forgotten about us," Brayton said.

Loki looked at the tightness around the prince's one good eye and knew he carried a great weight. Brayton had told them of how Meliakken had killed Savano and stolen her power. One more thing to add to the list Loki thought to himself. Suddenly Loki stood ramrod straight and his eyes went incredibly wide.

"By the gods!" Loki exclaimed as a tear slid down his cheek followed by several more.

"You felt it too," Dain said.

Loki turned his stricken face to his brother wizard who also was fighting back tears.

"Loki, what is it? What's happened?" Paolo asked with concern written all over his face.

It took several moments before Loki could find his voice.

"I can no longer feel my brother." He turned a tear-stricken face towards the king. "Redlin is dead."

Loki, can you hear me?

Loki turned his head slightly as if trying to hear better the voice coming to his mind.

Andros? Is that you? Loki asked.

Thank the gods! Loki, we need you, Andy said. *Meliakken*

killed my father and my mother is going berserk trying to kill him. Please come, I can't lose any more parents today.

Loki could hear the desperation and panic in Andy's voice.

Lad, you need to calm down and focus, Loki said. *We are coming to you, with a host of unicorns behind us. Don't despair son.*

"Talking to someone?" Dain asked noticing Loki had gone silent.

"Yes," he answered. "Andros was speaking to me. Meliakken has killed Redlin, and it appears the battle has begun."

"Then why are we just standing here?" Leah asked explosively as she extended her spear and pulled her talon blade.

"Do we know where they are?" Acacia calmly asked trying to get everyone to focus.

"My wife has a point," Paolo said. "Given the nature of Otherwhere, they could be anywhere."

"Sol, can help us," Sibila said laying a hand on Nyle's shoulder.

"Me?" Nyle asked. "How?"

"Part of the power of the goddess is in you my love," Sibila said. "And as you were able to make a connection to your son to bring us here, so also can you connect to the Braylynn's power that resides in her wizard."

"Lyson," Loki exclaimed, "of course. Lock on him and portal us there."

"Exactly," Sibila said smiling at the wizard.

"Can you do it Dad?" Cathal asked his father with concern at the amount of pressure being put on him.

"I guess there is only one way to find out," Nyle said as he closed his eyes.

Loki watched as Nyle started moving his hand in a circular motion as a small ring of fire appeared before them. He could see sweat starting to break out on his forehead as he sought for the link that would connect him to Lyson.

"I got it!" Nyle exclaimed as he started moving his hand faster, making the portal bigger and bigger. High enough and wide enough to fit the unicorns through fifty abreast.

Loki looked through the portal and his mouth fell slightly open at what he saw. Plunging himself into the source, a great anger welled up inside him at the death of his brother. That was two he had lost now and he vowed he would never lose another as they stepped through the portal to the chaos that awaited them.

Nyle had brought them very close to where the action was. Loki saw the dragons were flying in a uniform attack formation that was so intricate that it was hard to follow, but then all of a sudden it stopped, as if whatever was pulling their strings had stopped. He saw Luel assaulting Meliakken's shield with multiple energy bolts, coming dangerously close to coming in contact with the shield itself, which Loki was sure would kill her.

"Nyle," Loki called. "Can you isolate the faerie queen?"

Nyle nodded as he created a sphere of fire and threw it at the queen, encasing her inside. Luel started to rail against it.

"Let me out, damn you! Let me out!"

Loki saw Andros fly up next to her.

Mom, not this way. Dad, wouldn't want you to die this way. Please Mom, Andy pleaded with his mother.

Luel hovered inside the sphere as if seeing her son for the first time, allowing recognition to register. She closed her eyes and made the symbol of her house with her hands.

"You can let her out now my Sol," Sibila said. "The faerie queen is back in her right mind."

Nyle cut off his sphere as Luel allowed herself to settle to the earth where her son transformed back into his human self and caught her as she collapsed against him.

"Everyone stop!" Loki yelled in a voice that could be heard in every corner of the battlefield.

All the dragons landed as well as the host of faeries. The air was charged with magic. All of the power of Vasara was concentrated in one place, and whether it was Loki's commanding voice or just the atmosphere that had developed like the calm before the storm, everyone fell silent. That's when Meliakken started laughing.

"As I have said before Loki, you were always the sensible wizard," the god said.

"You will not find me sensible today Meliakken," Loki said in a dangerously quiet voice but still was able to be heard by everyone. "Today you will learn that a god can die."

Meliakken's laugh grew even louder and shook the earth.

"You are sensible Loki, but very naive."

"We will avenge my brother's death, you can count on it. That was your mistake Meliakken, for I think you have awakened powers that were dormant until now," Loki said looking at Luel and Donella.

"In all of my existence, Redlin was the symbol of the biggest thorn in my side. He was Trystan's puppet and friend, and I know his death has caused hurt to that god. My only wish is that I could resurrect his body and kill him over and over."

That was the wrong thing to say. Two screams happened simultaneously. The faerie queen and the Dragon Summoner were streaking towards the god.

"Nyle!" Loki yelled.

Nyle knew exactly what to do and created two spheres of fire and encased them both to prevent them from hurting themselves.

"Bring them here," Loki told him. "Andros!"

Andy ran over to where Loki was as Nyle lowered Luel and

Emilia to the ground.

"You must stop," Loki told them gently.

The queen looked at Loki with dead eyes, her body tense and shaking with rage.

"Do not presume to tell me what to do, Loki. He murdered my husband, my life. He murdered dear sweet Tera who tried to protect him. And where were you?" she said accusingly. "What is the good of this brotherhood of wizards if you can't protect each other?"

Luel was shaking harder now, the tears starting anew.

"All of you, listen to me," Loki said urgently. "You are giving into despair. He was my brother for eons beyond counting. I am not even sure I remember our first meeting, but he is as much my brother as my own blood. But he's gone now and my heart is ripped apart because of it. But one thing I do know without a doubt, Redlin would tell us to mourn him after it is done. I say again, do not despair."

Loki looked at Emilia and saw her eyes had become clear.

"What is it?" Loki asked her.

"Killian, he knew. He said those very words to me. He knew this would happen."

"He said the same to me," Andy said.

Their grief wasn't lessened, but Loki could see acceptance come into their eyes. The only one left was the queen.

"Well, Luel?" Loki asked.

"Are you asking me to stand down?" Luel asked, her eyes drawn down fiercely.

"No," Loki responded. "I'm asking you to not stand alone. There is not a single person here that could stand up to Meliakken. I'm not even sure if we can do it together, but together is the only chance we have at achieving success."

The hardness didn't leave Luel's eyes, but she acquiesced to the wizard's wishes with a single nod.

Loki walked closer to the god's shield. "I assume the reason you haven't killed us all yet is because you have some terms of surrender you want to share with us?"

Loki didn't care to hear his terms, he was just stalling for time. He looked around and saw the priests of the gods were forming a semi-circle around him. Why they were doing this he didn't know, perhaps they were being given unheard instructions. Pan stood directly behind him holding his decagram, his staff with the ten-pointed star affixed to it. The king of the Parma Wilds gave silent acknowledgement. For some reason it made Loki feel better that he was there. Meliakken drew Loki's attention back to him by laying out his terms.

"My terms are simple," the god began, "lay down all weapons and magical items, form a line and come to me as I absorb your power."

"I see no benefit in that for us to surrender," Loki said stroking his beard.

"The benefit will not be to you Loki, but to those that remain in this world with no magic. They will live as slaves, but they will live."

He saw Meliakken turn towards Zana.

"There is one exception," Meliakken said. "The Dragon Summoner will be last. She will watch all she loves die before her, then my apprentice will absorb her power."

Loki had been watching Zana closely. Her face showed all the signs of being completely under a god's will, but there was something, something in the corner of her eyes that was hers' as well as the very slight movement of her wings. Loki didn't know what that might mean. Zana had been betrayed once already by someone offering her power, he knew she had to be wondering if it could possibly happen again.

Everyone was quiet. A host of faeries were poised on one side. Loki could see Brie in the front, ready to lead her sisters into battle. On the other side were the unicorns, with Cathal and Brayton astride Tilmin and Fynbar.

Suddenly in the center of the field there was a great eruption, as if a large seal was broken open and out came thousands of Border Lands warriors on horseback. Loki looked on in wonder as the horses thundered around the entire company ten horses abreast. In the lead rank and slightly ahead of the rest was a woman. Her dark red hair was done up in a ponytail, the end coming to rest between the shoulder blades of her leather armor. One thing that struck the wizard with wonder were her legs. They were metal, black in color with slender lines of gold making intricate designs from the thigh to the foot. He could see her serpent hilt sword raised above her head making a circular motion which let Loki know she was a general.

"Neala!" Lyson yelled as he came to stand next to Loki.

"I take it you know her?" Loki asked Lyson as Neala rode over to them.

"Yes, I trained her. Last I knew she was guarding the great seal in the corridor."

Neala's horse reared and pawed the air before settling down next to the two wizards.

"It's good to see you again General," Neala said smiling at her former mentor.

"What happened to your legs?" Lyson asked while noticing them for the first time.

"Long story, and one that will have to wait until later given the situation here with that grumpy god over there," she said tilting her head in Meliakken's direction. Loki always admired the casual way these warriors went into battle. They would never shrink from a fight.

"She's right, we have a god to deal with. Well, Meliakken, things aren't looking too good for you right now," Loki said knowing there was no real meaning to his words, once again he was stalling for as much time as possible, hoping something would develop to give them direction on how this battle should go, because he had little hope for their chances.

Meliakken shook his head and laughed.

"I know what you are trying to do Loki," Meliakken said. "Stalling for time in the hopes for a miracle, there are no miracles anymore, your gods and goddess have abandoned you. They cannot even come back here anymore in their true form. That pesky goddess was the last to leave, and so left you all defenseless."

Meliakken scanned the forces arrayed against him.

"I almost feel sorry for you," he said. "And if circumstances were different, I might have even spared all of your lives."

His eyes narrowed and his voice took on a menacing tone.

"But your gods held me, imprisoned me, and I will take my vengeance on their creations." His tone once more returned to almost conversational. "It's nothing personal with you Loki, I hope you understand that." For some reason that struck the god as funny and he let out a maniacal laugh.

"So what happens now?" Loki asked. "We will never submit to you, you know that."

"I do, and I am glad you won't, because what comes next is going to be so satisfying to me. And believe me, this will not be a quick death, I will savor this."

The god snapped his fingers and there was a lightning strike followed by a loud crack. Suddenly the sky held nine shrikers that were circling and shrieking, but not yet attacking.

"Something to keep your dragons occupied," the god said.

He snapped his fingers again. A large portal appeared far in the distance behind them as the largest host of demons that Loki had ever seen started a slow march towards them. Some of the demons were walking, others were flying.

"We don't want your warriors, faeries or unicorns to feel left out."

"Is that all?" Loki asked with iron in his voice.

"Just one more thing," Meliakken said as he gave a nod to Zana.

Zana was holding a staff with a black stone attached. She leapt into the air, her wings beating a rhythm to give her altitude. It all seemed to happen so fast as she leveled her staff straight at Emilia and fired an energy bolt of pure blackness that sucked all the light in its path. Loki knew anyone hit with that would cease to exist and he was powerless to move quickly enough to counter it.

Chapter 25

Emilia saw Zana's energy bolt streaking towards her. She felt no fear. She did not move to the side or fly away. She stood there calmly, as if everything were coming at her in slow motion. She was sure it only seemed that way because all of her senses were heightened. Emilia thought she could hear Lyson scream her name. Watching her father be killed by Meliakken had changed her. The grief and anger had awakened in her a power she never knew existed. She was now able to override all the dragons' will at once, and she found it very easy to do so. Her own dragon, Chaos had also been affected and fought to be set free.

The pain of her father's death was like an open wound that was spewing blood, and she couldn't figure out how to close it, only now she didn't want to. She was feeding off its pain, making her both numb and coldly enraged. Emilia felt her eyes turning black as before, making everything around her grey. Color was gone and everyone was outlined in sharp defined lines. She could feel the rush of the blood through her veins and felt its raw power as it coursed through her body. As she tapped into it she was tapping into her very soul and the universe beyond. It filled her being, making her feel like a channel of incredible power. She had taken the comb out of her hair and transformed it into her staff with the pearl stone of the goddess. Pointing it at the energy beam that Zana hurled towards her, her own beam colliding with it only inches from her face. She felt the power and darkness coming off of it. Emilia knew that if Zana had possessed this power during their first encounter, she would surely be dead. She assumed it had come from Meliakken, but it was no match for the magic that Emilia now wielded.

Her wings opened up and slowly she started lifting off, drawing Zana's beam of darkness with her so no one would be accidentally hurt.

"You can stop this," Emilia said to her. Even though she was some distance away, Emilia was able to use her magic to make herself heard. "You can leave here and not one soul will harm you. You have my word."

Zana was still focusing all her energy on Emilia.

"Do you really think this is all the power I have?" Zana said with a growl. "This is but a small taste of what is in store for you."

Zana let the beam go as Emilia did too. They hovered some distance above the earth, circling as they faced off against each other. Everyone below watched, barely breathing to see what would come next.

"Leave Zana. Leave before your life is taken from you. Your crimes are many, but you don't need to be a pawn of gods or wizards. Leave sister."

Zana stopped circling and just hovered. Emilia could see what she had said had penetrated somewhat.

"I cannot," Zana said in a cold and distant voice. "He has my soul now. And do not call me sister. I gave up the right to be called that ages ago. I have no sisters."

"Then you leave me no choice," Emilia said.

"Good," Zana said. "Now we both have no choice."

With that, Zana took the spear off her arm and threw it with deadly accuracy at Emilia. Zana never missed a target when she threw her spear. But Emilia had a spear as well. One made by her grandfather, the master craftsman of his age. Grabbing her spear she extended it and letting it fly she yelled, "Nocte!"

The black spear sliced neatly through Zana's spear, the pieces falling to the earth as it sped towards Zana's heart. Zana quickly dove straight down but not before Nocte sliced her shoulder. This enraged Zana and her hands started moving in an intricate pattern. A ball of lightning was forming between her palms and she hurled it towards Emilia, encasing her body. Emilia's body went rigid with pain as the electricity assaulted her. She had underestimated the power that Zana now possessed. She had lightning thrown at her before and was able to repel it, but this was burrowing into the very marrow of her bones. She was no longer able to move her wings and began to fall. Emilia knew no one would be able to help her without getting themselves electrocuted. If she was going to get out of this she needed to focus she thought to herself. She needed to stop looking at the problem and start looking for the solution, which was difficult with all this chaotic energy flowing through her. Chaotic. Chaos. That was the answer.

Emilia reached deep within herself as the dragon tattoo on her leg started to blaze.

"Chaos, I need you," she said.

As if being let off the leash, Chaos erupted from Emilia's body, coming directly underneath her so that she rode on his back. The fiery red dragon absorbed all of Zana's electricity into himself while at the same time feeding healing energy into his mistress. He flew low along the ground as he tilted his wings and banked straight up. Getting back up to the level of Zana he hovered and let out an earth-shattering dragon's roar. The shrikers were still circling. Emilia knew they must be operating on some silent command from Meliakken to not become involved.

"Well, Zana, do you want to try this again?" Emilia said now feeling back to full strength.

"To the death," Zana said as she raised her arm and one of the shrikers flew beneath her and she settled onto its back.

Em, do you need help? Andy said speaking to Emilia's mind.

No brother, this is my task, she said with resolve.

Chaos screeched his challenge and the shriker screeched back as both propelled themselves forward like horses in a joust. Emilia was one with her dragon. Chaos was like an extension of herself and it would only take a thought to move him one way or the other. As they got closer, Chaos started to do a barrel roll as daggers of ice shot out of his talons. Zana's shriker was no novice to battle, and spinning in the opposite direction let loose with a barrage of lightning strikes. Emilia's staff was blazing as she stood on the back of her dragon. She had no fear of falling off, Chaos would make sure she didn't with his magic. Zana likewise was standing on the back of her shriker, a jet of liquid flame coming off her staff.

"Summoner," came Sibila's voice in her ears as if she were standing right next to her. "Beware the god fire, it can destroy your dragon, and you. Your shield will not help you."

Emilia didn't take the time to respond, but quickly had Chaos dive straight down as Zana's fire flew past the spot they had momentarily occupied. Emilia knew she needed to disarm Zana and get her staff away from her, for she knew all her power was being channeled through that. No doubt it was a weapon that Meliakken had given her.

Chaos was itching to get back into the fight and Emilia was hard-pressed to try and make him understand the danger. She looked behind her and saw Zana had taken up position there.

She had to do something Zana would not expect. Suddenly she had it, and she actually smiled at the simplicity of it.

Chaos, listen carefully, she said speaking to the creature's inner spirit. She started sending him images of fog. Once she felt he had the idea, Emilia looked behind her to judge the distance between Zana and herself. The timing would have to be perfect for this to work.

"Just a little bit closer," Emilia whispered to herself.

"This is the end, Donella," Zana said raising her staff. "This is where you pay the price for all you have taken from me."

"Now," Emilia said to her dragon.

Coming off of Chaos's wings was a contrail of white that obscured Zana's view. Emilia took Nocte off of her arm once more.

"Grandfather, please guide my spear," she prayed to the man who had forged her weapon with mastery and love. Eyeing a spot some distance away she aimed her spear and threw it, calling its name as she did. "Nocte!"

Now for the timing. Emilia counted down from ten. She could see Nocte had made its turn and was heading back to Emilia's hand. Judging the time to be right, she lay flat on Chaos' back and gave her command.

"Brake, Chaos, brake!"

Chaos pulled up with his wings fully extended allowing the wind to provide a level of drag as well as using his magic to propel himself backward as Zana and her shriker blew past them. Emilia stood up again and using her thought and connection to Chaos, positioned themselves directly behind Zana. Closing one eye, Emilia made tiny adjustments to their position as she held her hand out. Zana had been looking backwards at Emilia, bewildered at what they were doing. Emilia's face was grim when she looked at Zana, who turned to look in front of her, but it was too late.

Emilia's hand was raised in direct line with Zana's hand that held her staff. The hand that Nocte had just passed threw at the wrist, severing it from Zana's body. The staff went falling to the ground with Zana's fingers still clutching the shaft. The evil faerie's face went pasty white as she stared in horror at the loss of her hand, blood spurting out and running down the shrikers back. Emilia was about to fly over and cauterize her wound after Nocte returned to her hand when an angry shout came from below.

"You pathetic fool!" Meliakken roared. "I give you all this power and you can't even destroy a mediocre faerie. You are not fit for the station I elevated you to. You are worthless! You were worthless to Devon, you are worthless to me."

Emilia watched as Meliakken's words bit into Zana and her eyes closed and her head dropped to her chest in defeat and shame.

"Your life is over Zana. I am done with you!"

An invisible hand reached out and picked Zana up like a rag doll off the shriker's back and held her suspended.

"Think on your life for the few moments that you sail through the sky before your death."

Making a throwing motion, Meliakken threw Zana like a dead bird, her body flying through the air until she was taken from sight, to impact only the gods knew where. Every eye was transfixed as they followed the path of her flight. All eyes but one.

"Zana!" Finn screamed.

Finn went running, he appeared to stumble once before changing form. The golden dragon took flight and headed in the direction that the god had so viciously thrown the faerie that he loved.

"Finn!" Brion yelled. "Finn come back!"

***

"Let him go brother," Caleb said to Brion.

"We need him, Bull," Brion said. "You remember the trouble we had dealing with just one shriker. Could your sister bring him back?" he asked Andy.

Andy's gaze was still looking towards where Finn had flown off to. Emilia had settled back down to earth and stood next to Lyson who held her tight. Chaos at some point had disappeared.

"I'm sure she could," Andy said. "She's already proven she can control all of us at once, but I don't want to ask her to do that again."

"Why?" Brion asked.

"I don't know," Andy responded, "but something is telling me not to do it."

All attention was drawn to Loki as he started speaking again.

"It appears you have lost a key ally," Loki said to Meliakken.

Andy knew Loki was not meaning to talk about Zana as if she meant nothing. He was keeping the god in the dark of what he thought their chances were, making him believe that no perceived advantage or disadvantage matter in the least.

"She was a pawn, Loki. A tool to be used and discarded when it was no longer of any value and actually crossed over into a weakness."

Meliakken took a deep breath and sighed.

"Alright Loki, I've let you play your little game, the stalling is over. It's time for the battle to begin."

Meliakken brought his hands together in a mighty clap, and like hounds being released from their leashes, the demons attacked.

"Unicorns!" Brayton cried.

Andy watched as Brayton and Cathal led the unicorns in

a charge against the demon horde that was racing towards them, their horns gleaming in the sunlight and pulsing with magic. The faeries had also lifted off the ground and with spears extended flew off to meet the demons in the air.

"Warriors!" Neala shouted as every Border Lands warrior wheeled their mounts around to join the unicorns and faeries in battle.

Andy felt the temperature of the air had risen considerably with the heat of battle finally under way. Meliakken clapped his hands, and the shrikers erupted with shrieks and screams and started to attack.

"Brothers!" Andy yelled as every dragon ran for space and made their change. Climbing into the sky, Andy had two shrikers chasing him. So far they haven't hurled anything at him. He wasn't sure if they were just playing or what. He craned his long neck to look back as he completed a wide arc to the left when he noticed they had disappeared.

Watch out, Andros, Brion said to his mind as he engaged his own shriker, *they just disappeared behind you.*

Yeah, well two can play at that game, Andy said as he phased out.

Hey! Where did Andros go? Jace said as he was flying right next to him.

I'm right below you, Jace, Andy said. *I just phased, I'll explain later, if we live.*

In his altered state of phasing Andy could see the shrikers, they were just coming up on Brion's tail.

Brion! Fire directly behind you! Andy said.

Brion didn't hesitate and started firing lightning strikes at nothing he could see. One strike hit a shriker and forced it back into view. Jace and Gael were on it in seconds as Jace flew in from above and Gael from below, shredding it with fire. One set of its wings was incinerated and another severely damaged as it spiraled downward. Suddenly its head snapped back as if hit with something. As Andy looked closer, he could see protruding from the shriker's eye was the feathered end of an arrow. The rest of the shaft buried in its brain as it began its death fall.

Scanning below, Andy saw the source of the arrow. Standing on a rock holding a bow in her hand was Cleo. She touched two fingers to her brow and gave Andy a salute. Vasara's archer was on the field, and god help the enemy that stood in her way. Cleo had told him how Bart had given her the bow and the new powers bestowed with that. He felt a momentary pang as he realized Bart and his father were probably together now, although which paradise do wizards enter when they have left this world? Andy shook his head, he couldn't think of those thoughts just now, there was a battle to be won.

We could sure use your sister right about now, Caleb said as he tried to outmaneuver the shriker flying in his wake.

Em, we need you! Andy said as he phased back in where everyone could see him.

Andy saw her lifting off the ground, her staff blazing as she blasted a path through several demons that got in her way as she came to settle onto Andy's back. He could immediately feel her link up to himself and the others.

Are you alright? He asked her.

No, she said. *And don't pretend you are.*

I'm not, Andy responded. *But you know Dad would want us to finish this. To make sure all these lives weren't in vain, including his own.*

He could feel some of the tenseness leaving her body at his words, even though all the raw anger remained. Anger was okay, he thought to himself, as long as it had focus.

You're right, she said in a calm and deadly voice. *Let's finish this.*

Andy knew her eyes had gone black and she was tapping into that source of power that had been awakened with their father's death.

"Chaos!" she shouted.

Her dragon appeared next to Andy and gave a silent nod. The battle of the dragons was about to begin.

Chapter 26

"Well, Loki, looks like it's just you and this handful of misfits," Meliakken said with a laugh.

"There is a vast array of power here Meliakken," Loki responded as Dain and Lyson came to stand next to him.

"Not compared to mine," the god answered.

Loki noted that Meliakken seemed to be looking around, as if he expected someone to be here that wasn't.

"Was Meliakken now stalling?" Loki asked himself.

Luel's wings started to move as she lifted off the ground.

"What are you doing?" Loki asked her.

"I'm not going to do anything rash," she promised. "I'm just not going to be predictable."

The wizard watched as Luel flew to the opposite side of the god who had also followed her flight. Lyson extended his black wings to take flight.

"Now where are you going?" Loki asked him.

Lyson just smiled and flew off after the queen.

"I guess it's just you and me Dain."

"And what are we, fish bait?" came a cranky voice parting through the semi-circle of priests.

"This wouldn't be an end of the world event without you here Dim," Loki said smiling.

There was a loud cry of many voices as a force of demons had broken through the unicorns and faeries and were now heading their way.

"Should I deal with them?" Dain asked Loki as he readjusted his sword.

"Are you ever going to get rid of that sword?" Loki asked.

"Old habits die hard," Dain said smiling at him. "Just like old men."

"Was that a compliment or an insult?" Diminitus asked.

"Cleo and I will take care of the demons," Leah said as she flew by, stopping to kiss her beloved in mid-air before proceeding on. A contingent of faeries that had held back in reserve flew after her.

"I think it's time Loki, don't you?" Meliakken asked him. "Do you surrender, or do you die?"

Wait, a voice spoke to Loki's mind.

Loki stood stock still, letting nothing register on his face that he had heard something.

Wait, came the voice again.

"I'm going to take your silence as your answer not to submit. Say goodbye to this world Loki, and everyone in it that you love."

Get ready, the voice said. *Get ready to clear the circle.*

"Dain, when I tell you, grab Diminitus and propel yourself backwards out of the circle."

Dain to his credit didn't ask questions as he nodded his ascent. All of a sudden there was a loud crack and a flash of many colors.

"Now, Dain!"

Loki and Dain both used the source as they directed a force at the ground that propelled them up and backwards beyond the circle of priests, with Diminitus struggling and complaining as Dain held him fast. Everyone was momentarily blinded, but once they could see again, Killian was standing in the center.

Roland Capalbo

"Ha!" Meliakken screeched. "I knew you would turn up!"

"And to your demise you foul god," Killian said as he thrust both palms forward.

Just then the most remarkable thing happened. The priests of the gods raised their hands, palms pointing at Killian. The medallions were visible on their chest now and started to glow with each of the colors of the gods. The power flowed through their bodies into Killian who then channeled it into a single beam that flew straight for Meliakken's chest. Meliakken put his own hand up and his own beam shot forth to connect with Killian's. His eyes went wide and Loki thought he saw a small amount of fear there.

"What is this!" Meliakken roared. "This is not possible!"

Killian started to laugh. "Now you see it don't you."

"They can't be here, it is forbidden, it violates the magic the five themselves put in place."

"You have a lot of power, Meliakken, but you're really just a simple god after all."

"What are you talking about?"

"The five aren't here, but their power is, within these vessels," Killian said tilting his head to the priests behind him.

"The vessels!" Samara suddenly said right into Loki's ear because she was standing right next to him.

"What do you mean?" Loki asked her.

"Never mind," she said, and promptly disappeared.

"Where did she go?" Dain asked looking perplexed.

"That goddess has corrupted everyone here," Diminitus said crankily. "They all act just like her, popping in and out, talking in riddles."

"Dim, shhh," Loki said.

Meliakken started to laugh again.

"I believe you are missing one," Meliakken said. "Cael's

323

power can't be missed in the king of the fauns. Aditya's twins are holding their own," he said of Ava and Rhyan who weren't even breaking a sweat. "It's a shame that Fallon's priest is tied up here. I know the power of the Cath Priomh would have come in handy against my demon lords. I will say this about Raphael's priest," Meliakken said looking at Ala, "she has steel in her spine unlike any other."

"Damn right she does!" Diminitus shouted with pride. In spite of all that was going on, Ala was able to give her beloved a loving smile, as her eyes showed resolve and determination.

"But there is one missing, isn't there Killian?" Meliakken asked. "Where could Trystan's priest possibly be? Could it be that he is dead!"

Just then an energy bolt came flying in aimed at Meliakken's back. The god raised his other hand and countered the energy beam coming from both Luel and Lyson.

"Your power has grown faerie queen from the last time we met. I see you have truly harnessed the power of your father's stone. It's too bad one of my general's couldn't have wrested it from him before you killed him."

"Shut your mouth you filth. I lay the blame of his death at your door, same as my husband's," Luel spat at him.

"I love your anger. Makes you unstable and unable to focus."

"We shall see," Luel said as the jewel of the house of Caster blazed forth.

"Not enough Killian, not nearly enough to defeat me."

Suddenly there was a loud clap and every cloud in the sky scattered as if they were brushed away by a gale force wind.

"How about we throw in the power of the sun," Nyle said as he reached into the sun's core and brought forth his most deadly fire which raced towards Meliakken as it joined with the other beams of energy. The god was actually pushed back a fraction of an inch before he looked at Nyle with a deathly smile.

"Ahh, welcome Sol. You too I have been expecting. You defeated the god of monsters, but I am the god of everything. I think you are going to find yourself severely lacking today."

Loki was only a few steps away from Nyle.

"Are you giving him everything?" Loki asked him.

Nyle just nodded, his body aflame as he poured every ounce of power from the sun into the god.

"By the gods!" Dain exclaimed. "Is he a match even for the sun?"

"It would appear so," Loki said grimly, not liking their chances at all.

Suddenly there were lightning strikes coming from every direction. Loki looked up and saw the shrikers were trying to assault the priests of the gods as the dragons kept trying to engage them. It was an aerial combat that was dizzying to follow.

"Dain, we need to raise a shield!" Loki said.

"No!" a shout came close to Killian as Samara reappeared in the center. "Protect the vessels," she shouted as she threw her hands up and a dome the color of transparent blood covered the priests of the gods. The shrikers strikes impacted with the dome but could not penetrate it, thwarting their efforts.

"You insolent witch!" Meliakken roared. "I should have killed you when I had the chance."

Samara smiled at him. "I like you angry. Makes you unstable and unable to focus," she said throwing the god's words back at him. "Oh, and my father says hello."

"Nice touch," Killian said with approval. Samara winked at him. "Loki, Dain, we need you now."

"Dain, you go over on the far side by Tori, I'll go by Ala," Loki said.

As the wizards took up position, they raised their hands and added their power to everyone else's. Meliakken was still the portrait of control. He showed no sign of wavering, not even breaking out in a sweat if gods even sweat. Loki saw Diminitus walk over to his beloved.

"Ala, are you alright?" he asked with concern.

"I'm okay, Dim." She said touching his cheek. "I can feel him my love, I feel Raphael. It is like his very life force is flowing through me."

Her voice dropped to a whisper, but Loki could still hear her.

"The amount of power I feel," she said, "it's nowhere near full strength."

Loki was stunned. How were these people even able to handle what was pouring through them now if there was more to come.

Meliakken's laugh was measured and controlled. "Not near enough Killian, not near enough power at all."

Killian stopped talking. He was controlling all the forces being directed at him into a single beam. Loki found that truly remarkable, that one being could contain all those lines of power. But he knew Meliakken was feeling it too. He was no longer so indifferent with his comments. He had to concentrate to bring his focus to bear. Even still, Loki knew without Redlin to channel Trystan's power, they didn't stand much of a chance.

***

"Brayton!" Cathal yelled. "Watch your left flank."

"Tilmin, to the left," Brayton said as they charged a contingent of demons.

Brayton's sword was singing, slashing demons left and right as Tilmin's horn vaporized all that came in contact with him.

They succeeded in clearing a wide swath around themselves. Then Tilmin pulled up short and stopped.

"Sorry Tilmin, they came up on my blindside," Brayton said touching the patch on his eye.

It is of no moment your highness, Tilmin said graciously. *We would have gotten to them eventually.*

Brayton looked up and saw a faerie with chestnut-brown hair and red wings flying towards them.

"Brie!" Brayton called as the faerie landed beside them. "What's the word?"

"We could use some help over on the rise," Brie said as she pointed behind Brayton.

Brayton looked to where she was pointing and could see four lone figures standing on the hillside.

"Demon lords?" Cathal asked wiping the sweat off his brow.

Brie nodded. "They are guarding something, and we can't get any faeries near them. I've already lost a score of my best," she said, her face set grimly.

Suddenly there was a loud screech overhead. Looking up, Brayton saw the sky covered with monsters and faeries zig zagging, doing their deadly dance with their spears. Further to the east he could just make out the dragons in aerial combat with the shrikers. Like here, everything looked like a huge melee. More demons had spotted them and were starting to close their circle.

"Any ideas, Tilmin?" Brayton asked.

You are the Summus Re'em, Highness. If you don't know what to do no one does.

Brayton was really wishing Savano was here right now.

Fear not.

"What did you say?" Brayton asked.

"I didn't say anything," Cathal said. "You alright there brother?"

"Yes," Brayton said puzzled. He knew he heard a voice, and he knew he recognized it somehow. It wasn't Savano, he would know her voice in his head. It was someone else. Someone ancient.

You are my blood.

"What does that mean?" Brayton asked.

"Bray, who the hell are you talking to?" Cathal asked getting agitated. "I really hate when you get these visitors in your head that no one else can hear. I swear it must be a trait of the Taiyo line."

Brayton's eyes suddenly went wide. "Cathal, you are a genius!"

"What? What did I say?" Cathal asked clearly thinking his friend had finally slipped into craziness.

"Brie, can you keep those demons heading this way off our backs for a few moments?"

Brie gave a smart salute and lifted off. Giving a sharp whistle, a hundred faeries followed her headlong into the charging demons.

Brayton wrapped his hand around the horn that hung on his chest, closed his eyes and concentrated. When he opened them he was no longer in Otherwhere. It wasn't like the glade where Caomhnoir guarded the gate to the unicorn paradise, but it was a glade with a stream running through it. Lush grass lay on either bank with trees that had white flowers on the branches that reached to the sky.

"Well done, I knew you would find your way here."

Brayton turned around to the source of the voice. Standing under a tree stood a tall man with flaxen colored hair and cornflower blue eyes. His facial features closely resembled those of his father, and he figured probably his own, because he knew who he was.

"You are Taiyo, aren't you?" Brayton asked.

"In the flesh," Taiyo said with a sweeping bow. "Well, sort of anyway. Welcome kinsman. And I guess that kind of makes me your grandfather, many times removed of course."

Brayton smiled at that. He never thought of Taiyo as his ultimate grandfather, but it did stand to reason since he was a direct descendant.

"Well, Grandfather, can you tell me where I am?"

Taiyo laughed. "For some reason that makes me feel positively ancient, but I guess from your perspective I am."

Brayton smiled and found himself really liking this man. He had read Taiyo's history and his journals and knew the man to be whimsical and a wanderer. Seeing him in real life only reinforced that description. He knew it was also in him, it was a trait with all the descendants of Taiyo, that they venture out and see what there is to discover.

"As to where you are," Taiyo began in answer to Brayton's question, "I really have no idea. This is my first time to this place as well."

"Really?"

"Yes, I was asked to come here, by Trystan," Taiyo said. "I believe it is one of those in-between places, you know, not really anywhere but can connect to places that are somewhere."

Brayton had a hard time following that, but he let it pass.

"Why would Trystan send you here?" Brayton asked him as he scratched at the corner of his patch that had started to bother him.

"Would you like to have that healed?" Taiyo said pointing at his missing eye.

"You can do that?" Brayton asked stunned.

Taiyo nodded his assent.

Brayton thought about that. He marveled that Taiyo could

perform that kind of healing, but the patch on his face had come to mean something. It symbolized the fight of the unicorns on the Palatine Bridge, the battle against the warlocks and also Savano's death at the hands of Meliakken. He wanted to remember all that had happened, and his missing eye was a physical reminder of that. The unicorns went into battle because of him, and the patch on his eye felt like a part of him now.

"I think I will leave it as it is for now," Brayton told him.

Taiyo walked over and placed a hand on his shoulder.

"Believe me, I understand," Taiyo said with empathy in his eyes. "But time is short, and I must tell you the reason why I am here."

"The demon lords?" Brayton asked.

"Yes, you cannot get close enough to destroy them."

"Why is that?" Brayton said running his fingers through his hair.

"They are not like your every run of the day demon lords," Taiyo said. "These ones have been infused with some of Meliakken's power. You could almost say they are the kings of hell."

"Do you know what it is they are guarding?" Brayton asked.

"I do. They surround a crystal that is the color of the sun. It is shaped like an obelisk and is a man's height."

Taiyo looked intently at Brayton to give importance to his next words.

"It is a dimensions' breaker," Taiyo said.

"What does that mean?" Brayton asked perplexed.

"It opens the barriers between the demon world and any other world they choose to enter. If it stays open too long the break remains, and the demons can come and go as they please. They are close to achieving this."

"How can I destroy it?"

"The answer rests against your chest."

Brayton looked down at the horn on its necklace that rested against his chest.

"What am I supposed to do with it?"

"You must hurl it into the center of the crystal. The material that makes up the horn will cause the crystal to explode, which will kill the demons and seal the barrier."

"Will the horn be destroyed as well?"

"It will," Taiyo said.

"Would I no longer be the Summus Re'em?" Brayton asked.

Taiyo again placed his hand on Brayton's shoulder.

"The horn never made you the Summus Re'em, my boy. That has always come from within. It is who you were always destined to be."

Brayton felt better about that, but still sad to have to destroy something that he had worn around his neck since the day he found it in the crypt all those many years ago.

"How do I get close enough?" he asked. "None of the faeries have been able to get within a hundred yards of them without getting killed."

"That I am not able to tell you, only that the horn can guide you."

Suddenly a bird, startled from its nest gave a screech as it flew away into the sky. Brayton was following its flight before turning his attention back to Taiyo. But when he looked, his ancestor had vanished. He looked down at the horn as he held it in his hand.

"The horn can guide me, eh?" he asked himself. "I don't suppose you could tell me what to do?" he asked speaking to it.

What would you like to know? Asked a deep voice inside his head.

"By the gods!" he exclaimed. "You can speak?"

Of course, the voice said, *not that you have ever bothered to find out.*

Brayton swore the voice sounded slightly offended and had to laugh at that.

"I'm sorry," Brayton said sincerely, "my mind has been otherwise occupied."

It's alright, the voice told him, *no harm no foul. Thankfully, you discovered it now before doing what you need to do.*

"Why is that, and why have you never spoken before?"

It is the magic of this device, you must seek dialogue first. As for your other question, if you had destroyed the horn without connecting with me, I would have been destroyed along with it.

"What are you, and do you have a name?" Brayton asked.

Call me Cosain. As for what I am, say I am a guide or protector even.

"Protector for whom?"

I would have thought that was obvious, you.

"Cosain, can you tell me how to get the horn into the crystal without getting slaughtered by the demon lords?"

As Summus Re'em, you have the power to invoke tayaran, Cosain said.

Brayton looked perplexed and scratched his head. "What is tayaran?"

While on the unicorn you are astride, speak the word and you will see.

"And then what?"

Brayton paused to listen, there was no answer.

"Cosain? Well, so much for the guide."

Brayton focused and brought himself back to the battlefield.

"Where did you go brother?" Cathal asked him.

Are you alright, your highness? Tilmin asked him.

"Yes," Brayton said to both of them. "Tilmin, have you ever heard of tayaran?"

Tilmin craned his neck around to come in eye contact with the prince.

Only as a legend, Tilmin responded. *The only thing I know about it is that it has to do with flight.*

Brayton pondered that for a moment. What could flight have to do with unicorns, it made no sense.

Care to help me out here, Cosain? Brayton said to the awareness in the horn.

"I can see you are talking to your invisible friends again," Cathal said.

"Yes, except they aren't talking back. I think we are just going to have to rely on faith here."

"I always hate when you say that," Cathal said as he grabbed a fistful of mane. "Very well, let's get on with it."

"Let's go!" Brayton yelled as Tilmin pawed the air and wheeled around to gallop towards the demon lords, with Cathal and Fynbar close behind.

The horns of the unicorns were blazing as they threw up a shield of protection vaporizing any demon that came in contact with them. Brayton could see them getting closer and closer to the demon lords. Holding onto Tilmin's mane with one hand, he yanked the horn off its chain and closed his fist around it as he focused all his thoughts.

"As Summus Re'em, I invoke tayaran!" Brayton shouted.

For the briefest of moments a vision appeared before him of a unicorn mare all in black, her horn the color of the rainbows. Her head nodded as if giving permission, then reared on her hind legs as huge black wings unfolded from her body.

"By the gods!" Cathal exclaimed. "Bray, look!"

Brayton looked back at all the unicorns, and down at Tilmin. Fynbar likewise was in the same condition. The unicorns had wings. Brayton smiled to himself, he knew what to do now. He patted Tilmin's neck.

"Are you ready to fly my friend?" Brayton asked the unicorn.

How does one ever know if they are ready for something they are doing for the very first time in their existence.

In the midst of a battle against impossible odds, Brayton roared with laughter.

"Somehow I knew you were going to say something like that."

The first ever flight of the unicorns began. Those below watched in wonder as the entire unicorn herd galloped in a thunderous roar before soaring into the sky. Many of the more hideous demons that could fly broke off their combat with the faeries to meet this new threat.

"Strategy, brother?" Cathal asked as he flew close to Brayton. "We have quite the following of demons hot on our ass."

Brayton looked around as he tried to quickly put forth a plan to keep the demons off his back long enough to get to the crystal and hurl the horn into it. There was really only one thing to do, split their forces

"Cath, you take half the unicorns and engage those behind us, I'll take the other half and attack the crystal."

Cathal drew his sword, gave his prince a salute with the tip as he and Fynbar wheeled around to fly head long into the melee.

We have activity ahead, your highness, Tilmin told Brayton. *I can feel the drawing in of magic. I fear those demon lords are about to strike.*

Shield yourselves, Brayton mind spoke to the unicorns he was leading.

Just then, lightning strikes came in from everywhere. Some of the unicorns had fallen instantly. Whether it was because they didn't get their shield up in time, or some factor in the demon lords' magic that allowed it to slip through, the prince didn't know, but there was no stopping now. He felt this could turn into a death charge. Taiyo was right, these demons had more power than an ordinary demon lord. Some of that power was being displayed now as the three demons started to rise into the air, circling around the crystal and creating a cyclone so powerful it was throwing the unicorns flight into disarray.

Cosain, I could use some help here, Brayton said to his self-appointed guide and protector. *I see very little protection going on here.*

What do you mean? Cosain said to Brayton's mind. *You are doing splendidly!*

Is that supposed to be funny, the prince said as Tilmin tried his best to keep his flight going forward amidst the ever-changing wind currents of the cyclone.

Just trying to keep you calm Summus Re'em, because you will need that and laser like focus to achieve what you must. Deep breaths' princeling. Are you ready?

I'm ready, Brayton replied.

Center yourself, Cosain said. *Do not concern yourself with anything else but your objective.*

Brayton did that. He let the sounds of battle die away from his mind and focused on the three demon lords before him. Suddenly it felt like something clicked into place and a door opened in his mind.

Very very good! Cosain said. *Now you see it don't you?*

What is it? Brayton asked.

Your birthright. Reach forth and take it.

Brayton reached out with his mind. It was an energy source that had every color of the rainbow, almost like the colors in Caomhnoir's horn when he first met him guarding the gate to the unicorn paradise. As his mind connected with it, his body reacted violently.

You alright? Tilmin asked as he felt Brayton flailing on his back.

Brayton tried hard to hold onto the power that was fighting him like a wild stallion. That was it, he thought. He centered himself once more and reached out as he would to an unbroken colt, gently and passively. The power was reaching back towards him, tentatively, probing, and eventually submitting. It was now a part of him. He could feel a connection to every unicorn.

Oh my! Tilmin exclaimed.

You feel it? Brayton asked him.

Yes, Tilmin responded. *How is this possible?*

I don't know, but I seem to have a new-found power.

What else can you do with it? Tilmin asked.

We are about to find out, Cosain said.

Who is that? Tilmin asked as he heard Cosain's voice in his head.

We'll talk about it later, Brayton said. *So what happens now?* he asked Cosain.

Think according to your nature as Summus Re'em, came the reply.

Brayton knew he was running out of time.

"According to my nature, what does that mean?" he asked himself.

He pondered that. Cosain had said his nature as Summus Re'em, as the master of the unicorns. Unicorns. Then it hit him. Unicorns are at one with nature, they are so in tune with their grove and every living thing in it. The animals, water, sky, sun, everything. He knew what his power was.

That wasn't so hard, was it? Cosain said to his mind.

Tilmin, fly in the opposite rotation of the wind currents, Brayton said smiling to himself at Cosain's comment.

Brayton could feel Tilmin's puzzlement through his newfound power to link with him, but he banked down and left to come in line with the wind blowing directly at them.

Brayton reached out with both hands. It was then he realized that one other thing his power allowed him to do was not just have a mental link with the unicorns, but a physical one as well. He was in no fear of sliding off Tilmin's back, as if the unicorn became an extension of his own body.

His eyes suddenly flashed white and he was able to see the lines of force the demon's cyclone was making. Rainbow colored tendrils were snaking out of his fingers and connecting with those energy lines as he wrapped them up one by one. Nature was the most powerful natural force in the world and Brayton was straining trying to restrain it and bend it to his will. Like an unbridled colt, he needed to contain it or have it turn on him and destroy him. Tilmin was straining to keep them in the air but Brayton felt his stamina starting to slip.

Hang on Tilmin, I almost got it.

Tilmin was fighting too hard to stay aloft to answer. Suddenly the prince could feel a shift, the cyclone was slowing down. The demon lords shrieked their rage as they saw what Brayton was doing. They unleashed a barrage of lightning and metal shards at him. Being tied up with the cyclone, there was no way he could defend himself.

Tilmin, can you shield us? Asked Brayton breathlessly trying to hold everything together.

No, not against all of that!

Just at the last possible moment a wall of unicorns passed in front of them, absorbing the impact of the attack. Most of the energy and shards were deflected but not without cost. Some of the shards got through and embedded themselves in some of the unicorns' flanks. Brayton watched as they spun out below and impacted with the ground. A few others got caught in the cyclone only to be ripped apart in horror. Brayton heard a voice screaming. It was only after a few moments he realized it was his own.

A deadly calm with a great rage in its center buried itself deep in Brayton's psyche only to explode in one huge blast. Throwing his hands wide he shredded the cyclone and the air became dead. His eyes were blazing white-hot now, and to the demon lords he appeared to be ten feet tall as he stood up on Tilmin's back. Brayton was high above them as they hovered.

"Never again will you enter this world or any other", Brayton said with fierceness that could be heard in every corner of the battlefield.

He sent his thoughts to Tilmin, and the unicorn brought his wings closer to his body as they plunged downward, Brayton like a statue, standing with both arms thrust forward. The fury he unleashed upon them ripped through any shield they managed to throw up. He could see the fear in their eyes because they knew their doom was upon them and they were about to be wiped from existence. As Brayton poured forth his energy, he was reciting the name of every unicorn that had died in his cause. As Summus Re'em he knew them all. The very fabric of the demons' lives were being stripped from them one atom at a time. There would be no vaporous cloud that dissipates on the wind for them, only to reform at another time and place. Even as degraded as they were, the demon lords were still putting up a fight, until Brayton got to the last name on his list as he shouted it out loud.

"Savano!" he shrieked to the heavens.

The detonation as the demon lords ceased to exist reverberated through every ear drum. As Brayton released his energy he started to sway.

Do not falter now princeling! Cosain shouted in his mind. *If you do not finish this task all is lost!*

Brayton shook his head and righted himself. He could see the crystal looming closer.

I need to hit that thing in the center, Tilmin, Brayton told his friend.

Tilmin went low, to about ten feet off the ground. Seeing the direction he was taking, Brayton alerted a score of unicorns to fly directly in front of them in a v-formation, effectively plowing through any demons that were in their path.

Brayton held the horn tightly in the palm of his hand. He felt sadness at what he was about to do, but he knew that to save the world he loved it was necessary. With his new enhanced sight, he was able to see the barrier that the crystal was causing to deteriorate. In the very center he noticed a small hole.

"That is what I have to hit?" he asked aloud.

Yes, Cosain answered, and you can't afford to miss. *Regardless of where you hit it, the horn will be destroyed, but only in the center will the crystal be destroyed as well.*

Brayton licked his lips as sweat built up on his brow in concentration. He took several deep breaths to calm and center himself. Once again, he had to block out the sounds of battle going on all around him. He raised one hand, and with his mind, connected with the hole in the center. It felt like it kept moving, like he couldn't get a firm mental grasp. He calmed himself even further. Now he could hear nothing. It was as if he were in total silence, and even though he stood on Tilmin's back which was moving, he felt like he was on solid ground. A thousand feet, and the crystal was looming larger as they got closer. Five hundred feet, they were almost on top of it.

It's now or never, Cosain said calmly and almost fatherly as he whispered in the very vaults of Brayton's soul.

Brayton's arm reared back then came forward as he released the horn in a direct line at the crystal. He held his breath the entire time as he would if he were shooting an arrow. The horn slid smoothly and easily into the hole of the crystal. It started to hum in an erratic and violent manner, its color turning a sickly gray black.

Climb! Cosain shouted.

Brayton didn't even have to pass that onto Tilmin. He obviously heard it as he gave a powerful thrust of his wings and shot straight up.

Everyone, clear the area, quick! Brayton sent to the minds of all the unicorns.

Unicorns were flying in every direction. Suddenly there was a loud wailing screech coming from the crystal that continued to grow to the point that Brayton had to cover his ears. Then came the explosion. A huge section of earth was thrown skyward while at the same time every demon within a half-mile radius was instantly vaporized. The shock waves threw the unicorns off their flight and Brayton was suddenly falling off Tilmin's back and was hurtling towards the ground. His arms flailed uselessly as he clawed at the air.

"At least I accomplished my task before I die," he thought to himself.

Suddenly his outstretched hand was caught by another as Cathal hauled him up onto Fynbar's back.

"Saw you were in need of a ride brother, I hope you don't mind sharing mine," Cathal said smiling.

The prince smiled in return with gratefulness welling up in his chest for this man who was his first knight and protector. "No, brother, as a matter of fact I don't mind at all."

Then they both burst out laughing like the overgrown boys they were.

You did well, Summus Re'em, Cosain said. *You removed a great threat and received an incredible gift.*

And what gift is that? Brayton asked.

I would have thought that obvious, me of course.

Brayton started laughing again.

"What has you giggling now, brother?" Cathal asked him.

"Just something a friend told me," the prince said.

Well at least you are thinking of me as a friend, Cosain said. *That at least is a start, because we will be together for a very long time.*

Are you a part of me now? he asked.

Only marginally, Cosain said. *There are other things in other worlds that I am responsible for, but I am always here for you to call upon. But all of that would have ceased if you had not spoken to me and freed me from my prison.*

How did you happen to become trapped in the horn? Brayton asked.

That is a long story and doesn't really concern you. For now, just know that I am here, and I will be watching over you.

For some reason that brought Brayton great comfort. Just then Tilmin flew under Fynbar and looked up.

"Thanks for the ride," Brayton said to Cathal as he slid off Fynbar's back and onto Tilmins'.

Where to now? Tilmin asked him.

Let's see if we can lend a hand with the dragons, Brayton replied.

Brayton connected with the unicorns. Half would help the Border Lands warriors and the faeries as they battled the demons on the ground and in the air. The other half would enter the fray with the shrikers. He didn't know what kind of difference they could make against the shrikers with their magic, but whatever could be done, would be done.

Chapter 27

Andy was fighting hard against the shriker in front of him. They were both hurling energy bolts at each other while trying to maintain a shield at the same time. Suddenly the shriker dove and disappeared. Andy immediately phased, once he did he saw the shriker starting to strafe those below with fire. He released his own fire, hitting the back of the shriker as it howled in pain. The shriker started to fly straight up and Andy followed. It went visible and so did Andy, but he wasn't paying attention as he collided with Jace, who was following a shriker of his own, but didn't see Andy until it was too late. With their legs and wings tangled together, they spiraled to the earth, smacking their heads together leaving them dazed and confused.

Andy, Jace! Change! Emilia shouted in their minds.

The two dragon brothers cleared their heads enough to change back into their human forms. Now there were two men hurtling towards the earth and Andy was kind of wishing he had his dragon body to absorb the impact, because he had little doubt that his human body would not survive this free fall. Then as the ground was getting dangerously close, hands slid under their arms and held on tight. Andy saw that Emilia and another faerie that he did not know were beating their wings for all they were worth to slow their descent and gently land the dragons on the ground.

"You boys alright?" Emilia asked.

"Yes," Andy said, thanks Em, and.?"

"Aislynn," the red winged faerie responded, tipping her talon dagger to her head in salute.

"Thank you Aislynn," Jace responded since it was he that Aislynn had saved.

"My pleasure," she said as she smiled and winked before lifting off to rejoin the battle.

"Sorry about that Jace," Andy said.

"No worries, brother," Jace said. "Not the first time one of us has collided with another, I'm sure it won't be the last."

Just then Abby ran up to Andy and threw herself in his arms, hugging him fiercely.

"Just what did you think you were doing?" she said with fire in her eyes.

Andy saw she was holding the sword her father had given her that would shoot lightning bolts at whomever she thrust it at. Her face was smudged with ash and he could see she was not just idly sitting by and watching the battle rage around her.

"I'm sorry love," Andy said. "This whole phasing thing is still kind of new to me."

Abby's face softened as she accepted his explanation, but Andy knew she would always worry about him as he flew the skies without her. Just as he would worry about her on the ground without him there to protect her. He took this one short moment they had to kiss her soundly on the lips, this put her in much better spirits.

Jace was looking up and saw the aerial combat that raged above them.

"We need to get back up there," Jace said.

"Yes," Andy replied, "although I don't know how we are going to tip the balance. Thankfully, we haven't lost anyone but neither have the shrikers."

"We could really use Finn right now," Jace said looking at Emilia.

Emilia just shook her head. Andy knew his sister would not override their wills again. Jace sighed.

"Very well, let's get this done," Jace said, "and hopefully we survive it."

"Wait!" Emilia said, she held up her hand to make them pause as she tilted her head as if listening.

"What is it Em?" Andy asked looking concerned.

Emilia suddenly looked to the south and pointed.

"It's Brayton," she said excitedly, "and the unicorns!"

"By the gods!" Jace exclaimed. "When did they get wings!"

"My guess is just recently," Andy said running his hands through his sandy brown hair. "Time to fly!"

Andy gave Abby a quick kiss and ran to make his change followed by Jace and Emilia who settled onto Andy's back. Andy sent his thoughts out to Brayton.

Brayton, can you hear me?

I hear you Andros, we are coming to help, Brayton replied.

How do we coordinate this? Jace asked. *These shrikers follow no discernible pattern and the risk for accidents is only too great.*

I can guide the dragons through my link to prevent most of that, Emilia said

And I believe I can help with the rest, a voice said that Andy did not recognize.

Who is that? Andy asked.

Cosain, at your service Chief Dragon.

I'll explain later, Brayton said.

Cosain, what did you have in mind? Emilia asked as Andy was swerving left and right trying to avoid demons. One blew up right in front of him from an apparent lightning strike. He looked down to see Abby give him a tip to the brow with her sword in salute before sprinting away to help protect the circle of priests of the gods.

Link with your dragons, Summoner, then link to me, which in turn will link to the Summus Re'em, who will be linked to the unicorn host, Cosain said. *It will seem automatic and will prevent friendly casualties.*

Andy could feel Emilia's amazement of what they were about to do through the link.

We have to engage, so we should do this now, Jace said as he started firing energy bolts above and below him, hitting a couple of broadsides on a shriker flying below with Chaos hot on its tail.

Emilia stood up on Andy's back with her arms spread wide and her staff blazing. She was tapping into that newly awakened power. In a matter of an instant all the dragons were linked to her in tighter bonds than he had ever felt before.

Very good, Summoner, Cosain said. *Now reach out to me.*

It took Emilia a few tries, but she finally made contact with Cosain, who in turn connected to Brayton and all the unicorns. The impact of that coming through the link was like nothing Andy had ever experienced before. His dragon eyes went wide, and his flight faltered before he was able to right himself again. Suddenly he felt something he hadn't felt since this battle had started. Hope.

It felt like the shrikers were everywhere at once. Their ability to disappear was maddening. Chaos helped a lot in this since he could follow them whether they were visible or not. Andy could follow them as well, but he could only really focus on the ones he had engaged.

Em, got any strategy here? Andy asked his sister.

As a matter of fact I do, she replied. *Brayton, can you split your unicorns up so you have like five or six buzzing around those shrikers like flies and draw them apart from each other?*

Yes, we can do that, Brayton replied.

Harass them, don't get into any direct assaults, Emilia said.

I see where you're going, Brayton said.

So do I, Brion echoed.

You do? Andy asked, *because it is still a little fuzzy to me.*

It's very simple brother, Emilia said. *The unicorns will keep each shriker busy to allow the dragons to come in for the kill attacks.*

Can we start this sooner rather than later, Caleb said flying low, swerving left and right with a shriker hurling lightning strikes at him, several hitting his tail. Just then Irwyn flew in, perpendicular to Caleb, and fired ice shards at the shriker, scoring a direct hit that sheared off one of the shriker's four wings causing it to spin away.

Thanks Irwyn, I owe you one, Caleb said.

No problem brother, the silver-colored dragon said as he peeled off in search of another target.

We are almost there, Summoner, Brayton said. Cosain, you ready?

I'm ready, Cosain replied. *I will keep you all from killing one another.*

Why doesn't that make me feel better, Caleb said as he climbed higher.

Let's go, Emilia said standing on Andy's back as her staff blazed with the power of the Goddess.

Andy started a roll, and amazingly Emilia didn't fall off. He could feel the link to all his brothers as well as the unicorns that had suddenly reached them, and being smaller and more agile than the shrikers started their aerial dance of flying on top and under the demon spawn. It was like Emilia said, they were flies, annoyingly buzzing and drawing the shrikers further and further apart from the tight ring they had made while fighting the dragons.

Andy spotted a target. Brayton had moved one of the shrikers off to his left and was raking it with their horns as they flew by, the beast shrieking in pain. The shriker started spinning, sending energy bolts in all directions, most missing the unicorns, although a couple found their mark and sent several to their deaths. When some would fall, Brayton would bring in more. Andy felt it was his turn to do some disappearing.

Hold on Em, I'm going to phase, Andy said.

Andy phased out and disappeared from view.

This is so freaky, Emilia said looking around.

I'm going to fly higher, then dive at that thing, coming visible at the last possible second.

I'm ready, she said kneeling on his neck with her staff pointed level in an attack position.

Once Andy reached the height he wanted, he dove straight down. The shriker had no clue at what was descending on him. The distance was closing rapidly. Making sure he left enough time to swerve away, Andy phased back. Both he and Emilia sent a barrage of energy at the shriker, ripping its body to shreds. Just then Chaos blew right through the middle of the shriker, carrying any remnants in his wake to float away on the wind.

Yes! Andy said excitedly. *That's one.*

Shall we go find another? Brayton asked.

That is an excellent idea, Andy replied as he saw Brion starting to engage his own shriker.

Andy felt the best strategy would be that as one shriker was defeated, the dragons and unicorns would move to help the next dragon, with the ratio of dragons to shriker constantly increasing in their favor. Andy felt certain of victory against these monsters with the unicorns there to help them. He gave a powerful thrust of his wings as he raced up to where Brion was dealing with his shriker.

Hang on Em, we're phasing again.

"Let's do it!" She shouted.

Andy laughed at her enthusiasm for the hunt as he disappeared from view, letting his enemies guess where he would appear next.

Chapter 28

Luel had both hands extended. Her father's jewel on her crown was blazing and almost blinding to look at. All her focus, all her energy was being poured into her magic as she kept the assault against the god firmly in place. Her body and mind were on autopilot, fighting without really thinking. Her spirit however was somewhere else entirely. She felt herself going into an altered state. Her spirit was visiting those places that held great significance for her, all of which involved her husband. The first time she ever met him, he was rummaging through the queen's library at Cavanah Hall. She watched him as he sat for hours pouring through manuscripts. Stray wisps of his hair kept falling in front of his eyes, making him constantly run his fingers through his hair like a comb. Her hand kept rising unconsciously as if she would brush them away. A spark was born in her breast that day for this man who would become the very center of her world, and she his. Image after image kept coming and she communed with them all. She wondered how she could possibly go on. Part of her did not want to.

Luel, a voice said in her mind. She knew instantly who it was.

Father? Where are you, why can't I see you?

There is no time my daughter, Eriyn replied.

He's dead, Father. Meliakken killed my husband, he killed Redlin!

Luel couldn't see her father, but she could feel empathy and sadness coming from him. Even though her spirit was traveling, she knew her eyes were streaming tears down her cheeks.

Luel, listen to me, Eriyn said with the gentleness and kindness of a father's love. *Your spirit must engage with your body and mind. You are nowhere near releasing the jewel's full potential, and you will need to in order to come close to defeating Meliakken.*

I don't know if I can go on, Father, not without him.

Luel, a new voice said, a woman's voice.

Luel knew her body was shaking violently now. She could faintly hear Lyson screaming her name. The voice that she heard was her mother.

Mother? By the goddess, mother, is it truly you? I am so sorry for that day.

The day that was forever seared in Luel's mind was the day her mother told her to flee while she was swarmed over and killed by a band of alfar.

My dear sweet daughter, it is time to let that go. I know the pain that you are going through right now, but you need to set that aside, if not for yourself, then for your children. Remember this, a mother will sacrifice everything for her children, everything.

Luel could feel that the presence of both her mother and father had left. They had done for her the one thing she wasn't currently capable of doing for herself, and that was giving her perspective. She thought of Andy and Emilia, fighting with everything they had to save this world they now called home. She could not call herself a mother if she didn't do everything that was in her power to protect them, just as her own mother had protected her.

She brought her spirit back in line with her body and mind. She looked over and saw Lyson looking back with concern written all over his face.

"Are you alright?" he asked as he kept the energy hot against

Meliakken, his black wings keeping a steady rhythm to hold himself in place.

"I am now," she responded.

She looked at Meliakken. The god, feeling her eyes on him turned his attention from Killian to her.

"Discovered something, Majesty?" Meliakken said with an arrogant sneer.

Luel suddenly felt the anger go hot white inside her. When she first saw her husband killed at the hands of this deity, the jewel in her crown had responded to her emotion and tapped into an energy source she had never felt before. Now she was tapping into it again. Her father had told her she was not even close to releasing the jewels potential. That struck something with her. Release. Let out. She let herself puzzle on this for a moment. To let out was to set something free, to open the door. Door. Suddenly realization dawned on her. She closed her eyes and focused solely on the jewel, and in her mind's eye, she saw it, the door. When it came to her father's house, the house of Caster, there was always a door. And as she expected, there was the pattern her father had taught her since childhood on how to open. The door was blue just like the jewel and the pattern was white spidery lines. Luel traced the pattern one more time and she heard an audible click.

"What was that?" Lyson asked.

Apparently Lyson had heard it too, she thought. The door slowly opened. Once fully opened, she could see a blue sphere racing towards her at an incredible speed. As it got closer she reached out with her mind, body and spirit. Once it connected with all three, she found she could not contain the raw power that was threatening to rip her apart, so she did the only thing she could, she channeled it straight at Meliakken and watched as his head snapped back upon impact.

The god regained his composure and cast dagger eyes at the faerie queen.

"Discovered something did you?" Luel asked smirking and feeling like she could crush the world. A blue nimbus surrounded her body as she hovered in place.

The god was no longer smirking or sneering. She could tell that for the first time, Meliakken knew he would have to work for this victory. Vasara would not just lay down like an obedient dog and play dead.

"You are feeling very strong and powerful," Meliakken said matter-of-factly. "But even with what you have tapped into, it still falls short."

Luel knew he spoke the truth, but they were a lot closer now than they were a few moments ago. She just needed to keep it going and not let up and pray to the goddess for a miracle.

***

Loki could feel the beads of sweat that were forming on his brow. He looked up and watched the aerial combat of the dragons and the unicorns. The dance they were engaged in was incredible and hard to follow. It appeared there were fewer shrikers. The action up there was so fast moving it was hard to tell how many of the foul beasts had fallen. Glancing behind him was a melee of epic proportions. A horde of demons were locked in heated combat with Border Lands warriors, unicorns and faeries.

Listening to Meliakken's engagement with the faerie queen, he knew something to be true; they did not have enough power to offset the power of the god. Loki had spoken to each of the five gods when they had walked the land in physical form. They had told him about the struggle it took to subdue the evil god and imprison him. Had it not been for Braylynn, the landscape of Vasara would look very different than it does today, if it even existed at all.

"So much power here," Loki thought to himself as his gaze swept over everyone that had any magical abilities and were currently directing it at the god, and yet it was still not enough.

"I really wish you were here brother," Loki said to himself as he looked up at the sky as he thought of Redlin. "At least you are in Trystan's paradise now, or wherever it is we wizards go. I expect I will be joining you soon."

This was the longest that Loki had ever channeled the source. He didn't know if there was a limit, but he could feel the strain of it starting to settle into his bones. He looked over at Dain. The poor lad never even had a chance to reach his first century he thought. Dain likewise was struggling to maintain contact. Loki could feel despair starting to take hold of him, the very thing he had warned Luel and Donella about. He shook his head to clear his thoughts, then thoroughly berated himself for his weakness. They may be destroyed he thought, but it wouldn't be because he gave up. He plunged himself even further into the source and opened himself up totally and completely, holding nothing in reserve. Suddenly he heard Meliakken laugh.

"Are you ready to concede, Killian?" Meliakken asked. "Stop right now and I swear I will let everyone live, after I absorb their power of course."

For a split-second, Loki almost thought that sounded like a reasonable request, such was the power of Meliakken's voice.

Now it was Killian's turn to laugh.

"After all our years contending against one another, you don't think I can tell a lie once you speak it," Killian said. "There are only two possible outcomes here, either we will die, or you will."

"Do you really think you could destroy a god?" Meliakken said smirking as he made a subtle twist with his hand.

"By the gods!" Dain said as he was pushed back about ten feet, although he didn't lose contact with the source or the power he was funneling to Killian's energy. "Did you feel that?" he asked Loki who also had been pushed back.

Loki nodded at his brother wizard. Meliakken had been toying with them, evidenced by the fact he could so easily force them back.

"That is what we are here to find out," Killian said in answer to the god's question. "If you look skyward, you will see most of your pets have been destroyed."

Meliakken just shrugged. "Like Zana, they were just tools, they served their purpose which was keeping the dragons occupied."

At the mention of the evil faerie's name, Loki couldn't help but wonder at her fate.

***

As soon as Meliakken had flung Zana half-way across Otherwhere, Finn had flown after her, picking up her staff that still had the hand clutching the shaft that Donella had cut off with her spear. Seeing the way the god had so brutally cast her aside had caused something to snap inside the golden dragon. He knew now he could never forsake Zana, no matter what she had become. Their destinies were intertwined, and it was the reason why he was winging his way to her now, not knowing whether she was dead or alive.

His long neck was scanning back and forth, searching the ground for any sign. He almost missed it, but as he flew over a field of tall grass, he could see a line of grass that looked like it had been flattened by some object, and it was at the end of that line that he found her, face down and unmoving. Changing back to his human form he ran to her. Sliding on his knees, he grabbed her and pulled her into his lap. She groaned from the pain. Her face was cut and bleeding and one of her wings had sheared off.

"Thank the gods you're alive!" Finn exclaimed.

Zana's eyes fluttered as she looked up at him.

"Finn," she said weakly as her hand brushed his cheek, "let me die."

"No!" he shouted, tears starting to fall down his stubble cheeks. "Not again, you will not push me away again. Where you go, I go."

She smiled a warm sad smile at him. He could see her eyes were clear for the first time in eons.

"You cannot go where I go, my love. For I go to pay for all my crimes, of which there are many."

It was not lost on Finn that she had called him her love. A sob escaped his throat as he held her tightly against his chest. He could feel the hopelessness of the situation. Her body was broken and death would be here soon to claim her. The thought of going on in this life any longer without her was more than he could bear.

In the vaults of his mind, he heard a voice, a woman's voice. *Fly*, she said.

"Fly? Fly where?" he asked.

Zana looked at him puzzled as she slipped in and out of consciousness.

Meliakken, she said. *Use Cael's gift.*

Finn was stunned. How did she know about his other gift? Suddenly it dawned on him what it was she wanted him to do, and it rocked his very core. Then he looked down at Zana who had closed her eyes. His tears were splashing on her face as he thought how peaceful she looked. He pushed her dark hair behind her pointed ears. It had all come to this. They would be together, but not in this life. Cael must have seen this day coming and had given Finn the one gift that could possibly make a difference. The god had poured a part of himself into the young dragon to give him this ability. The ability to penetrate any god shield. Finn believed Donella must have known he had this gift from his thoughts as she tried to make him kill Zana in her madness.

Finn slowly started to caress Zana's cheek and call her name as he poured some of the healing energy of the source into her body. There was so much damage.

"Zana, can you hear me? I need you to wake my love."

"Finn?" she asked sounding confused. "Is it time to go? Is it time to die?"

Finn bit his bottom lip as he took a deep breath to calm himself.

"No Zana, it is not time to die. Not yet. I need you to use your power one last time, and then we can both sleep."

One thing that Finn was good at with the source was healing. He was pouring all his energy into closing her many wounds, stopping the flow of blood from draining out of her body. He could see her awareness getting stronger and stronger, but there was a lot of damage internally, he would not be able to save her. The best he could do was keep her alive until they did what they had to do. Zana was sitting up now, alert and coherent.

"Finn, what are you doing?"

"We are going to take vengeance on the one who has manipulated everything from the very beginning." Finn looked dead serious at Zana. "Including you."

Zana hung her head in shame.

"That wasn't Meliakken, that was me. She looked up at him with tear stricken eyes. "Leave Finn, I am not redeemable."

"Maybe you aren't," Finn said. "Maybe I am too for forsaking my brothers and coming to the place where I belong, at your side. But that doesn't mean we can't strike a blow at our enemy for all he has done. I want you to fly with me, just one last time, just one last time, Zana."

Zana looked at him with sadness and tears in her eyes. She was thoroughly broken in body and spirit.

"Finn, I don't know if I have anything left in me. I barely have the will to want to continue living. The only thing I want right now is the love I lost and the forgiveness of my goddess."

Finn cupped her face and gently kissed her lips, something he hadn't been able to do in over fifteen hundred years. Zana's eyes went wide and she kissed him back fervently. She broke off the kiss as she started to cough so violently, blood spraying the front of Finn's dragon clothes.

"Easy love, I've got you," Finn said as he crushed her body to his. "As for the things you want, your love was never lost, it has always been right here," he said pointing to his chest. "As for forgiveness, who's to say what is to come."

Zana took a deep breath and gathered her strength.

"I will go with you," she said at last. "For good or ill, we will make our last stand together."

Finn started to see the fire come back into her eyes, the fire of the faerie warrior he met that first day by the lake and in his soul knew his life was forever wrapped up with hers.

"Together my love, we leave this world together."

Zana looked down at her legs that were twisted at unnatural angles, then turned her head to try and see where her wing had once been.

"I don't know how I am going to get on your back," she said.

"Don't worry," he said, "I will take care of that. You will need this."

Finn handed her the staff that she took with the hand that remained. Zana looked at the stump on her other arm that Finn had cauterized and stopped the flow of blood.

"I can feel its power," Zana said. "His power."

"What's wrong?" asked Finn sensing her hesitancy.

"If he senses what we are about to do, he could take over my will. He could make me destroy you."

"I'm willing to take that chance," Finn said resolutely. "Something tells me if we don't do this, Vasara fails."

He looked back to where he knew the battle was raging but could not see it.

"If that happens, it won't really matter, nothing will."

Zana saw his determination and fed off of it.

"I'm ready if you are," she said.

"I'm ready," he said as he started to give himself room to change.

"Finn, wait!" Zana cried.

"What is it?" he asked coming back with a concerned look on his face.

"If this is the end, please kiss me one more time. Please, Finn, I desperately need this. I need to feel like a faerie again, like a woman," she said with tears streaming down her face.

Finn also had tears in his eyes as he sat down and embraced her, kissing her deeply. In that one moment, nothing existed but them. In the space of a few minutes of a kiss they had created their own paradise.

Finn broke their kiss and ran to give himself some room to make his change. The golden dragon now stood where the man once was. Reaching forth his talon, he gently picked Zana up and sat her down on his back.

Are you alright? He asked her.

Zana laughed, but it was the laugh she used to have at the

beginning. Before the thirst for power, before Devon, when she was truly free.

"Considering that we are probably winging our way to our deaths, and my body is a broken mess; yes, I'm alright."

Okay, Finn said, *here we go.*

Finn thrust his wings powerfully, gaining as much altitude as he could. His only plan was to get high enough and then descend on Meliakken before he had a chance to see what was coming at him. It was an insane plan, but it was all he had. He looked back at Zana who had put all her trust in him in this one final blow. He prayed it wasn't in vain.

Chapter 29

Loki was not feeling too good about their chances. As Meliakken displayed an increase in his power, the priests of the gods had answered in kind.

"Ala, are you at your limit yet?" Loki asked Raphael's priest.

She just looked at him and nodded. Loki was afraid of that. There was no way they could overcome him. The wizard could see that this was not exactly a cake-walk for the god. Meliakken was being put to task as he was hit from all sides. They just needed a little more. They needed Trystan's power.

"Killian," Meliakken called out to his long-time enemy. "This is your final chance to surrender now before I bring everything to bear."

Killian laughed.

"This has always been your way, Meliakken," Killian said. "If there is even the smallest doubt that you may be overcome, you try and win by default."

"And yet obviously I have never been overcome, have I?" the god said smirking.

Loki thought he would like nothing better than to wipe that smirk off Meliakken's face. They needed more power. Meliakken had effectively taken the dragons out of the fight as they still battled the shrikers with the unicorns. And even though the demon horde was lessened, the faeries and warriors were also otherwise occupied. But Loki felt they still might not have been able to contribute to this altogether different battle occurring right before him. The air was hot and charged, there wasn't anyone here that was not dripping with sweat as their power continued to rage, except Meliakken of course, but then do gods sweat, Loki wondered.

For the first time in his life, Loki was at a loss on what he should do. It seemed like every available option was already on the table and there was nothing left. They were about to die, and there wasn't a thing he could do about it. There wouldn't even be anyone left to sing the songs of all the brave souls that perished here. Loki accepted his fate. If it were to end here, he couldn't think of a better band of people to exit this life with than those that were here with him today. He scanned the area, noting each face, imprinting them on his mind in the hope that he would remember in the next life, wherever that happened to be. His run in this life had been a long one, several thousand years in fact, and he hoped the gods looked kindly on him in that he did the best he possibly could. He was ready.

"Killian," Loki said getting ready to tell him they should just end this once and for all.

Killian looked over at him, and with all the power of Vasara pouring through him and the end of the world looming, he gave the wizard a wink and a smile.

What did that mean? Loki wondered. He didn't have long to find out.

"I grow weary of this," Meliakken said. "You have been a good adversary, Killian, but this meeting shall be the last."

The god started to grow in size, towering over everyone as he began to bring his full power to bear.

"Meliakken, wait!" Killian said.

"Are you ready to surrender?" the god asked in a booming voice.

"No," Killian answered. "I offer you a chance to leave. You are free of your prison, you can continue on, go find your own world."

Meliakken gave a great and maniacal laugh. Loki was amazed how he was able to laugh and still maintain the level of power he was throwing at them.

"Are you insane!" Meliakken roared. "Can you not feel it even now? I feel all of you at the limit of your power, but now it is time to raise mine!"

Suddenly there was the cawing of many birds, loud and from all directions.

"Hold fast," Killian whispered to his allies.

Meliakken however was looking in all directions. The sound was there but there were no birds.

"What is this?" the god asked, "a trick?"

There was a bright flash that momentarily blinded everyone.

"A trick?" a voice said that everyone recognized. "Why I believe it is, and the oldest one since time began."

"Redlin!" Loki shouted.

"Now, Redlin!" Killian commanded.

The wizard of the brotherhood of the three, father of Andros and Donella, husband of Luel the faerie queen and priest of the god Trystan, finally brought the god's power to bear as he flooded Killian with its energy. Killian momentarily threw his head skyward with the impact and then focused the added energy at Meliakken whose own energy was pushed back towards him and hit his psyche like a physical blow.

"This is not possible!" the god screamed furiously. "I would have felt you creating any kind of illusion."

"You are right," Redlin said defiantly. "I didn't."

"I did," came a young girl's reply as she stepped out of Redlin's shadow.

"Tera," Dain exclaimed astounded.

Of course, Loki thought to himself. The birds. Tera's gift was the ability to make bird sounds, which worked to distract Meliakken long enough to make their dramatic entrance and giving him no time to prepare a counter strike. The god was doing all he could to keep the beam of energy from moving one inch closer to him.

"I would like to know how you did that young lady," Loki said with a raised eyebrow while still being able to maintain his flow of energy.

Tera flew over to him and kissed him on the cheek. Suddenly something sparked inside of Loki, hope. Hope that they might actually win.

***

Redlin kept his focus on Killian and delivering Trystan's much needed energy. Because of Meliakken's arrogance, he had made a grave mistake. The evil god felt he could toy with them thinking that he was dead. Redlin didn't even know what was going on until Tera had spirited him away just before Meliakken arrived and created her illusion. It was all her, he had had nothing to do with it. There was a bright flash and when his eyes had opened, he felt like he was in another universe. They stood upon an island, but there was no water surrounding it, only stars.

"Tera, where are we?" he had asked her.

Tera had looked at him with tears in her eyes as she pushed her silver hair behind her pointed ears.

"Killian had told me this was the only way. The only way to save you and Vasara."

"What do you mean?"

"Everyone thinks you are dead."

"By the gods, Tera! What have you done?"

"You remember Killian had given me this?" Tera asked holding up the charm. Only now he could make out the image where before he couldn't, and he was awed by what he saw. Depicted on its surface were planets, moons, suns, stars, black holes and supernovas, except they weren't stationary. They moved as if in some cosmic dance, and in the very center was the image of a door.

"This is what brought us here," Tera said. "It also unlocked a power within me to create the illusion of us that Meliakken has just destroyed."

The implication of that had hit Redlin.

"Luel," he said wide-eyed. "Emilia, Andy and Abby."

Tera had been on the verge of tears, and some had started to slide down her cheeks.

"I'm sorry," she said in anguish. "Killian told me this was the only way to unlock the hidden powers of the Queen and Donella while at the same time tricking Meliakken."

Redlin had suddenly felt something, or rather the lack of something.

"I can no longer feel Loki or Dain, which means they cannot feel me." Redlin ran his fingers through his hair in frustration. "Loki will tell them with certainty that we are dead."

Redlin could see the moral struggle Tera was going through in what she had done. He laid everything aside for a moment, the battle, Vasara, everything and tried to reassure his young friend.

"Tera, listen to me," the wizard said as he placed both hands on her shoulder. "You are an instrument of the prophecy, and you fulfilled that which only you could do."

"But it's going to cause so much pain," she said with her bottom lip quivering.

"Yes it will," he said seriously. "But I know my family, they will not let the pain bind them in despair. Let your mind rest easy, this will be alright I promise."

Tera looked up at him gratefully and then proceeded to hug him fiercely.

A fire blast from Meliakken brought him out of his musings and back to the present. Suddenly he caught a movement out of the corner of his eye. Circling and moving into his field of vision was his wife, and she looked anything but happy to see him alive.

When this is over, you have a lot of explaining to do, husband, she spoke to his mind. Even in his head he could feel her anger, but there was something else that was overriding it all, love and relief.

I'm sorry love, he responded. *I will make it up to you I promise.*

Luel smiled at that and nodded, letting it drop, for now they had a god to deal with.

Dad! Is that really you? Andy's shout came to him. *What happened?*

Later, Son, said Redlin as he looked up to see Andy and Emilia engaging the remaining shrikers. *You and your sister finish up there, we will deal with what's down here.*

We are on it, Dad! Emilia's happy reply came back.

Redlin looked to his left and saw Abby beaming as she gave him a silent salute with the sword he had given her many years ago. He now focused all his thought and energy on Meliakken, when adding the power of the ring that Trystan and Eriyn had made for him, his energy beam turned black. He locked eyes with Meliakken and saw pure hatred there, and death. But they were evenly matched now, neither side could break contact without destroying the other, and the gods only know how this will end.

"What say you now, Meliakken?" Killian asked. "Shall you retire to some unknown universe in need of an evil god?"

"You shall die for your insolence, Killian. And everyone with you. I have one last card to play."

Redlin wondered what Meliakken could possibly have up his sleeve.

Killian gave a chilling laugh that set Redlin's hair on edge. He could not have imagined how things would've gone if Andy hadn't been the first to free the Key and secure Killian's alliance to them. The wizard definitely did not want this being for an enemy.

"I know the card you think you have," Killian said to the god, "but I think you will find you are unable to play it."

Doubt appeared in Meliakken's eyes, but he made no move to try anything different than he was already doing. They were in a stasis now, neither side gaining an advantage. Everything was perfectly balanced and there was nothing else to throw at him.

Meliakken showed no signs of weakening and neither did Killian. The priests of the gods however were a different matter. Redlin could see the strain of channeling so much power was starting to have an effect on them. Could they keep this up indefinitely he wondered. Even Tori, who he always considered the strongest of them all given her abilities, was struggling.

Redlin, look up high on the horizon, came Loki's voice in his mind.

Redlin slowly turned his head to the right so as not to attract the attention of the god. Coming towards them was a bright golden light.

Is that a falling star? Redlin asked looking at his brother.

Loki shook his head sadly. *It's a last weapon.*

The color drained from Redlin's face at what that meant.

***

Finn kept up a steady rhythm as his wings beat the air. Zana was quiet and laying on his back. Looking down he could see the outer edges of the battle coming up. Faeries, warriors and unicorns were engaging demons of all kinds. He swung his neck around to look at his love. She had her eyes closed as if she were sleeping. Finn knew she was nearing the end of her strength as death hovered at the door.

Zana, can you hear me? We are almost there.

Zana pushed herself up to a sitting position, still holding the staff in the hand she had left. Peering below she could see the melee playing out. Finn could feel the remorse radiating off her, the weight of centuries of pursuing evil power had left her hollowed out.

"Finn, I'm scared," she said at last.

There is nothing to be afraid of, we will go through this together.

"It's not this I'm afraid of," she said as a tear escaped her eye.

Of what then?

She looked at him with such a feeling of loneliness.

"I am afraid I will never see you after this."

Finn didn't know how to respond to that. He didn't know himself what came after, he only knew of what he could do right now, and right now was Meliakken.

Let's not think about that now love. Let's do the one thing that only you and I can do, destroy Meliakken. We do that, it has to count for something in the hereafter.

Zana looked at him and Finn felt her heart start to swell.

"I will do what I should have done centuries ago, trust you."

Finn could feel her love and her absolute trust as she surrendered every part of her heart and soul to him, he wasn't about to let her down. It was time.

Zana, I'm going to do something, but I don't want you to

be afraid. I'm going to change a little bit, but it won't harm you. I need you to release the power of your staff at just the right moment.

"What are you going to do?" she asked sounding concerned.

Have you heard of last weapon? He asked.

He felt her body go rigid on his back, and there was no mistaking the sorrow in her voice that she knew what it was.

"Yes, from Layla," she replied as she lay back down on his back to hug him one last time.

***

Andy was just coming off a dive with Emilia on his back and had started to climb again. As he did so, something bright caught his eye. Swinging his long black neck behind him, he could see a golden glow streaking towards them. Brion was flying next to him when he asked him about it.

Brion, what is that coming up behind us? Andy asked.

Brion looked behind him as he shot several energy bolts at a shriker passing below them.

By the gods! It's Finn, he exclaimed.

Why does he look like a star about to explode? Andy asked.

Because he is doing last weapon, Caleb said as he flew up to where they were.

What is that? Andy asked.

Loki never told you? Brion asked sounding surprised.

There were three shrikers left and the unicorns and the others were doing a good job of keeping them occupied.

Told me what? Andy asked.

It is a last weapon a dragon will ever use, Caleb answered him, *themselves.*

Instead of channeling the source outward at an enemy, you channel it into your very being, Brion explained. *Upon impact you implode, sucking in and destroying everything around you.*

Are you saying Finn is doing a kamikaze?

I don't know what that is, Brion said, *but if it means sacrificing yourself, then yes.*

We need to stop him! Andy exclaimed.

It's too late, Caleb said with sadness in his voice. *Once you start the change, there is no turning back.*

Andy could not believe this was happening. He had just got his father back and now he was about to lose a brother.

Why would he do this? He asked.

He must have felt there was no other choice, or he's getting instructions from someone, Brion said.

Someone is on his back, Caleb said, *but I can't make out who.*

It's Zana, Emilia said, *and she has her staff.*

You don't think she is making Finn do this, do you? Andy asked.

No, Emilia said. *I can feel through the link that Finn is in his right mind. I also feel Zana's link to him, she is not controlling him.*

Andy felt Emilia was holding something back but he didn't pursue it.

What he is doing is pointless, Caleb said. *He's not going to be able to penetrate the god's shield.*

Yes, he can, Emilia said.

How do you know that, Em? Andy asked.

Andy could feel shame coming from his sister.

Because in my madness, when I discovered I could override everyone's will at once, it was then I could delve deeper into everyone's thoughts and emotions than ever before. I went the deepest with Finn because I knew of his feelings for Zana. It was then that I saw his second gift, given to him by Cael, the ability to penetrate a god's shield. I tried to use that in an effort to destroy Zana.

Then that's it, Brion said. *He plans to dive straight into Meliakken, destroying them both in the process.*

Suddenly the shrikers broke off their attack against the dragons and started heading towards Finn. It was Caleb who sounded the alarm first.

We have to stop them! Caleb shouted to everyone's minds. *If they collide with Finn he will destroy himself before he can reach Meliakken.*

That's their plan! Andy said, understanding suddenly came to him. A great rage had settled into his being. All the death and wanton destruction of this evil god had come to a head. He was still recovering from the supposed death of his father while at the same time trying to wrap his head around the fact that his brother was about to commit suicide and there was not a thing he could do about it. One thing he did know, he was not going to let his death be in vain.

Brothers! He shouted to their minds. *We need to stop the shrikers and clear a path for Finn!*

Andy was in a battle frenzy now, every nerve in his dragon body was on fire and more alive than at any other time in his life. He wheeled hard left and started to soar further upward chasing after the shrikers with eight other dragons hot on his tail.

Hold on, Em, he told her.

Don't worry about me brother, she replied.

Brayton, we need you, Andy sent his thoughts to the prince. *Keep every demon and shriker away from Finn.*

I hear you, Andros, Brayton replied. *Cathal will clear out the demons while we help you with the shrikers.*

This was it then, Andy thought to himself. It all came down to this. Looking down he could see the battle going on with Meliakken was so evenly matched, no one was gaining any ground. It could be this one act that ends it all once and for all. The love and pride he felt for his brother was so intense right now, there was no way he was going to let him down.

Andros.

Finn? Andy asked.

Yes. I am speaking only to you.

Why? Why are you doing this? We could find another way.

There is no other way. There is not much time. I need you to do something for me, Finn said.

Andy could feel his dragon tears sliding along his scaly hide.

What can I do, Brother?

Tell the others goodbye for me, I can't bear to do it. And also talk to your mother.

My mother?

Yes, about Zana. Please ask her to forgive her and have her ask Braylynn to forgive her.

Andy understood what Finn wanted, and he would do it without hesitation.

I will take care of it, Andy said, *I promise.*

Farewell, Andros.

Farewell, Finn, Andy said choking back a sob.

Em, let's finish these bastards, Andy said to his sister as he started spewing liquid fire at the shriker right in front of him, bathing it in flames.

Suddenly it wasn't hot enough and he reached as deep as he could go in channeling the source. The shriker was screaming in agony as all four wings started to turn to ash. Andy followed it down, never letting up. Emilia poured white-hot goddess fire from her staff that blew the shriker apart, leaving no sign that it ever existed.

Two more to go, Andy said as he pulled up looking for an enemy.

Are you alright? Emilia asked concerned.

No, Andy said as he lined up his next target and let loose with all he had.

***

Redlin could feel things were about to come to a head. He assumed the dragon that had employed the strategy of last weapon was Finn. His heart went out to his son's brother. Finn was the most introverted dragon, but once you got him to open up his soul was rich and beautiful. This path of self-sacrifice was totally in line with his nature. Suddenly Killian was speaking again.

"Your chance to flee has now past, Meliakken," Killian said. "Even now your doom is speeding towards you."

Redlin noticed that the god had not taken his eyes off Killian and was not even aware that Finn was hurtling towards him.

"I think not," Meliakken said. "I have one power that I have held in reserve until now, and once unleashed, there will be nothing left to testify to your existence."

Killian again did that low measured laugh that let a person know this was not a being to be taken lightly.

"I know of your wildcard," Killian said. "And the fact that you think you can use it shows how lacking in total understanding you are of Vasara and its creatures."

Meliakken closed one eye and squinted the other at Killian. Redlin could tell the god was weighing if Killian might know more than he.

"Go ahead, Meliakken," Killian said. "Call forth the power of the queen of the unicorns."

There was the longest of pauses. Finn was getting closer and still Meliakken did not notice. He was having difficulty wondering if he had made a grave error.

"Did you not wonder why Savano let you take her power?" Killian asked. "She could have easily released it the second you killed her, but she allowed you to absorb it. Should I tell you why?"

Redlin looked up and saw all the dragons speeding towards

Finn. Apparently the shrikers were trying to disrupt Finn's plan. Meliakken's head started to turn upwards.

"Should I?" Killian screamed, drawing the god's attention back to him.

Meliakken's face turned angry and red. Angry that he needed Killian to tell him where his fault lay.

"Tell me you bastard!" Meliakken roared.

Killian's voice went calm and gentle, like an eerie calm before the impact of a great storm.

"Because a unicorn's power can never be used for evil, to do so would cause it to recoil and start to destroy you from the inside. Just by absorbing it, even now it begins to suck some of your own power into itself, merging and turning it from evil to good. Oh Meliakken, you sealed your own fate. You had a chance to escape, now you will learn that a god can die."

"You lie! I am the god of worlds! My power is limitless. Even what you have assembled here is not enough to destroy me!"

Meliakken was raving now, his mouth starting to froth. Suddenly his head snapped back as a beam of white-hot energy slammed into him. The god looked up and his eyes went wide. Redlin was stunned to see Zana sitting on Finn's back, her staff in her hand as she obliterated everything that came in their path. The wizard didn't think that once Finn impacted with Meliakken that any of them would survive. Redlin did not know the effects of last weapon or what it could do, Loki was the master of dragon lore, not him. Then he heard Killian speak to Samara.

"Protect the vessels, protect us all."

Samara's hands started to move in a very fast and intricate pattern, and Redlin had a hard time following it. Suddenly transparent spheres started to appear above everyone.

"You'll know when it's time," Killian said to her.

Redlin could feel the power of Trystan running through him, hot and laser focused. His body was glowing and looking over at the other priests, they were similarly glowing in the color of their god's energy. There was no way any of them could break contact with Killian, if they did it was game over. The timing of this had to be perfect with Finn's impact. Redlin knew that just as they could not break contact, nor could Meliakken. To meet the threat from above meant he had to ignore the threat in front of him. The god had held all the cards until this very moment.

The wizard could see that Andy and his brothers had cleared a path for Finn, all the shrikers were destroyed, now they were cleaning up any flying demon lords foolish enough to make a last stand.

Finn was a glowing golden star now that hurt the eyes to look at him. Zana kept up a steady beam of energy centered on the god's chest. Veins of red and black started to appear on Meliakken's face. Redlin knew the end was near if none of them faltered, Meliakken knew it too. The god gave one more desperate plea.

"Zana!" Meliakken shouted. "Destroy them! Destroy them and I will make you the goddess of this world. I will restore you and leave. This world will be yours' to do as you will. You can have your revenge at last!"

Then Redlin heard the most amazing thing. It was not ravings, madness or anger that came from Zana's mouth. The tone was almost like a healing balm, like a warm breeze between summer and spring that carried with it the hope of better things to come.

"No Meliakken," Zana said to the sputtering god. "It is time to lay my burden down and face the justice of my crimes. My life is over, and so is yours."

Redlin's heart was in his throat as Finn and Zana slammed into the god.

"Now, Samara!" Killian shouted.

Samara brought both her hands down, bringing down the protective shields that surrounded everyone. With the power of the source combined with the power of Zana's staff, Finn hit the god. There was at first a concussion of air that blew everyone a goodly distance away from where they were currently standing. Then there was a loud crack that blasted everyone's eardrums as all that energy was sucked inward creating a miniature black hole, that ripped apart anything that fell into it. Demons that were close by and not protected by any shield were clawing the ground as the hole pulled them in. The dragons were flying erratically, roaring their grief at the loss of their brother. The scene was utter chaos. Of Meliakken, Finn and Zana, there was no sign.

Then the black hole started to change. It had been a thing devoid of all light, but now suddenly there was a pinpoint of gold, and it seemed to be getting larger, as if something were flying out of it. As it got bigger and bigger, Redlin couldn't help wondering if something more insidious was about to be released, but then the gold light escaped the darkness and shot skyward with a streak of black down its middle. Onward it went until it had left Vasara's atmosphere and hurtled towards the heavens. The wizard couldn't help but wonder if that was possibly Finn. It was his color, but even if it was him it was anyone's guess what he may have become or where he has gone. One thing Redlin did know was that the quiet young dragon's life in Vasara was over.

Chapter 30

Andy noticed an eerie silence as he hovered above the battlefield. A gold streak had just flown into the heavens and now all was quiet. There wasn't a single demon left on the field. Whether they were killed or simply vanished he did not know. Everyone on the ground had been thrown back in the shockwave and were picking themselves up.

Did we win? Andy asked no one in particular.

I believe we did, Emilia said sounding drained.

Not all of us, Caleb said soberly.

Andy knew he meant Finn and Zana. He had heard what Zana said at the end, he found himself more shocked than anything else.

She redeemed herself, Emilia said.

How did you know what I was thinking? Andy asked as he started his descent with his brothers.

I felt it through the link, Emilia said, *plus I was thinking the same thing myself.*

Andy remembered what Finn had asked of him in regards to his mother and Braylynn, but he wondered what his sister thought.

Could you forgive her, Em?

I already had when I took her hand off. She took accountability for her actions, but I sometimes wonder how twisted she would have become if it weren't for Meliakken's and Devon's influence. I guess we will never know.

Andy landed on the ground as Emilia flew off his back and into Lyson's arms. He made his change just as Abby came running over. He lifted her off the ground and brought her into a crushing embrace. She was sobbing, and he had tears flowing from his own eyes and down his cheeks. She grabbed the sides of his face and planted a solid lingering kiss on his lips which he returned with passion. As the kiss ended, Andy snaked an arm around Abby's waist as they surveyed the scene before them. All the unicorns had landed and stood rank upon rank behind them. The faeries had assembled behind their queen, his mother, the jewel in her crown returning to its normal tranquil blue. Andy heard the thunder of hoofbeats. He turned to look towards the horizon and saw the Border Lands warriors galloping towards them, raising a cloud of dust in their wake.

"Is it over?" Abby asked her husband as she leaned on her sword and brushed the stray locks out of her eyes. Andy had noticed she had a cut over one eye, although it didn't look deep. "Your sister can take care of that," she said noticing where he was looking.

He smiled at her. They had been through so much together, putting their lives on the line countless times for this world that they loved. Now all he wanted to do was fly her back to their house in Dragonsgate, sit on the porch with a hot cup of coffee and feel the autumn breeze on their faces.

"To answer your question, I believe it is finally over."

Andy was suddenly overwhelmed. He didn't know who he should run to first, his mother, his father. His brothers were very downcast at the loss of Finn. Never has a dragon died before. Nia had run over to Gael and crushed him to her. Leah, with a bandage on her leg from a wound a demon had inflicted on her no doubt, was lifting Dain off his feet as they hugged each other tight. At a moment like this, everyone needed the presence of a loved one. Even his mother and father had found each other's arms and didn't look like they were letting go anytime soon. Abby and Andy walked over to the place where Meliakken had stood. There was nothing but scorched earth.

"To answer your question, he's gone," Killian said walking up behind him.

"I didn't know I had asked a question," Andy told him.

"Your heart did, and I heard it."

"Is he dead then?" Abby asked.

"It is not the same for a god, Death's Mistress. You could never call back his spirit because it no longer exists."

Andy looked around again. It was all very quiet. There was no cheering, no celebration. It was as if everyone's soul had been purged of all iniquity and made new. Like they were the gold in the crucible that was burning away all the dross until all that remained was pure gold. It was like this was now a holy place and everyone was showing it reverence and respect.

"You are not too far off the mark," Killian said.

"Reading my thoughts again?" Andy asked. Killian just nodded. "I know it has been asked before, but what exactly are you Killian?"

"And as I said before, Andros the black, that is for another story and does not concern you," Killian said giving him a wink and a smile.

Eventually everyone started talking again, but it was more like a low murmur as they all caught up with what each person had gone through. Andy couldn't begin to tell his father how relieved he was that he was alive. Tera was about the only one showing any kind of excitement and enthusiasm. She flew from person to person, giving and getting hugs and kisses, talking a mile a minute the whole time. Andy laughed in spite of it all, she at least was back to her old self and yet at the same time, she wasn't. That seriousness and resolve of the burden she carried still lingered in the corner of her eyes.

Andy noticed his brothers had gathered around the spot where Finn and Zana had spearheaded into Meliakken. He walked over and joined them.

"He told me to tell you all goodbye," Andy said.

Brion looked at him with understanding.

"He was never one for showing his emotions," Brion said, "and yet I believe he was the most sensitive of all of us."

"I didn't know him as long as the rest of you, but he made it a point to come see me at least twice a year," Andy said looking at the point of impact, as if he might see Finn's image in the ashes. "We would go camping for three days and just fish and talk."

"I think a part of your gift as a person, Andros, is your ability to draw people out," Jace said. "He was our brother and we loved him, but he kept his personal life close to his chest if you know what I mean."

Andy nodded, he did know.

"Where do we go when we die?" Elek asked.

Andy wondered if having the same dragon color as Finn gave them a special bond.

"Faeries go to Bralynn's paradise, the warriors to Fallon, and so forth," Elek continued, "but where do we go?"

Nobody answered because a dragon had never died before. Andy suddenly had an idea.

"I could ask Abby to try and reach him," he said.

Andy told them how the death dagger had made her Death's Mistress and was able to communicate with those who have passed on. It was Caleb who shot it down.

"I think we should leave him be," Caleb said. "Let him have his peace. If anyone has earned it, he did."

After everyone thought about it they had to agree. Even Andy felt it was time to let him go and continue his journey.

"I know one thing," Daragh said, "this will be a wound that will be a long time closing."

Everyone nodded their agreement.

"I feel totally drained," Jace said. "When can we leave here?"

Andy was just thinking the same thing. Suddenly he was wanting to be home with his wife in Dragonsgate, and he turned to do just that.

***

Luel was holding tight to her husband, as if she would never let him out of her sight again. After being reunited with him, she proceeded to let him know just how much anguish he had put her through. Tera, she had praised and hugged her fiercely for saving the life of her husband as she trusted her to do. And even though Tera was young in the reckoning of faerie years, the queen had elevated her to a position of a trusted advisor. Luel had laughed at how that had stunned her into silence, for a few seconds anyway. Now Luel used her gift that allowed her to hear many conversations at once. Brayton and Cathal were over with their parents and some heated discussion seemed to be happening.

"I won't do it," Brayton said to his father. "You are the king, father, your people need you."

"They are your people too son," Paolo said as he put a hand on his shoulder. "For the ten years that Zana had us imprisoned, your mother and I discussed this many times. You have ruled in my stead without hesitation, never once forsaking your duty. The people love you. You will be an excellent king, you already are."

"And if I refuse?" Brayton asked while scratching an itch around his eyepatch.

"That is always your choice," his father said, "but you won't, will you?"

Brayton ran his fingers through his hair and sighed, knowing his father had made up his mind.

"No, I won't," he said finally. "Are you still going to live in Kensington?"

"For a little while," his mother said.

Acacia had just sheathed her rapier for the first time since the battle had started. From her vantage point in the sky, Luel had seen Acacia holding her own against any demons that had tried to penetrate the shield Samara had erected to protect the priests of the gods.

"Eventually we want to go back to the village you were born in just beyond Black River," she continued. "After that, who knows," she said looking lovingly at her husband as she snaked an arm around his waist.

"What about you Cathal?" the prince asked his friend.

"I'm going where I have always been, brother. Right at your side," Cathal answered him.

Nyle walked over and embraced his son.

"I'm proud of you," Nyle said. "Now it is your time to be First Knight."

"And what will you do Dad?"

Nyle looked lovingly over at Sibila.

"I think it's time I learned how to live again," he said as Sibila put an arm around his waist and he around hers. "When the sins of my past continued to haunt me daily, I buried myself in duty as penance, denying myself every joy. Now that someone has shown me how to lay that down, I'm going to start living that joyful life, as well as trying to harness my full abilities. Who knows, they may come in handy again," he said winking.

"Oh they will my Sol, they absolutely will," said Sibila giving him a kiss on the lips."

Luel's attention shifted over to Lyson who was talking to the Border Lands general who had brought the warriors into battle.

"Why are you giving me this, Neala?" Lyson asked as she extended her serpent hilt sword to him.

"Because, General, I have failed you and Fallon in letting Ansgar break open the last seal and kill my entire regiment."

Lyson took the sword, then walked closer to her as he grabbed the sheath strapped to her waist and slid the blade home.

"Neala, there is no shame or dishonor here. We were trained to face demons and demon lords, not gods and the perverted mutants they create."

He lifted her chin and looked in her eyes.

"There is no fault here. You did your duty and stood to the last, and above all you lived so that Fallon could restore your legs and bring you to us when we needed it most. I would love to know how he did that?" Lyson asked.

"It wasn't Fallon," Neala said striking a fist on her steel legs making them ring with an ominous boom. "At least not directly."

"What do you mean?" Lyson asked her.

"A man came, dressed like a warrior in leather armor with a greying black beard and the whitest teeth I had ever seen. He said his name was Chrys."

Lyson's eyes widened in wonder.

"Do you know him?" she asked.

"No. I have only read about him, long ago in a book that has disappeared from the library at Lyonsdale."

"Who is he?" she asked.

"It is not so much who he is but what. His name means first disciple and the nearest I could figure out from what I read, he is one of Fallon's angels."

"Do the gods have angels?" Neala asked.

"Apparently Fallon does," Lyson said running his fingers through his hair while pondering what this could mean. "How were you able to travel here?"

"Through the hole that was opened when Ansgar broke the seal," Neala answered. "There was something else, he called me Nentoka Viajera."

"Are you sure that is what he said?" Lyson asked.

"Yes, does it mean something?"

"It is a being of legend," Lyson replied. "I actually came across it in the library of the faerie queen. Loosely translated it means Underworld Traveler. I have a feeling that to get here you had to travel through the underworld itself. By the gods, Neala! Do you know what that means?"

"No, what?" she asked with a little apprehension in her voice at what Lyson may reveal.

"It means you can pass through the realm of the demons. The underworld touches all worlds, which further means you have the power to go anywhere."

"Why did this happen to me?" she asked.

"I don't know," Lyson said placing a hand on his one-time student, "but my guess is that you were born for this moment. What happens after and what you are able to do with these new abilities is anyone's guess. I'm afraid I won't be able to help you in this. If any instruction is to come, it will have to be revealed by Fallon himself, and it will be in his time I'm certain."

She looked a little downcast at being different now from all other warriors.

"Neala, listen to me. Just because I can't help you doesn't mean you are alone."

Neala smiled and brightened at that.

"If anyone can help you," Lyson continued, "it's Tori. She knows what it is like to go from a warrior to something so much more. Go see her when you can."

"I will," Neala promised.

Luel's attention had shifted again. Her son and Abby were over talking with Bowen. The captain of the Grey Morning had shown he could still handle a sword in defense of the world he loved.

"What will you do now, Captain?" Abby asked him.

"That is a good question lass," Bowen replied. "I have actually been giving a lot of thought to retirement."

"Is that something you could do my friend?" Andy asked stunned. "The sea is your life."

Bowen burst out laughing. "You know me too well Edward!" The captain said slapping him on the back. Andy had told his mother how when Bowen first met Andy, he had given his middle name to help hide his identity from Devon and his minions. She smiled at the memory and the friendship that was born from it.

"No laddie, I'm not going to quit the sea," Bowen said. "But I will be retiring from service as a merchant vessel."

Bowen looked down at the spyglass Killian had given him.

"I believe I will try my hand at exploring," he said. "This device has certain abilities that I know are there but haven't tapped into yet. Who knows, maybe I will find a nice quiet little island somewhere and truly retire. I'm keeping my options open," he said winking at them.

"I really hope we get to sail together again," Abby said touching his arm fondly.

"Don't you worry lass, you will always have a berth aboard my ship for as long as I have a deck under me. Also, the lads would most assuredly mutiny if you didn't come aboard and sing for them at least once a season."

"That brings up a point, Captain," Andy said. "How will you pay your crew?"

Bowen smiled at them both. "When I said exploring, I didn't mean just for Islands."

"Treasure hunting?" Andy guessed.

"Indeed lad. Remember that map that Braylynn had given me which at first I took for a treasure map but took me to the island where you and your family had entered Vasara for a second time."

Andy nodded as he recalled flying from the island they had landed on after going through the door at Lyndhurst Castle back in his other world and encountered the Grey Morning as she sailed for what Bowen thought would be untold riches from a grateful goddess.

"I had been looking at that map just prior to this whole business with the demons and noticed it had changed. New islands are visible on it now, and it is my intent to see if maybe Braylynn isn't such a trickster after all."

"I wish you the best of luck my friend," Andy said shaking his hand as Abby gave him a hug.

Luel then heard a voice in her head. It was Killian.

Majesty, I need to speak to you and your husband, Killian said.

Luel looked over and saw Killian standing next to the key, Tallika. How or when she showed up, Luel had no idea.

"What happens now?" Redlin asked Killian as they walked a ways apart from the others.

"Do you remember when you first saw me in your vision you asked me what my name was?" Killian asked him.

"Yes, you said for now, it's Killian, after, who knows."

"Well remembered master wizard," Killian said smiling. "This is your final task. Now that the battle has been decided, you must choose my new name, but choose wisely, for I will be bound by its aspect."

Luel watched as her husband pondered and struggled with a name to choose, and she was sure that like herself, he was wondering why he had to choose one. After all, what was wrong with the name he already had.

Redlin suddenly smiled as understanding lit up in his eyes.

"Aylward, your name is Aylward."

Suddenly a great white light descended and bathed Killian, now Aylward in its radiance as his head was thrown back and his arms spread wide in some form of baptism. As the light subsided, Luel could see that his eyes were no longer golden, but blue like sapphires.

"Well done wizard, you figured it out and chose wisely."

"Figured out what?" Luel asked her husband clearly puzzled as she looked back and forth between the two. Tallika just looked on with a grateful smile on her face.

"He is taking Meliakken's place," Redlin said to his wife.

"He's what?" she asked incredulously.

"Not like that love," Redlin said smiling as he put his arm around her.

"May I?" Aylward said.

"Please," Redlin said with a slight nod of his head.

"When Vasara was in the midst of its creation, that is when Meliakken attempted to wrest control of this world from the gods and goddess. Little did he realize that he became woven into the very fabric of that creation. But now with his demise, that power that originally got absorbed from him needs to be replaced or its absence will tear apart the world."

"And you are that replacement," Luel said seeing where this was going. "You are here to fill that void."

"Exactly," Aylward said.

"But why is the name important?"

"Because it will determine his true nature going forward," Redlin answered.

"And its meaning?" Luel asked.

"Defender," Tallika answered as she lay a hand on Aylward's shoulder.

Luel nodded her head in understanding. The queen suddenly felt very tired, as if she had been carrying a two-ton boulder for a hundred miles and was finally able to set it down.

"I know you are weary," Aylward said reading her thoughts. "All tasks are accomplished, no more deeds to be done. It is time for you to go home."

"We will need to bury our dead," Redlin said soberly.

"That has already been taken care of, and with dignity," Aylward said.

Luel looked around in astonishment. All of the creatures and humans that had perished in the fight to free Vasara were gone and the ground free of blood and gore. In the center of the battlefield there was now a large white pyramid that seemed to appear out of nowhere. Luel was pretty certain that the dead were buried inside and underneath. Her eyes welled up with tears as she thought of her sisters that would not be making the journey back to Laurel Hollow. They were in Braylynn's paradise now and free from pain, and she took solace in that knowledge.

"I'm ready to go home," she said wearily as her husband pulled her tight against his chest, his own tears seeping into her hair.

Aylward threw his arms open wide as he called forth his magic and portals started to appear to various parts of Vasara. It was a somber crowd that filed into their respective portals to begin their journey home. The jubilation and celebrations would wait for another day. Today was to remember those that gave their lives so that others might live, and it was out of respect for them that everyone passed into their homelands in silence.

Chapter 31

Andy was in his backyard setting up tables. It was a cool fall day, and he had a fire going in the outdoor hearth for the guests that were coming, in case they wanted to warm themselves. He felt a momentary pang of sorrow as he remembered the day he and Ben had built it. Even knowing what Ben was now, the memory was still a pleasant one. He put his hands on his hips and surveyed his land. This was just like a backyard barbecue that he would have had on any given Saturday in New York. Every now and then he wondered how his friends were, what they might have grown up to be. That world was forever closed to him now. Suddenly he heard footsteps behind him. Without turning he knew who it was. Abby laid her cheek against his back as her arms circled his waist.

"Thinking?" she asked.

"Yes. I was just wondering what might be happening back in New York."

"I'm pretty sure the Yankees are still losing, and the Red Sox are the team of the decade."

Andy burst out laughing. He would never forget that his beloved favored the baseball team that would be the forever arch enemies of his Yankees.

"Maybe Dad could find that out," he said.

"I don't think I would trust his answer," she said. "He has the same biases as you when it comes to baseball."

She turned him around and kissed his lips soundly.

"Speaking of which, where is he and your mother?"

"I'm sure they will be here soon," Andy said. "When I talked to him at the source, he and Mom had spent the last month secluded away somewhere."

"You think they went back to Otherwhere?"

"I'm not sure, but Dad kind of hinted at that," Andy said.

"Ho Andros!" a voice called from the back porch.

Looking back towards the house Andy saw that Ava and Rhyan had arrived. He didn't get to speak to them much after the battle and he was overjoyed they were here. Abby and Andy quickly walked up the steps and onto the porch to properly greet their friends.

"I was hoping you could make it," he said to them.

"We never pass up on a meal that Abby prepares," Rhyan said winking.

"Or the company of good friends," Ava added smiling.

"How are things in Fenner?" Abby asked as she pointed to chairs inviting them to sit down and offering them wine.

"All is quiet now," Rhyan said leaning her bow and arrows against the house next to Ava's. "While we were in Otherwhere, the clans were busy fending off demon attacks."

"By the gods!" Andy exclaimed. "I would have thought most of the battle would have occurred in Otherwhere, but I guess that wasn't the case."

"No, and it wasn't just Fenner, other cities encountered the same thing," Rhyan said. "But from what I understand, something that Brayton had done ended it."

Andy had spoken to Brayton about how he had used his unicorn horn talisman to destroy the crystal that allowed the demon lords to rip into the barriers between worlds and give them free rein.

"Do you still have your god medallions?" Abby asked seeing

that they weren't wearing the golden discs around their necks.

"No," Ava said. "As soon as we stepped through the portal back to Fenner they disappeared. Either they were no longer needed or couldn't be taken out of Otherwhere, maybe both."

Andy found that extremely puzzling and wondered what that could possibly mean.

"Is it alright for me to be here?" said a voice from around the corner.

"Samara!" Andy jumped up and ran to hug her. "Of course it's alright, I invited you."

Everyone else got up and hugged the witch of Vasara, making her feel welcome.

"Why would you not think it alright to be here?" Abby asked.

Samara sat down in one of the chairs and accepted the glass of wine that Abby offered her.

"It's just that there are so many people that I have wronged over my long lifetime, which I have been coming to terms with for quite a while now." Here she looked at Andy. "It actually started the first day I met you."

"I remember that day, when you branded this into my skin" Andy said holding up his palm showing the brand of the death dagger.

"I am sorry about that," Samara said before Andy stopped her.

"Samara, we were all acting according to the dictates of the prophecy. I don't hold any of this against you, I never did. And I could feel in that moment that you sought a better way."

A single tear slowly rolled down Samara's cheek as her eyes lit up with gratitude.

"And you, Death's Mistress? Can you forgive me the hurt I caused the one you love, as well as being the instrument that took your own life when the death dagger brought you to the door of death itself?"

Abby walked over and hugged Samara again. After letting go she looked in her eyes with all seriousness.

"As my husband says, we were all following the prophecy. And that one act has in turn given me the greatest gift possible, which is I get to spend a very long and happy life with the man I love," Abby said.

"I think everyone here, and all that come today will feel the same Samara," Rhyan said. "A new age has dawned, and all past sins are forgiven and forgotten."

"Thank you," Samara said gratefully.

"So what is next for you?" Andy asked her. "Will you return to your Blood Forest and remain there?"

"I will still live there," Samara said. "It is my home and a gift from my father for protection. But it will no longer be closed, nor will it be required to enter my service for anyone who seeks my advice or help. But in the short term, I'm going to travel to my father's forge that Meliakken destroyed and see if I can rebuild it."

"If you want any help or company," Ava said with a wink, "just give us a shout."

"I may just do that," Samara said smiling.

"Count Andros and I in as well," Abby said.

"Where the hell is everyone?" came a shout from the front of the house.

"That could only be Diminitus," Abby said smiling.

"We are in the back," Andy yelled.

Three figures emerged from around the corner of the house, Diminitus, Ala and Pan. Andy saw that the king of Parma was carrying his decagram staff. After much hugging from everyone, they sat in chairs in the yard as Andy and Abby gave their guests some refreshment.

"You have redeemed yourself missy with this superior wine," Diminitus said raising his glass in Abby's direction.

"Ouch! What was that for?" Diminitus asked as he rubbed his shoulder after Ala smacked it.

"Abby has done nothing to be redeemed for Dim and you know it," Ala said with a raised eyebrow.

"Hmmph," he said grumbling.

"What's the news out of Parma?" Andy asked Pan.

"All is quiet there for a change," the one-time king of the fauns responded. "Even the alfar have taken to stop harassing travelers. It is like a universal peace has broken out."

Here Pan paused as he ran a hand along his horns. "There is something though."

"Oh, what is that?" Andy asked.

"The door to Otherwhere at Raven Rock is open, and there appears to be no way of closing it."

"Killian…I mean Aylward you think?" he asked. Andy kept forgetting he had a new name now.

"That's what I am thinking, but I have not seen him to ask him," Pan said.

"What is he, Pan?" Andy asked.

"I'm certain he would tell you that is not needful for you to know," Diminitus said taking another sip of his wine as he draped a leg over the arm of the chair and made himself comfortable. "But I feel like I should know."

"Why do you say that?" Rhyan asked.

"Because he said he knew me when I was very young. There are parts of my early youth that I can't seem to recall. I do remember something though. The image of a man with golden eyes reaching down to pick me up. Whether he was saving my life or just helping me up off the ground I don't recall. In fact that is the one and only memory I have of myself as a young man, and I have none as a boy. It's like it was purposefully erased for some reason."

"I know that I've only ever known you as a grown man," Pan said.

Another Vasara mystery shrouded in the past, Andy thought to himself.

"Ho! Where is everyone?" a female voice from the front asked. It sounded like Tori, Andy thought.

"In the back!" Diminitus yelled. "Really lad, you should have told everyone where the party was located to prevent all this yelling back and forth."

Andy had to laugh at that as Tori and Cleo appeared from around the corner of the house. Cleo had the bow that Bart had given her slung across her shoulder. When Emilia had told him of Bart's message when he gave the bow to Cleo, Andy felt an enormous sense of peace knowing that his friend was alright. Tori looked a little pensive around the eyes and took her off to the side to talk to her.

"Everything okay?" Andy asked her.

"Yeah, I'm fine. Why do you ask?" she said as she ran her fingers through her long dark hair like a comb. It wasn't done up in a ponytail as Andy was used to seeing it. Andy looked at her with one eye squinted.

"I think I have known you long enough and been through enough life and death situations with you to know something is occupying your mind."

Tori stared off into the woods for a moment. She unconsciously re-adjusted her shoulders as if she were wearing her twin swords,

"I was talking with Neala about her ability to travel to the underworld and her being Nentoka Viajera. She and I are alike Andros, we both know what it means to be different. I was able to help her though, the way you once helped me to accept what I am."

"I am glad for that," Andy said sincerely. "So what happens now?"

"To tell you the truth I don't know. With Meliakken gone it made me wonder, is there really a need for us? But then I thought, if Fallon didn't want us to have these powers, I imagine he would just take them away. Both of us feel there is more to do yet. I have a feeling Neala and I will be traveling together."

"And what about Cleo?" Andy asked looking back at Vasara's Archer.

"She'll come with us of course," Tori said matter of factly, "she's not likely to remain behind without an argument."

"Why do I get the feeling you are going to embark on some kind of grand adventure," Andy said shaking his head.

"Care to join us, Andros the Black," Tori said winking.

And there it was, Andy thought. It was like they had come full circle from the first time they met and Tori had named him for what he was, chief among dragons.

"I think Abby wants to see how long this peace lasts before we need to go out and save the world again," he told her.

Tori burst out laughing and slapped him on the back causing him to rub his shoulder that seemed to be throbbing now. It was then that he realized she had hit him on the raven brand that Devon had burned into his skin. Sometimes he would forget it was even there. Andy thought in wonder at all that had happened since that first fateful day he stepped into Vasara.

"I think you left me, Andros," Tori said giving him a sidelong glance.

"What? Oh, sorry. I was just remembering."

"Been doing a lot of that myself," Tori said. Suddenly Tori shook her shoulders at the coolness of the day. "Come on, let's go back and get some wine before this conversation turns melancholy."

"That sounds like a good plan to me," Andy said.

It was then that he looked down at Tori's sleeve and saw an angular head poking out. It would appear Percy was seeking a little warmth himself as he drew his head back in. Andy took that as a sign that he should get a fire going before Diminitus started shouting about how chilly it was so far up north from his home in Parma.

It wasn't long after that Andy's brothers showed up, along with Emilia and Lyson. The yard was getting quite full, and he loved it. Abby was over talking to Nia and Gael. His wife had developed a deep friendship with his brother's beloved, and he was sure that given the long lives ahead of them that friendship would only continue to grow. Andy gazed towards the far corner of the yard where Abby had her little flower garden and walking path. The path was crushed stone as it made a little circuit around the various plants and statues. Brion was there staring at something. Andy looked over at Emilia and noticed she was looking at him too, then she turned her attention to Andy and gave a slight tilt of her head in Brion's direction. Both walked over to where he stood and saw he was staring at a statue. It was a golden dragon in flight and on its back was a faerie with her hand raised and a talon spear in her fist, mounted on a white marble base. Brion turned as he heard footsteps behind him.

"I don't believe I've seen this before, Andros," Brion said pointing down at the statue. "Although that is actually not surprising since this is probably the first time I have ever seen Abby's garden up close."

"Finn gave that to Abby as a present for her garden when we first settled here," Andy said.

"Do you know where he got it?" Brion asked.

"He told me he made it hundreds of years ago, but didn't have any real place he wanted to display it, so he gave it to Abby."

Brion seemed stunned at that. "He made this?" Brion asked surprised. "He must have used magic."

"No," Emilia said bending down to run her fingers along the exquisite lines of the statue. "I would be able to feel the dragon magic within it if that were the case. This was done by hand. Plus, I have seen some of the work of my grandfather, and there is a certain quality you can only get when it is done by the hand of a master craftsman."

"I never knew," Brion said. "I wonder when he learned to do that."

"Finn and I used to have long talks in this garden," Andy said. "He never expressed his emotions too openly, but I could tell he had the heart and soul of an artisan."

Thinking of his brother that was no longer there brought a sharp pain to Andy's heart. Finn was grumpy at times, but he had the gentlest spirit that Andy had ever seen.

"I suppose the faerie is meant to represent Zana," Brion said.

"He never told me, and I never asked," Andy said, "but like you, I thought the same thing."

"It's amazing that he still cared for her even after what she had become," Brion said.

"Sometimes with love, you don't feel like you have a choice," Emilia said. "It's like something that was always meant to be. I will tell you this, the Zana that killed Meliakken was not the Zana we fought and contested against for so long. Maybe that was enough to earn her some kind of redemption."

Andy remembered Finn's request to have his mom speak to Braylynn on Zana's behalf. His mother didn't hesitate to do as he asked. What the outcome was, Andy had no idea, but he felt Finn and Zana deserved to be at peace. Andy suddenly heard a melody. Turning back toward the others he could see Pan was playing an achingly beautiful light tune on his pipes.

It was then answered by another set of pipes on the air, but he could not see who played them. Suddenly there was a sound like the crack of a whip followed by white light.

"By the Gods!" Diminitus yelled as Tera, Redlin and Luel suddenly appeared right next to him. Dain, Leah and Loki were also with them. "Enough of this popping in and out unannounced!" Diminitus said. "You people are worse than the goddess!"

"Dim, try and calm down," Ala said, "you are going to give yourself a heart attack."

"Me?" he exclaimed. "Well I…"

"Shhh," Ala told him putting a finger to his lips that silenced him.

"I don't suppose you'd care to tell me how you did that?" Lyson asked.

"Sorry brother," Loki answered, "but there are some secrets the wizards of the five need to keep." Loki smiled and winked at him.

"Pay him no mind Lyson," Luel said. "Those boys had nothing to do with it. It was Tera and I, and to some degree, Pan. And before you ask, I will tell you how when we are back in Laurel Hollow. There are some secrets that only belong to the servants of the goddess."

The last part she directed at Loki as she winked back at him. Andy had to assume their mode of delivery had to do with Tera's new abilities. His father had told them how she had been able to whisk them away to a whole separate universe. He truly felt like there was going to be many more stories to tell once all the dust had finally settled.

It was turning out to be quite a crowd. Everyone was eating, drinking some wine and just relaxing in the yard. To have everyone he loved here had Andy feeling more at peace than he ever had before. Looking over towards Abby's garden again he saw Loki walking the path. Watching his old mentor reminded him of when he first learned he was a dragon, and how it was Loki who taught him how to be one. Loki didn't even turn around as he spoke, he just bent down to smell a flower.

"So lad, feels like we ended right where we started doesn't it?" Loki asked.

Andy knew what he meant. It was here where everything started and where his first quest began. It was Loki who was so much a father to him as his real father. He looked up towards the mountains where Loki had helped him accept life as a dragon, and in doing so made him a much better man.

"I guess it does," he responded sitting down on a bench next to the path. Loki came to sit next to him. "What happens now?"

Loki laughed. "Are you eager to go and find a new adventure?"

Andy chuckled at that.

"I suppose with Vasara's greatest threat out of the way we will have never ending peace."

Loki suddenly got serious.

"Maybe for a little while lad, and maybe for several hundred years or more, but don't count on everything to always be rosy."

"Well, I'm sure the prophecy will help us out in the event something goes south."

Loki was shaking his head.

"What?" Andy asked.

"The prophecy is no more lad. It had an end point, and Meliakken was it."

"What do we do now?" Andy said stunned.

"I suppose we solve Vasara's problems for ourselves," Loki said matter of factly. "I believe the gods never intended for us to be constantly relying on the prophecy to bring together all the necessary elements to meet every earth-shaking event."

"I suppose that makes sense," Andy said scratching his head.

"Think about it lad, have you ever seen so many beings in one place with so much power at their fingertips. The gods and that finicky goddess, don't tell her I said that, have given us all the tools necessary to meet any threat should it arise. We are the stewards of this world, Andros, and it is up to us to keep her and her inhabitants safe," Loki said putting an arm on Andy's shoulder.

It was a very sobering thought and Andy pondered it before speaking again. Was Meliakken truly the end of everything or was this just the beginning of something more.

"What will you do now?" Andy asked his friend.

Loki took out a pipe and lit it, taking a deep draw before letting the smoke out. Once again Andy was back in the dragon's cave, he was so confused and feeling alone at the time, but there was Loki, sitting in his chair and smoking his pipe, making him feel safe and at ease. The wizard was a rock that Andy realized he had come to rely on for his own stability.

"I will probably do what I always do during times of quiet, travel from town to town, telling stories and inviting myself to somebody's house for dinner," he said winking as a ring of smoke encircled his head.

"Is that all?" Andy said laughing.

"No," Loki said suddenly getting serious. "I've been speaking with your father and Dain. We are going to see what we can do when we combine our powers."

"Like when you made the wizard's bridge?" Andy said.

"Exactly," Loki said before suddenly going quiet.

Andy knew why Loki had stopped speaking. The last time the wizards of Vasara came together to create something magnificent, one of their brotherhood had turned totally evil, Devon.

"And what about you lad? What's on the upcoming agenda of Andros the Black."

"Loki, please. I get enough of that from Tori," Andy said laughing. "Abby has a lot of projects that are going to keep me busy for the immediate future."

"That's why I never married," Loki said waving his pipe. "Women always have a long list hiding somewhere on their person just waiting for the right moment to haul it out, no offense to Abby of course, but you know what I mean."

Andy just smiled. "I truly don't mind if it makes her happy."

"And after that?"

"I actually hadn't been thinking about it until I talked to Tori earlier. She plans on probing the underworld with Neala. After talking with Abby, she feels the two of us need to go with them. I think it has something to do with being Death's Mistress."

"I tell you, that whole thing baffles me."

"Really?" Andy asked surprised. "I thought you knew everything."

"Just because I've lived a long life doesn't mean I've studied everything in the world that there is to know about it."

Andy thought on that, especially since he was about to live thousands of years himself. The thought alone struck him so profoundly. For now though, he was just going to be in this moment with his friends and family.

"You boys want to hear a story of Vasara's beginnings?" Abby asked as she came to the head of the path.

"Who's telling it?" Loki asked warily.

"Redlin of course," Abby replied.

Loki groaned. "I was afraid of that. Well lad, let's refill our wine glasses and pick out a comfortable spot. If I know your father, this will be a long tale."

Andy, Abby and Loki walked back up to where the fire was blazing. The sun was just starting to set, and everyone was gathered around. His father had a drink in his hand and his cloak was drawn about him with his feet propped up on an ottoman. Andy thought he resembled what he imagined a bard in a medieval tavern would look like. Puffing on a pipe and about to spin his tale, his mother was sitting next to him. She wasn't wearing her crown and Andy was curious enough to ask her why. She said she didn't feel it necessary, and that she wanted to come here just as his mother and not the queen of the faeries.

Emilia and Lyson sat on one side of Redlin, while Andy and Abby sat on the other. It struck Andy how similar this felt when they would sit in the gazebo in their backyard at their house on the Hudson River, and his father would tell them stories that he had made up. Andy wondered now if they were truly made-up stories after all.

His brothers were lounging on the ground with their legs drawn underneath them. One thing Andy found interesting was Tori sitting next to Daragh. Could there be a connection forming there he wondered? If there was, Daragh would pick up on it immediately giving his empathic abilities. But then again, maybe not. Andy remembered Daragh's strict rule about reading friends. However, if there was one brother that was any kind of match for Tori, Daragh was it.

Suddenly there was a very quiet and gentle tune blowing on the wind. Andy looked over and saw that pan was playing on his pipes, another set of pipes joined it as Tera matched his melody. His father raised his glass in a silent toast, taking the music as his cue to begin.

"There was nothing but darkness," Redlin began, "but there always is in the beginning..."

Epilogue

She could hear water, she knew the sound of water. On her face she could feel a warm breeze as well as the sun's rays hitting her body. What she didn't understand is why she couldn't see it.

"I'm blind," she said aloud.

"No, you're not," a musical voice answered, a woman's voice.

"Who is that? Who's there? Why can't I see?"

"You can see, you just need to open your eyes."

"My eyes are open," she said.

"Let me help you."

A hand touched her forehead and a bright light exploded behind her eyes. Suddenly she realized her eyes were closed. Slowly she opened them and audibly gasped at what she beheld. She was at the base of a huge mountain, with a waterfall cascading out of the cliff face into a large deep pool. The water was crystal clear and she could see the bottom far below. Looking up she could see the peak of the mountain was high, but there was no snow or ice on it. Around the pool was lush grass with white and purple wildflowers ringing the edge. Birds that she had no memory of inhabited the various trees spread throughout.

"Can you see a little better?" the voice asked.

She turned towards the voice and saw a woman with pointed ears and hair the color of honey wheat. Her eyes were cornflower blue with wings to match.

"Yes, I can see. Thank you," she said.

"Who are you?"

She thought for a moment. She did not know who she was, or what she was. Her mind was blank.

"I don't know," she answered. "I can't remember."

"Can't remember, or perhaps you choose not to remember."

"Does it make a difference?" she asked. Why was this creature asking all these questions she wondered? For some unknown reason her spirit was tired and all she wanted to do was sleep forever.

"I'm afraid you can't do that," the pointed eared woman said.

"Do what?" she asked.

"Sleep."

"You can read my mind?"

"All thoughts are open here."

"Do you have a name?" she asked.

"Call me Saorise," she said.

"Saorise, where am I?" she asked feeling fearful. A dread was creeping upon her and suddenly she felt very alone, as if some impending doom was about to descend upon her.

"First, you must know who you are. Go over to the pool of hidden thoughts and peer into its waters," Saorise said.

She started to shake as she hesitantly took a step towards the pool. Fear gripped her heart and she stopped, fearful of what she might see.

"What if I can't do it?" she said keeping her eyes on the ground.

A hand was under her chin and lifting her head up. How Saorise had gotten in front of her she didn't know. Saorise's eyes were boring into her own and she saw eternity there.

"If you don't move forward, then you are truly lost, but I will walk by your side if you wish."

"I do wish that," she said gratefully.

They walked to the edge of the pool. Taking a deep breath, she looked into its watery depths. Her face went ashen as hundreds of horrific acts were played out before her in which she was the main character. Tears were streaming down her face and her spirit screamed to look away, but she knew she could not. After the last scene faded she sank to her knees and sobbed.

"Who are you?" Saorise asked in a stern and commanding voice.

"I am Zana," she said with all the condemnation that came with that name. "Is this hell? It's not too horrible if it is."

"It is not," Saorise said. "It is judgement."

Zana lowered her head.

"I was afraid of that. Are you my judge, Saorise?"

"No," a voice said behind her that was not Saorise, "I am."

Zana's heart filled with dread. She did not want to turn around because she knew who that voice belonged to.

"And I," said a male voice that she did not recognize.

It was useless to prolong that which was inevitable. All her actions had brought her to this place and it was time she was judged for her crimes. Standing up she turned, her black wings unfolding from her body as she pushed her hair behind her pointed ears. Standing over six feet tall with hair the color of summer gold and streaks of autumn red, wearing a sleeveless dress of forest green was her goddess, Braylynn. Standing next to her was a man with close-cut hair, almost a buzz cut, wearing what looked like an animal vest and pants to match. He had a wineskin slung over one shoulder and carried a staff. He looked like someone who would be at home in the wilds. If Zana had to guess who this god was she would have to say Cael.

"Your guess is correct," said the god reading her thoughts.

Zana felt nothing but remorse and shame and wished she could crawl under the nearest rock.

"Did you see your life in the pool?" Braylynn asked.

"I did Moth...I mean Braylynn," Zana answered. She had wanted to say Mother, but she gave up that right a long time ago.

"And how do you plead with what you saw?" Cael asked. "Guilty or innocent?"

Zana wasn't exactly sure why Cael was here.

"I am here because you were indirectly involved with the death of one of my dragons," Cael said reading her thoughts once again.

Of course he meant Finn. Pain and loathing entered her heart as she thought of the demise of her beloved. Finn had made the ultimate choice, but she knew he would not have made that choice if it were not for her.

"I am guilty of all of it," Zana said bowing her head. "The only thing I can say is I would undo every act if it were in my power and beg forgiveness from everyone I have ever wronged."

Braylynn and Cael both nodded to each other.

"We will pass judgement soon, and once we speak the word it cannot be unspoken," Cael said.

"Before we do," Braylynn said, "Is there anyone who would speak on your behalf."

"I speak on her behalf."

Zana turned around to where she heard that voice. That voice she hadn't heard for over fifteen hundred years. That voice that she had silenced forever by her own hand.

"Layla," Zana barely managed to get out. Her heart was banging violently against her chest and her breathing was coming in gasps. She was afraid to move. She didn't have too. Layla ran up to her and caught her as she collapsed in her arms sobbing.

Once the sobbing had subsided, Zana looked long at her one time friend. Her auburn hair shone with a kind of otherworldly radiance, her yellow wings moving back and forth ever so gently. Zana's face was moist with tears, and she could see Layla's was as well.

"Layla, I am so sorry. I don't know how you could ever forgive me, but I beg for your forgiveness."

"Oh Zana," Layla said pressing a hand to her cheek. "I forgave you long ago, and prayed daily for your redemption."

"I can attest to that," Braylynn said, "my ears still ring from her incessant verbal assault on your behalf."

Zana smiled though it was hard to focus, her eyes being blurry from her tears, so she wasn't entirely sure what Braylynn's current mood was from her facial expression.

"I don't understand," Zana said to Layla. "I took everything from you, how could you ever forgive me?"

Layla looked intently into Zana's eyes. "I saw when the darkness entered you my sister, but I thought our friendship would be enough to pull you back out. On that I was wrong. But I knew that faerie who had saved my life countless times and I hers was still buried deep inside, and I knew one day she would come back."

Zana closed her eyes. Layla had called her sister. That one word had brought back all the invisible connections that bound all faeries together and to hear it was like a healing balm that washed over her. Zana hugged her sister fiercely, afraid to let go but let go she must and face what was coming to her. She turned to face Braylynn and Cael.

"I am ready to…" Zana started before Cael held up his hand to stop her mid-sentence.

"Is there anyone else who will speak on your behalf," Cael said in a booming voice.

Of course, Zana thought to herself. Layla spoke on her behalf for Braylynn, but who was there to speak for her with Cael. There was no one.

"I speak on her behalf," a voice behind Cael spoke.

Zana's heart was in her throat as Finn stepped from behind Cael and came into full view. Zana did not hesitate. She choked back a sob as she flew straight into Finn's arms, burying her face in his neck as her head lay on his shoulder, soaking his body with her tears. Finn didn't say a word, he just held her and poured all his warmth and strength into her. How long they stayed that way Zana didn't know. It could have been minutes, it may have been eons. Nothing existed in that moment but them, and she wanted it to last as long as she could make it. It was Braylynn that brought them back.

"Zana, it is time for your judgement," the goddess said. "Layla, Finn, come stand before us."

Zana held Finn's hand as they walked around to face the deities directly. Layla came up on Zana's other side and grabbed her hand. The two she loved the most were standing right next to her, ready to help her face what comes next.

"Layla, what have you to say?" Braylynn asked.

Layla looked at her friend and sister. "Her crimes are inexcusable, Mother. They are worthy of banishment or worse."

Zana's head fell. To hear the accusation from Layla's lips was devastating to hear even though it was deserved.

"However," she continued, "we grew up together, fought together, and saved each other's lives more times than I can count. I would also argue she was unduly influenced by an evil god and wizard. I have to wonder, would any of us have been able to stand up under that kind of direct power? Also my goddess, I submit that the Zana that did those things no longer exists. In the end she forsook all of Meliakken's offers of godship and dominion, proving that my friend and sister of old has come back to me."

Zana could see Braylynn's face was neutral, giving no hint to which way she was leaning.

"Finn?" Cael said.

Finn looked at his beloved and smiled.

"The love I have for Zana was put in me for a reason, as if it were meant to be," Finn said. "When she turned to darker ways and I thought I had lost her forever, I felt that love would wane with time. I found that not to be true."

Zana's eyes were filled with tears and made a path of twin streams down her face, but they were not tears of sadness.

Finn turned his face towards the god.

"In my fifteen hundred years of sleep and exile there was only one thought moving through my head the entire time, Zana. In my mind we just sat together holding hands, nothing more. Lord, that thought made fifteen hundred years seem like an instant."

"I understand your love for her, my son" Cael said intently, "but how does that excuse her crimes?"

"Because of the second gift you gave me yourself," Finn said. "Otherwise, why give me the ability to penetrate a god's shield if you had not seen a possible future in which Zana and I would bring Meliakken low. That in and of itself tells me you knew she could be pulled back from the darkness and into the light by the greatest force there is, love."

"Well said my son," Cael said as he looked towards Braylynn. "You know my thoughts, Sister."

"I do, Brother," Braylynn said as Cael nodded and then disappeared.

Braylynn brought her attention back to the three individuals in front of her.

"Layla, you may leave now daughter."

"Yes, Mother," Layla responded as she gave Zana a fierce hug then slowly faded from view. Zana wondered where one goes when they do that.

"Finn, would you give us a moment alone?" the goddess asked.

"Of course," Finn responded as he walked a good distance away out of earshot.

Braylynn was silent for several moments before speaking again, her eyes boring into Zana's.

"There was a period of time when I would never have allowed you back into our sisterhood, you know that right?"

Zana lowered her eyes, not able to look at her because of her shame and guilt. Then she felt a hand under her chin as the goddess brought her eyes back to the level of her own.

"You do right to hang your head, it means you accept your guilt and feel remorse. Do you know when I started to have hope in you again?"

Zana shook her head.

"When Donella spared your life after Devon tried to take yours. Then after the battle of the warlocks and before I left Vasara forever, I asked Donella and her mother the Queen to spare your life if they should encounter you in battle again. Both have spoken for your redemption to me recently after the battle with Meliakken."

Donella. The faerie whom she had made her most dire enemy and whose destruction she had planned every single day since they met, was saving her life at every turn, and now she was trying to save her soul. Zana's heart truly broke, any hardness that had remained was shattered once and for all and she crashed to her knees as her wings furled and the sobs wracked her body. Then she felt a warmness wash through her unlike anything she had ever felt before as Braylynn lifted her up and cradled her in her arms.

"Welcome home daughter," the goddess whispered into her pointed ears. "Everything is alright now, I won't let you go."

The joy and euphoria that filled Zana's body had cleansed her from head to toe, making her anew as she was welcomed back into the grace of her goddess.

"What happens now, Mother?" Zana asked. "I don't know what to do."

"You have all of eternity to figure that out my dear," Braylynn said patting her cheek. "For right now though, I think there is a young dragon over there waiting to speak with you."

Zana turned around to look at Finn. He was looking up at the waterfall, following the drops of water as they cascaded down.

"What do I…" Zana began, then stopped when she turned around and saw that Braylynn was gone.

She looked back to Finn and remembered the first time she met him. It was at a pool much like this one. All of a sudden she was afraid to move, afraid she would find this to be a dream if she did. But then Finn turned towards her and held out his hand and she knew this was no dream. She glided over to where he stood and as she came down, Finn folded her up in his arms.

"I think we are back where we started, my love," Finn said.

"I was thinking the same thing," Zana said as she buried her face in his chest. "Finn, I'm sorry."

"Shhhh," Finn said laying his head on top of hers. "That life is no more, this one has just begun."

He sat down on the grass and cradled her in his lap as they listened to the water rushing over the rocks.

"Finn, I never stopped loving you. Not even once," she said looking up at him.

Finn just smiled at her as he looked in her eyes and combed his fingers through her long black hair.

"I know my darling. My love has also remained steadfast."

"What should we do now?" Zana asked.

Finn looked around at the area they were in.

"This place seems pretty familiar for some reason. What do you say if we just stay here for a little while. You don't have anywhere you need to go do you?" he asked with a wink and a smile.

Zana laughed a musical laugh. Suddenly she stopped as the enormity of that hit her. It had been hundreds, perhaps thousands of years since she had laughed, and it felt amazing to be able to do it again. She buried her face in his chest once more and closed her eyes as she breathed him in and said, "No love, there is nowhere I need to go. This is the only place I ever need to be."

www.ingramcontent.com/pod-product-compliance
Lightning Source LLC
Chambersburg PA
CBHW030351030726
47497CB00002B/281